# THE PERICLES CONSPIRACY

---

MICHAEL KINGSWOOD

# CONTENTS

# ABOUT THIS BOOK

Captain Josephine Ishikawa changed the course of history, but no one knows about it.

She and her crew had an encounter while returning to Earth from the colony worlds, and upon their arrival the government swore them to secrecy about it.

With the powers that be in charge, Jo did her best to put the incident out of her mind and set about getting her starliner, Pericles, through a major overhaul and back out to the stars.

But the circumstances of their return to Earth along with the mysterious death of her Chief Engineer has caused the news media to ask questions, prompting Jo to wonder whatever became of the beings she rescued out in the depths of space, and of the promise she made to their dying parents.

If you like action and intrigue, The Pericles Conspiracy is sure to keep you on the edge of your seat, and leave you wanting more.

***

Enjoy the book! After you're done, please come to Michael's website and sign up for his mailing list at michaelkingswood.com/newsletter-signup/. Guaranteed to be spam free, he uses it to announce new releases and special promotions for his fans.

1
______

## PICK-UP LINES

La Chupacabra was almost empty.

A few patrons sat at tables along the wall opposite the bar and two more were at the bar itself: a plump middle-aged man in dirty work coveralls at the near corner and, at the far end, a slender woman with short-cut black hair dressed in dark business attire.

The bartender idly wiped down the taps halfway down the bar, and a lone waitress chatted with a patron at one of the tables.

Vidscreens behind the bar displayed the latest headlines and sports scores, but the volume was muted. A tune from the middle of the pop charts played over the bar's speakers, just loudly enough to make it difficult to hear a conversation from more than a few feet away.

He would have expected more business, considering it was hump day. Just two more days until the weekend after all. But he was just as happy for a sparse crowd. He hated having to search through a throng to find his mark.

As it was, a quick survey as he paused at the tavern's entrance revealed this evening's objective. He smiled slightly and walked to the far end of the bar.

He paused as he reached the chair around the corner of the bar from the slender woman. He cleared his throat, but the woman already noted his presence, favoring him with a slight frown and a quirked eyebrow.

"Is this seat taken?" he asked.

She shrugged and looked away, back to the closest vidscreen, where, from what he could tell from the closed-captioning, some talking head was pontificating about what effect the latest elections on Centauri would have on interstellar trade.

Her choice of programming made sense, considering her occupation.

As he sat down, he was struck by the woman's appearance. Ten year-long shifts as Captain on a starliner, plus the time to move up through the ranks to reach that station meant she had to be in her early to mid 50s at least. Still, he could have sworn she still had a few decades before she reached her middle years: she did not look a day over forty.

Her bio said she was the product of a marriage between a Japanese man and an English woman. In his experience, women from east Asia tended to age well, but even still he was impressed.

The bartender sauntered over.

"What'll it be?"

"Bud Light."

He noticed the woman smirk ever so slightly before taking a sip of her drink as the bartender moved back to the taps. He figured she would prefer to drink something more exotic from one of the colony worlds, but unless he missed his guess, she was drinking a Seven and Seven.

Hardly the height of sophistication itself, and not exactly a perch from which to scoff at his beer.

"You ever study ancient history?"

She glanced back at him and rolled her eyes.

"I'm not looking for company right now."

"Sorry. Don't mean to impose."

She sniffed and turned back to her newsvid.

A moment later the bartender returned with his beer. He accepted it with a smile of thanks and tapped the paypad on the bar. His database implant interfaced with the pay system and applied his standard tip rate automatically. The bartender looked surprised, then pleased, and voiced his thanks before moving away.

Tipping well was often useful for opening doors, he found.

He sipped at his beer for a few minutes, watching the newsvid with only the vaguest of interest. It was a moot discussion; whatever effects the election caused had already occurred more than four years ago.

Folks on Earth were only now hearing about it, of course. But whatever changes they made in response would also be extremely time late in reaching Centauri ears.

So what was the point?

Glancing back at the woman, he noted that she too looked a bit amused at the discussion. Of course, she would know the futility of it more than most.

Time to try again.

"So I was reading the other day about an ancient Athenian ruler. Guy named Pericles."

She stiffened slightly when he mentioned the name, but quickly recovered, sipping her drink again without bothering to look at him.

"Is that right?" She sounded annoyed.

"Very interesting man." He took another drink of his beer. "He took over while Athens was rebuilding from the Persian wars. He fostered the arts, built the Acropolis, endorsed Athenian expansionism. During his reign, Athens became the greatest political force in the region. But then, of course, he pressed too far. Made Sparta nervous. And so, the Peloponnesian War. He didn't live to see it, but eventually Athens fell beneath Sparta's military might."

"Fascinating. Look, I *really* don't want company, so..."

"I heard a story about another Pericles recently."

She froze, her expression suddenly becoming wary. He continued on.

"Starliner by that name comes in from the Gliese system, just like normal. But there's nearly a week's delay in unloading the cargo. The crew is sequestered. Interviewed by government agents, they say. All but the fourth shift are out within a week. That shift's sequestered for more than a month. Six months later, Malcolm Ngubwe, the fourth shift's Engineer, dies under, shall we say, mysterious circumstances? Then that same shift's pilot, one Carlton Hersch, and his wife Alison, the shift's doctor, leave the starliner company for work planetside." He shrugged. "Not so unusual, except he was in line for promotion to Captain. Strange time for a career change, isn't it?"

"I don't know what you're talking about."

"Yes you do." He leaned toward her, noting her expression shifting from wariness to nervousness. "What happened out there to cause so much fuss, Captain Ishikawa?"

She swallowed, pulling away from him.

"Who are you?"

He tapped his thumb and forefinger and waited for a moment.

When nothing happened, he sniffed in annoyance. He figured she would have upgraded to the interactive database implant by now. She had been back long enough, and those implants made forgetting names a thing of the past.

He always kept old-style holocards, though, just in case.

Pulling one from his pocket, he slid it across the bar to her. His credentials were plainly visible: Jeremy Reynolds, Investigative Reporter, Star News.

She picked it up, her eyes narrowing as she read it. Then she stood, dropping the card onto the bar.

"I've got nothing to say to you, Mr. Reynolds."

She turned to leave, but stopped as Jeremy grabbed her arm gently.

"There are rumors of a new strain of disease onboard. The public has a right to know the truth, Captain."

She hesitated, then pulled away from his grasp.

"Good night, Mr. Reynolds."

With that, she walked away at a brisk pace. She was out the door quickly, and never looked back.

Jeremy remained in his chair for several minutes more, finishing his beer and shrugging off the bartender's quip about him striking out. There was definitely something there. And he intended to find out what it was.

---

As the door to La Chupacabra slid shut behind her, Josephine Ishikawa let out a breath she did not realize she had been holding. It had been two years, and she thought sure interest about her last shift on Pericles had died by now.

Dammit, that's all she needed, some reporter prying into things.

Muttering angrily to herself, she stalked to the lift at the end of the hall and punched the down button.

La Chupacabra was on the third floor of a commercial tower on the east side of town. Far enough from her usual stomping grounds that she was unlikely to run into anyone from work.

Not that she didn't like the people she worked with, but she generally preferred not to mix business with pleasure. Besides, she saw way too much of them when they were stuck together on a starliner, millions of Astronomical Units from the nearest rock.

A short lift ride later, she hit the streets.

Quito was *the* major hub for travel to and from low earth orbit in the Western Hemisphere. Its location, essentially right on the equator, was ideal. Add in its status as a political hub and its relative proximity to major shipping ports, and it was natural that, as mankind became a spacefaring species, it, along with Mogadishu and Kuala Lampur, would move into the limelight.

That would likely change once the space elevators were completed; the western anchor point was further east, in Brazil, away from the fault line in the Andes. But that wasn't scheduled for completion for another decade or more - a worry for a later time.

For the planetbound, anyway. But Jo, like other starfarers, had a different perspective on the flow of time than most people. In another two years, once Pericles' overhaul was complete, she would hop aboard to Gliese once again. The next time she returned, though only two and a half to three waking years would have passed for her, Earth would have seen over forty.

Some found that disconcerting; culture shock alone accounted for a large percentage of the Company's attrition among new hires. But Jo found it fascinating, being able to observe the flow of history from a position outside the normal timeline. She very much looked forward to seeing the changes when she returned next.

But for now, she was here, and Quito was booming. Towering skyscrapers, filled with stylish and pricey condominiums. Fine restaurants on every street corner, catty-corner to the omnipresent Starbucks. Shopping establishments that ran the gambit from thrift stores to the highest of high-priced.

Quito had it all, and with it, congestion. It wasn't worth it to even try to motor yourself anywhere, even if it did not cost an arm and a leg to park.

A cab stand was situated a half-block down from La Chupacabra's building. Jo flipped up her collar and hurried the short distance, hunching over in the early evening drizzle in a vain attempt to avoid getting wet. The forecast had been for clear skies, so she had not brought an umbrella.

She should have known better than to trust the weatherman.

Fortunately, the queue was short and covered with a simple plasti-glass canopy, so she was able to avoid the rain while she waited. Within a few minutes, she found herself settled into the cab's passenger compartment. Fortunately, it was an older cab and still had a slot that accepted holocards.

She inserted her card and said, "Home."

The cab acknowledged in a deep male voice and pulled away from the stand. Jo would give even odds whether the voice was from a voice-actor or just simulated. Either way, she suspected it was supposed to make a lady feel secure, or maybe sound sexy. She had heard the female voice that played for heterosexual male passengers.

Hopefully they found her as silly as Jo found the male.

Settling back into the passenger couch, Jo watched the buildings pass, and her thoughts began to drift. She remembered the mixture of wonder and fear when Carl called her to the bridge and she saw what he had found. The exhilaration of applying her crew's capabilities to an unexpected problem. The terror when it seemed like it was all falling apart, and then the relief when it didn't.

She decided two years ago to put it out of her mind. Even without the security debriefings and non-disclosure agreements, she knew her part of the job was finished. There was nothing else she could do, and it wouldn't serve any purpose to dwell on their encounter. Then, when Malcolm died, it was just one more reason to move on. She had done a good job of it.

Damned reporters.

The cab stopped, and she stepped out.

Her building was a smaller condo complex on the south side, not far from the spaceport. More industrial, with less fancy decoration and greenery, it wasn't a choice neighborhood. But she hated long commutes, so it suited her purpose.

Her condo was on the sixth floor. The ride up on the lift seemed slower than normal. Or maybe she was just more anxious to get home than usual. It had been a crappy end to a crappy day, and she wanted nothing more than to soak in the tub and hit the rack.

As she entered, the lights automatically turned on and soft music began to play, streaming from her favorite mix site.

As the music started, the televid wall in her small living room lit up with a slideshow from Jo's travels during her career in space. Vistas from a dozen worlds flicked past in time with the music. The eternal terminator on Gliese, where the famed Granite Trees with their massive trunks leaned far into the constantly-blowing hurricane-force winds and sent their branches with their hauntingly beautiful flowers straining toward the star that forever lingered on the horizon. The barren mountains of Barren's Holdfast, accessible only in a suit and even then only with permission from colony administration and after extensive EVA training. The Vine Peaks of Talos, rising higher than a number of mountains on Earth and formed entirely by a single growing plant that housed its own micro-ecosystem and dozens of unique species.

Jo smiled slightly as she took in the slideshow for a moment. It was good to be home after a long day, but there was where her heart truly lay: out among the stars, on a ship at her command.

Then her smile faded as a dialog box opened on the televid wall. There was a message from Harold Jameson, the Chief Operating Officer of the starliner company and her boss at the moment.

"Crap," she breathed, and tapped the televid control pad.

The dialog box turned into an image of Harold, bald head and all, looking tired but alert. Seeing her, he perked up and scowled.

"Where the hell have you been, Jo? And when the hell are you going to get an implant?"

"Never. I don't want a bunch of electronics in my head that will be obsolete by the time I get back from my next run in forty years."

"Then why can't you turn on your mobile, like every other civilized person on the planet?"

Jo rolled her eyes.

"What do you want, Harry? It's late."

Harold's scowl faded, replaced by a focused, businesslike expression, with a hint of anxiety that only someone who knew him as well as she did would notice.

"I need you back here ASAP. We're manning the ECC."

Jo's fatigue was instantly replaced by a surge of adrenalin, and annoyance. So much for her trip to Boston tomorrow.

"What's happened?"

"Wu Shin will fill you in when you get here. Hurry."

The video feed switched off, and the televid switched back to the classical music playlist. Swan Lake began playing, along with the slideshow of landscape photos from the planets she had visited during her time with the starliner company.

Jo left the condo before the first ten bars had finished.

2

# EMERGENCY CONTROL

Corporate Headquarters of McCallister Stellar Transport was located just outside the Quito launch complex fence line, on the south side of the city.

A sprawling campus of just over twenty acres housed the corporate buildings nestled together inside a guarded wall: a large center tower that stood some fifty stories in height, seven smaller outbuildings, and the cargo warehouses at the back of the campus along the fence line with the launch complex.

The entire campus, with the exception of the warehouses with their railway terminals and sprawling parking lots for heavy lift trucks, was carefully maintained and planted with the finest greenery available on any of the known habitable worlds. Paved walkways joined the various buildings. No vehicles were allowed inside the campus except for the chief executives' and the cargo trucks, but the truck roads were concealed from sight behind carefully planted trees in front of stout concrete walls.

It was a quick five minute cab ride from Jo's condo in the light evening traffic; this time of night, more vehicles were going from the campus than towards it.

She could have walked it in about half an hour, and most days she did. But between the weather and the urgency of Harold's message, she hopped into the first cab she could find.

The guards at the campus entrance noted her identity as she

approached and waved her through with only a cursory glance. Supposedly the process would be quicker and easier with the new implants, but she never had any problem with the identichips in her security badge or holocard.

The Emergency Control Center was located on the thirtieth floor of the main tower. The lift from the ground floor brought her up with barely a whisper.

The noise inside the ECC was quite a bit louder.

Large status displays dominated the wall directly to the left of the entrance. A glance showed her they were being updated by the latest feeds from the stellar Lagrange point navigation satellites as well as those from a pair of starliners: Chamberlain and Leonov. Workstations for the various support organizations were scattered around the floor below.

Directly opposite the status displays, on a raised platform above the support workstations, the command table was fully manned by the usual people, except for the Incident Commander's station at the center. Li Wu Shin, her principal assistant, was sitting there, and looked relieved when she walked in the door.

"Jo, where've you been?" Wu Shin asked, echoing Harold's earlier words as she walked up to the incident commander's station. He stood up, tapping the control console to log out from the command and control voice network as he did.

Jo didn't bother to answer Wu Shin's question; it didn't matter anyway. She settled down into the command chair and inserted the earbud resting there specifically for her use. Most of the other principals had database implants, so they didn't need one.

"What's the situation?"

Wu Shin leaned over her shoulder as he filled her in.

"The Hephaestus suffered a containment breach in her fusion core. Took out the after third of the ship. They managed to close off the airtight bulkheads, but they're without propulsion and adrift."

"Son of a bitch. Any casualties?"

"The Shift Engineer and a Reactor Tech were in the access tunnel troubleshooting the problem when it blew."

"And the passengers?"

"Cryo-suspension is uninterrupted. All indications are they're fine, for the moment."

Jo breathed a sigh of relief.

"When did this happen?"

"Earlier today. The distress signal reached us this afternoon."

"Have we notified next-of-kin?"

"The casualty assistance office is beginning the process, but they have not yet made contact."

"Very well."

Jo tapped the command screen and called up the Hephaestus' manifest. "They only left two weeks ago. Their velocity can't be that high yet."

Wu Shin shook his head.

"No, a little under twelve thousand kilometers per second."

That was something, at least.

The most dangerous portion of any starliner's voyage was the initial acceleration away from port. When the plasma generators that powered the main engines were in standby, the ship's reactor plant operated at only a fraction of its rated power. But during acceleration, it gradually increased its power output until it reached one-hundred percent, in order to achieve an even acceleration as relativistic effects increased the ship's mass.

And it did so for just about a full year, in order to achieve nominal cruising speed of ninety-five percent of the speed of light.

If anything were to go wrong, it was most likely to happen at those higher power levels. And while a rescue from a mishap during the deceleration phase was relatively simple, a mishap during acceleration was a different matter entirely.

Two months out from the originating star system, it would be virtually impossible to mount a rescue, since the distances involved, and the speeds required for intercept, were beyond the capabilities of most conventional rescue vessels.

And, of course, by the time the ship reached the destination star, if it ever did, everyone onboard would be long dead.

Jo inwardly gave thanks for small mercies, that this disaster had not occurred a few weeks from now. Two public funerals would be bad enough. At least there was still a chance to avoid five thousand.

"Have you had a tug powered up?"

Wu Shin nodded. "Tugs T-3 and T-8 will be underway in fifteen minutes."

Jo nodded and waved him away. He took a seat at a support console behind the command table.

Tapping the control console to log into the command and control voice network, she spoke up.

"This is Captain Josephine Ishikawa. I have relieved as incident commander."

---

AFTER THE INITIAL burst of activity, the next several weeks within the ECC were less frantic and exciting, but by no means easy.

There were countless details to manage, from interfacing with the various levels of government to rerouting incoming starliners into a holding orbit so the tugs could have unimpeded access to the docking facilities to offering official condolences to the families of the dead crew members.

And, of course, there were the press conferences.

As Incident Commander, Jo was obliged to sit beside Harold each afternoon and field questions, each more inane and brainless than the last. How the hell was she supposed to know what the people stuck onboard Hephaetus were feeling about their situation? How the hell did that news bimbo think they were feeling?

Each press conference was an exercise in frustration, and she often left with her jaw aching from grinding her teeth so hard.

She understood where the reporters were coming from. They had their deadlines and were fighting for ratings so they could keep their jobs. But really, would it kill them to at least review basic physics before coming up with their questions?

But after the first week, with nothing new happening and nothing more dramatic to do than wait for the tugs to rendezvous with the stricken vessel, Harold, at the press corps' request and to Jo's relief, moved the press conferences from daily to twice a week.

There was another brief flurry of press interest when the tugs made up with Hephaestus and began the long, slow process of re-directing the starliner back toward the Sol system.

But when it all went according to plan and no one else was killed, their interest quickly faded once again.

When Hephaestus docked, it was almost anti-climactic. The news media noticed, of course. But the coverage was light, limited to blurbs on the evening news shows and little else.

Of course, the docking was not the end of the job by any means. But with the crisis stabilized, it was time to stand down the ECC. The normal command and control system could handle it from here.

Jo had spent the last two and a half months living out of the ECC and her personal office on the thirty-fifth floor. She slept on a couch in her office, and showered and changed clothes, using spare clothing she kept in her office for just that purpose, in the employee gymnasium, which was located in one of the outlying buildings on campus. She was more than ready for a long bath in her own bathtub, and then a little vacation.

Before the crisis hit, she had planned to go up to Boston, to visit Carlton and Alison. They had both been as disappointed as she when she cancelled, but they understood. They had lived the starfarer's lifestyle their whole lives up until a year ago.

It still seemed strange to think those two wouldn't be returning to space with her when she got underway again, in a little more than two years. And to think that when she returned, they would both be in their late seventies, suddenly, from her perspective, older than she was.

It was odd, and more than a little sad, for her. But it was their decision, and they had made it for their own reasons. Who was she to judge?

As soon as she finished the last details in the ECC, Jo called Harold and informed him that she was going to take her vacation. He raised no objections so she booked herself on the next flight to Boston, leaving early the next morning.

Alison was thrilled when Jo called to tell her the news. It was obvious Alison wanted to chat more, but as much as Jo enjoyed the discourse, she was exhausted. So she begged off, promising they would have all the time they needed to catch up when she arrived.

**3**

---

## OLD FRIENDS

Carlton Hersch met Jo at the baggage claim in Logan Airport. She was just turning away from the carousel, pulling her checked bag behind her, when he saw her and waved with a grin. She returned the grin in kind, her face brightening as it always did when she smiled, and gave him a hug in greeting.

"Looking good, Cap'n," he said, then winced at the look of reproach on her face. "Sorry. I mean, you look good, Jo."

Try as he might, and no matter how often she told him to do otherwise, he always found himself addressing her by her title when talking to her, almost without realizing it. Serving under her command aboard Pericles for five years was hard to get past, but he was out of that game now, wasn't he?

"Good to see you, Carl," she said, the reproachful look changing to a familiar, friendly smile. "How are Alison and the kids?"

"She's fine. Tim's enjoying first grade a lot. He has a girlfriend." Carlton found himself shaking his head in amusement at that. "Malcolm's starting to say a few words. Or at least I think they're words."

"You didn't have to come all the way out here to meet me, you know. I've ridden the T before."

Carlton waved off the comment dismissively. "Least I can do. You've had a tough few weeks."

They stepped outside into the crisp winter afternoon. Carlton noticed Jo shivering, heck nearly convulsing, as she pulled her jacket tight about herself.

Too much time along the equator's making her blood thin, he thought. Not that he didn't find it a bit chilly for his taste, as well.

He was parked in the short-term lot. It only took a few minutes to reach his car. Jo whistled appreciatively when she saw it, a brand new Mercedes, painted in a green so dark it was nearly black.

"Not bad, Carl. The Airline's treating you well, I see."

He chuckled. "Alison paid for it."

Alison was an Attending at Beth Israel Deaconess Hospital and made much more money than he did as a senior instructor at Delta's Orbital Flight Academy.

He could not complain about his work schedule, though.

The drive from Logan to his and Alison's house took a bit less than an hour. It was after rush hour, but someone from out of town would not believe it from the number of vehicles on the roads. Most people commuted on the T, or in automated taxis or public transport buses, but even still the roads through town were almost always packed.

Eventually, he turned right off the Riverway onto Longwood Avenue and drove into the residential area adjacent to the medical district. It was like driving back in time. The rest of the city had long ago turned into towering skyrises, but here the residents still maintained old, quaint homes on quiet, wooded streets.

They pulled into the driveway, and Carlton helped Jo with her luggage.

Alison was waiting on the porch, beaming a wide smile. She and Jo embraced fondly, and walked into the house, chatting away already.

Typical, Carlton chuckled to himself as he trailed behind and lugged the bags up the stairs and into the house.

Alison had dinner ready: a marvelous concoction of braised beef, simmered greens, seasoned mashed potatoes, dinner rolls, and a fine Cabernet that they had decanted earlier in the afternoon.

And, of course, mashed up baby food for little Malcolm, who proudly wore his meal on his bib before Alison finally gave up trying to pilot any more starships into the tiny docking bay that was his mouth.

After dinner, the ladies took Malcolm to the family room while Carlton took Tim upstairs to get ready for bed. The usual routine of bath, pajamas, and bedtime story went off without a hitch, and before long Carlton kissed his son on the forehead goodnight and shut the door.

When he got back downstairs, Alison and Jo were deep into another bottle of wine. Malcolm was lying on Alison' s lap, drowsy eyes halfway closed in sleep that he was clearly fighting.

Carlton gestured to the little guy. "Want me to carry him up?"

"No, he's fine. Come join us," replied Alison, pointing to a filled glass that was sitting on the end table next to his chair.

Settling down into his chair, Carlton took a sip from his glass and smiled. It was a Malbec from Argentina, one of his favorites. "So, ladies. What are we talking about?"

"Not much. Just reliving some old sea stories."

Carlton always found it funny how starfarers called tales of what happened onboard the starliners "sea stories". There was no denying that many nautical traditions had translated over into the culture and procedures of operating spacecraft.

All the same, to still use the term after all this time was strangely amusing.

The conversation lasted late into the night, only interrupted for a few minutes while Carlton carried Malcolm upstairs once he was good and fully asleep.

But after a while, Carlton noticed Jo drifting off into her own world. Frowning, he glanced at Alison, who shrugged slightly.

"Jo, is everything ok?"

She gave a little start. "Oh? Yes, fine, thank you. My thoughts were just wandering."

"Where to?" queried Alison.

Jo took another drink of wine and was silent for a long moment. Then she sighed and asked, "Do either of you ever think about our last shift?"

Surprised, Carlton shared another look with Alison. "Of course we think about it. How could we not? But, well..."

Alison picked up his slack. "It's out of our hands now, and we're not supposed to talk about it. So we don't."

Jo nodded slowly. "I hadn't thought about it for a long time. I've purposely kept myself from thinking about it. But a few weeks ago, a reporter came by, asking questions."

Alarm bells went off in Carlton's mind. "You didn't tell him anything?"

"Of course not. You haven't heard from him have you? Jeremy Reynolds."

Both he and Alison shook their heads. "Does he know anything?"

"Just conjecture, and even that is far from the truth. It got me thinking though."

"Well that's something, at least." Carlton shook his head. "What did Harry say about it?"

Jo took another drink. "I haven't told him yet."

Alison's eyes widened in shock, and Carlton knew his were as well. "You haven't? Jo, you know the protocol on this."

"I know, I know!" Jo stood up and strode over to the window. From her gait alone, Carlton could tell she was annoyed. "I'll tell him when I get back. But look," she turned back to them, fully back in the present and talking in her 'I mean business' tone. "This guy might come calling."

"I wouldn't be surprised if he did," replied Carlton.

Jo stayed with them for three days, but they never again spoke of what happened on their last shift aboard Pericles, or of Jeremy Reynolds.

It was a fun visit. She had been to Boston before, but it had been years. So for those few days, Carlton and Alison got to be tourists in their own town, showing her all the sights.

Jo's flight back to Quito departed early in the morning of the fourth day. Once again, Carlton drove her. They sat in silence for most of the trip to Logan, listening to the morning news. When they pulled up into the passenger offload area, Jo smiled and clasped his hand.

"Thanks for your hospitality, Carl. It's been great seeing you two again."

"You too, cap'n. Don't be a stranger."

And then she walked away, into the terminal.

Carlton waited a minute, in case she forgot something in the car. But she didn't return, so he drove off. When he got back home, he found Alison just returning from dropping Tim off at school.

"She make it ok?"

Carlton nodded. "Ought to be in the air by now."

"You're heading back up to Luna tomorrow morning, right?"

"Yes, but only for a week this time. Should be back for Tim's birthday."

"What will I do without a babysitter during the day?"

Carlton chuckled and shook his head. "Good to know I'm loved for who I am."

Alison smiled and gave him a kiss on the cheek. "See you this afternoon." And then she headed out for work.

Carlton spent the day taking care of Malcolm, as he did most days when he was at home and Alison at work. It was a pleasure, for him and Malcolm both. The little guy cooed and giggled as they played, and occasionally babbled the beginnings of a word.

But as the day wore on, Carlton's mood grew darker. As he looked at his little boy playing, the conversation from four nights ago came to mind, and he started thinking about what had happened onboard Pericles.

And about his friend, the man his son was named after.

And then there were the things they had been given, and what they had been asked to do. What had become of those things, he wondered, after the government took over?

He would probably never know.

---

THE LIFT DOOR OPENED, and Jo stepped out onto her floor.

Pulling her suitcase behind her, she walked slowly toward her condo, yawning into the back of her hand as she went. It had been a long flight, made the worse by weather delays over Columbia. It was almost 1 o'clock in the morning, more than three hours later than she thought she would be getting home, and she had a meeting at 8:30.

She reached her door and pressed her holocard against the door control. The identichip interfaced with the locking mechanism and the door slid open.

"Hello, Jo."

Shocked, Jo jumped backwards, landing in a defensive stance as she turned toward the deep voice.

It registered in her head that the voice was familiar in the same instant that she saw the man standing there, leaning casually against the hallway wall.

He was tall, dressed in khaki slacks and a dark blue collared shirt. He had a lean runner's body, dark skin, and close-cut black hair that grew in tight curls. His face was narrow, but not unattractive. His eyes were dark, his gaze direct and intelligent. As she landed, he grinned, revealing gleaming white teeth.

She knew him at a glance, but there was one problem: he was dead.

4

# BACK FROM THE DEAD

"**M**alcolm!" Jo exclaimed in disbelief, her fatigue forgotten in the shock of seeing him.

"It's good to see you," Malcolm replied.

"What do you mean, it's good to see me? You're supposed to be dead! Where the hell have you been?"

Malcolm's smile faded and he pushed himself off the wall. With a quick, furtive glance both ways down the hallway, he stepped toward Jo and spoke more quietly.

"I need your help, Jo. Can we talk inside?"

She was tempted to say no, to tell him to go away. If he had faked his death—and what other explanation was there—he was certainly up to no good, and that was trouble Jo did not need.

But he had been a good friend, and once, long ago, more than that. She found herself nodding, and then following him into her condo.

As usual, the lights turned on as they entered, and her classical mix began to play along with the slideshow of alien landscapes. She closed the door and rolled her suitcase over to the closet. When she turned back toward Malcolm, he was watching the slideshow with a far away look in his eyes and an amused grin on his lips.

"Remember that time on Talos, when we took that picture? You almost..."

"Stow it, Malcolm," she said, placing her hands on her hips and assuming the tone she reserved for times when a subordinate was being particularly stupid. "What are you doing alive, and who the hell did we cremate, a year and a half ago?"

Malcolm looked sidelong at her, saying nothing for nearly a full minute. Then he nodded, as if coming to a decision, and sat down in her stuffed chair. He drew a deep breath before replying.

"The body was a homeless man." Seeing her expression, he raised his right hand in a placating gesture, and quickly added, "We didn't kill him. We found him dead in a back alley. Probably drank himself to death."

"Bullshit. They verified the body through DNA analysis."

Malcolm's eyebrows rose high onto his brow. "Well, I'm here. Clearly they were mistaken." He made a powerful case, she had to admit. "We knew they would run tests, so we made sure to set the fire in a manner that would render the body unidentifiable. But as a little extra insurance..."

He raised his left hand, and Jo's breath caught in her throat. His little finger was gone, cut off except for a small bump where the last knuckle would be. "It doesn't take much to leave a lot of DNA."

Jo sank onto the couch and shook her head in disbelief. "Why would you do that? And who is we?"

Malcolm leaned forward, resting his elbows on his knees. "Do you remember when we docked? The debriefings?"

"Of course I do. What does that..."

"Almost from the beginning, I realized that the government was not going to do right by our new friends. When they brought out the non-disclosure agreements and swore us to secrecy, I knew for sure."

Jo snorted, and Malcolm frowned slightly.

"Don't believe it? I studied the incubator, and the technical documents, for almost nine months before we turned over the watch and went back into cryo-suspension. I checked with the others when we woke up before docking and no one else had bothered to even look at it. I knew more about what those creatures gave us than anyone else alive, so why wouldn't the Agency accept my help, unless they meant ill?"

"You faked your death because your ego was bruised?" Jo knew she sounded incredulous, but it seemed appropriate.

Malcolm shook his head vigorously. "it's not about *me*!" He stood up suddenly, and paced over to the window. "I tried, Jo. After we were released, I tried to get them to listen..."

This was getting ridiculous. "Listen? Listen to what? You don't have security clearance. You're just an Engineer on a starliner, or you were. And a damn good one. But why would they need your help when they have world-class PhDs on their payroll? Especially when you were going out of your way to be a pain in the ass!"

Malcolm turned back at her, looking startled.

"Oh yes, I heard about the little stunt you pulled at NSA headquarters. What were you thinking? You're lucky they didn't lock you up!"

Malcolm waved off her comment. "They wouldn't have done that. Too much press if they did. Too many questions." He walked back to the sitting area and took his seat in the chair again. His expression was serious as he continued, his eyes taking on a fierce light. "But then I met some people. I don't know how they heard about it, or how they found me. But they had suspicions about what had happened up there, and they confirmed my worst fears about what the government was up to."

"Some kooks tell you a tall tale, and you buy it?"

"Of course not. I thought they were crazy at first too, just as you think I am."

"I don't think you're crazy."

He smirked. "Yes you do. But they showed me evidence of what the government had done in the past in other cases, and it was compelling. When I showed them my copies of the technical documents - "

"Copies? You made copies of what they gave us?"

Malcolm nodded. "I knew they'd be confiscated, but I wanted to continue studying them, so - "

Jo threw her hands up. "And you wonder why the Agency wasn't going to trust you? Did you ever even *once* think about just trying to work within the rules?"

"The Agency's rules are about exclusion. About keeping information away from the populace. About keeping them enthralled with bread and circuses while the government - "

Jo stood up. "I've heard enough of this. I don't know what happened to you, Malcolm, but I'm tired and I've got an early day tomorrow. Take your conspiracy theories and leave."

She turned away, toward her bedroom door.

"The government has no intention of sending those eggs back, Jo."

Malcolm's words stopped her in her tracks. She looked back at him over her shoulder. His face was stricken, almost as though he was in physical pain.

"What are you talking about? Of course they will."

He shook his head. "No. They've got the eggs in a lab, and they're running tests on them. When they've learned all they can, the eggs will be discarded. Meanwhile, the government is using the technology in those documents to build weapons to use when we encounter them again."

Clenching his fists as he rose, Malcolm took a step toward her, and Jo backed away without realizing it. Now he looked enraged, ready to commit violence.

"They entrusted us with their eggs—*with their babies*—and the government is using them like lab rats!"

This had gone far enough. Malcolm's rapidly changing moods were making Jo more than a little nervous. "I'm going to bed now, Malcolm. Please show yourself out. Don't make me call the police."

He recoiled as if slapped. For a second, Jo thought maybe he was going to lash out at her. But then he slumped, looking defeated, and, nodding, he turned toward the door. He half-turned as the door slid open, and he looked like he was going to say something else. But he must have seen in her face that she didn't want to hear it. So, with a sigh, he walked out of her condo.

As the door slid shut behind him, Jo let out a tense breath. What had happened to him? He used to be poised, decisive, passionate, brilliant! Now...well, he was still passionate, that much was clear. But the rest? He was twisted, hardly resembling the man she once knew.

Jo locked up and went to bed. But she was unable to sleep for a long time. Instead, she replayed the encounter in her head over and over. She couldn't help but feel sorry for her old friend.

<br>

JO PUSHED past Harold's secretary, ignoring his protests that Mr. Jameson was in a meeting and wasn't to be disturbed.

The double doors to his forty-fifth story office were solid, probably mahogany, and beautifully stained. She shoved them open, and they swung through their full range of motion, smacking into the walls within his office with a loud crash.

Harold was seated at his coffee table with three other men, all dressed in fine business suits. They were going over documents on the display screen built into the table, but all looked over in unison at the noise, surprise turning to chagrin on the faces of the three guests as she walked in. Harold's face was a thundercloud.

He stood up, pulling off his reading glasses and glowering at her.

"Jo, what - "

She gave him no time to complete his sentence. In her best no-nonsense tone, she said, "I need to talk to you, Harry. Right now."

Harold knew her well enough to recognize that tone. His expression moderated a bit, but from the tightness around his eyes, Jo could tell he was very annoyed.

Well, it was about to get worse.

"Will you excuse us for a moment, gentlemen?" Harold said to his companions.

The three men looked from Harry to Jo and back, then the fellow who seemed to be the leader nodded. They stood, the younger of the three pausing to turn off the display, then walked out.

All three of them gave Jo appraising, and questioning, stares as they walked past her.

Harold closed the doors behind them and turned to face her. "Alright, Jo, this better be good."

"Malcolm Ngubwe is alive."

Harold's jaw dropped open, the annoyance leaving his face, replaced by confusion.

"What are you talking about? He was confirmed dead a year and a half ago."

"Then I guess it was a ghost that came by my condo last night."

Jo stepped over to the televid control on the wall across from Harold's desk and touched her holocard to it. A moment later, her homepage came up, and she tapped her video cache twice.

The feed from the security camera outside her door came up on the televid screen, showing her encounter with Malcolm, or at least the part of it that occurred in the hall.

Harold stepped toward the screen, his eyes widening. "My God, it *is* him. How?"

"He faked his own death."

"But, why?"

Jo felt an upwelling of sadness for her friend as she related the substance of their discussion to Harold.

She was circumspect about the eggs, and the other items they brought back on Pericles. Harold did not know the details about what happened up there. He took over as COO three months after Pericles docked, and he was not cleared to learn the details. As far as he was told, and from what Jo could tell as far as he cared, something had happened that the government cared about. But it was not safety related and it did not affect the operation of his starliner fleet except for a short delay offloading that one ship, so he had not asked questions.

He knew better than that.

All the same, he looked quizzically at Jo as she came to the end of her tale. "I know you can't say what could possibly have gotten him so riled up, and I really don't want to know, but...?" He left the rest of the question unspoken.

Jo spread her hands in an expression of helplessness.

Harold waved a hand, as though dismissing his own question. "Well, the authorities are going to want to know he's alive. And if he's as unstable as you say..." He shook his head. "Pity how people fall apart sometimes, isn't it? Well, I'm sure when they catch up to him they'll get him the help he needs."

Harold checked the time and paused for a moment. Jo could almost see him computing the time difference in his head.

"It's four o'clock in Geneva now. Better let Chandini know."

He reached toward the controls for the intercom to his secretary, but froze as Jo spoke again.

"There's something else, Harry. A reporter's been asking questions about what happened on Pericles."

"What? Who?"

Jo shrugged. "A guy named Reynolds. Jeremy Reynolds, from Star News. He approached me at a bar."

"When did this happen?"

"The night the Hephaestus had her accident."

Harold slammed a fist onto the top of his desk. "Goddamnit, Jo! That was almost three months ago, and you're just telling me now?!"

"It slipped my mind in the furor of trying to save over five thousand lives. Sorry. Next time I'll get my priorities straight."

Harold managed to look a bit sheepish as he nodded, conceding the point. "True enough. Well, hopefully no harm no foul. Brace yourself though, Jo. You know the Feds aren't going to like this one bit."

With that, Harold tapped the intercom control. His secretary's voice came through.

"Yes, Mr. Jameson."

"Steven, get me Deputy Director Chandini of the NSA."

There was a long silence on the other end of the intercom. For a moment, Jo wondered if Steven had heard the order. But then he spoke again, his voice quavering as though he were suddenly very nervous.

"Yes, Mr. Jameson."

The intercom clicked off, and memories from Pericles' docking rushed into Jo's mind, primarily the interviews with the NSA agents who took charge of her crew's debriefing.

They were cold and aloof, seemingly ready to find fault with her people and haul them away at any moment; a far cry from the customs agents from the Interplanetary Commerce Administration that starliners normally dealt with. They were cordial, almost warm in a professionally familiar sort of way.

But the NSA people...

They were in the law enforcement and solar system security business, and on the murkier side of law enforcement at that.

It made sense for them to take over, considering what happened, but dealing with them was uncomfortable, to say the least.

And Chandini herself... Jo had to stop herself from wrapping her arms over her chest, protectively. Chandini was not someone to be trifled with.

Jo glanced over at Harold. From his expression, she could tell he was thinking the same thing she was: it was going to be a very long day.

# 5

# THE AGENCY

I t took several minutes for Steven to make the connection, but finally he came back over the intercom.

"Deputy Director Chandini on the line for you, Mr. Jameson."

Harold thanked him and tapped another part of his desk controls. The display screen on his wall came to life, and Jo found herself looking eye-to-eye with the Deputy Director.

A woman in her late middle-years, probably into her nineties from the look of her, she had darkly tanned skin and long hair that still showed black in a few places beside wide streaks of silver. Seeing Harold, she smiled in greeting, but Jo noticed that her eyes were sharp as razors.

"Harry. To what do I owe the pleasure?" Chandini asked.

Harold cleared his throat and gestured toward Jo. "Ms. Chandini, I believe you remember Captain Ishikawa?"

"Of course. Good to see you again, Captain."

Jo inclined her head politely, but remained silent. This was Harold's conversation to lead, and Jo hoped to have to say as little as possible.

"We've got a situation here that you need to know about. Last night, Captain Ishikawa received an unexpected visitor at her home. Malcolm Ngubwe."

"Ngubwe." Chandini said his name slowly, almost like she was tasting it. For a moment, she was motionless, then her eyes flashed with recognition as both eyebrows rose on her forehead. "Isn't he dead?"

"Apparently not. I'm sending you a video feed from Captain Ishikawa's home security camera now."

Chandini looked away from them, toward something off-screen. Her lips pursed as she saw the video, but she didn't say anything. She looked back toward them, her expression expectant.

Harold cleared his throat. "Apparently, he faked his death, and has fallen in with some sort of conspiracy theorists. Captain Ishikawa and I are concerned that he may attempt something foolish, and harm himself or others."

"Understandable. Captain, did he give any indication as to what his plans might be?"

Jo shook her head. "No, ma'am. But he was definitely angry over what happened after we docked Pericles. Whatever he's up to, it has something to do with that."

Chandini nodded, her expression becoming grim. Her eyes flickered toward Harold. "Harry, would you leave us alone for a moment?"

Harold looked taken aback. For that matter, Jo was surprised as well. That sort of request was unheard-of.

To his credit, Harold handled it well. "I can, ma'am, but - "

"I do apologize, Harry, but you're not cleared to hear the questions I need to ask the Captain, or her answers."

Jo could tell Harold was put out by the suggestion. He looked side-long at her, his mouth turning downward into a scowl, and she shrugged, putting what she hoped was an apologetic expression on her face.

Harold sighed and, turning his eyes back toward Chandini, he nodded, then walked out of his office.

Chandini shook her head slightly, then fixed her eyes on Jo. "I'm going to secure mode, Captain. Let me know when you're ready."

"Yes, ma'am. One moment."

Jo went over to Harold's desk, a large wooden monstrosity, and found the controls. Tapping the secure broadcast button, she nodded to Chandini. "Ready."

Chandini moved her hand, presumably to press something off screen.

The seal of the United Earth Coalition flashed in the center of the screen for a moment, then retracted to the lower left corner. The display was now ringed in a yellow line, and the words "Top

Secret/Rama" were written in yellow on the top and bottom of the viewable area.

Jo blinked. "Rama?"

A slight smirk crossed Chandini's face. "We changed the code name recently. Someone in Classification is a fan of ancient Science Fiction literature." The smirk faded, Chandini's face returning to a business-like expression. "Now then, what did he say to you?"

Over the next several minutes, Jo related the substance of Malcolm's visit, the previous night. She left nothing out. It would have been foolish to do so, considering not just Chandini's power, but also her ability to apply resources to get Malcolm the help he needed.

When Jo finished, Chandini's expression was troubled, almost to the point of being distressed.

"Son of a bitch," Chandini breathed.

Jo nodded agreement. "I don't know where he got such crazy notions into his head. I can only surmise that his new friends are at least partly to blame."

Chandini appeared lost in her own thoughts as Jo was speaking. She only roused herself when Jo came to an end.

Chandini nodded, saying, "Yes, of course. He definitely needs help, that much is clear." She paused for a moment, then asked, "Do you know of anyone else he may have spoken with?"

Jo started to shake her head, then stopped. "I'm not sure. But he may have spoken with a reporter."

Jo thought she saw alarm on Chandini's face. "What makes you think that?"

"A reporter found me a couple months ago, asking questions about Pericles."

Chandini's eyes widened, and her lips compressed in anger. "Why have you waited so long to inform us?"

Jo shrugged. "He didn't know anything. It was obvious he was on a fishing expedition. And then the Hephaestus went down, and it slipped my mind to tell anyone. Besides, freedom of the press - "

"Is not absolute."

Jo blinked in surprise. Given the Constitutional protections the press received, a high public official like Chandini making an assertion like that was impolitic, to say the least.

Chandini must have seen the skeptical look on Jo's face. Her lips compressed slightly and her eyes flashed with irritation before she spoke again. "A wise man in ancient America once said, 'The Constitution is not a suicide pact.' Those creatures you encountered constitute a clear and present danger, not just to the security of Earth, but of every colonized world. If word of your encounter were to get out before we had a plan to deal with them..."

Chandini shook her head. "You think the Hephaestus incident was a media circus? That wouldn't even compare. There would be cultural upheavals, panic, religious crises... No, the consequences of not handling this first contact correctly are too horrible to contemplate. You know this."

Reluctantly, Jo nodded. She wasn't entirely convinced things would be as chaotic as Chandini seemed to think they would be, or that the creatures were as hostile as she and others assumed, but Jo had lost that argument long ago.

"Who was this reporter?"

"Jeremy Reynolds, from Star News."

"Well, he works for an editor, who has a boss. I'm sure we can get his efforts pointed in other directions. And in the future, you will inform us of inquiries like this promptly, is that understood, Captain?"

Chastened, Jo nodded. "Yes, ma'am."

Apparently satisfied, Chandini said, "Going non-secure," and pressed something offscreen. The yellow border around the display and the Top Secret banners disappeared. "Tell Harry he can come back now, please."

Jo went to retrieve him, and he returned quickly. Chandini was suitably brief. "I'm informing the local office in Quito about Mr. Ngubwe. You should be hearing from them later today. I expect your full cooperation with their investigation."

"Of course, ma'am," Harold replied.

Chandini inclined her head, as though receiving supplication, and broke the connection.

Jo let out a humorless half-chuckle. "She didn't even say goodbye."

---

THE AGENTS ARRIVED JUST after lunch, and were ushered up to Harold's office, where he and Jo awaited their arrival.

There were two of them, a man and a woman. The man was a bit taller than average, with the kind of powerful looking body that comes from many hours in the weight room and dark hair and tanned features suggesting a Central or South American origin. He was handsome, but no more so than half the men Jo walked past on the street.

The woman, however, was stunning: tall, with a slender, toned body and legs to forever, wavy dark brown hair, lightly tanned skin, and a heart-shaped face that would, and did from what Jo could see, draw every male eye in the area.

Both were dressed conservatively, in dark suits that were almost cliché in their similarity.

The woman took the lead, shaking hands with Jo and Harry ahead of her partner. "Good afternoon, Mr. Jameson. Captain Ishikawa. I'm Special Agent Jaqueline Moore. This is Special Agent Jesús Calderon."

"Nice to meet you both," replied Harold, and he gestured toward the chairs around his coffee table. "Please have a seat."

"Mr. Jameson, we mostly have questions for Captain Ishikawa. If you don't mind...?"

"We can just go to my office, Harry," Jo offered, but Harold shook his head.

"I'm sure they'll want to speak with both of us once you're done, correct?"

Agent Moore nodded, and Harold, putting on a smile of acceptance that Jo saw right through, left his own office for the second time that day.

Once the door shut, Agent Moore gestured to the chairs, and the three of them sat down around the coffee table. Agent Calderon pulled out a tablet and stylus, and punched in a few commands. Then he nodded to Agent Moore, who looked at Jo with a half-smile.

"Now then," she said in a crisp, businesslike tone, "would you please recount your conversation with Mr. Ngubwe for the record, Captain Ishikawa?"

"Of course," she replied.

For the third time that day she told the story.

It was becoming a bit irritating having to repeat herself, especially since she had no doubt the entire conversation with Deputy Director Chandini had been recorded. But Jo was careful not to let her irritation show.

If she had learned one thing over the years, it was that government types don't like to have it pointed out when they were behaving stupidly.

The two agents kept their faces neutral during the telling and they sat still, except for Agent Calderon's note-taking. When Jo was finished, Agent Moore nodded slowly.

"Did he give any indication where he'd been for the last year and a half, or where he was staying?"

Jo shook her head. "None, but I think I can guess what he's thinking about doing."

Agent Moore's eyebrows lifted. "Oh? What's that?"

Jo gave her the patented Ishikawa 'What are you, an idiot?' stare. "He's going to find a medical research lab, convince himself it's the one doing all those dastardly things, and break in or something."

"You sound as though you believe him."

"What?" Jo shook her head emphatically, irritation welling up yet again. "No, I said before that he seemed unstable, and probably delusional." This lady was dense, and if she was in charge, Jo didn't have much confidence that Agent Calderon was much better. It was good to know they were getting the varsity team on this case.

"Alright." The two Agents shared a look, then Agent Moore said to Jo, "I think we can have Mr. Jameson rejoin us now."

Once Harold returned and had joined them around the coffee table, Agent Moore spoke again.

"These sorts of investigations are always difficult. Finding one person, particularly a person as intelligent and resourceful as Mr. Ngubwe, is hard enough when he doesn't believe anyone is looking for him. But after last night, he must assume that you came to the authorities, and has begun taking precautions."

That made sense. Malcolm had always been clever, and the fact that he had managed to convince the entire world he was dead for more than a year spoke to how well he had transferred his skills to the underworld. "So what would you like me to do?"

"For now, nothing. Continue to go about your normal routine. We may occasionally stake out your house overnight, and with your permission we'll place a tap on your communication lines..."

"What? Why?"

"It's unlikely, but he may try to contact you again. If he does, we need to be able to track him. We can get a warrant if you prefer, but that will take more time. Also, since he's likely been living in the underworld since he disappeared, he may have contacts who can hack into the court records. If there's no record of a warrant, there's nothing to tip him off."

Jo and Harold shared a look. He looked uncertain about this line of discussion.

For that matter, so did Jo. There were Constitutional restrictions on wire tapping for a reason.

At the same time, Agent Moore's point about hackers was a good one, and it's not like Jo had anything to hide. After a moment's thought, she nodded.

"Ok, go ahead. But I want a list of what you install, and where."

"And you'll have it."

The rest of the conversation was more nuts and bolts, and boilerplate. She was to report if she had any further contact with Malcolm, as she expected. There was a brief discussion about possibly asking her to wear a wire at some point, but Harold objected to that, and Agent Moore tabled the topic for a later date.

Finally, after about an hour, the two Agents stood and, promising to stay in touch, shook hands with them and left. As the door closed behind them, Jo quipped, "Well I feel safer already."

Harold looked sidelong at her, as though he was wondering if she was being serious. She returned his look with a smirk, and he chuckled.

# 6

# EDITORIAL DEMANDS

Jeremy exhaled in consternation as he stepped through the doors to Star News' headquarters.

Another dead end.

He spent the last week tracking down Sven Godenburg, one of Pericles' two fourth-shift pilots, eventually tracking him to the McCallister branch office in Stockholm. Godenburg had been as much a stone as the others to this point.

Jeremy had never seen a group so unwilling to talk, but that couldn't last forever.

He figured to try Carlton and Alison Hersch next, in Boston, but he received an unexpected call from Lou Greenfield, his managing editor, telling him to get back to New York pronto. So Jeremy dropped everything and took the redeye from Stockholm, just landing in Kennedy Airport this morning.

Jeremy hated long flights. His equilibrium was all off, his internal clock shot to hell. It was not going to be a fun day.

Lou's office was in the back corner of the press room, past dozens of cubicles and a hundred or more people who were hard at work, scrambling around in seeming chaos. Jeremy nearly knocked a young intern over as they both rounded a cubicle, and he jumped out of the way with an apology, earning a shy grin in response.

The girl walked off, and Jeremy paused for a moment, admiring the sway of her hips, and the way her slacks showed off her shapely, firm backside. Maybe being summoned back to headquarters wasn't so bad after all.

His reverie was broken by Lou's gravelly voice. "Stop ogling the interns and get in here, Reynolds!"

Jeremy gave a start and smiled ruefully, but paused before he turned fully, as the intern looked over her shoulder and gave him a much bigger, warmer smile.

He saw her fingers move, then a block of text appeared in his vision. Supplied through the database implant, her name, Kelsey, appeared next to her head and below that, her voice, mail, and homepage contact data.

She mouthed "call me", and then went back about her business. Jeremy's smile as he entered Lou's office was genuinely cheerful.

"Hey Lou, what's up?"

"Shut the door and have a seat."

Uh-oh.

Lou hardly ever shut his office door, unless he was getting ready to chew some ass. Jeremy thought hard as he sat down, but couldn't come up with anything he'd screwed up lately.

He didn't have long to remain puzzled, though. Lou came around his desk and sat on the edge, facing Jeremy.

Just from looking at him, you could tell Lou was an old-time news man. He had the look down pat: the wrinkled collared shirt with the ugly tie hanging loosely from his neck, the dark pants that were held up by suspenders, a deeply receding hairline, and even a bushy mustache that was more grey than brown.

Plus, piercing green eyes that fed straight into a finely-tuned bullshit detector. Right now, they glimmered in a manner that made Jeremy want to squirm in his seat.

"You've been burning through a lot of travel money the last few weeks."

Jeremy opened his mouth to speak. Those expenses had all been approved...

But Lou beat him to it, continuing as he raised a calming hand.

"I don't necessarily have a problem with that, especially if this thing you're working on ends up being as good as the Grynmoor corruption piece."

"Trust me, Lou. It's big. Huge! I'm talking Pulitzer Prize big."

"Yeah, yeah. Great. What is it?"

Jeremy hesitated. "I'm still working that out, but there's a major cover-up going on. I'd rather not say anything else until I have it more wrapped up."

"Hmmph. How many sources do you have?"

"Just one. Anonymous."

Lou threw up his hands. "Then you don't really have *anything*, do you?" Shaking his head, Lou stood and walked back behind his desk. "Sorry, kid, but I'm pulling you off this...whatever it is you're working on. I've got something else for you."

Jeremy ground his teeth. He hated when Lou called him kid, almost as much as he hated having his toes stepped on. "Be reasonable, Lou."

"I've been more than reasonable. You've blown through how many thousands of credits chasing this thing, and you've got one anonymous source? There's nothing there, Jeremy, so drop it."

"But..."

"No buts about it. Here's what I want you working on."

Lou tapped his desk controls, and the display on the wall lit up with the image of an older man, married from the ring on his finger, with his arm draped over the shoulder of a very young and very buxom blonde. She distinctly was *not* wearing a wedding ring.

"You're pulling me off the biggest story of the year to investigate some schmuck who's cheating on his wife?"

Lou grunted. "He's not just any schmuck. He's Vladimir Zuchov, the head of the Securities and Exchange Commission, and she supposedly has strong mob connections."

"Great." Jeremy stood up, his irritation growing by the second. "This is bullshit, Lou, and you know it."

"Sorry you feel that way, but that's how it is. Go get to it."

Jeremy slammed the door behind him as he stormed out of the office.

---

Lou watched the door slam shut and sat back in his chair, frowning. Jeremy was right: this *was* bullshit. But there wasn't a whole lot he could do about it.

Orders were orders.

Sighing, he turned to his desk controls and tapped in the command to call his boss, Julian Deveraux, the owner and publisher of Star News. It took a minute to get through Julian's secretary, but soon enough his image appeared on the small display screen in Lou's desk.

"Is it done?"

Lou nodded.

Julian sighed and leaned back in his chair, rubbing at his temples with his fingertips. "How did he take it?"

"How do you think he took it? He's pissed off, and I don't blame him! What the hell is going on here, Julian?"

"You're just going to have to trust me on this, Lou. He's about to ruffle some feathers, and I need you to hold him back for a little while, until I can work things out."

What the hell did that mean?

Lou had been in the news business for over forty years, and had worked for Julian for twenty. He had never seen Julian back down from a story before, not for anything or anyone. The fact that he was doing so now was unsettling, to say the least.

"Jesus, Julian. What the hell kind of feathers are we talking about here?"

"Just trust me, will you Lou?" He both looked and sounded stressed out. Something was seriously wrong, but Lou could tell he wasn't going to say anything more.

"Ok, Julian. I hope you can work it out soon, though. It's going to be hard to keep him reined in for long."

Julian nodded. "I know. That's why we love him. Do your best."

The display went blank, and Lou leaned back in his chair. He clasped his hands behind his head and his thoughts raced. For the life of him, he couldn't figure what the hell was going on.

---

JEREMY LAY AWAKE LONG into the night, staring up at the ceiling of his tiny bedroom as his thoughts wandered.

Normally, he would have been asleep by now, especially after the workout Kelsey gave him. He glanced to his left, where she was already asleep, nuzzled up to him with a contented smile on her face, and couldn't help but smiling faintly himself.

But the smile didn't last, as even having a hot, nubile young intern in his bed didn't ease the consternation Jeremy felt over his re-assignment.

Jeremy muttered, "Fucking Lou," but must have done so more loudly than he thought, because Kelsey stirred and opened her eyes.

She looked up at him sleepily, and leaned over to kiss him lightly.

"You ok, handsome?" she asked, and he shrugged.

"Yeah, fine."

Kelsey frowned, and Jeremy knew his annoyance was showing. Sighing, he spoke again.

"It's just Lou. It still pisses me off, that's all."

"Well, you're the best investigator he's got, right?"

Jeremy nodded.

"So maybe he thinks this is really important, too important for anyone but his best. I'd be flattered, if I were you."

She wasn't serious, was she?

But from the earnest expression on her face, Jeremy could tell she was.

Ah, to be a naive intern again.

He smiled and kissed her on the cheek. In spite of himself, he felt a little bit better from her trite attempt to encourage him.

"Thanks, Kelsey," he said. "That actually makes me feel a bit better."

She beamed, then gasped softly. "I just thought of something! I could help you with the story!"

Jeremy shook his head. "No."

"Why not?"

"Because you're an intern. Interns do paperwork around the office. They don't come out on tricky investigations."

Kelsey's smile faded, replaced by a scowl. Without warning, she threw the covers off and got out of bed. Jeremy, perplexed, wasn't going to complain about the view as she bent over to snatch up her undergarments. Moving in the abrupt manner that broadcasts a woman is furious, she donned her panties and jeans.

"You are an asshole, Jeremy Reynolds," she snarled. The sway of her breasts as she bent over again to pick up her bra and shirt took some of the sting out of those words, but not much. What the hell was going on here? Quickly fastening her bra, Kelsey pulled her shirt over her head and stomped into her boots. "I let you *fuck* me! The least you could do is let me in on your story!"

Jeremy, shocked, watched in silence as she snatched up her coat and stormed out of his bedroom. A moment later, he heard his front door slam.

He shook his head, then burst out laughing. That was the most ridiculous thing he had ever seen!

Lou's antics forgotten, at least for the moment, Jeremy slumped back into his pillow. He fell asleep to the sound of his own guffaws.

# 7

# DISCOVERY

Jeremy stalked into his apartment and flung his coat onto the couch, impotent frustration lending extra force to the toss.

The last two weeks had yielded nothing. His new assignment was a complete joke, and he suspected Lou knew it. He had gone into Lou's office to present the data, certain that when he saw it, Lou would acquiesce and let him get back to the real story. Photos, documents, even the report from the private detective Jeremy hired to tail Zuchov for over a week: not a one of them showed any contact with the girl in question.

Jeremy had even tracked her down, and if she was involved with a mob kingpin, that kingpin had strange taste in contacts. He discovered her name was Chelsea Singletary. She was a hair stylist at the salon Zuchov's wife went to twice a month, and apparently was friends with Mrs. Zuchov, because they had tea together last Wednesday.

All of it pointed to a big, fat zero. There was no story there, none.

But Lou merely scrolled through the pictures on his televid display, scanned the documents, and shrugged. "Keep digging," he said.

Keep digging! Jeremy was digging his career straight into the crapper! What the hell was Lou up to? He had never been this obtuse before!

"Fuck it," Jeremy said to himself as he pulled a beer out of the refrigerator in his kitchen.

Plopping down in his stuffed chair—its upholstery was faded and the seams were fraying in numerous places, but it was comfortable as hell—he popped open the beer and, with a wave of his hand, turned on the televid screen on his wall.

One of those silly cop shows was on. Normally, Jeremy hated cop shows, but at that moment, he couldn't bring himself to care. For the next hour, he let his brain vegetate. He downed the beer, then another, then started a third, hardly paying any attention to the program on the televid.

He just sat.

The electronic beeping of his doorbell intruded on his meditations, and he sat up in surprise. It was a Tuesday night. None of his friends typically did anything on Tuesdays, and he had made no plans. Who was at his door?

Setting his beer down on his end table next to the two empties, he went over to the door and touched the security panel. The video feed from the security camera outside the door sprang to life. The hallway within the camera's field of view was empty.

Was this some kind of joke?

Curious, Jeremy cracked the door open, then, still seeing nothing, opened it fully. He looked both ways down the hallway, and aside from the doors of the neighboring apartments, the wall lamps and potted plants at intervals along the corridor, and a trash bin near the lift off to the left, there was nothing.

He was just about to close the door again when he looked down and saw a small package lying on the ground.

He picked it up and turned it over in his hands. It was a box, about ten centimeters long, five wide, and maybe half a centimeter deep. Jeremy gave it a shake. Something rattled around inside.

He stepped back into his apartment, and the door shut behind him. Settling back down in his chair, he found the seal and pulled the box open. Upending it, a small black rectangle, made of metal, dropped out into his palm, along with an earbud that was connected to the rectangle by a cord, of all things.

Curious, he turned the rectangle over, and saw that on the other side were written instructions. "Put the earbud in your ear and press this button."

This was just becoming silly. One of his friends was definitely pulling a prank on him.

But what the hell, he figured he could use a laugh. With a grin, Jeremy put the earbud into his ear and pressed the button.

His smile faded as a garbled voice, clearly electronically disguised, began talking into his ear.

"Mr. Reynolds, it is very likely that your apartment is bugged, and you are being surveilled. Do not react to what I am about to say. When this playback is finished, the device is programmed to erase itself. All the same, I would ask that you take precautions to more thoroughly dispose of it."

There was a pause, and Jeremy, for a heartbeat, thought one last time that this had to be a prank. But then the voice started up again, and he knew it was not.

"You've been asking about what happened aboard the Pericles. If you wish to learn the truth, come to the Tavern on the Green at one o'clock, tonight. Come alone, and wear a Yankees ballcap. You will receive additional instructions there."

The voice stopped, and a few seconds later, smoke began rising from the corners of the device. The voice wasn't kidding abut the thing erasing itself.

Jeremy glanced at the chronometer on the wall. 2230. Then he looked over to his other wall, to all his Mets paraphernalia.

Why did the voice have to be a Yankees fan?

Oh well, no use griping. If he hurried, he could probably find a store that sold a Yankees ballcap and make it to Central Park on time for the meeting.

Feeling energetic and excited for the first time in two weeks, Jeremy grabbed his jacket and headed out the door.

---

THE OVERCAST SKY precluded any moonlight, making Central Park especially dark, even with the snow on the ground. Jeremy, feeling like an ass in his newly-acquired Yankees ballcap, crept down the path toward the Tavern on the Green. He looked around carefully as he approached the famous restaurant, but didn't see anything out of place.

As he stopped in front of the Tavern, he smirked. He had never actually been inside the place. Hell, he had never been this close to it, despite having lived in New York most of his life. Funny how things work out.

He clicked on his chronometer display, tucked nicely at the lower left corner of his vision by the database implant.

Five minutes after one.

Whoever he was supposed to meet was late, and it was freaking cold. Jeremy stomped his feet and crossed his arms over his chest to stay warm, his mood getting more foul by the minute.

The soft clump of boots striking pavement drew Jeremy's gaze off to the left, where a shadowy figure walked down a path toward him.

That must be his guy.

Jeremy walked toward the person, who stopped when they were about two meters apart.

They looked at each other for a long moment.

For his part, Jeremy couldn't make that much out about his contact. He was medium height, and stocky, and was dressed in wool overcoat and fedora. Those had made a comeback in the last few years, but still looked exceedingly old fashioned to Jeremy's eyes. Shadows from the hat partially concealed the man's face, but Jeremy could tell he had a mustache and a wide nose.

"You left Quito too soon, Mr. Reynolds," the man said, by way of introduction. His voice was deep, and his accent had the sound of central Asia.

"Is that so?"

The man nodded. "I'm sorry you were disappointed in your interview with Captain Ishikawa, but did you really expect anything different?"

Jeremy frowned. How did this guy know about that?

There were only a few other people in La Chupacabra that night, and Jeremy was sure he would remember if any of them resembled him. This whole thing was beginning to make him a bit uneasy.

But then again, he had been in nervous situations before; that's how you get the big story.

Jeremy shrugged and assumed a carefree smile. "Never leave a stone unturned if you want the story. You can never tell who's going to give you the scoop."

"Too true. And have you had any better luck with the others?"

This was becoming annoying. "I have one more couple to try."

The man snorted. "You'll get no help from the Hersch's. They've drunk the Kool Aid more deeply than even Captain Ishikawa has."

Jeremy rather doubted that. "You'll forgive me if I decide to find out for myself."

"As you wish. When you're ready, come back to Quito. My associate is eager to speak with you."

The man turned and began to walk away. Was that it?

"A lot of good your associate will do. The only other person on that ship was Malcolm Ngubwe, and he's dead."

The man stopped and half-turned toward Jeremy. It looked like he smirked, though it was hard to tell in the half-light.

"Is he?"

---

JEREMY STRODE into Lou's office, an excited grin on his face.

"I've got a source, Lou."

Lou blinked in surprise, not so much that he had a source, but that Jeremy seemed to have regained his normal zeal for the job. Well, there's nothing like bringing down a crooked public official to do that.

"Good. Zuchov's clever, but arrogant. I'm sure that - "

Jeremy sniffed and made a dismissive gesture. "Yeah, whatever. There's nothing worth printing there. I'm talking about *my* story."

Oh no. "Look, kid, I know the Zuchov story isn't that exciting, but - "

Jeremy leaned over, resting his hands atop Lou's desk. "It's not any kind of story *at all*, Lou, and you know it."

Lou scowled and stood up. "No, I don't know it. If I knew it, I wouldn't need my best reporter on it, would I? I don't care if you don't like the Zuchov story. That's the story you've been assigned, and I expect you to work it!"

Lou realized suddenly that he was raising his voice. Through the windows to the main press room, he saw several sets of eyes turning toward the office, perplexed and curious.

Jeremy stepped back and shook his head. "I'm flying to Quito tonight. When I get back, I'll have the story of the year."

He turned to leave, but stopped when Lou replied. "You walk out on this story, and you can forget about coming back to work here."

Jeremy looked back at him, a bemused expression on his face. "Are you *threatening* me, Lou?" Shaking his head, he left the office, pushing the door shut behind him.

Son of a bitch.

Lou slumped into his chair and wiped his brow. He was afraid this would happen. Reynolds always had been impulsive. Muttering to himself, Lou jabbed at the desk controls, and a moment later Julian's face appeared on the display.

Sighing, Lou said, "We've got a problem."

# 8

## LA CASA BLANCA

nother bar in Quito.

This one, La Casa Blanca, actually *was* an old white house in the southwestern suburbs of the city. It was a charming construction, two stories tall with a wide wrap-around porch. But when Jeremy stepped inside, the quaint charm was replaced by the usual modern accouterments.

The first floor had obviously been gutted to make room for the large bar in the middle of the room, and the booths lining every wall. Swinging doors in the back no doubt led into the kitchen, and there was a spiral staircase leading upstairs to Jeremy's right.

Even though it was a Sunday night, the place was bustling. Every stool at the bar was filled, and several groups of patrons dressed in club attire stood around talking.

Waitresses moved through the crowd with practiced ease, balancing trays full of drinks or food over their heads as they made their way to the orders' destinations.

Loud music, the kind with a heavy beat but not much in the way of melody, pumped out of speakers in the walls, and a few couples were dancing off to the left on a small dance floor.

Jeremy grinned. This was his kind of place.

He arrived in Quito early Thursday morning, having flown through the night. Bad turbulence prevented him from getting much sleep on the plane, but he had long since learned that the secret to adjusting to a new location and time zone after a long plane flight was to just stay up until normal bed time at wherever he found himself. It made for a long and tiring day, but it did the trick.

All the same, he was just as happy to not receive word from his contact with the broad nose until this morning.

Jeremy had not gone out of the way to announce his presence in town, but he had not exactly hidden it either. It was partly a test, to see if this guy was as good at ferreting out information as he seemed to be, but also a ploy to hopefully allow Jeremy time to rest before getting down to business.

It worked in both respects.

The note left at the front desk of his hotel was plain enough to not arouse suspicion, but sent a clear message. Meet the contact here at 2330, in an upstairs booth in the back corner.

Jeremy mounted the spiral stairs and made his way to the second level.

It was quite different up here.

The beat from the music below thumped up through the floor, but the background noise was quite a bit softer, allowing people to talk without having to shout to be heard. The lighting was lower, more intimate. Tables were set up all around the floor, with lit candles in the center of each. Ringing the room were booths that were separated from each other by high wooden walls that stretched nearly to the ceiling. Each booth area had a narrow entryway and a curtain that could be drawn, blocking out the rest of the room.

It was easy to see why his contact had chosen to meet here.

Jeremy made his way through the crowd, noticeably more sparse than the one downstairs, and toward the back. Several of the booths had their curtains drawn, but one in the right hand corner in back was partially open. Through the gap in the curtains, Jeremy saw a figure sitting there, waiting.

This must be it.

Taking a deep breath, Jeremy slipped into the booth and pulled the curtain closed.

The booth was gloomy, the candle on the table having been extinguished. The man across from him was tall, lean, with dark skin and short black hair. He was dressed simply, but his collared shirt was freshly pressed and seemed to be made of high quality fabric.

The contact nodded in greeting as Jeremy got settled, then pulled a small device out of his pocket, set it on the table, and pressed a small button on its top.

Jeremy had seen that sort of thing before: a bug jammer. It would disrupt any electronic listening devices in the immediate area. And make the voice and video recording functions in Jeremy's database implant useless.

The man obviously saw the look of chagrin on Jeremy's face, as he chuckled softly. "Sorry for the inconvenience, Mr. Reynolds, but I can't take the chance that you're bugged. And I don't want any records of this meeting, even if they're kept by someone as trustworthy as yourself."

Jeremy thought he heard a hint of irony in the man's voice, there at the end.

"You have some information for me?"

The man nodded. "I was hoping to not have to meet you face to face. If things had gone differently..." He cut himself off with a rueful shake of his head, "But then I suppose we both underestimated how stubborn Jo can be."

The familiar way the man spoke piqued Jeremy's curiosity. "Ishikawa? I've met far tougher than her."

"Don't be so sure, Mr. Reynolds. She can be quite surprising."

"You talk as though you know her."

The man grinned, white teeth shining plainly in the gloom. "I know her better than most. In some ways, better than she knows herself."

Jeremy shrugged noncommittally, and waited for the man to get to the point.

A soft chuckle said the man understood Jeremy's silence. He fished into another pocket and pulled out a portable televid unit, with a set of wired earbuds plugged into it. Setting it on the table, he pushed it across to Jeremy. "You'll want to have a look at that."

Curious, Jeremy put the earbuds into his ears, then picked up the device and pressed play.

---

THE VIDEO WAS OBVIOUSLY FILMED on a hand-held, since the image bounced around periodically, but it clearly showed a half-ring of five people, all dressed in the light blue coveralls that starliner crews wear when underway, armed with slugthrowers and a pair of plasma rifles, facing a pressure door, with a sixth, a woman, standing ahead of the others.

"Alison, are you filming?" Jeremy recognized Captain Ishikawa's voice, and when the woman in front turned her head to look at the person filming, it was clearly her.

"Yes," answered a woman whose voice he didn't recognize, but he reasoned she must be Alison Hersch.

"Alright. Malcolm, open the hatch."

The camera moved over to a tall dark-skinned man as he pressed his hand against the door controls.

Jeremy blinked and pushed pause, his eyes flickering up to the man across the booth from him, the same man who was on the video. The same man who had been cremated a year and a half ago.

"Malcolm Ngubwe?" he breathed.

Ngubwe nodded, and Jeremy felt a shiver go up his spine. He pushed play again, and looked back at the televid.

The pressure door slid open, and Jeremy realized it was an airlock. He should have realized that from the start...

His breath caught in his throat. What the hell was this he was watching? This couldn't be real, could it?

On the video, four creatures, dressed in loose grey jumpsuits, waited in the airlock. They were short, powerfully built, and not human. They stood hunched on two legs, and had two arms, but there the resemblance to humans ended.

Even though they wore breathing masks, Jeremy could see they had features that made them look like cats: long snouts with sharp teeth and peaked ears atop their heads, short tails between their legs. But they weren't furry; instead their yellow-orange skin, streaked with green, shimmered as the creatures moved.

Were they scaled, was that it?

Captain Ishikawa said, "Welcome Aboard", and one of the aliens...they could only be aliens...moved its hand.

Someone shouted, "OH JESUS!" and the distinctive sound of a plasma rifle being fired rang out.

The alien that had moved was struck and collapsed back into the bulkhead. The video swung erratically as shouts ensued, along with a pair of menacing roars. It was hard to see what was going on.

He heard Captain Ishikawa scream, "NO! Stop!"

The video stabilized and centered on Captain Ishikawa, one of the aliens gripping her by her throat as it held her a quarter of a meter off the deck. Its free hand was drawn back to strike, and Jeremy could see vicious-looking claws protruding from the tips of its fingers.

"Don't shoot," ordered Captain Ishikawa in a strangled tone as she waved for her people to stand down.

The video panned over to show a man Jeremy recognized as Carlton Hersch slowly lowering a slugthrower.

Past him, Ngubwe had another crewmember pinned to the floor in a submission hold, a discarded plasma rifle lying on the deck nearby.

The video moved back to Captain Ishikawa, and showed the alien peering at her closely, then looking around at the other humans, particularly Ngubwe and the man he had pinned.

Then, with a barking sound, it released her and retreated a step. She slumped, clutching at her throat and coughing, but waved away an offer of support from Hersch.

The next several minutes on the video showed the aliens tending to their wounded comrade and helping him...it?...back through the airlock door, presumably to their ship. Then two more aliens walked in, pushing a large black device that hovered in the air.

Hovered! How the hell did *that* work?

The same alien who had earlier almost killed Captain Ishikawa now gestured for her to join it next to the device.

She did, with obvious caution.

The alien spent a moment showing her something on the side of the machine, some sort of control panel, Jeremy presumed, as it slowly lowered to the deck, then hovered, then lowered again as the alien touched different places.

The camera holder moved to get a better angle, and Jeremy was able to see that the device was topped by a transparent cover that appeared frosted over. The alien made a vocalization that was a mixture of a hiss and a bark and pressed something else on the controls. The cover cracked open, and fog that resembled melting dry ice issued from the device.

The alien opened the cover more fully and pulled out a small object. A bit larger than a baseball, it was leathery, orange-green in color, and wrinkled. The alien cradled the object close to its body and gave it a long, lingering, and strangely gentle caress. Then, looking at Captain Ishikawa, the alien pressed its free hand to its belly.

Alison Hersch spoke, sounding almost shocked. "An egg," she said.

Jeremy heard at least one other crewmember gasp.

The alien replaced the egg into the device and closed the lid, which immediately frosted over again. Then it pulled a long black device out from behind its belt. It showed the device to Captain Ishikawa for a moment, then pressed it. A three-dimensional image appeared in the air above the device.

Was that a hologram? Amazing!

Whatever it was, the image was clearly a star chart. It showed a flashing green dot, and a curved yellow line going to a small star not far away. The alien pointed at the small star and a second line, this one blue, appeared, going from that star to a larger star system, quite a bit further away. Then the alien pointed at Captain Ishikawa, laid its hand on the large device with the eggs, and finally pointed at the larger star system.

Captain Ishikawa shook her head. "Sir, we can't - "

The alien cut her off with a mixture of a growl and a whistle. Then it pointed again from her to the egg machine to the star.

Captain Ishikawa sighed, and nodded.

Jeremy couldn't believe what he was seeing. Had the alien just asked Captain Ishikawa to take its eggs back to its star system? Why?

On the video, the alien touched the device in its hand again, and the star chart disappeared, replaced by an image of that same alien, their Captain presumably, talking in its alien language of barks, hisses, growls, and whistles. The alien only let the video go on for a short time before bringing up the star chart again and pointing at the distant star system. That had to be a message for the aliens' brethren back home.

The alien pressed the device again, and a single dot appeared, with a strange symbol next to it. Then two dots appeared next to a different symbol. Then three, four, all the way up to eight. Then the symbols reappeared in various combinations, along with other, new symbols. Finally what looked like an entire page of alien symbols appeared. The alien waved its hand through the page and another page appeared. Then another. And another.

On the video, Jeremy heard Ngubwe's voice, speaking in hushed awe. "It's their mathematics."

The image in the air blinked out, and the alien pointed first at the device in his hand then, slowly, to each human crewmember in the room, even the man Ngubwe held pinned to the floor. Then it held the device out to Captain Ishikawa, who took it with an expression of trepidation.

The alien then made another hiss-bark, and its only remaining companion turned and walked back into the airlock.

Once its companion was gone, the alien made a strange hand gesture and inclined its head to Captain Ishikawa, Then it, too, turned and walked out of the airlock.

Jeremy heard a man's voice asking, "Where's he going?"

Then the video stopped.

Jeremy pulled the earbuds out of his ears, and they fell limply onto the table.

Was what he just saw real?

He looked up at Ngubwe, who stared at him with an earnest expression, and said the only thing he could think to say.

"Holy shit."

# 9

# DANGEROUS KNOWLEDGE

They sat in silence for several minutes after the video ended. The enormity of what he had just seen weighed on Jeremy's mind like a cinderblock around the ankles of a mob drowning victim.

Finally, Ngubwe leaned forward over the table and broke the silence, speaking softly enough that his words barely made it to Jeremy's ears.

"Their ship was adrift. Crippled. They managed to escape before it blew and made it over to us in a lifepod. When they came aboard, they realized they couldn't survive on Pericles long. Our gravitation and atmosphere were too different from theirs. So they gave us their eggs, a map of where to take them, and a message to explain what happened to their people. And they paid us, with technical schematics and the mathematical means to translate them. Then they got back in their lifepod and blew it up, so they could die with dignity."

Somehow Jeremy figured the aliens' thought processes weren't exactly as Ngubwe presented them, but he didn't press the matter.

"This is unbelievable! Why wasn't anyone told about this? It's... It's the biggest thing since..."

"It's the biggest thing *ever*," Ngubwe finished for him.

He was right.

A couple dozen colonized worlds and a hundred or so more that were at best marginal for sustaining human life had revealed a plethora of exotic flora and fauna, but no creatures that could be said to even come close to human intelligence. A few could give a great ape a run for its money, or a dolphin, but most were no more brainy than the average rabbit hopping down the bunny trail.

Or whatever they really do.

To actually meet intelligent beings, and beings who clearly were more advanced than humanity was...to say it was historic would be to say that the odds of surviving a fall from ten thousand meters were unfavorable.

Which made it even more confusing that no one had been told about it.

"Then why...?"

"There is much more to tell, but we cannot talk about it here. Too many eyes and ears."

"Well great, let's get out of here."

Ngubwe shook his head. "The people you need to meet are otherwise engaged tonight. Meet me tomorrow night, same time, at the train yards near the launch facility."

Jeremy highly doubted the other people were actually unavailable. More likely Ngubwe and his compatriots had planned this first meeting to size him up and try to determine if he was on the level before deciding to trust him fully.

It was not so unusual. During the Grynmoor corruption investigation, his primary source had required three separate meetings over the span of a month before he would even begin to give Jeremy the first hints of how deep the scandal went. Compared with that story, this was proceeding at light speed, and with a lot less expense.

Jeremy nodded agreement.

Ngubwe pushed himself to the end of the booth seat nearest the curtain and peaked out the curtain. Apparently satisfied, he took back the televid player and the bug jammer. He moved his thumb over the control switch, then paused, looking at Jeremy with serious eyes.

"Be very careful, Mr. Reynolds. This is a more dangerous game than you know. You are probably being followed already. If not, you should assume that you will be, and take precautions. There are people who will go to great lengths to stop this information from becoming common knowledge."

Jeremy nodded, not bothering to remind Ngubwe that he was a

professional, and knew what he was doing. Besides, he was a journalist, and that afforded him a lot of legal protection.

Ngubwe wouldn't appreciate hearing that, though. He clearly had faced a lot of heat, otherwise why fake his own death? Jeremy could understand him being a bit paranoid.

Ngubwe returned the nod. "Until tomorrow night, then."

With that, he turned off the bug jammer and slipped through the curtain.

---

JEREMY REMAINED in the booth for a long time, his thoughts racing.

He had known there was something big hiding in the shadows, but this? This was not the story of the year, it was the story of the millennium! The Pulitzer would not be enough to express how important this story was, and he had the exclusive scoop.

How the hell had no one else thought to look into this before him? Granted, Pericles' arrival drama was not broadcast extensively back when it happened, but it had been two years.

Jeremy could hardly believe his luck.

He needed to call Lou, and let him know this was not a wild goose chase. Maybe he would be less pissed when he heard that.

Jeremy tapped his thumb and ring fingers together, and his contact list appeared in his vision: a vertical list of names, complete with a thumbnail picture of the person's face beside each, and a blinking cursor next to the first one. Flicking his index finger along his thumb caused the cursor to scroll down the list, until it stopped next to Lou.

Jeremy hesitated, suddenly unsure what to tell him.

This was not the sort of thing to just go blurting out on the phone, even if Ngubwe was wrong. But especially if he was right.

Again he cursed the bug jammer. If he had been able to make a good recording, he could mail the video and audio to Lou as evidence. But without that...

Jeremy shook his head and stood up from the booth seat. He would call Lou tomorrow night, after the next meeting with Ngubwe.

The upstairs area was more crowded than it had been, to Jeremy's surprise. Then he noted the time and realized with surprise that it had been well over an hour since he slipped into the booth for the meeting. It had not felt that long.

Jeremy's thoughts were still wandering as he descended the spiral staircase. He did not even notice the woman near the bottom of the stairs until she bumped into him, spilling her drink all down the front of his shirt.

"Oh, I'm so sorry!" she exclaimed, a look of surprise that quickly turned to embarrassment on her face. She had a cocktail napkin in her hand, and began dabbing at the fluid that was running down his torso.

Jeremy gently pushed her hands away, grimacing in annoyance from the unexpected wetness and cold. "It's ok, really."

"I'm such a klutz," she said, still looking and sounding distressed. "Let me make it up to you."

It suddenly registered with Jeremy that the woman was a knock-out. Tall, only slightly shorter than he was, with lightly tanned skin, wavy dark brown hair past her shoulders, a slender and firm figure that was accentuated nicely by her dress, legs that never quit, a lovely heart-shaped face, and stunning eyes that sucked him in.

Despite his annoyance at her clumsiness, he felt an instant attraction.

"It's really ok, miss..." he let the sentence fade away into a question.

"Oh. I'm Jaqueline, but my friends all call me Jackie."

He shook her hand in greeting and was pleased to find her grip was firm, confident. "Jeremy. Jeremy Reynolds."

"Are you sure I can't make it up to you? How about I buy you a drink?"

Any other time, Jeremy would leap at the offer, but he needed to collect his thoughts. Besides, tomorrow promised to be one hell of a day. He shook his head.

"Sorry, I've got work, but maybe..."

Jackie snorted, a teasing smile appearing on her face. "All work and no play makes Jeremy a dull boy," she quipped. "Come on, just one drink. I promise I won't bite. Hard."

She was a little minx, wasn't she?

Oh what the hell. It's not like he was going to write any of his story right then and there, or in the morning. Grinning, he nodded.

"Ok, one drink. But first you need to find me a bigger napkin."

Jackie laughed and, grasping his hand, led him toward the bar.

It was shaping up to be one hell of a night, indeed.

---

JEREMY DID NOT REGISTER much about the ride back to Jackie's place, except for her.

The ride could have lasted for minutes or hours. Almost as soon as they shut the cab doors and entered the destination address, she was on him. Deep forceful kisses the likes of which he hadn't experienced in years. Freely roaming hands. Jackie teased him with a flash of skin, but when he tried for more, she demurred, gesturing to the cab's security cameras. By the time they arrived, he was mad with desire, ready to burst his pants.

Jackie's flat was on the twelfth floor. They kissed and groped each other the entire way up the lift, then down the hall to her door.

They spilled into her flat, and he pressed her against the wall. As the door slid shut behind them, he cupped her breasts gently and moved his kisses to her neck. She moaned softly, and he found the zipper at the back of her dress. A quick tug, and the zipper came undone, allowing her dress to fall to the floor.

Jeremy backed away a half-step to take in the view.

She wore no bra. Her breasts were perfection: B-cups, with small, perky nipples. She wore a black thong, with a barely translucent front that hinted at what was there without revealing too much.

For a short moment, he just looked at her, thinking he had to be dreaming. She was far and away the best-looking woman he had ever been with.

Then, with a grin, he bent over and took her nipple into his mouth. She gasped, then moaned again, running her hands through his hair and holding his head in place. After a long few minutes, he moved to the other breast, but she pushed him backwards.

He stumbled, landing on the couch he hadn't even noticed when they came in. Slowly she stepped out of her panties, revealing a short landing strip of brown hair between her legs.

Then she bounded forward and landed on top of him. Her fierce kiss pressed him back against the couch, and she tore open his shirt, not even bothering with the buttons. She worked down his neck with kisses, then to his chest. She lingered on his nipples, giving them little flicks with her tongue while she moved her hands down and began rubbing him through his pants. Now it was his turn to moan.

A heartbeat later, she was kissing his belly while undoing his belt. Then she pulled his pants and boxers down to his knees. Gentle caresses of his member had him gasping. Then she took him into her mouth, and it was all he could do not to explode right then. The things she was doing with her tongue!

After what seemed an eternity, she slowly came up for air. He shuddered with pleasure as her lips dragged over the tip. She grinned at him, swirling her tongue around his member and getting yet another moan in response. He wasn't going to last if she kept this up much longer.

"Are you ready?" she asked in a sultry tone.

He nodded eagerly, and she gave the tip of his penis a little kiss. Then her gaze moved from his face to something behind him, and she nodded.

Suddenly a gloved hand clamped over his mouth, and he felt cold metal press against the side of his neck. Ecstasy turned to panic in a heartbeat. He saw Jackie back away then he felt a burning line draw across his throat.

His hands went reflexively to the wound, but his lifeblood spurted out regardless. He flailed on the couch, but couldn't move far with his legs entangled as they were. He tried to cough as blood began filling his lungs, but was unable to manage it.

Why?

He mouthed the word as the room began to grow dim, the sounds incomprehensible. He could vaguely make out Jackie calmly getting dressed and speaking to someone out of view.

Then everything went black.

# 10

# WE INTERRUPT THIS PROGRAM

Jo was halfway through spreading cream cheese on her morning bagel when the news broke.

At first it did not register; there were murders every other day, after all. Then Reynolds' face appeared on the vidscreen and she dropped the knife. Moving quickly, she turned up the volume control and reversed to the beginning of the report.

"Tragic news this morning, as a well-respected member of the news media was found murdered. The body of thirty-one year old Jeremy Reynolds, a highly respected investigative reporter for Star News, was discovered in the west Quito apartment of known narcotics dealer and gang leader Henry Friedheim, also found dead at the scene. Police found weapons and residue from a number of narcotic compounds as well. Although the police have not released an official report as of yet, sources close to the investigation tell us they believe Mr. Reynolds was involved in a narcotics deal gone bad. Star News has not responded to requests for comment. We will follow this story closely, and bring you more as information comes in. And now, a look at the weather for the next - "

Jo turned the broadcast off, a chill traveling down her spine. For a long moment, she just looked at the blank display screen. Then, her breakfast forgotten, she strode briskly to her door.

STEVEN ANNOUNCED JO'S PRESENCE, and she waited for a couple minutes before Harold told him to admit her. She walked into Harold's office to find him sitting behind his desk, reviewing a document on his desk display.

He looked up as she came in. "Morning, Jo. What can I do for you?"

"Did you see the news this morning?"

He shook his head. "I had an early meeting. Why, what's up?"

"Jeremy Reynolds is dead."

He looked confused for a moment, and mouthed Reynolds' name. Then a light came on in his eyes, and he nodded. "The reporter who talked to you right? Damn. He was a young guy, didn't you say?"

Jo nodded. "Thirty-one. He was found dead here in Quito, in some drug dealer's apartment."

"Really? What do you think was he doing there?"

"No idea."

"Well, that's too bad. Hope he didn't have any kids."

With that, Harold went back to reading over his document.

"That's it?"

With a sigh of consternation, Harold looked up again. "What do you mean, that's it? What do you want me to do, break down and cry over the guy? I didn't know him from Adam, but he was making some trouble for us. So yeah, I'm sorry he's dead, but I'm not going to lose sleep over it."

"You don't think it's weird that he dropped dead here in Quito, just a few weeks after he approached me, after we discovered that Malcolm's still alive and apparently on the prowl here also? Star News is based in New York, so what was he doing here?"

"From the sound of it, I'd say he was investigating the drug trade and got caught somewhere he shouldn't have been."

"That's what the news reporter surmised, too."

"Probably because that's what happened." Harold's eyes narrowed as he looked at her, then he groaned. "Ah, Jesus. You're not going all conspiracy-theory on me, are you, Jo?"

Jo looked askance at him and shook her head. "Of course not. It just seemed odd, that's all."

"Well, I wouldn't dwell on it, if I were you. I love you Jo, but you're not the center of the universe. I'm sure whatever Reynolds was doing had nothing to do with your little adventure up there."

Jo shrugged and walked out. Regardless of what Harold said, she was not so sure.

---

JO COULD NOT STAY cooped up in her office with her mind racing, so she left at lunchtime.

She spent the afternoon walking in the Parque La Panecillo. As sunset approached, she settled down on a bench and watched as Sol slowly dropped behind the towering mountains to Quito's west.

As it always did, the orange-pink of the sunset juxtaposed with the shadows cast by the mountains touched something within her. It made her feel small, but also somehow in tune with the natural cycle of things.

She often came here to think when she was confused, or troubled. The natural surroundings and breathtaking views helped her get to the bottom of her troubles, normally.

But not this night. The news story about Jeremy's death kept intruding on her thoughts.

It was difficult to believe the story that he was in Quito investigating the drug trade. For one thing, why Quito? Important as the city was, it wasn't a great hub of drug manufacturing and trafficking. Just a few hundred kilometers away were half a dozen better places to go for that sort of thing than Quito.

But far beyond that, the thing that caused her doubt was what she had seen in his eyes that night in La Chupacabra. She only met him that once, but he had made an impression: a smart, driven, determined young man who was not going to be put off from reaching his goal just because Josephine Ishikawa put a roadblock in his way.

So why would he abandon the Pericles story and shift gears so quickly?

Even if all the other members of her crew held their silence—and there were a couple that Jo was not so sure about in that sense—she felt sure he would continue to search for some way to break the story open.

Try though she might to come up with another answer, Jo kept coming around to thinking that Jeremy's death had something to do with Malcolm and the crowd he ran with these days.

Which is why she was not surprised at all when she stood, turned around, and saw Malcolm standing there, watching her.

"Hello, Jo."

Jo looked at him, standing there so calmly, and irritation flared up within her. "Dammit, Malcolm, can't you take a hint? I don't want to see or have anything to do with you."

"I know. But events have left me no choice but to ask for your help again."

"What events are those?"

Malcolm looked down at the ground for a moment. "I met with a friend of yours last night. Jeremy Reynolds."

"I knew it! What did you do to him?"

He looked back at her, a flash of anger in his eyes. "I didn't do anything. You're the one who killed him."

"What are you talking about?"

Malcolm took a step closer, and Jo found herself tensing her muscles to fight off an attack before she realized what she was doing.

Foolishness! Malcolm would not harm her.

At least, she did not think he would.

"You told the NSA that I came by your condo." She opened her mouth to retort, and he continued, "Don't try to deny it. We both know it's true. Did you also tell them that Reynolds was asking questions?"

Jo nodded, "Of course. It's standard security protocol, you know that. But that doesn't mean - "

"You warned Carl, back on the bridge when you and he first detected the aliens' ship, that the NSA might make us all disappear if we screwed up the first contact protocols, remember?"

"No, I said we'd get in trouble if we let word spread too far about them."

Malcolm didn't reply. He just looked at her with his direct gaze, and slowly Jo got a sinking feeling in her chest.

Could it be true?

No. Rumors about inconvenient people disappearing were just that, no matter that she had used them to remind Carl about security requirements. And yet...

And yet, Jeremy was dead, and she had told them about him.

"Do you have proof, Malcolm?"

"Of course not. There's never proof. But last night, I met with him and showed him a copy of Alison's recording - "

"You did *what*?"

Malcolm gave her a long-suffering look, and after a moment, Jo's ire lost some of its fury. Did she really expect him to do anything else, after what he had already done?

Malcolm continued. "We were supposed to meet again tonight, and I planned to show him the other evidence I've found. The proof of the things I told you about before." He turned to the side, staring at the Virgen Del Panecillo, the last remnants of the sunset coloring the statue in beautiful pinkish hues. "I'd hoped he would write the story, blow the thing wide open, and they'd be forced to admit the truth and do the right thing. But now..." He shook his head.

Jo did not really know how to respond. His words triggered feelings of guilt within her, despite telling herself that what happened was not truly her fault.

Malcolm saved her from having to say anything by turning back to her and speaking first.

"Come with me tonight. I'll show you what I meant for him to see, and you can decide what you wish to do with it, in honor of his memory."

Jo shook her head. "No. Whatever it is you're into, I don't want to be involved."

Malcolm smirked. "You're involved already, whether you like it or not. They're following you, you know. Your house is bugged."

"I know that. I signed the consent forms, and they gave me a list of the bugs they installed. I've got nothing to hide."

Malcolm chuckled, his eyes flashing in amusement. "Ah, Jo, how trusting you are. That list is far from complete."

Jo crossed her arms over her chest, annoyance growing within her again. "If they're following me, how come they haven't shown up to arrest you?"

"If they catch me, Jo, they won't arrest me any more than they arrested Reynolds. They don't follow you all the time; they have other leads to follow, and they're not sure about you yet. But from time to time, if you look carefully, you might see one of them."

"I guess I won't have to worry about being mugged, then."

Malcolm looked incredulously at her for a moment, then burst out laughing.

Jo had forgotten how vibrant, how full of life, he sounded when he laughed. Despite herself, she found the corners of her mouth turning upward into a grin as some of his mirth carried over onto her.

His laughter fading, Malcolm returned her smile and asked again, "Will you come with me, Jo? I promise, if you're not convinced after what I have to show you, you'll never see me again."

All at once, Jo came to a decision.

Part of her was sure she would regret it, but a deeper part, the intuitive part of her mind she had long ago learned to trust to guide her in making difficult command decisions, told her she would regret it more if she did not.

Jo nodded, and Malcolm's smile widened.

# 11

## THE UNDERGROUND

Malcolm had a car waiting near the entrance of the Parque, an older model that would pass unnoticed in just about any corner of the city.

Motioning her to remain within the Parque, he looked around carefully as he crossed the street to the car and took a few moments to look beneath it, behind every tire, and under the hood. Then, apparently satisfied, he opened the passenger door and gestured for her to come quickly.

Feeling a bit of a fool, Jo complied, racing across the street and ducking into the car. Malcolm closed the door for her and then hopped in himself. He grinned at her as he closed his own door and started the car.

"Going a little overboard on the cloak and dagger, aren't you?" Jo quipped, and instantly wished she had not.

"Can't be too careful, Jo. Friends of mine have found car bombs before. One died because he wasn't looking."

The smile she had been wearing disappeared and she felt her heart rate begin to increase. Maybe this was a mistake, after all.

Then Malcolm fished into his pocket and held out a bandana.

"What's this?" Jo asked.

"A blindfold. For my protection, and for yours. You can't be made to tell something you don't know."

"You know what? Never mind." Jo opened the car door, and Malcolm grasped her arm.

"Please, Jo, trust me. I'm not going to hurt you, nor will any of the people you meet tonight."

She knew she should get out of the car and walk away, but Malcolm's expression was so earnest, so full of need, that she couldn't bring herself to walk away. With a disgusted sigh, she pulled the door shut and took the bandana.

"Thank you," Malcolm said, and put the car into gear. Jo tied the bandana over her eyes and slid down in the seat to wait out the ride.

THE RIDE WAS long and bumpy, with many turns. In reality it probably did not last as long as Jo thought, sitting there in her blindfold, but it felt like an eternity.

Of course, seeing how careful Malcolm was, how willing to believe he might be followed or car bombed, she figured he probably turned many more times than necessary, to throw off a tail. And, she was forced to admit, he probably did it to confuse her sense of direction, so she could not retrace the drive even if she wanted to.

Finally the car came to a stop, and Malcolm said, "You can take off the blindfold." She eagerly complied and sat up straight to take a look around.

The car was parked in a small, two-car garage. The parking area next to them was dusty, and filled with clutter: boxes, a work bench, tools, the usual sort of things that people put in garages instead of cars. Looking behind them, she could see that the garage door was closed. The only other way out was through a small door to their left.

"Here we are," Malcolm said as he turned off the car's motor. "Are you ready?"

Jo nodded, and they got out. At the door, Malcolm knocked thrice, then once, then four times. Jo shook her head and smirked in amusement. Three, One, Four: the secret knock was the number pi. Cute.

Malcolm noticed her smirk and shrugged. "We're almost all engineers, here," he said.

The door cracked open, and a nasally man's voice said, "Who's that with you, Malcolm?"

"Josephine Ishikawa," Jo announced.

The man behind the door grunted, then the door closed again. Jo heard a muffled electronic beep, followed by a series of rattles and thumps. Slowly, the door opened wide, and she was able to make out the man who had greeted them.

He was short, wiry, in his early middle years, maybe sixty at the most. His face was long and scrawny, his nose a little bit too large for the rest of him. He wore loose-fitting overalls and work boots.

And he held a plasma rifle, pointed right at her chest.

"What's she doing here? You were supposed to bring the reporter," he said, his squeaky voice managing to sound menacing.

Jo blinked in surprise. He didn't know?

Apparently not, as Malcolm replied, "Reynolds is dead. She's all we've got, now."

"Fuck," the man said, and lowered the rifle. "All right. Come on, then."

The little man turned and vanished around a corner, and Malcolm, gesturing for Jo to come along, followed him.

They walked down a short corridor that ended at a narrow staircase leading down. The stairs descended for longer than Jo expected, stopping at one landing and bending right before continuing down again.

They finally ended, after what Jo estimated to be a fifty foot descent, at another door, this one more solid looking, with a sliding view hole at chest level and an antique intercom box to the side. Looking up, Jo could see a small camera in the corner, looking down at the area before the door, and wondered at the purpose behind the view hole.

Then the view hole opened and the muzzle of another plasma rifle poked out.

That answered that.

After a brief exchange of words, the second rifle withdrew. A moment later, the door opened and the small man gestured for Malcolm and her to enter the room beyond.

---

Jo STEPPED through the door and her jaw dropped in amazement.

The room she walked into could have been transported to McCallister headquarters without missing a beat. In fact, the controllers in the

ECC or Flight Control would probably look with envy at some of the equipment they had here. Satellite tracking stations, communication downlinks, interactive star charts, and command summary displays dominated the wall to her right.

Off to the left, through a set of plastiglass sliding doors, it looked like there was a lab of sorts. Or at least, several men in lab coats were working around work benches in there. Further back, past the working men, was another set of doors marked with containment seals like were used for a clean room.

In the center of the room, a command station similar to hers in the ECC was set up, facing the display screens. Past that, the wall opposite her was plain, with two standard sliding doors leading to more rooms.

A solid thunk from behind them drew Jo's eye as a tall, powerfully built man, dressed similarly to the first but much more effective in the role of imposing security guard, closed the door behind them, leaving the smaller man to his post outside.

Seeing her gazing at him, he grinned at her, a broad smile that suddenly made his severe features warm, handsome, and inviting.

Jo felt a sudden heat rush to her face as she realized she had let her gaze linger on his impressive figure longer than she intended, and she quickly looked away.

Jo caught Malcolm looking sidelong at her with an amused expression on his face. "Lars has that affect on a lot of women."

"Shut up," Jo replied. She had to force herself not to grind her teeth in annoyance, both at him and at herself.

A soft chuckle drew her attention back to the command station, where a plump woman in jeans and a green blouse was just getting up from a chair.

A bit taller than Jo, she wore her extra pounds in a manner that only accentuated her natural curves. Add to that a pleasant face with an inviting smile, and Jo supposed she probably did not have much difficulty attracting men, if she wished to.

The woman stepped up to them and extended a hand toward Jo. "Captain Ishikawa, I've heard a lot about you from Malcolm. I'm Becky." She had a bit of the Land Down Under in her accent, unless Jo missed her guess.

Jo shook hands, and was impressed at Becky's firm, confident grip. "The pleasure is mine," she replied. "Are you in charge here?"

Becky shrugged her shoulders. "More or less." She and Malcolm shared a quick look. A moment of awkward silence followed.

Finally, Malcolm cleared his throat.

"Anyway, Jo, you probably want to get down to it."

"That would be nice."

Becky blinked, then nodded and led them over to the command station.

"This is a pretty impressive setup," Jo remarked.

And it was. The displays on the far wall showed a complete readout of every satellite in Earth orbit, from the smallest weather bird to the five large spacedocks in their geosynchronous positions. But beyond that, Jo saw starliners on departure vectors, shuttles running to and from the various orbital stations and Luna, pleasure craft of every kind...everything she would need to manage an orbital traffic control station. How did they get all this?

"It ought to be," Becky replied. "We paid enough for it."

"Surely this isn't a licensed traffic control station."

Behind her, Malcolm half-snorted, half-chuckled, and Jo found herself flushing slightly. Becky glanced at him and frowned slightly, then shook her head.

"No. Everything here is strictly passive: receive only. The Feds would shut us down in an instant if they knew we were online."

"Passive only? That doesn't make sense. How do you - ?"

Becky interrupted, "Every vessel and satellite transmits its location and velocity every several seconds via special coded sequences in its Stellar Navigation Transponder." She looked at Jo with incredulous eyes. "You didn't know that?"

Jo blinked, embarrassment flooding through her like a tsunami. She felt her cheeks flushing, and she nodded quickly. "Yes...of course. I just..." She managed a half-smile and shrugged. "I wasn't thinking about that." Clearing her throat, Jo changed the subject. "Where did you get the funding for all this?"

Becky and Malcolm exchanged glances, and were silent for a long moment.

Finally, Malcolm ran his hand through his hair and replied, "We provide...services...to people who would rather not have their comings and goings monitored by the government. Some of them pay quite nicely."

He almost sounded embarrassed. For that matter, Becky avoided looking her in the eye.

"So...narcotics dealers," Jo said. "Looks like the news broadcast was right about Reynolds' death, after all."

Becky perked up, her nostrils flaring and her lips compressing into a snarl as she drew breath to retort. Then Malcolm placed a calming hand on her shoulder, giving it a slight squeeze.

At Malcom's touch, Becky's ire seemed to leave almost as suddenly as it flared up. He spoke in an earnest tone.

"That's not how it is, Jo. Yes, we sometimes assist gangsters. But we mostly help honest people who have fallen afoul of the law through no fault of their own, or legitimate businesses who find themselves unable to do business effectively with all the regulatory and bureaucratic hoops they're forced to jump through."

As he finished, Becky reached up, taking Malcolm's hand into her own as it lay on her shoulder, and exhaled slowly, her shoulders losing their tension. Jo found her curiosity piqued, seeing the strangely intimate physical exchange.

Were they involved as more than just compatriots?

"So, what does this have to do with me?"

## 12

# EVIDENCE

"We keyed in on the Pericles situation shortly after you docked," Becky said as she tapped the control pad at the command station.

On one of the display screens that lined the far wall, a video clip began to play. Jo recognized it as the news footage from Pericles' arrival.

She recalled there had been minor media attention when they did not unload immediately, but it had quickly faded. The video was nothing special: just a long panorama of Pericles' two and a half kilometer long hull and the two counter-rotating rings which contained the ship's main living and cargo storage spaces.

"Who is we?"

Becky looked sidelong at Jo and hesitated for a moment before answering. "A group of concerned citizens. Over the years, we've observed the Coalition government becoming more closed and secretive, taking a more oppressive stance toward the civil and economic rights of the citizenry. A number of us, who value liberty and would not see it perish, gathered together to monitor the government's activities and bring its misdeeds to light."

Oh boy.

Jo had heard about these kooks, or at least about people like them. Conspiracy theorists who saw malice in every act, no matter how mundane. From what Jo gathered, there was little to be said to convince them otherwise, either.

"And have you found very many misdeeds?"

Becky nodded. "More than we feared we would. But none matching what they did with the eggs you brought to earth aboard your ship."

Jo rolled her eyes, looking from Becky to Malcolm. "Malcolm made that same claim to me before. Do you have anything to back that up besides conspiracy theories?"

Becky glowered at her, and opened her mouth to reply, but Malcolm beat her to it.

"After what happened to Reynolds, do you still believe the Coalition is on the up and up?"

Jo hesitated. Was she sure they were wrong? What happened was awfully coincidental, after all. No, that was not enough. "You haven't shown any evidence to make me think otherwise."

Becky jumped back into the discussion, gesturing toward the video of Pericles.

"At first, all we had was suspicion. The government's behavior after you docked was completely irregular. Which was odd, but the virtual news blackout at the same time made us certain something was amiss. Then we met Malcolm, and he described what you encountered out there."

Jo glanced at Malcolm. She was sure her continued disapproval showed, but he returned her gaze with a level stare of his own. "I can't imagine you just took him at his word. What convinced you, the video Alison shot?"

Malcolm shook his head. "I didn't have a copy of the video when I met them, just the technical schematics. Those were enough for them to believe my story, at least at first." He gestured to the back of the room, where the men in lab coats were working. "The group's engineers were just as intrigued as I was when I first saw the documents. Working together, we made more progress in three months than I had made in nine aboard Pericles. And since then..."

In spite of herself, Jo felt a surge of curiosity. "What have you discovered?"

Malcolm smiled, an expression of wonder and eagerness that made him seem a young boy for a moment. "It's amazing, Jo. Because the aliens only have three fingers and a thumb, they use a base-eight number system - "

"We knew that much on the ship."

He nodded. "Of course. You remember how difficult it made deciphering the documents, though. How frustrating it was. Well, about six months ago, we finally learned enough of their mathematical language to translate the schematics. Jo, they're plans for an artificial gravity device!"

Jo felt her eyebrows rising high onto her forehead.

Malcolm's grin grew more broad, and he bobbed his head. "You see it, don't you. With such a device we could build more efficient ships that won't require spinning rings. We could build new propulsion systems, hovering systems, you name it. It's so exciting!"

"That's a year after these people met you." Jo looked back at Becky. "You're very trusting. That was a long time to go without any real evidence to back up his claim."

Becky shrugged. "If there's one thing we've learned, it's the value of caution, and of patience. Malcolm made himself more than useful during that time. And if his claims amounted to nothing..." she spread her hands "...we at least got good work out of him."

Beside her, Malcolm smirked slightly at Becky's words, but she did not seem to notice. Or at least, she ignored it.

"But it didn't come to that. Within a few months, we received confirmation, of sorts. One of our informants within the NSA passed word that something strange had been unloaded from Pericles. Something not on the shipping manifests. If it had been narcotics or other contraband, the news would have been awash with reports of your arrest and trial."

"That's a big leap to make, from narcotics to alien beings and their artifacts: right past common sense to the fantastic. You didn't think it could possibly be anything else? You don't seem that dumb."

Becky glared at Jo again, then tapped, more like jabbed, the control pad, and the display shifted. The video of Pericles was replaced by an image of a long corridor, lit by recessed lighting in the ceiling. The image bounced around slightly, as though the cameraman was walking.

"We investigated very carefully. It took many months to learn where the NSA brought the eggs. But finally, just a few months ago, we managed to get a person inside," Becky said. Despite her obvious irritation, Jo noted that Becky's voice was calm and serious, and found herself impressed. Becky at least was not a complete amateur.

"So this place is where, exactly?" The corridor could be in any number of buildings Jo had seen over the years.

"Deep in the Australian outback. Far from observing eyes."

"Uh-huh. And who is this person doing the filming?"

"Just someone who works there and decided he didn't like what was happening. You'd be surprised how many government employees come to us for just that reason. He, however, was...a bit more emphatic about it."

Jo held off replying, as the mole turned a corner and approached a wide antechamber that contained a security checkpoint. Half a dozen men, armed and armored in the latest government issued gear, manned several scanners of various makes. The image bobbed, and Jo realized the bobbing was caused by the mole nodding to the security foreman. She blinked in surprise.

"He recorded this through his database implant?" Jo asked, feeling even more incredulous than she sounded. "How? Secure facilities have building-wide bug jammers so people can't do that sort of thing."

Becky crossed her arms over her chest and smirked. Her voice was positively smug as she replied. "It wasn't too terribly hard to design an algorithm to overcome that. It has a pre-programmed lifespan, so it will delete itself and be undetectable later, but it's more than sufficient to get the recordings we need." She lost some of her smugness as she added, "Unfortunately, it'll only record video, not audio. But it's better than nothing."

Jo had to concede that was a pretty impressive feat. From what she had learned during her security indoctrination, that sort of thing was supposed to be impossible.

On the display screen, the mole left the security checkpoint behind and walked through a pair of double-doors and onto a narrow walkway that ringed a large, open room. The mole looked down over the railing that ran along one side of the walkway, and revealed that the room was two stories deep. Jo could see from this high vantage point that it was divided into thirds. The nearest area was set up like a lab of some sort. Over by the far wall, it looked like there was a machine shop or something. The central third of the room was covered, preventing a recording of its contents.

The mole turned away from the work floor and moved over to a set of spiral stairs at the far end of the walkway. Quickly descending to the ground level, the mole passed by a round fellow in a lab coat who was waiting at the bottom of the stairs and stepped into a work area.

The image panned slowly around and Jo could see it was much more than the machine shop she'd taken it for from the overhead image. There were lathes, drill presses, and all the other sorts of machines one would expect from a shop set up along one wall. But the rest of the work area was filled with computer workstations and electronic devices of all kinds.

That was not unusual, of course, but Jo could see no less than three clean room containments and a vacuum chamber, and along another wall a series of pages containing odd symbols. It took her a second to realize those pages were recreations of the pages of mathematics she had seen in holographic form aboard Pericles, projected from the alien leader's black rod.

At least thirty people, all wearing lab coats, were working in the area. A few nodded familiarly to the mole, but he did not pause to engage them in conversation.

Instead, the mole walked over to the wall dividing the work area from the central, covered area of the room. A single door in the center of the wall provided access. The mole stepped through and into an airlock. A few seconds passed, probably for the airlock to shift over to the internal atmosphere, then the mole pushed open the inner door and stepped into the second area.

It was wide open, with hardly any furniture. In the center of the chamber rested the aliens' incubator, or egg stasis unit, or whatever the right term was. About two meters long, a meter wide, and a meter and a half tall, it was colored black with the exception of the control panel on one side and the frosted-over transparent lid on top. It appeared the same as when Jo saw it last.

"Everything looks in order," Jo said, not trying to keep the doubt out of her tone.

Becky cast an annoyed look her way. "Wait until you've seen the rest," she replied in a biting tone.

Jo sniffed.

The mole walked past the egg machine, and Jo saw that it was not as intact as it first appeared. One whole side of the machine had been removed, revealing its innards. Numerous probes and leads ran from a console set up nearby into the machine, to monitor or sustain its function, Jo surmised.

That wasn't so very surprising. The researchers would want to learn how the machine worked, but also would not want to disturb its function if they could help it.

The mole did not linger, but instead made his way through another airlock door which again stood in the center of the far wall.

"Son of a bitch," Jo breathed. She did not need to look away from the display to know that Becky wore a deprecating smirk as she voiced the words.

The laboratory beyond the airlock was clean, antiseptic even. Yet it was also ghastly.

In an anti-microbe containment not far from the door sat an egg. An elderly man with a kindly face that did not match what he was doing had his hands stuck into gloves built in the wall of the containment. He was cutting into the egg with a scalpel. Another containment several meters away contained what Jo had to presume was an alien embryo. It was dead, dissected. Nearby, three lab-coated men stood looking at an electronic microscope display of what could only be a part of the embryo and chatting amongst themselves. One of them laughed.

Jo felt sick.

"Seen enough?" Becky asked.

Jo nodded, and Becky tapped the control pad again. The video playback stopped.

13

# DELIBERATION

"Why? Why would someone do such a thing?"

Malcolm spoke before Becky could reply. "Do you really need to ask, Jo? Power. And fear. They see threats everywhere. They long ago sold their souls, and they assume everyone else has as well. It's especially easy to assume the worst of intentions in this case, because the creatures involved are not even human are they? Therefore, they can justify doing just about anything and not feel even a heartbeat's guilt or remorse."

Jo wanted to retort, to deny the truth of Malcolm's words, but any arguments that sprang to mind rang false even before she gave them voice. Finally, after a long moment of silence, she sighed and nodded.

"Do you understand now why I had to leave?"

Jo looked back at Malcolm as he spoke. His gaze was gentle despite the stern, determined set of his jaw.

"No. You didn't know this until a couple months ago."

"But he suspected. And he was pushing. Hard," said Becky. "We overheard high level chatter with his name on it. Chatter that made it clear if he didn't stop, he would be in serious danger. So we approached him to let him know he wasn't alone and to make him aware of the threat." She smiled faintly. "He didn't believe us, at first."

Malcolm shrugged, his gaze dropping for a moment as though he was embarrassed. "I was naive. With what I already suspected, I shouldn't have been, but..."

"But it's hard to really believe those who are supposed to be the people's servants would fall so far," Becky finished for him. "Until you've seen it happen."

"What convinced you?," Jo asked.

"After they warned me, I started paying more attention. I noticed the same people around me wherever I went. At the market, on the train, in restaurants..." He scowled. "I realized I was being followed. It wasn't hard to put two and two together from there. Becky's friend left contact information. I got in touch, and we made a plan. You know the rest."

Jo nodded.

The fire had been very convincing. No one ever questioned that Malcolm had died there, asleep in his apartment. Oh, there had been whispers around the office about how unlikely it was for a short to cause a fire of that intensity. But no one seriously doubted he was dead. A bunch of rocket scientists were not all that smart after all, apparently. Jo found herself suppressing an amused smirk at the thought.

"I had hoped to show all of this to Reynolds," Malcolm continued. "Once he saw the truth, he would go to press, and the conspiracy would be laid open for all to see. The government would have no choice but to do the right thing and send the remaining eggs home. But now..." Sighing, he shook his head. "You're our last hope."

Jo blinked. "Me? What are you talking about?"

"No one else in our crew will talk. And even if they did, you have the most gravitas among us. If you're not onboard, the word of a subordinate crewmember can be discounted. That's why we waited until we had definitive proof. I wanted you there with me to confirm what happened to Reynolds. Now, with him dead..."

"Hold on a minute. There are plenty of other news agencies out there you can go to. For that matter, why don't you just post it up on the internet yourself? Between that video and Alison's..." Jo stopped speaking, confusion welling up within her. "For that matter, you said you didn't have Alison's video before. How did you obtain it to show it to Reynolds?"

Becky answered, gesturing at the screen. "The mole. He managed to smuggle a copy of the video out. Nearly got caught, but he made it."

"Ok, fine. So why not upload - ?"

"We tried that, Jo." Malcolm's tone was somber, dejected almost. "As soon as we got both videos, we made an edited version that explained what was going on and uploaded it. It wasn't easy, because our organization does not operate any computers that are attached to the network. We had to go through an outside entity. But the Feds have bots on the Net, trolling for this sort of thing. Within a few minutes of our upload, the bots deleted the file and initiated a denial of service attack on the connection. An hour and a half later, agents raided the company's offices and confiscated all of their data storage drives." His eyebrows lifted high on his head. "Remember that?"

Jo did indeed remember a combination SEC/NSA raid on a local investment banking firm. They had been accused of insider trading and securities fraud, or something like that. But that company had very quickly been cleared of all charges and allowed to resume operation. It had taken them some time to get back up and running, though. They lost a lot of money and more clients. From what she had heard, they were now a shadow of their former selves, small time players at best.

"Ok, let's say I believe you. What are you proposing?"

Becky exhaled, tension seeming to leave her in a rush. "You and Malcolm will hold a press conference and reveal what happened onboard Pericles to the world, as well as what's happened since. I believe we can guarantee most of the largest networks in the world will be in attendance. It will be exceptionally difficult to shut down a gathering like that, or make it disappear."

"Then what?"

"Then," Malcolm said, "we wait to see what the government does, and whether we'll have to take more...drastic...action."

That sounded rather ominous. Jo inhaled and looked away from Malcolm and Becky. As her gaze swept over the room's displays and equipment, she found herself focusing on the readout of a starliner leaving Gagarin Station. From its displayed trajectory, it was on a heading for the Talos colony.

As she considered the vessel's course, memories welled up, of the Vine Peaks of Talos and of the days she'd spent there with Malcolm, so many years ago. Other memories followed. Dozens of exotic locales and celestial phenomena, more than most planetbound ever dreamed of seeing, passed through her mind's eye.

Jo felt blessed to have been born a starfarer.

Some starfarer natives, in their teen years, rebelled and left, choosing the life of the planetbound over the one they'd been born into.

But Jo had never even considered that. The magic of traveling the stars had called to her from her earliest memories.

To do what Malcolm suggested would put the life she had always lived in jeopardy. If it went wrong...

The notion of spending years in prison, followed no doubt by never being allowed aboard a starliner again, was unacceptable. It was a big risk. But at the same time...

Jo looked back at the image frozen on the main display: the dissected alien embryo. Could she just let that go?

"I don't know," she said. "I need some time."

From the corner of her eye, Jo saw Malcolm and Becky exchange glances. Becky wore an annoyed expression, but when Malcolm replied, his tone did not reflect his partner's opinion.

"Fair enough. But time is something we're running short on. Before too much longer, they'll call that portion of the project complete and dispose of the remaining eggs. When that happens..." Malcolm spread his hands in a helpless expression.

They stood in silence for a long moment. Then Malcolm cleared his throat and spoke again. "Come on, Jo. I'll drive you home."

---

MALCOLM DROPPED Jo off a kilometer from her condo, in a small park that was devoid of streetlights. They sat for a moment in the car as Jo removed her blindfold and collected herself.

"I'll be in touch in a day or two. I hope by then you'll have decided to do the right thing," Malcolm said.

Jo looked away, not sure how to respond for a moment. Finally, she just nodded and stepped out of the car.

The darkness masked their identities, but as Malcolm drove off, Jo could not help but feel nervous as the night closed in around her. This area of town was not particularly crime-ridden, but it was not the most secure either. She had read about a woman being attacked in this very park seven or eight months ago.

Pulling her light jacket tight about her body, Jo hurried through the park toward the main street. Not normally given to flights of fancy, she nevertheless found herself suspecting eyes were upon her. And were those footsteps behind her? Her breathing became rushed, and her brisk walk became a slow run, then a sprint. Surely the man behind her would catch her before she took her next step!

Jo emerged from the park next to a streetlight and almost collapsed next to it, panting from exertion. Leaning against the metal framework of the light for support, she looked back over her shoulder, half-expecting to see a burly, lecherous attacker emerging from the undergrowth behind her.

Instead, there was only the nighttime breeze moving the tree limbs in the park with a gentle rustle.

Jo managed a short laugh as relief flooded through her. A heartbeat later, chagrin and embarrassment followed. She wasn't a silly girl, scared of the world, and unsure of herself. She was a grown woman, successful and strong! She commanded a starliner crew who followed her orders without question, and respected her judgment implicitly. What was she doing, jumping at shadows?

Annoyed with herself, Jo pushed off from the street light and, pushing her hair back from her eyes, walked down the street toward her condo, standing as straight and tall as she could manage. But, confident exterior or no, she couldn't shake the feeling of impending danger.

It must have been the things Malcolm and Becky showed her. Jo wasn't about to admit it to them, but the video had shaken her to the core. She had always proceeded from the assumption that the government was a force for good. Keeping the order, providing a stable structure where people could live, pursue their passions, and conduct business that benefitted not just themselves but everyone else. These were good things, necessary things, that people needed government for.

But she had hardly ever lived under this particular government's thumb. Jo was forced to admit, as she walked through the night, that she had been very insulated in her little world aboard ship. If she saw some injustice here, or on one of the other colonized worlds, she often would just shrug it off. It did not concern her, because she would be gone in a few months, or a couple of years at most. As one of her mentors once said, she could stand on her head for two years if she had to. That was nothing.

All the same, she had never before been confronted with an injustice, a duplicity, of this magnitude. And from the very people she'd trusted to do the right thing! When she had left the security debriefings, Jo felt sure the NSA, and the other government bodies that would inevitably become involved, would do whatever analysis of the aliens' artifacts was necessary, then hurry the eggs on to their homeworld. That was the decent and right thing to do, wasn't it?

Jo had upbraided Malcolm for his cynicism, for his distrust. She had actively helped push him out of the loop, recommended against his being included in the team the NSA put together to perform their analysis. In the brief time between her crew's release from debriefing and when the Deputy Director asked her opinion, Malcolm had simply become too distrusting. Outright paranoid.

And now, it turned out he was right all along.

Jo blinked in surprise as a familiar doorway appeared off to her right. Had she reached her building already? Snorting in a mixture of disgust and self-deprecating amusement, Jo turned and walked into her building.

The lift ride was slow, as always. During the wait to reach her floor, fatigue suddenly set in. It had been an exhausting evening. Glancing at the chronometer on her wrist, she was shocked to find that it was 2 o'clock in the morning. It had been an exhausting *night*! And she had an 8 o'clock meeting with Jan Sholsburg, the navigation training department head, tomorrow. He planned to pitch his latest idea for new hire training. She had not been looking forward to sitting through the presentation, since Jan was, at his best, dry as a stack of well-seasoned firewood. As tired as she knew she would be in the morning, the briefing would be intolerable. It was too late to get out of it now, though.

Jo stifled a groan as the lift doors opened. Wanting nothing more than to grab what few hours of sleep remained for her, she hurried down the corridor to her doorway and pressed her identicard against the controls.

She crossed the entryway in a rush and was just opening her bedroom door when she heard a deep male voice behind her.

"Good morning, Captain Ishikawa."

Jo whipped around, her fatigue forgotten as she instinctively dropped into a ready stance. Her weight settled evenly between her feet as her hands raised into a guarding position before her torso, the way her father taught her all those years ago, and her eyes quickly scanned the room.

The man was sitting on her couch, apparently taking his ease. She recognized him at once: Special Agent Calderon, of the NSA. Red hot anger rushed through her, replacing her momentary fright.

"What the hell do you think you're doing here?" she demanded through gritted teeth. "Get out!"

Agent Calderon either didn't hear her demand, or he just ignored it. She suspected the latter, as he replied, "You're out quite a bit later than normal tonight."

"Like that's any of your business. Get the - "

Before she could repeat the command, Agent Calderon tsk'd softly, shaking his head. "It is very much our business when someone who is supposed to be helping our investigation goes off the reservation."

A chill went up Jo's spine. What did he know? But she maintained a straight face, her anger at his presence overcoming the uncertainty she suddenly felt.

"I don't know what you're talking about. You've no right to be here. Get out, now, or I'll call your superiors and have you brought up on charges."

Agent Calderon laughed, a mirthless chuckle that did not touch his eyes, hard as agates beneath his bushy brows. "You have it backwards, Captain. You have no right to keep us out. And if anyone should be worried about prosecution, it is you." He stood up quickly, his powerful frame moving with a fluid grace that Jo would not have expected him to be capable of. "You're going to have to come with me."

Jo snorted. "The hell I am."

Agent Calderon shrugged, the movement of his shoulders somehow concealing the movement of his right hand as it dipped into his jacket pocket. Jo did not even notice it until the hand emerged, carrying a small plasma pistol that he proceeded to point straight at her heart.

"I'm afraid I'm going to have to insist," Agent Calderon said in a quiet, no-nonsense tone.

**14**

---

## INCARCERATION

The room was moderate sized, not that much smaller than the bedroom in her condo. It was sparsely furnished with a single table in the center of the room that had two chairs facing each other and another, smaller, table off in the corner. The wall next to the second table was clearly a console of some sort, but it was dead and resisted any of Jo's attempts to turn it on. The walls were bare and painted white, as was the single door in one of the corners.

Jo could not see any video or listening devices, but she had no doubt there were several present. This was an interrogation room, after all.

Or so she assumed.

Agent Calderon had been polite, but firm, the entire drive to NSA's Quito field office. He never laid a hand on her, though he made it clear without saying it that things would go badly for her if she did not do exactly as he ordered.

Despite the unspoken threat, Jo could not bring herself to be afraid of physical harm. He was a federal officer, after all, and they did have rules.

She followed him into the field office and, when he directed her through a nondescript door on the second floor, she entered without question. And found herself locked in this room.

Alone.

By the chronometer on her wrist, that was two hours ago.

Her initial nervousness, her worry over what the NSA knew or suspected and how much trouble she was in, had long since given way to irritation, then annoyance, then anger.

Not to mention a steadily worsening need for the bathroom. If someone did not show up soon, there was really going to be hell to pay!

No sooner had that thought crossed through Jo's head when she heard the click of the door lock retracting. Then the door swung open and Agent Moore walked in. Dressed in a stylish pants suit that was elegant in its simplicity, the NSA agent paused just inside the door and looked Jo over for a moment.

"Please take a seat, Captain," Agent Moore said, her tone polite and businesslike. Then she sat down herself and placed her briefcase onto the table.

There was no point in making a fuss, so Jo sat down as instructed.

The two women sat in silence for a long moment.

Jo's anger faded a bit, replaced by a slowly growing amusement. Did this girl really think that silence was going to intimidate her? Memories of her father—dead for almost ten waking years now—and the discipline he taught flashed through her mind, and it was all Jo could do not to laugh.

This lady had no idea what it was to embrace silence, to commune with one's own subconscious for hours. Agent Moore had another thing coming if she thought a little silence and a weak stare-down was going to intimidate her.

After a short while, Agent Moore cleared her throat and flipped open the latches to her briefcase. "I must say, Captain, I'm very disappointed."

"Well you bought the suit. Next time, bring a friend along when you try on clothes."

Agent Moore scowled, her eyes narrowing with what could only be irritation. She pulled a small tablet from the briefcase and set it down on the table between then. Tapping the screen to life, she made a few more gestures, and a video began to play.

Jo's spirits sank as she saw the images on the screen. There was Malcolm, talking with her in the Parque. And then, in the soft-green tint of a low-light camera, the image of herself getting out of his car and walking through the park near her condo.

What the hell? Jo looked from the screen to Agent Moore, astonishment leaving her speechless for a moment.

Agent Moore's eyebrow quirked upward, and she said, "Yes, we had you under surveillance. Mr. Ngubwe very effectively lost our pursuers when you left with him, but he was...less careful...when he dropped you back off again. He led us right back to his compatriots." Her tone became amused, mocking at the end there.

Jo sat back in her seat and crossed her arms over her chest, suddenly feeling vulnerable.

Agent Moore leaned toward her, pressing her advantage. "What did you think you were doing, Captain? I told you to contact me if you heard from Ngubwe again, and instead you got into a car with him!"

Jo spread her hands in a gesture that she hoped was placating. "It seemed the right thing to do at the time."

"The *right* thing?"

Jo shrugged and looked from Agent Moore to the door. "I think it's time I spoke to a lawyer."

A loud snort was Agent Moore's initial reply. "A lawyer? No lawyer would have you, Captain."

She stood from her chair and walked over to the side wall. A hearty smack on the console mounted there made the wall flash, then turn on. Jo was only halfway surprised to see that most of the wall was, in fact, a display screen.

A slideshow of images appeared on the wall display, and Jo's breath caught in her throat. Lars, the handsome muscular guard, sprawled on the ground in an expanding pool of blood. Becky, her face bruised and battered and her hands cuffed behind her back, being led into a police cruiser. Other faces, people she recognized from her brief stay with Malcolm's organization though she could not recall their names, flashed past in various states ranging from dead to beaten or merely defeated, hopeless.

Jo looked, aghast, from the display to Agent Moore, her jaw dropping open.

Agent Moore smirked. "I suppose we should thank you. We've been searching for this particular cell for almost four years. They were very adept at avoiding detection." Her eyebrows rose in time with her words. "Until you came along."

Jo sunk back into the chair, the enormity of what had happened crushing down upon her. Guilt welled up, threatening to overwhelm her, as she considered the shattered lives on display before her. Frantically, she sought the peace of meditation that her father had taught her all those years ago, but it would not come.

Lord, she was a fool!

"You're a fool, Captain," said Agent Moore, echoing Jo's own thoughts as she sat back down into the chair across from Jo. "If you'd played it right, you could have gotten credit for this take-down." Agent Moore's smirk became a twisted grin as she went on. "Hell, they'd probably have given you a medal and a reward credit. But as it is?" She shook her head. "You're an accomplice. A co-conspirator."

Agent Moore put the tablet back into her briefcase and snapped it shut, then stood and walked to the door. The door swung open easily at her touch. She paused and looked back at Jo with eyes that almost appeared pitying.

"Such a waste. You could have been off in your precious starliner in a few months, a rich and respected woman." She sighed, shaking her head again. "I hope you're not claustrophobic."

At Agent Moore's gesture, two lean, muscular men stepped into the room. They moved around the table toward Jo.

She backed away, but quickly found herself pressed up against the wall. The two men wore identical stern yet apathetic expressions as they drew nearer.

The man on the left reached out to grab her, and muscle memory from hundreds of hours of training in her youth took over. Jo caught his hand and twisted it around and upward, putting him into a wrist lock that made his eyes bulge in surprise and pain.

The other man, his expression losing its apathy, bounded forward, but Jo forced the first man in front of him with a hard push against the back of the elbow on his trapped arm.

The two men collided and fell to the ground in a tangle of arms and legs.

Jo leapt away from them and turned toward the door. She froze as she found herself looking down the barrel of another plasma pistol.

"Don't make this harder on yourself than it already is, Captain," Agent Moore said, her tone icy as she flicked off the pistol's safety.

Jo swallowed. To her right, the two men were regaining their feet, their faces dark with chagrin.

For a heartbeat, Jo considered making a try for it, but just as quickly shelved the idea. There was no way she could cross the three meters between her and Agent Moore without getting a plasma ball in the face.

Besides, even if she made it, where the hell was she going to go? It was not like they would just let her walk out of the field office.

With a deep sigh, Jo raised her hands in submission.

Agent Moore nodded to the two men. They grabbed her by her upper arms and, one on each side, pulled her out of the interrogation room.

Agent Moore led them down the corridor, then down a flight of stairs into the Field Office's basement. A uniformed guard sat behind a desk at the bottom of the stairwell. He nodded familiarly to Agent Moore as she strode past and watched Jo with appraising eyes as she followed.

They trouped down another corridor and through a set of security doors into a long hallway lined on each side by small, sturdy doors with numbers on them. Agent Moore opened a door numbered '37' and pointed inside.

The men shoved Jo forward and she stumbled into the room.

Jo's first thought was one of relief. For one thing, her arms had begun to tingle from lack of circulation from the tightness of the men's grips.

For another thing, there was a toilet in the room.

Her next thought was one of disgust, because the room was nasty. The only furniture besides the toilet was a ratty cot along the far wall which was covered with dirty sheets. There was graffiti on the walls and grime in the corners.

What the hell kind of holding cell was this?

Then the door closed behind her and the lights went out, leaving her in near total darkness.

15

———

# HOLDING PATTERN

For a moment, Jo stood there in shock and growing panic.

Alone and helpless in the dark, she began to imagine all manner of horrors stalking her. Berating herself for being foolish and trying to focus her thoughts on the remembered layout and dimensions of her cell helped a little, but not much.

Unbidden, fear kept welling up within her, joining with the guilt that weighed on her mind already and threatening to reduce her to a weeping, huddling caricature of herself.

In the end, though, her bladder accomplished what willpower failed to, as immediate physical need drove her psychological turmoil down to a manageable level, at least for the short term.

It took several moments to stumble and feel her way, first to the cot, then to the wall, and then finally around to the toilet.

That taken care of, Jo stumbled over to the cot and sat down. She tried not to cringe at the remembered grime on the blankets, but in the darkness did it really matter if they were dirty?

Then all at once, exhaustion from a very long night combined with the stress of everything she had learned and experienced that evening crashed down upon her.

Sleep took her before she could think another thought.

LIGHT, bright against her eyelids, caused Jo to wake.

Groggy and disoriented, she couldn't register what was going on for a moment. Bright, blinding light streamed through a rectangular shape...a door? People, their features indiscernible as they were silhouetted in the light, stepped into the room and, bending over, grasped her by the forearms.

She found herself lifted onto her feet.

The figures all but dragged her suspended in the air between them as they led her from her cell. They turned left outside and began walking down a long, monotonous corridor.

Where the hell was she? In her half-dreaming state, Jo couldn't figure it out for the longest time.

But finally she began to gather her wits about her and regain her footing. She glanced right and left as she moved with the two guards, but she might as well have stared at the floor.

The passing walls were the same drab color and bare of decoration. Every few paces they passed another pair of doors. She stopped noting the numbers on them when they passed seventy-five. How many souls were incarcerated here in cells devoid of even the hint of light?

She shuddered to think about it.

After several minutes, she and her escorts reached the end of the corridor and turned right. Before long, they came to a plain wooden door that had a picture of the blindfolded Lady Justice painted on it. Jo tried not to ponder the irony of that picture given the nature of her accommodations as the two men pulled her through and into the room beyond.

It was a courtroom.

A man in a bailiff's uniform nodded familiarly to the two fellows who served as Jo's escorts and handed a tablet to the man on her left.

The man scanned the text on the screen and nodded, then touched his thumb onto the bottom of the screen. The tablet beeped. Apparently satisfied, the bailiff made a gesture for Jo to follow him.

She complied, noting that the two guards took seats next to the door.

She had come in through a side entrance, near the jury box, which Jo noted was empty. The observation gallery behind the counsels' benches was empty as well, except for a small grey-haired woman sitting in the back row.

Jo didn't linger on her for long. Instead, her gaze was drawn to a stately-looking man in black judge's robes who was seated opposite the counsels. He had the stern look of a fellow who sees miscreants all day long and has allowed that experience to tarnish his view of all mankind. Or he just had a good game face.

"Prisoner Ishikawa," the Bailiff said quickly as he led Jo around to the Defendant's bench. "Your case is next on the docket. Please wait here until you are called." He gestured to a seat two rows behind the Defendant's bench.

Jo sat down without bothering to reply.

Another prisoner was standing before the judge. Tall but pudgy, the man had an unruly mop of red-gold hair and was wearing a plain yellow jumpsuit. Beside him was a young man in an obviously cheap imitation of a quality business suit. The youngster couldn't have been older than twenty-five. Jo hoped for the defendant's sake that was a younger relative who'd come to lend moral support, and not his attorney.

"Trial is set for January 24th at ten o'clock," said the judge, and he rapped his gavel onto the plate on top of his desk.

The defendant turned to the youngster next to him and shrugged. Then the two of them shook hands and the defendant turned and walked past Jo toward the main entrance doorway. Jo watched him stroll out and felt a pang of jealousy.

"Josephine?" The sound of her name turned Jo's gaze away from the departing man and back toward the speaker.

It was the youngster.

He smiled at her—at least he had a nice smile, and gorgeous deep green eyes—and extended his hand. "I'm Wesley Thompson. I'm the public defender. This is the preliminary hearing. Lots of procedures to follow, t's to cross, and i's to dot. It can get pretty thick with legalese, so just relax and let me do the talking, ok?"

Before Jo could respond, a bailiff near the judge's raised lectern spoke loudly, "Docket Number 24483, United Earth Coalition vs Josephine Yukio Ishikawa."

Thompson gestured for Jo to move forward and she obliged.

Following him to the defendant's bench, she took a moment to size up the prosecutor. Tall and willowy, with legs that never quit, an overly large bust that strained against a business suit that was perhaps a size too small for her to be wearing in public, and striking features framed by flowing golden locks right out of a fairy tale, Jo hated her on sight.

Then she spoke, and her nasal voice made Jo smirk slightly. Miss Stunner was not so perfect after all, was she? It was a petty thought, Jo knew, but she couldn't help but taking satisfaction in it.

So it took a moment for the prosecutor's words to settle in.

"What did she say?" Jo asked quietly, disbelief making her breathless.

Thompson glanced sideways at her and shook his head, a look of annoyance flashing across his face for a heartbeat. "Let me do the talking," he said.

"How does the defense plead?" asked the judge as he turned his severe stare on Jo and her attorney.

"Defense pleads guilty, your honor," Thompson said, to Jo's amazed disbelief.

"The hell I do," Jo burst out. "She didn't even read the charges!"

The loud CLACK of the judge's gavel striking its plate drew her gaze back to him. "The defendant will remain silent," he said, an unspoken threat in his tone and his stare.

"Your honor, I..."

"*Enough*! Bailiff, remove the prisoner!"

"I told you," Thompson said softly, with a rueful shake of his head.

Rough hands grabbed her from behind. Jo looked over her shoulder to see the first bailiff. She struggled against his grip, but his fingers were like iron as they grasped her arms and she found herself being dragged away.

"This is a travesty," she yelled. "I demand - "

She reached the door then and her two earlier guards moved forward. One grabbed her on either side of her jaw, and she felt her mouth being forced open. Then he forced a rag into her mouth and his compatriot wrapped a cloth around her head to keep the gag in place.

Gag she did as the thug tied the cloth in place a bit too tightly and the rag in her mouth tickled the back of her throat.

Jo doubled over involuntarily as her stomach heaved and she tasted bile, along with a tangy, metallic flavor from the fabric in her mouth.

Her head began to swim. Jo saw Thompson shaking his head, a regretful, almost pitying expression on his face, as the door swung shut behind her. Somewhere in her rapidly fading consciousness she realized the rag was probably drugged.

Then she faded out completely.

---

Jo awoke some time later, though it took a while for her to realize she really was awake in the darkness of her cell. Finally, the smell of food convinced her that she was not just dreaming.

She struggled to a seated position, but fell to her knees the moment she tried to stand. Whatever drug had been on that rag was a strong one.

That would have been fine, but she contacted something made of metal as she fell. She heard a ringing clang as whatever it had been flipped up and then clattered back onto the ground. Groping hands soon enough discovered what happened: she had upended the plate of food as she fell.

Jo gritted her teeth and resigned herself to not eating after all. But rumbling from her abdomen and a feeling like her stomach was a giant empty hole in her belly eventually compelled to eat her meal off the floor. Whatever small satisfaction having a less empty stomach brought was overwhelmed by a feeling of shame that welled up within her as she sat back up on the cot.

Had she been reduced to behaving like an animal so quickly?

She fell asleep again a short while later. The sounds of her own weeping acted as a twisted lullaby.

# 16

# VISITATION

Most of a day passed before the two thugs returned and led her out of the cell again, though that day was marked only by the changing time display on Jo's wrist chronometer and the periodic deliveries of food through a slot at the bottom of her cell door.

Eating in the darkness was difficult and messy, but based on the flavor of the food Jo suspected maybe she was just as happy she couldn't see it.

She spent most of her time on the cot, trying unsuccessfully to not think about her situation.

Her mind kept whirling back through the events of the last several days, visiting every conversation, every decision she made that had led her here. And she found she would make the same decisions again, even the decision to go with Malcolm in the park.

A big part of herself wanted to lash out at him, and at her own stupidity for going with him. But that part of her mind was silenced by the memory of what Malcolm and Becky showed her, in their headquarters.

And then, after the evening meal, by her memories of her encounter with the alien beings aboard Pericles. The exhilaration of discovery, the terror when it looked like the encounter was going to collapse into violence. The feeling of crushing responsibility when the alien leader's request for their eggs became clear, and the awed respect at the way the adult aliens met their fate.

The crushing burden of responsibility. It was hers. She had accepted the aliens aboard her ship, allowed them access. She had allowed them to place their offspring into humanity's hands—into *her* hands.

She did the best she could, under the circumstances. Pericles only had enough fuel for the deceleration burn on approach to Sol and to maneuver within the solar system, and she had a little over five thousand passengers under her care, to say nothing of the monetary value of the cargo in her holds. Jo could not have changed course to the aliens' system then and there under any circumstances, not without sacrificing the lives of everyone on the ship. So she had trusted that the authorities would do the right thing once she reached Earth.

Apparently not.

It was the only choice she had, but that did not change the fact that she carried some measure of responsibility for what was happening to those eggs.

She was the one who said yes.

The feeling of revulsion she experienced when she first saw Malcolm's video returned, more pronounced than before because it was tinged in guilt.

She fell asleep amidst those feelings, and only awoke when the cell door swung open and the thugs entered.

When they took her this time, they turned left when they reached the end of the corridor. The corridor turned twice then ended at a set of double doors that led into a long, narrow room. The room was split in two down the center by a row of cubicles that was bisected by a wall of transparent plastiglass.

Jo had seen enough crime shows on the televid to put two and two together: it was a visitors' gallery. But it was empty except for her and her guards.

They led her halfway down the room and deposited her into a chair in one of the cubicles. Then they left. But they didn't go far, only about four meters, before they stopped, their backs against the wall and their faces locked into stern, expressionless facades.

Jo sat in silence for a long several minutes. Finally, a door on the other side of the plastiglass wall opened and Harold walked into the room. He did not look happy.

In spite of herself, Jo felt a flash of nervousness as he sat down across from her.

Harold tapped the table in front of himself, and a dialogue window popped up on the plastiglass between them.

"You look like hell, Jo," he said. His voice sounded a bit hollow, almost metallic, as it came through the window.

Jo shrugged. "Harry, I - "

"Save it. What the hell were you thinking?" He shook his head in disbelief. "What did that guy do to you that you decided to whack him?"

A chill went down Jo's spine. "Wha-"

Harold raised a hand to silence her. "I saw the video, ok?"

Just a few hours earlier, that would have made Jo relieved. But...Harry thought she had killed someone? Who? What video had he seen?

"I'm sure you had a reason for it," Harold continued, "but you've really put us in a bind here."

"Listen to me, Harry. I didn't kill anyone. It's a setup."

"Yeah? By who?"

Jo leaned forward and spoke in a softer tone. "The NSA. They - "

Harold snorted. "I told you not to go all conspiracy theory on me. Why would they, or anyone else for that matter, want to set you up?" He shook his head again. "You'll have to come up with a better defense than that."

Jo sat in shocked silence for a moment. Then, with a sinking feeling, she shrugged and leaned back in her chair. "That's all I've got."

Harold scowled at her response. "Well you'll have some help. I've got our legal team spinning up. I'll probably catch hell from the Board for it, but you're one of the best we have and I'm not going to leave you in the lurch."

Harold stood up and put on a grin that Jo presumed was supposed to be warm and comforting. It only made him look like a hooligan. Still, the knowledge that she wasn't completely alone helped.

A little.

"Don't worry. We'll get that public defender replaced by someone who knows what he's doing. I'm sure we'll have a favorable decision faster than you can say 'Gliese'."

With that, Harold turned around and strode out of the room.

---

It was days before Jo met her new lawyer.

By then, she had almost become accustomed to the conditions in her holding cell. There is something that happens to a person as a routine sets in. The person gets used to it, comes to rely on it. To be comforted by it.

Jo had experienced that several times in the past with new hires on the ship. First they were awkward, uncomfortable with the conditions onboard, but after a while they grew used to them. Most grew to like it; a few to love it.

But though she had seen that adaption before in others, and experienced it herself many times before, she never would have thought she would get used to conditions like she found herself in now. All the same, she found herself counting the minutes between each feeding, relishing the small amount of light that came in as much as the food. It became the highlight of her daily routine, almost a joy.

The rational side of her found that extremely troubling. It meant she was slowly becoming institutionalized. She began to wonder if they left her in this state for long enough, would she just confess to whatever they said, to avoid leaving the comfort of her routine? She scoffed at the thought, but could not rule it out completely.

So it was with a mixture of relief and fear that she encountered a disruption to that routine some days later.

First, the guards brought her to a small room, empty except for a shower nozzle. They told her to strip down, tossed her a bar of soap, then watched as she bathed.

She could have refused. Maybe should have.

But she stank, even to herself, and she felt grimy and crusty all over. So she endured their stares, and the lukewarm water of the shower, and managed to find some enjoyment in washing off the accumulated dirt of a week or more.

Her clothing was gone when she finished, replaced by the orange prisoner jumper that she was used to seeing on the televid.

That had taken long enough.

The guards did not rush her, but Jo wasted no time getting dried and dressed. Without the small distraction of the shower, she felt their eyes on her acutely.

Then they led her out. But instead of turning down the long corridor of cells to her home, or what passed for it, they led her to a small room that did not look all that different from the interrogation room. Except it was not an Agent waiting for her, but a grey-haired man who looked to be in his late nineties. He was dressed in a dark grey business suit with a blue and white striped tie.

He stood when the guards led her in and nodded in greeting.

The guard on her left fished a small tablet from his pocket and gave it to the man. He scanned it and nodded again, then pressed his thumb against the screen before handing it back. With that, the guards stepped out of the room and the door slid shut.

There was a brief pause while Jo and the man looked at each other.

He had sharp grey-blue eyes that twinkled with intelligence. His face was lined as any middle-aged man's face would be, but he had more smile lines than most. He looked vaguely familiar.

"Captain Ishikawa. I'm Jerome Middleton. I work at the firm Ernst, Middleton, and Young. McAllister Transport hired me to handle your case."

Middleton extended his hand and Jo shook it. His grip was firm, confident, unyielding, as Jo would expect.

At the mention of his firm, she remembered where she had seen him before. He and his partners had handled the defense of a high-profile celebrity who had been accused of murdering his wife and her lover a year or so ago. As Jo recalled, the defendant had gotten off. Suddenly her position did not seem quite so helpless.

"Glad to meet you, Mr. Middleton."

"Please, call me Jerome."

He gestured toward one of the chairs, and she took a seat. He did the same, across the table from her.

"Your case," Jerome said, "is a tricky one. The laws governing - "

"Could you start by telling me what I've been accused of?"

Jerome blinked, then nodded. "Forgive me. I forgot you have limited experience with the current legal regime. The charges in cases such as yours, that touch upon matters of Planetary Security, cannot be read in open court, for security reasons."

He leaned over and picked up his briefcase, which lay on the ground next to his chair, and sat it on the table to the side. Snapping it open, he pulled out a ream of, of all things, paper documents.

Jo's eyes widened in surprise. Jerome noticed and smiled again.

"There are also no electronic records kept. It would not do to have sensitive material leaked inadvertently."

He shuffled through the documents for a moment, then pulled a single page out. "Now then, you are charged with conspiracy to commit treason, conspiracy to reveal sensitive material, and the second degree murder of one Lars Hamilton."

Jo blinked in surprise. "Lars? They're saying I killed Lars?" She leaned back in the chair. In spite of the dire situation she was in, she found herself laughing. "What possible reason would I have to do that? I've met him once."

Jerome shrugged. "In these sorts of cases, it is not necessary to show motive. They have you on tape interacting with and then shooting him."

"What? How is that possible?"

"The terrorists' lair..."

"They are not terrorists."

Jerome raised an eyebrow at her, then shrugged again. "Their lair had multiple security cameras. No less than three show you entering and leaving in company with a known fugitive, then returning a short while later, as Mr. Hamilton was leaving, and gunning him down in the street outside."

Jo could not believe what she was hearing. "How does that make any sense at all? The NSA took me into custody as soon as I got home. The timetable does not work at all, never mind the fact that I was not there to be recorded in the first place." She leaned forward and tapped the table with an index finger. "You need to change my plea. That idiot of a Public Defender did not even consult with me..."

She trailed off as Jerome shook his head. "I'm sorry, but that is not possible. In these sort of cases a plea, once entered, is firm."

Jo looked at him, stunned. "So I'm screwed."

"Not necessarily. Your case is now moving to sentencing. If we play our cards right, we may be able to get the judge to be lenient."

"What does lenient mean?"

"That depends entirely on you." He pulled another sheet of paper out of the stack and perused it for a moment. "The prosecutor is willing to accept a minimal sentence, in recognition of your status in the star-farer community, if you assist in the remainder of the investigation and prosecution."

"What is a minimal sentence?"

Jerome shrugged. "Could be anything from 5 years with some probation to time served. It all depends on how valuable your assistance is to the prosecutor."

Time served! She should be so lucky. But... "What else is there to do? The NSA already raided their headquarters."

Jerome shook his head, his expression sad. "Apparently the terror - " He stopped and corrected himself. "The suspects were ready for the raid on their lair. All but a handful managed to escape, though agents confiscated all of their equipment and data files. The prosecutor believes you may be able to assist in capturing the remaining fugitives. Or, barring that, there are other cells in existence besides this one. You could assist in taking them down."

Jo snorted. "I don't see how. Malcolm came to *me*, not the other way around. I doubt he would come again after all that's happened."

"Nevertheless, the offer is on the table. I suggest you take it. The alternative..." He spread his hands. "Well, let's just say the prison system is very unpleasant these days."

Jo swallowed, then nodded. Whatever it took to get out of there.

# 17

# TO BE A MOLE

"I don't see how I can be of any further help."

They were back in the original interrogation room. Jerome sat at Jo's right this time. Agents Moore and Calderon sat opposite them. Agent Moore raised an eyebrow in response to Jo's statement.

"Ngubwe is among those who escaped. You and he are...friends." She said the last with smirk and a tone of distaste.

Jo snorted. "We stopped being friends a year and a half ago."

Agent Moore waved her hand in a dismissive sort of way. "From your perspective, perhaps. But he still trusts you."

"I doubt he does anymore."

"You may be surprised. There are any number of ways we could have discovered the cell's hideout. He is likely counting his blessings that he was not there when we executed the raid. I expect he may try to contact you again."

Jo shook her head. "He's not that stupid. He has to know that I've been in custody for the last several days."

Jerome cleared his throat softly and gave Jo an apologetic look. "Actually, you've been on the Gagarin Station, overseeing the deployment of a new array of navigation satellites. McAllister made a press release to that fact the day after your arrest." He smiled slightly. "Damage control, you understand."

Jo's initial surprise gave way quickly to understanding. She had supervised a few spin sessions designed to mitigate potentially damaging events in the past. It just made sense. If McAllister could get out ahead of the news cycle, they stood a better chance of controlling the narrative. And limiting any negative impact bad news would have on the stock price, of course.

All the same, the Mendeleev Cluster deployment was routine in nature. It had been scheduled for months and had been proceeding on schedule and on budget. Her supervision had consisted solely of receiving periodic status reports from the Mendeleev team; with everything proceeding smoothly there was no need to insert herself and there were other things that required her attention.

Idly, Jo wondered how McAllister planned to handle the crew on Gagarin Station. They had to know she never came aboard, and the Mendeleev team certainly would know she was not personally overseeing their deployment. Of course, they were all operating under Non-Disclosure Agreements; it was a standard part of the employment contract. But still, people talk and the presence of a specific person at the launch would likely not fall under the NDAs.

Jo suspected their year-end bonuses would be quite a bit higher than normal.

But that was neither here nor there.

"So what's the plan?"

Agent Moore replied, "Now you go back to work. You'll go about your normal duties and behave as though none of this happened. You will submit a detailed report on your activities to myself or Agent Calderon each day. Sooner or later, Ngubwe will contact you again. When he does, you will agree to meet him and inform us. We will handle the rest."

"That's it?"

Agent Moore smirked. "Not entirely. Obviously we cannot let you wander around unsupervised. You are, after all, a convict." Outrage welled up within Jo; she was no such thing! But then she caught herself. With a guilty plea on her record, she was indeed a convict now.

Son of a bitch.

The two agents exchanged glances and Calderon stood. His broad hand snaked inside his jacket and for a heartbeat Jo thought he was going to pull his weapon. When he instead produced a small syringe, she let out her breath in a sigh.

Then he began to walk around the table toward her, and tension rose up within her. She pushed back from the table, her chair scraping softly across the floor, and said, "What do you think you're doing?"

"Josephine," began Jerome, but Agent Calderon spoke over him.

"This is a monitoring device. It will let us know your location at all times and keep us apprised of your vital functions so we can render assistance if you are accosted."

Jo felt her skin crawl as she looked at the syringe with revulsion. She had refused to get a database implant not just because she did not trust it would be any use by the time she returned from her next run to Gliese but because she felt strongly the need to keep at least part of herself private. The implants potentially opened everything to prying eyes.

And now the NSA wanted to put a bug inside her?

"Hell no," she spat, looking from Calderon to Moore and then to Jerome fiercely.

"Then we have no deal," Agent Moore said flatly. "You can go back to the criminal justice system and take your chances at the sentencing hearing." She leaned forward, her dark eyes flashing in the light from the lamps in the ceiling. "But the prosecutor will recommend the strictest punishment."

Jo swallowed hard. She had no doubt the prosecutor would get whatever she asked for, and the strictest punishment meant Jo would likely never again see the outside of a prison unit. They had her over a barrel and there was nothing she could do about it.

"You'll take it out once this is done?"

Agent Moore nodded. "Before you launch on your next starliner run."

Jo blinked. "Pericles won't be ready for another twenty-two months, maybe twenty-three. And then there are space trials and workups before she can be certified for another commercial run. That's a very long time to..."

"We can no longer trust your judgment in this matter, Captain. The directive came down from the highest level - you will not be released without monitoring. So," Agent Moore clasped her hands on the tabletop and fixed Jo with an unblinking gaze, "what will it be?"

---

"It's good to have you back, Jo," Harold said.

She sat in his office, in one of the chairs surrounding his coffee table. His apparently genuine smile and pleased tone should have been complimentary but for some reason Jo found them disconcerting. Maybe it was just the stress of the last several weeks and the discomfort of her new implant - she found herself rubbing at the muscle of her shoulder where they injected it every now and then, almost like a nervous tick - but Harold's greeting rang hollow to her.

Jo shrugged and managed a weak smile in response, but said nothing.

Harold's smile slipped slightly. Silence reigned for a few moments, then he cleared his throat softly. "I'm glad to see Jerome was able to work everything out. He's a miracle-worker sometimes, that one."

"Yes, he was very helpful. Is there anything I need to know before I get back to my duties?"

Harold's smile broadened again and he shrugged slightly. "Wu Shin covered things pretty well. There were no big crises, except for the Mendeleev deployment, but you know all about that, right?" He winked conspiratorially at her.

Jo rolled her eyes. "The deployment was successful, yes?"

Harold nodded.

"Well that's something at least. I guess I'll go get caught up then."

She moved to stand, but Harold stopped her with a light hand on her knee. "There *is* one thing we need to discuss, Jo."

"Oh?"

"Chandini told me you're going to be working with the Agency as part of your deal." He paused for a moment, then took a deep breath. "I don't know exactly what you're into, but be careful. She is not happy with you at all, and that can be...dangerous."

Jo cocked her head to the side and smirked. "Harry, if I didn't know any better, I'd say you were worried about me."

Harold snorted. "I *am* worried." He stood and walked over to the window. He had a great view of downtown Quito and the mountains to the east and north from his office. For a long moment, he just looked out there. Finally he seemed to come to a decision about something. He inhaled and nodded, then turned back to Jo. "Get whatever business you have with them done as soon as you can. Then I'm putting you on the next starliner out of here."

Jo stiffened, almost feeling as though she had been slapped. "But...Pericles..."

Harold scowled. "You don't have time to wait for Pericles, Jo. Agrippa departs for Talos two months from Thursday. I'm transferring you to her, assuming you're done with whatever the NSA needs you to do by then. Captain Dorsey will take your place on Pericles."

Chagrined, Jo stood and stalked over toward Harold. "You just can't swap the Captains of two different crews," she said. "The crews have their own ways of doing business, their own cultures. It takes..."

"I can, and I am. No argument, Jo!"

Jo just stared at him for a moment. Harold had been planetside for years, but he had flown in starliners for the first several decades of his career, even commanded a starliner and a colonial field office. He knew the upheaval he was about to set off. It was hard enough when Captains changed out in the normal rotation, but at least in that case there was time to prepare for it. Doing it this suddenly... The two crews in question would take months, if not years, to get back to their current levels of performance.

She shook her head. "I appreciate your concern, Harry, I really do. But I think you're overreacting."

Harold shook his head. "You've not lived here very long, Jo. I've seen what can happen to people the NSA finds inconvenient or dangerous. Trust me, you want to get off this rock as soon as you can. I'm half-tempted to put you on the Kennedy, and to blazes with what Chandini wants."

Jo blinked. Kennedy was set to depart at the end of the week. Harold *was* worried. Christ...

Part of her wanted to take Harold up on the offer, to blast away from Earth and all of the trouble that had reared up around her. But she had no doubt that would get Harold into a lot of trouble. Possibly her other friends here as well. And beyond that, there was still the matter of the eggs. She could not just flee without knowing how that situation had been resolved.

She shook her head.

"No, Harry, I have to take care of this first."

He nodded. "Yes you do. But then it's Agrippa, in two months. Got it?"

Jo sighed and nodded acquiescence. Harold looked relieved.

**18**

---

## OUT OF THE FRYING PAN

"We will handle the rest."

Agent Moore's words echoed in Jo's mind as she walked into the Parque La Panecillo again. Without realizing what she was doing, she found herself touching the seam of her jacket where the NSA agents had implanted the listening bug. As it registered, she jerked her hand away.

It almost felt dirty, touching it.

It took most of a week, but Agent Moore was correct; Malcolm made contact. Jo had spent a hard week in the office getting the Kennedy ready for departure. By the time she got home after spending most of last night in McAllister's traffic control center watching the starliner depart—and secretly wishing she was aboard—Jo was completely drained, both physically and mentally.

So she was completely unprepared to walk into her condo and find a message waiting in her televid queue. At first she thought it would be Wu Shin or Harold, but when she tapped the control pad to start the message, the screen showed a dark figure sitting before a darker background. She could not make out the figure's features, but his overall build and the way he carried himself resembled Malcolm. A voice, garbled from electronic distortion, was no help in identifying the person either. It simply asked her to meet in the Parque at 2230 the next night.

She had spent a restless night tossing and turning in her bed only to wake an hour earlier than normal feeling as though she had not slept at all. Looking at herself in the mirror as she brushed her teeth put the lie to that feeling, as the shadows beneath her eyes were much improved from the day before. She still felt like hell, though.

And no wonder, with everything that had happened.

She had been distracted most of the day, only paying cursory attention to the weekly briefing from her department heads. Her thoughts kept wandering to what she had learned in Malcolm and Becky's command center and to what she had gone through since.

Agent Moore had again assured her, during their preparations this afternoon, that she was doing the right thing, but Jo was not sure. What *was* the right thing to do? Her heart told her that betraying Malcolm and his compatriots was wrong, that they were on the right side in this matter.

And yet...

Images sprang into her mind, memories she had not recalled earlier from her encounter with the aliens aboard Pericles. Twin burns, as though made by plasma torches hundreds of times stronger than any torch in any of the shipyards she'd seen, running perfectly parallel across the port side of the aliens' ship. Gasses venting to space through those two burns where the hull had been breached. She and her crew had speculated at length on what could have caused those burns. The only thing they had come up with was a weapon of some sort.

If the aliens had been engaged in a battle before she met them, there was a lot more to their situation than met the eye. Given that, was it not prudent for the government to do everything it could to learn as much about the aliens as it could? The Coalition's first responsibility was the security of its citizens, after all.

But that did not justify slaughtering the aliens' children. Did it?

Further self-debate stopped as she rounded a corner and emerged into a clearing below the Virgen. Malcolm sat, apparently calm and collected, on a bench a short distance away. His clothing was rumpled as if he had slept in it, and he looked tired. Jo stopped, almost turning to leave before he noticed her, but Agent Moore's stern warning from earlier in the day about what would happen if she did not come through sprang to mind and she hesitated.

The brief hesitation sealed the deal. Malcolm turned his head and spotted her. The quick flash of a smile graced his face as he stood. By the time he walked over to her, though, his expression was all business.

"Hello, Jo."

Jo managed a smile of greeting. "Malcolm."

He looked at her closely, his head cocking to the side as though he could sense something was wrong. "Are you..."

"MALCOLM NGUBWE!"

Agent Calderon's voice barked through the evening air, bringing Malcolm up short. Calderon stepped into the open from the trees to Jo's right. At the same time, another agent, Jo never got his name, emerged from the left.

Malcolm's eyes widened and he looked at Jo, a shocked, stricken look on his face. She felt a wrenching in her gut, almost a physical pain at the hurt her betrayal had caused him.

"I'm sorry," she whispered as she backed away and the two agents advanced toward him.

Malcolm turned and ran, but he only went a few paces before he was brought up short by Agent Moore and a fourth as they sprang from concealed positions on the other side of the clearing. They leveled plasma pistols at Malcolm and he froze, raising his hands above his head.

"On the ground. Now," ordered Agent Moore in a clipped, businesslike tone. Malcolm obliged, slowly going to his knees and then onto his belly. Agent Moore and her backup advanced toward him quickly, the man pulling a pair of handcuffs from a pouch on the back of his belt.

Agent Calderon remained in position as they moved, covering them over the sights of his pistol. "We've got it from here, Captain. DiStefano, take her back to the truck."

DiStefano, the man who had arrived at Jo's left, nodded in response to Agent Calderon's command and holstered his sidearm. Then he stepped to Jo's side and placed a gentle hand on her arm that nevertheless directed her away with a forceful intensity. "This way, Captain."

Jo complied with DiStefano's direction and walked away. She looked back over her shoulder once and saw Malcolm, on his knees with his hands cuffed behind his back. In spite of his situation, he did not look defeated.

Then she lost sight of him as they turned the corner. Had she done the right thing? She was not sure, and the thought that she had no choice was small comfort.

"How long do cases like this take to go to trial?" she asked.

DiStefano sniffed. "What?"

"How long until the trial?"

He snorted but did not answer.

Jo stopped, a sudden chill going up her spine. That snort had been far too dismissive. They couldn't intend to... Unbidden, Reynolds' face appeared in her mind and Jo found that she could not tell herself that they *wouldn't* just get Malcolm out of the way and to blazes with the trial.

It took DiStefano two steps to realize she was no longer beside him. Turning with a scowl, he said, "Come on, let's go."

"What are they going to do with Malcolm?"

DiStefano looked at her like she was an idiot. "He's out of the picture now. You need to worry about what happens with *you*." He stepped over to her and she found herself craning her neck to meet his eyes. He was very tall. "Don't do anything else stupid and you'll come out of this smelling like roses."

"But..."

A sharp sound came through the trees from the clearing and Jo's heart skipped a beat. That was a plasma pistol!

"Malcolm!"

Jo turned back to the clearing, needing to see. She heard DiStefano moving a heartbeat before she felt his hands slide beneath her upper arms, then over her shoulders and up toward the back of her neck.

She reacted instinctively, straightening her arms, dropping to her back on the ground in front of DiStefano, and kicking upward before he could close the full-nelson lock he was trying to put on her. Clearly not expecting resistance, he froze in surprise as she slid from his grasp, then doubled over as the toe of her boot struck him just above his navel.

DiStefano stumbled away and Jo sprang to her feet. Perhaps she should have run, but she remained frozen in place, surprised.

She had not practiced very much over the last several years, but she clearly had not lost *all* of the skills her father had taught her, so very long ago. The slight pleasure she felt at that discovery was quickly eclipsed as she realized what just happened. She had assaulted an NSA Agent!

Then she lost the opportunity to think.

DiStefano righted himself and turned toward her. His hand snaked into his jacket, where he wore his plasma pistol in a shoulder holster, and he spat, "BITCH!"

Jo's eyes widened as his hand came back out, weapon held in a tight grip. He had a murderous look in his eyes.

Only a couple meters stood between them. Moving with a desperate speed, Jo sprang toward him as he leveled the gun. Her hand struck his the instant he pulled the trigger. The pistol barked, deafeningly loud at such close range, but the superheated ball of gas that launched from its muzzle passed harmlessly to the side. Jo grabbed onto DiStefano's gun hand and forced it down and to the side. The pistol barked a second time as he reflexively fired again.

His face was a mask of fury as he pulled back forcefully against Jo's grip. She felt his hand slipping and knew he would be free in a heartbeat. Once that happened...

Jo twisted her body, using her weight to pull against DiStefano's arm, straightening it. Then she struck upward with the palm of her left hand. It struck the back of his elbow before he could adjust to her changing tactic.

The sharp snap of breaking bone and DiStefano's sudden howl of pain ended the fight. His hand spasmed and the pistol fell onto the ground at Jo's feet. Shifting her weight again, she kicked his feet out from under him and he landed on his back with a "HUFF" of air leaving his lungs.

She picked up the weapon and turned toward the fallen agent. His eyes, so hostile and superior a heartbeat before, were wide with surprise, pain, and sudden terror. He raised his good hand in a pleading gesture.

"Don't..." he coughed, slowly regaining his breath. "Don't shoot."

Jo stood frozen in shock over what had happened. Her gaze went from DiStefano to the hand which held his weapon. It was trembling visibly. What the hell was she doing?

He saw her sudden uncertainty and seemed to regain some confidence. Drawing a deep breath, he said, "Don't do anything you can't pull back from." His words were quick, his tone anxious but also practiced, professional. "We had a misunderstanding is all. Put the gun down and we can still work this out."

"Yeah right. I'm not a total idiot." Although a not-so-soft voice in the back of Jo's head screamed at her that she was indeed an idiot. A complete and utter fool.

From the clearing behind her came shouts and the sound of another plasma pistol discharging. What was going on? Jo peeked over her shoulder but saw only trees.

A shuffling from DiStefano drew her eyes back to him. He had snaked his good hand down toward his ankle. Seeing her eyes on him, he froze.

"What's that? A backup?"

He nodded slowly, watching her with wary eyes.

"Take it out and throw it to me. Slowly."

DiStefano scowled, but did as she ordered. The weapon landed on the ground at her feet and Jo slowly bent her knees. Taking her left hand from the grip of her pistol, she snatched it up then quickly straightened. Then she tucked the backup behind her belt in the small of her back.

"Do not move from this spot, Agent DiStefano," she warned, and she backed away, slowly at first, then more quickly.

"Don't be a fool, Captain. He's done, but you don't have to be."

Jo put a tree between herself and DiStefano, then turned and ran back toward the clearing.

# 19

## INTO THE FIRE

Jo pushed a low-hanging branch out of her way and stepped into the clearing, her heart pounding in her chest and Agent DiStefano's plasma pistol in her right hand alongside her thigh.

The scene in the clearing made her stop in surprised shock.

Agent Calderon was on the ground, groaning through gritted teeth and grasping at his left knee, which was scorched and blackened by what Jo assumed was a plasma shot. His pistol lay on the ground about three meters from him; a kilometer away for all the good it would do him. Agent Moore stood in a shooter's stance almost directly in front of Jo, her pistol held in both hands and trained on Malcolm and the third agent.

Malcolm stood behind the third agent. Jo could see the metal bands of the handcuffs around his wrists, but the chain between them had been severed somehow. He had his left arm wrapped around the agent's neck, pinning the agent close to his body. In his right hand, he held a plasma pistol pointing at the agent's temple.

"Put down the weapon, Ngubwe," Agent Moore said, her tone crisp and professional, though it also carried a hint of frustration.

Malcolm shook his head and took a step back, dragging the agent with him. "Back away," he shouted in return.

Agent Moore showed no sign of complying. She moved forward in time with Malcolm, her pistol never wavering as she sighted in on him. Malcolm was almost a full head taller than the agent he held captive. Jo imagined it would not be hard for Agent Moore to shoot him in the head, if she meant to.

Malcolm called out, "Put your gun down and back away." He was beginning to sound desperate.

Jo saw Agent Moore flex her hands on the grip of her pistol and cock her head slightly. She was getting ready to fire.

Before she realized what she was doing, Jo took two steps forward, out from beneath the canopy of branches and into the open, and raised the pistol she was holding, pointing it at Agent Moore's back.

"Do what he says," she ordered in her best Captain tone.

Agent Moore froze and glanced back at Jo. Malcolm's eyes widened in shock.

"Jo..."

"What the hell do you think you're doing?" Agent Moore said, her expression and tone growing harsh with sudden fury.

"The right thing. Finally," Jo replied. She stepped forward and to her right, keeping the pistol trained on Agent Moore. "Put down your weapon and back away."

The agent swallowed, her eyes flickering between Jo and Malcolm. She flexed her hands on her pistol again and she swallowed.

"Have you gone mad? You're killing yourself, do you know that?"

Jo shrugged and moved over to Malcolm's side, being careful to keep Agent Moore in her sights. As she walked, she put on her command face and said, in her best Captain voice, "If I'm already dead, I guess I'll have no problem taking you with me. Put. Down. The. Gun. Now."

For a moment, Jo had the sinking feeling that she might actually have to follow through on the threat. It was easy enough to say it, but contemplating actually pulling the trigger...

She was not sure if she could really do it.

Apparently her doubt did not show through on her face, because Agent Moore's expression changed from cooly in control to doubtful. She licked her lips and glanced to the side where Agent Calderon still lay in obvious agony—he was out of the fight even if his weapon had been near to hand—then back toward Jo. Their eyes met and Jo saw the doubt become fearful certainty. A few seconds passed then, ever so slowly, Agent Moore raised her hands and tossed her weapon off to the side.

"Good. Now turn around and get on your knees."

As Agent Moore complied, Jo looked over at Malcolm. He looked haggard, and no wonder after the last few moments. Jo did not want to look in a mirror herself right then. What the hell *was* she doing?

Malcolm gave her the briefest of smiles and said, "This way, Jo."

Moving as quickly as he could with the agent in his grasp, Malcolm backed away toward the trees on far side of the open area. Jo followed and in short order they stood beneath the overhanging branches. Agent Moore had not moved, no doubt expecting a plasma shot in the back if she did.

"Now what?" she asked.

In response, Malcolm twisted his foot between the agent's legs and pushed forward, sending the man sprawling.

"Don't move," Malcolm ordered. Then he turned to Jo and said, "Let's go."

Malcolm sprinted away. Jo hesitated only a heartbeat before running to join him.

---

"WHAT MADE YOU CHANGE YOUR MIND?"

Jo gritted her teeth and clung to the handle on Malcolm's car door as he took a turn at a higher rate of speed than she would have preferred. As in their last meeting, he had parked not far outside the Parque. This time he did not bother with the blindfold or the security walk around, though. They just hopped in and he floored it.

Tires squealed as the car skidded for a moment, then Malcolm righted it and sped away north down Bahía del Caraquez. They passed a hospital on their right, then he turned the car hard to the right again, onto Ambato.

"Where are we going?" Jo asked, not bothering to answer his question.

"We established a new safehouse north of the city," he replied in clipped tones. "If we can get on Highway 35, we should make it there relatively quickly."

And that would be the reason Malcolm picked such a late hour for their meeting. It was not just some cliché cloak-and-dagger act, after all. A getaway in Quito's middle-of-the-day traffic would have been laughable. But now, they just might make it. Except...

"That's not going to happen," Jo said, a sinking feeling in the pit of her stomach that was caused by more than Malcolm's hard turn to the left onto Venezuela.

Malcolm glanced at her and, seeing her expression, grinned and let off the accelerator. "You're right, of course. It wouldn't do to get pulled over for speeding, would it?"

Jo shook her head. "No, but that's not what I mean. I... Aw crap. Don't hit anything for a second." She unhooked her seatbelt and leaned forward then shrugged out of her jacket. Quickly checking that she had everything from its pockets, she rolled down her window and tossed the jacket out into the night.

Malcolm raised one eyebrow. "Bugged?"

Jo nodded. "But that's not all." She rubbed at her shoulder and imagined she could feel the bump from the locator concealed there. "They injected me with a locator device."

Malcolm's other eyebrow rose and he glanced at the shoulder. "Crap," he said, echoing Jo's words. "Ok, I know a guy who can take care of it." His eyes flicked to the rearview display and he frowned. "If we can make it to him. They'll probably follow us at a distance, set up roadblocks..."

His frown deepened as he turned right onto Jose Mejia. The intersection with Highway 35 lay ahead, but he did not seem to be relaxing at all.

Jo swallowed despite the dryness in her mouth and tried to suppress the anxiety within her. They were not caught yet; there was a chance they could still get away. Wasn't there? "We're not screwed are we?"

Malcolm glanced at her. His frown lessened and he shook his head. "Not yet. But we'll have to move quickly."

Keeping one hand on the wheel, Malcolm reached into his jacket pocket and pulled out a mobile communicator. He tapped its screen to life and made a selection. A few seconds later, the electronic beep which announced his call being answered sounded over the car's internal speakers, followed by a male voice.

"Robert, do you know what time it is?" The man's accent marked him as a local to the Quito area. His voice was deep and gravelly, and he sounded sleepy and more than a little annoyed.

"I've got an emergency, Raúl."

"What else is new." The man on the other end of the line grumbled something unintelligible then inhaled deeply. In her mind's eye, Jo imagined him sitting up, throwing his feet over the side of his bed, and rubbing his eyes as he woke up fully. Finally, he said, "Alright, what's up?"

"I need an internal locator removed. Right now."

"What???"

"I'm serious, Raúl."

The man groaned softly. "Robert, that's a tricky procedure. I need special tools, a lab... It's not just something I can throw together."

"Well you're going to have to. They're after us and we don't have a lot of time. I'll be at your place in ten minutes."

"What? Hell no, don't come here." The man inhaled loudly again. "Meet me at the usual spot in twenty. Ok?"

Malcolm glanced at the rearview again and nodded. "Alright. Twenty minutes."

The speakers went silent as the call ended.

Jo looked at Malcolm in confusion. "Robert?"

Malcolm chuckled. "I don't advertise who I am very widely, Jo. Raúl is a good man, but also a tad," he looked at her with a raised eyebrow, "shady, if you know what I mean. But if there's anyone who can get that bug out of you, it's him."

"That's a comfort."

Well, it was not, really. But Jo was committed now. Even if she was not sure she had done the right thing by siding with Malcolm, there was no going back. She was just going to have to trust him, and his 'shady' friend. Wonderful.

She took a deep breath. "Where are we meeting him?"

"In the short-term parking lot at the airport." Malcolm must have noticed the confused look on her face, because he chuckled and continued, "It's controlled airspace, so it's not likely we'll be pursued or observed by aerial units. And there's always a lot of people coming and going, even at this hour." He winked at her. "Makes it easy to blend in."

"Ah. That makes sense, I suppose."

The airport was a bit over twenty kilometers away, past a line of peaks east of the city. Throughout the drive, Jo expected to see the flashing blue lights of police cars in the rearview, or blocking the highway ahead. But there were none. As Malcolm pulled off the highway Jo managed to relax a little.

Maybe Agent Moore had been so delayed by Calderon and DiStefano's wounds that she decided to wait. More likely not, though.

Thinking about it, Jo decided she would not likely use the local police unless she had to; a public spectacle was the last thing the NSA wanted. So there would likely be no flashing lights and squad cars.

But they did want the rest of Becky's cell, and Jo had the locator in her shoulder. Maybe Agent Moore would wait after all, hoping Malcolm and Jo would lead them to the rest of his companions before they got someone to remove the locator.

Jo dismissed the thought. Agent Moore had never struck her as particularly clever, but she was not a complete idiot. She would have to know that Jo would try to get the locator out first thing.

Which meant the agents were on their way, and Jo would likely not see them until they were on her. So much for relaxing.

# 20

# TAKING FLIGHT

In spite of the hour, the short term parking lot at Quito International Airport was still about a third full. The last flights would not depart and arrive for another hour or so. That was some comfort; they would stand out completely in an empty parking lot.

Malcolm drove through the swing-arm gate and into the lot. Sitting in the passenger seat, Jo looked over at the terminal and, for a moment, the irony of the airport naming convention struck her. It's not like there still were nation states to speak of; just the Coalition itself and its member states, then the various provinces and localities beneath them.

Yet still people called some airports International and some Regional. It was funny now that she stopped to think about it, just like starfarers using nautical terminology onboard ship.

Jo supposed it was comforting, or something, to harken back to old traditions like that. But still, funny.

"Look for a yellow van," Malcolm said, bringing Jo back to the present. He turned down the first row of parked cars and drove slowly down it, peering side to side intently.

Jo shook herself back to alertness. This was no time to be daydreaming. Or nightdreaming, she smirked to herself as she glanced at the car's chronometer.

They traversed the parking lot twice without spotting the van.

Malcolm frowned and pulled into a spot near the exit gates and turned off the car's lights. He left the engine running, though.

"I guess we wait," Jo said. "This guy *is* reliable, right?"

Malcolm half-shrugged. "He's not the most punctual person ever. But he knows his stuff and is good in a pinch."

Jo turned to look at the parking lot entrance, an anxious knot beginning to grow in her belly. This was bad. They needed to keep moving, not sit around where Agent Moore and her comrades could catch up to them. But moving would not do much good unless they removed the locator.

Crap.

Jo found herself wringing her hands as the minutes ticked by, no matter how many times she forced herself to stop. Finally a yellow van pulled up to the entrance gate. She perked up and nudged Malcolm, who followed her gaze to the van and nodded.

"That's him," Malcolm said.

The van meandered around the parking lot for a few moments, almost as though the driver could not decide where to park. Finally it pulled into the space next to them. The driver did not get out.

Malcolm looked at Jo seriously. "All set?" he asked.

She took a deep breath and nodded. Malcolm returned the nod and turned off the car's engine. "Make sure you have everything," he said. "We may have to leave in a hurry." Then he opened the car door and stepped out.

Jo did a quick check of her belongings. She did not have much: just her handbag and the weapons she took from the agents in the Parque. Hardly enough to make it for very long on the run. But there was not much choice was there? Shaking her head, she got out of the car.

Malcolm stood at the passenger-side door of the van. The window was rolled down, but Jo could not see inside from her angle. Malcolm nodded in response to something she did not hear and the side door in the rear of the van slid open.

The inside of the van was set up like a lab, a first aid station, and a communications center all rolled into one. Surprise made her not notice the man who stepped back from the driver's seat until he spoke.

"Are you going to introduce me, Robert?"

The man, Raúl no doubt, was short and slender, with thin limbs and a pencil neck that clashed with his unexpectedly broad shoulders. He kept his black hair tied into a ponytail at the nape of his neck and had a short beard on his face. He wore jeans and a t-shirt depicting the logo for a band that Jo had never heard of, and sandals on his feet. His skin was well tanned, though he looked pale compared to Malcolm, and his eyes were dark behind wire rimmed spectacles. Jo was surprised by that; glasses were almost unheard of these days, with the ease of corrective surgery or implants. But then, a person without a database implant was a rarity too, so who was Jo to judge?

Malcolm gestured toward the man in the van and said, "Jo, meet Raúl Ramirez, a legend in his own mind."

Raúl made a sound that was halfway between a snort and a chuckle and reached with his right hand toward Jo. She shook it and was pleased to find he had a strong, confident grip. She smiled in a manner that she hoped was friendly and said, "Nice to meet you."

Raúl returned the smile with a broad grin. "The pleasure is mine, Jo." Releasing her hand, he looked from Jo to Malcolm and rubbed his hand together. "Well, if you'll join me inside, we can get down to business."

They stepped up into the van and Raúl tapped a control panel. The door slid shut silently, cutting out the outside world. Once the door closed, Raúl looked Jo over again.

"I assume you have the locator, no?"

Jo nodded and pointed at the meat of her shoulder.

Raúl nodded. "Sub-cutaneous injection, huh?" He looked back at Malcolm. "How much time do you have?"

Malcolm spread his hands in a gesture of ignorance. "No idea. They could be coming around the corner any minute for all we know."

Raúl shook his head and gestured toward the racks of communication gear in the front of the van's cargo area. "No one's mentioned you on the police bands."

"And they won't," Malcolm replied. "It's an NSA operation."

"Hijo de puta," Raúl muttered. More loudly, he said, "That's going to cost you double."

Malcolm scowled and opened his mouth, no doubt to protest, but Raúl beat him to it. "Double, Robert, or you can get the fuck out right now. I don't need to spend any more time in the lockup."

Malcolm and Raúl traded stares for a brief moment, then Malcolm nodded.

Raúl smiled again. "All right. Robert, drive the van. Stay on the main roads where there's still traffic."

Malcolm nodded and moved up to the driver's seat.

Raúl turned back to Jo. "Have a seat and roll up your sleeve. This should just take a minute."

As Jo moved to the bench at the very rear of the van, she felt the engine start up and the vehicle begin to move. Then she lost her balance and fell onto the bench with a thud as Malcolm hit the breaks a little too hard.

"Hey," she shouted.

"Sorry. Brakes are tighter than I'm used to," came the reply from the front.

Raúl shook his head and smirked. "Many men have trouble with control when it's tighter than normal, am I right?" He winked at her and raised his eyebrows in a lecherous manner.

Jo glowered and almost smacked him, but thought better of it before doing so. He must have realized it though, because his smirk faded quickly, replace by a wary, almost disappointed expression.

"Let's just get on with it, Raúl," she said, and rolled up her sleeve until the fabric bunched up around the top of her shoulder and armpit.

The van moved forward again as Raúl pulled a drawer of various tools out from a bin in the wall. He fished around inside for a moment, then emerged with a portable MRI and what looked like a pair of pinchers.

Jo recognized the MRI unit from the medical supplies onboard ship. They were extremely expensive; more than she earned in a run from Sol to Gliese and back. Where the hell did Raúl get it? He did not look the type to be rolling in money.

Jo almost asked but realized she probably did not want to know.

"Alright. Hold still for a second," Raúl said. He attached the clamps on the MRI to either side of the meat in her shoulder then spent a brief moment adjusting some of the machine's settings. After a moment he nodded to himself and tapped the control pad. The MRI began to hum.

In Jo's experience, portable MRIs did not require much time to warm up, but this one seemed to take forever. Although, she was forced to admit it could have been her nerves that made to seem to take as long as it did. Finally, the unit made a soft beeping sound and Raúl tapped the control pad again.

A display built into the wall of the van flashed to life, revealing a false-color image of the inside of Jo's shoulder. She blinked, fascinated, and leaned forward to see better. She had seen MRI readouts before, but never before one of her own body. It was a very different experience.

"Ah. There's the little bugger," Raúl said in a slow near-purr of satisfaction, and pointed to the lower left quadrant of the scan.

Even with his direction, Jo could not find the locator for a long moment. When she finally did, she was underwhelmed.

"That's it?" she said incredulously. The thing could not have been more than two millimeters long, maybe three.

Raúl nodded. "It does not have to be large. It gets its power from the electric potential within your body and only transmits when queried from elsewhere. When it transmits, the Feds triangulate its position using the web nodes nearby."

Interesting, but right then Jo could have cared less how the thing worked. Get it out, already, she wanted to shout. Instead, she just nodded.

"Now," Raúl said as he began adjusting his pincher tool, "if I'd had more time to prepare, I would have a good anesthetic ready." He looked up from his tool with an apologetic expression. "As it is, I'm afraid this may hurt a little."

Oh great. Jo gritted her teeth and nodded again. Might as well get on with it.

Raúl made one last adjustment on his pinchers, then hefted them and leaned forward. He paused for a moment, studying the MRI display again. Then he nodded to himself and moved the pinchers toward Jo's shoulder.

A sudden lurch sent Raúl stumbling forward onto Jo. They both slid across the bench into the van's wall with a painful thump, followed by a metallic rattle as the MRI unit became dislodged from her shoulder and fell to the floor. The MRI display went black.

"What the hell, Robert?" Raúl shouted as he and Jo extricated themselves from each other.

Malcolm's voice was strained as he replied, "I think they've found us."

"Son of a bitch," Jo and Raúl said in unison.

# 21

# AROUND THE BEND

"Are you sure they're on to us?" Jo shouted.

The van lurched again as Malcolm turned quickly, nearly knocking Raúl and Jo over again. Then the van's motor noise grew louder as he accelerated.

Finally, he answered, "Pretty sure. I passed two sedans going the other way. They stopped in the middle of the road and made u-turns, so either they're NSA or they both *really* want to stop at McDonalds." He gestured ahead and to the right, where they were about to pass a pair of the famous golden arches.

"Small chance of that," Jo muttered. More loudly, she said, "Can you lose them?"

"In this?" Malcolm sounded incredulous, earning a scowl from Raúl. "Did you get the locator out yet?"

Raúl muttered something in Spanish, probably a curse. "I was about a minute away before you did that. Now I have to get re-set up."

Malcolm cursed as well then nodded. "They're about a hundred fifty meters back and coming up fast. I'll do my best to lose them, but it won't matter if you don't get that chip out."

Raúl squatted to retrieve the MRI unit and gestured for Jo to sit again, muttering, "You think I don't know this? You came to me, remember?" under his breath. When he looked back up at Jo, he was still scowling. "Alright, it's probably going to hurt more since we're in a bigger hurry. You up for it?"

What was she going to say, no? Jo nodded and held out her arm.

The van lurched again, more mildly as though Malcolm had just changed lanes abruptly. Jo wedged herself into the corner as best she could while still allowing Raúl access to her arm.

Reattaching the MRI took longer than it did the first time, or maybe it just seemed that way because of the new tension in the air. Raúl had to readjust the clamps a couple times before it would stay; maybe one of the clamps got bent when it fell? At least the image came back after he energized the unit, just as clear as it had the last time.

Another lurching came, along with the squealing of tires, as Raúl adjusted his pinchers and Jo nearly fell to the floor again. But she managed to keep herself still by pressing hard against the wall of the van with her outstretched feet. As Malcolm completed the turn, the van rocked and for a moment it almost felt as though it was going to go over. Wouldn't that be a wonderful end to the night? But then it righted itself and he drove straight again.

Jo really wished she could see what was going on outside. The tension of being chased and apprehension over the advertised pain to come was bad enough, but all the rocking and rolling was beginning to make her head spin. She normally did not get motion sickness, but for whatever reason she felt a mild nausea coming on. Maybe it was the -

A sharp pain in her shoulder distracted Jo from that line of thought. She heard herself crying out and bit down hard, gritting her teeth again. She favored Raúl with a glare that would send one of her crew members scurrying away to hide, but he did not notice. His gaze was locked onto the MRI display, which now showed the ends of the pinchers pushed deep into her muscle but not quite to the locator. Worse...

"Is that thing *moving*?"

Raúl nodded and Jo's nausea was joined by a sudden terror. In a near panic, Jo had to force herself not to rip the equipment off of her shoulder and jump off the bench, and to hell with this procedure. But then that would mean leaving that...thing...inside her. Shuddering as reason pushed panic down, she focused on Raúl.

"I missed it. They are designed to resist removal," Raúl explained. "If their sensors detect tampering, they activate and burrow in deeper." His eyes left the display and met hers for a moment. His expression was almost pitying. "Sorry about this."

He actuated the pinchers and agony ripped through Jo's shoulder.

Unable to hold back a scream, she felt as though she had been run through by a pair of red-hot pokers. Then just as she had almost recovered, the pinchers twisted and jerked, sending another lance of pain through her shoulder. She gasped and slumped back, breathing in and out with quick heaving breaths.

The interior of the van spun for a moment before she could right herself. Finally she took a deep breath and sat up again, wiping tears from her eyes with the back of her right hand. The pain had reduced to a dull throb, maybe a four or five on a scale of ten. Normally that would be enough to be far more than annoying, but compared to the fifteen she just experienced it almost felt like heaven.

She looked over at Raúl and demanded, "Tell me you got it."

He nodded and held up the pinchers for her to see. They were covered with a thin coat of blood and grasped a small metal object between their tips. Seeing the blood prompted her to grasp at her shoulder with her hand. When it came away blood-free she raised one eyebrow in surprise.

Raúl smiled ever so slightly. "It's treated with a coagulant, so the wound seals almost immediately upon removal."

Jo nodded. That was standard for invasive medical instruments these days; she should have figured it would be that way with Raul's pinchers as well.

Raúl turned to his lab bench and deposited the locator into a small cup with a threaded top, then screwed a cap onto it. "It will keep its charge for a few hours, so you'll want to get rid of it somewhere." Turning back to her, he held out the cup.

She took it and was about to say thanks when the van lurched again, this time from an impact. There was no way she could have stopped herself from falling off the bench this time. She found herself sprawled on the floor with Raúl on top of her.

"What was that?" Raúl demanded.

Malcolm jerked at the wheel, trying to get the van back under control as it veered from side to side. "They're right on us," he said in a strained voice. "The one on the left just hit us in the quarter panel with its fender."

"Goddamnit," Raúl said, "I just had this van refurbished." He pushed himself up and off Jo then bounded forward toward the cockpit area.

Jo followed, a bit more slowly. She worked her shoulder gingerly; it worked but it would be uncomfortable for a while, she suspected. She reached the cockpit just as the van lurched again, this time to the left, and was barely able to brace herself against the back of Malcolm's seat to prevent falling over.

Raúl strapped himself into the passenger seat and cursed. Jo could see why. The two side view displays showed the pursuing cars on their flanks. At least three people sat in each car, no doubt armed.

This was bad. Very bad.

The car on their left began moving forward as Jo looked up at the street ahead. And saw traffic moving across their street at the next intersection. Her heart leapt into her throat.

"Red Light!," Jo screamed at the same instant that Raúl, watching the sideview displays, shouted, "Hit the brakes!"

Malcolm slammed on the brakes and the van abruptly slowed to the sound skidding tires and the smell of burning rubber. Jo stumbled forward and pressed her palms into the dashboard to keep from falling into the windshield. They fishtailed and stopped just before the painted line marking the stopping point for the red light.

The two pursuit cars shot ahead of them into the intersection. The car on the left, already accelerating, had to swerve to avoid crossing traffic but made it through and slammed on its brakes.

The car on the right was not so lucky. A car traveling from right to left hit the pursuit car broadside, sending it careening away, the entire passenger side caved in. A second car, traveling the opposite direction, struck the first, and then was struck in turn by another car coming up behind it.

Jo, Malcolm, and Raúl sat in silence for a moment, stunned.

"Right, right! Turn right," Raúl shouted, pointing in that direction. He had a point; the pileup had stopped traffic from left to right and they had a clear avenue of escape in that direction.

Malcolm nodded and hit the accelerator again. The van lurched forward and turned hard to the right. In her peripheral vision, Jo saw the first pursuit car maneuvering to turn around; they would not be in the clear for long.

Very soon they were in violation of the speed limit and quickly gaining on the traffic ahead. Another intersection loomed; the light was green. A small sedan ahead signaled its intention to turn right. Raúl pointed at it.

"We need to ditch the tracker. Follow that car, Robert."

Malcolm nodded and slowed so as to not overtake the vehicle, then got into the turning lane. Raúl turned to Jo and held out his hand. She blinked, unable to comprehend his meaning for a moment. He shook his hand insistently and looked back at her in annoyance.

It clicked. She still had the tracker.

Feeling like an idiot, she handed the small device to Raúl. He took it out of its container and put it into a different case, which he pulled out of the glove compartment.

Jo glanced at the rearview. Still no sign of their pursuers. Malcolm turned right, about a fifty meters behind the sedan.

"Get up beside him," Raúl ordered. He rolled down his window as they got up next to the other car and tossed the tracker out. Its new case struck the top of the sedan and stayed put; apparently it was magnetic.

"Pretty slick," Jo murmured, earning a quick grin from Raúl.

Another intersection loomed ahead.

"Turn left here," said Raúl.

Malcolm complied and soon they left the sedan, and the tracker, behind. Jo let out a sigh of relief and sunk back onto her heels between the two cockpit seats.

"I thought they had us there, for a moment," she said breathlessly.

"Yes, well, they didn't," Malcolm said. He looked calm, but Jo noted more than a hint of relief in his tone.

Raúl sounded only angry. "You're fucking paying for the damage to my van, pendejo," he said, wagging a finger at Malcolm.

Malcolm just nodded. "Of course. It'll take a bit of time to get..." He stopped talking as his eyes locked on the rearview display.

Jo glanced over and felt her spirits sink like a stone. The pursuit car passed the intersection behind them, following the sedan as planned. A couple seconds later, however, it came back into view, speeding in reverse. It skidded to a stop facing down their street then accelerated straight toward the van.

"Oh shit," she breathed.

**22**

---

## AGAINST A WALL

"**S**on of a bitch," Malcolm swore, and he floored it. The van surged ahead, but the pursuing car was smaller and probably souped up with a law enforcement motor. They were not going to outrun the agents, not in this rig.

Malcolm took a right hand turn so quickly that the passenger side wheels came up off the road momentarily. Jo slid into the van's wall, jarring her sore shoulder, and winced.

"Be careful, Malcolm. It won't do us any good to crash!"

Malcolm blanched and sent her a reproachful look. Raul's look was more speculative.

Jo gasped as she realized what she had just done. Stupid, stupid! It's not like she had not been in stressful scenarios before. Why was she losing her cool this time?

The answer came to her as soon as she asked the question. She had been in hard situations before, even a few life-or-death ones. But she had never faced a high probability of arrest and incarceration before. Sure, she had been arrested just a couple weeks ago, but she had not really believed any harm would come to her when it happened. This time...

That was no excuse, though. Malcolm had not told Raúl his real name for a reason, and she had just blown it for him. She flushed in embarrassment as she gave Malcolm an apologetic look. He did not see it, though; he was focusing on the road.

He made another right hand turn at the first intersection, but did it slower this time and under more control. Jo noticed the pursuers entering the last intersection as the van completed the turn and blanched. The agents almost certainly saw them.

Malcolm turned to the right again at his first opportunity and Raúl said, "Whatchu doing, man? You're just making a circle."

"If we're lucky," Malcolm replied as he jerked the wheel hard to center the van on the road before flooring the accelerator again. "They'll miss at least one of these turns. If that happens, they'll continue on and we'll be going the opposite direction."

Raúl snorted. "Don't matter, man. They're probably calling in the local cops for help."

Jo snorted and Malcolm shook his head. "No they're not. They want to keep this under wraps."

Raúl looked inquisitively at him and Jo could see he was doing some figuring in his head. It would not be a big stretch to put two and two together. He just might decide it would be worth it to turn them in, maybe get a reward. Jo flexed her fingers unconsciously, the way she used to do before starting a sparring session with her father.

"It didn't work," Raúl said, his tone one of near panic.

And he was right. In the rearview, the pursuit car rounded the corner and sped toward them, making up ground at an alarming rate.

Malcolm swore under his breath and glanced at Raúl, then Jo. "Any ideas?"

Jo shook her head; she had nothing.

Raúl pursed his lips in thought for a moment then pushed himself out of the seat and slid past Jo into the back of the van. "I might have something back here that can help," he said. He began opening one locker after another and hurriedly sifting through the contents. "It's here," he murmured. "I know it's here."

"Help him," Malcolm said, but Jo was already on it. She went to the the lockers on the other side of the van from Raúl and started looking inside them.

"What am I looking for?"

Raúl replied, "Looks like a thick magic marker, except it has a button on one side and a transmitter element at the end."

Jo blinked. "A transmitter?"

"It sends out a burst of electronic noise that's tuned to disrupt a car's computer systems. Cops use it to avoid high speed chases."

Jo shut the locker and moved on to the next one. "You mean like we're in right now?"

"Yeah. Wonder why they haven't - "

Raul's words were cut off by a loud crunching sound as the van shuddered and spun off course. He and Jo fell to the floor as tires squealed, a motor revved, and Malcolm shouted a curse.

The van continued to skid. Jo looked forward and saw, through the windshield, a hardware store on the side of the street. They were heading straight toward it.

Malcolm clawed at the wheel, but only managed to turn the van a fraction of the amount needed to avoid crashing.

They hit the storefront a few degrees from broadside, smashing through the display windows with a loud crash. The van tilted, then rolled over onto its side as impact absorbing foam flowed from the walls and ceiling. All Jo could see was pink foam, the only sounds were the squealing of the van's steel body as it slid further into the store and repeated crashes as it knocked over display cabinets, countertops, and machinery.

Then there was another tremendous crash and the van stopped.

———

THE FOAM ABSORBED the worst of the impact, but as she got to her hands and knees Jo nevertheless felt bruised and battered all over. Raúl lay in a heap in front of her, his left arm bent at an unnatural angle. From up in the cockpit, Malcolm groaned softly.

Jo got to her feet and staggered over to Raúl. Her movements were slowed by the foam as much as by pain. She had to force her way through the stuff. Supposedly it would dissolve in a few seconds, now that the collision was over, but for the moment it was a serious impediment. Finally she got to him and crouched down.

"You ok, Raúl?" she asked as she felt for his pulse.

At her touch, Raúl jerked up to a sitting position. "What the fuck..." he began. Then he let out a strangled cry and doubled over, clutching at his broken arm. "Hijo de puta," he muttered through clenched teeth.

"Can you stand? We need to get out of here."

He nodded and Jo helped him to his feet. It was beginning to get easier to move; the foam must have begun to dissolve.

"Malcolm, can you move?" Jo called.

In response, Jo saw two feet rise out of the foam and begin kicking at the windshield. Once. Twice. Three times. Then the bottom—or rather the passenger side—of the windshield popped out of its frame, leaving a gap they could probably crawl through.

Good enough.

Jo put her arm around Raul's shoulder and helped him forward while Malcolm got to his feet. He took in Raul's condition at a glance and grimaced. Then he slipped through the gap in the windshield and pulled it out a bit further from the other side.

"Let's go!" Malcolm hissed.

Jo helped maneuver Raúl through the opening. As broad as his shoulders were, it was a tight fit. He ended up jarring his bad arm on the way out, and for a moment there Jo thought he would either pass out or refuse to go on.

Then Malcolm, who had stood up to look over the van toward the street, hissed, "They're almost here. Move your ass."

That was apparently all the encouragement Raúl needed. He gritted his teeth and began moving again. Jo helped him with a vigorous push that left him sprawled on the ground, then followed him out.

The store was a wreck. No big surprise there, but the destruction was still impressive to look at. Shelves were toppled, products smashed. A column had smashed the rear portion of the van and was itself split and leaning over at an acute angle. The ceiling, about three meters tall elsewhere in the store, was sagging around the pillar; it clearly had been a load-bearing structure.

Jo straightened and looked over the the hulk of the van. And cringed. The sedan that had been pursuing them was a crumpled hunk of metal wrapped around a light pole on the other side of the street. One person lay sprawled on the sidewalk, where he had apparently been thrown from the sedan on impact. The remaining passengers, three of them, were clawing through slowly dissolving foam and out the sedan's windows. Two were strangers, but Jo recognized Agent Moore without difficulty.

"What happened?" Jo breathed as Malcolm helped Raúl to his feet.

"They came up faster than I expected and rammed us," he replied.

Agent Moore and one of her companions made it out of the car. He took a moment on his knees to catch his breath, but she was up on her feet in a flash, plasma pistol clutched in both hands, the barrel pointing toward the street for the moment.

"Ngubwe! Ishikawa! There are more units on the way. You can't escape, so come out with your hands up."

Jo found herself sliding her hand to the small of her back, where she had tucked DiStefano's weapon. If Agent Moore thought she was going to just surrender—a certain death sentence at this point—she was sorely mistaken.

Malcolm's hand on her shoulder stopped her from pulling the weapon. "Not like this, Jo. Come on, out the back."

Jo nodded and the men moved out. She waited for a moment, just long enough to see the third agent make his escape, then she turned to go.

She found Malcolm and Raúl at the back of the shop. They looked distressed. It only took a moment to figure out why. There were two doors in back. One led to a small office, the other to a bathroom. There *was* no rear entrance and, at first glance at least, no windows either.

"Oh no," Jo breathed. She looked over her shoulder. The streetlights outside cast long shadows from the three agents as they approached the overturned van. They were getting closer. It would take a moment for them to climb over the van, but then it would be all over. "What do we do?"

Raúl leaned against the wall and winced, then shut his eyes and shook his head. Malcolm's eyes went to the ground and he sighed.

"I guess we get arrested."

# 23

# OVER THE ROOF

The words hit Jo like a ton of bricks. Get arrested. Yeah right. Agent Moore and her colleagues had no interest in arresting them; that was obvious from DiStefano's remarks. Removing them from the picture? Absolutely. Arrest and trial? No way. Not anymore.

"Like hell," she said.

Turning back toward the front of the store, Jo crouched down behind a fallen shelf and took aim with DiStefano's pistol. At least go out fighting. It would be a useless gesture, no doubt, but it was something.

A small part of Jo's mind wept for lost opportunities. If she had just stuck to the deal she would probably be home by now, and off on Agrippa in a few weeks. Back to her normal life, with these troubles far behind her.

And the government would continue the alien egg program to its ultimate conclusion. Sooner or later, the creatures would learn what happened. These sorts of things always came out. When it did, there would be no containing their anger. Jo imagined the rage humanity would feel if the tables were turned; it would be murderous, and entirely justified. Such a betrayal of their most helpless ones could not be forgiven.

But almost worse than that, Malcolm would be imprisoned or, more likely, dead. And it would be her fault. She could try to justify it by thinking of her own predicament, but in the end it would have come down to the fact that her friend was dead because she betrayed him while he was trying to do something she now agreed was morally and ethically right. There was no way she could live with that.

So she took her place and silenced that part of her mind. She did not regret her choice.

Malcolm crouched beside her and she passed him the other pistol she had taken from DiStefano. He smiled faintly and settled down to wait with her.

"Never thought it would come down to *this*," he said. "I just wanted to blow the lid on it, not..." He trailed off and shrugged. It did not matter now, did it?

The shadows of the agents' movements on the other side of the van grew larger. Jo could hear their footsteps, slow and cautious but relentless in their approach. They would have to climb over the van to get at them; that was something at least. The store was narrow enough that the van, lying on its side, blocked most of it off. Fallen shelving and displays took care of the rest.

"I think we can hold them off for a while," Jo said. "They'll have to come over the hood, because of how the ceiling is sagging..."

She blinked, her train of thought stopping as she looked back at the sagging ceiling. Then the column, nearly falling over where the van plowed into it.

Son of a bitch.

There were other columns throughout the store. Some were damaged, most were intact. And the building the store occupied was just one story tall. Hope surged back into her.

"Malcolm, the columns!"

Malcolm looked quizzically at Jo, then followed her gaze to the columns. His eyebrows rose high onto his forehead. He was an engineer; he saw it immediately. Raising his pistol, he took aim and looked back at her from the corner of his eye.

"On three?"

Jo nodded and sighted in on the bent column near the van.

Malcolm counted down. Jo saw Agent Moore's face appear over the side of the van the moment he reached three. She dropped back to the ground as Jo and Malcolm opened fire.

Jo's column went first. It was already all but destroyed by the van's momentum and only took two shots from the plasma pistol to give way. Malcolm's was undamaged, so Jo shifted fire to help him. Their combined fire reduced the column in a few seconds.

They stopped shooting and waited.

The agents on the other side of the van were shouting something, to each other or to them, Jo did not care; she paid them no heed. She watched as the second column buckled, then fell over, and felt a thrill of victory.

A low groan issued from the ceiling as members that were not designed to hold the total weight of the ceiling and roof above were suddenly required to by the loss of the columns. The ceiling began to sag a bit more and for a moment Jo's feeling of victory began to fade.

Maybe it would hold up after all.

Then it all came tumbling down in a roar. A huge cloud of dust billowed up as ceiling tiles, beams, cross braces, lamps, electrical wiring, insulation, roof shingles, and all manner of other materials fell. The collapse went on for a full minute, and then there was a sudden quiet, almost deafening in its own right after the sound of the collapse.

Jo took a deep breath and found herself coughing as she got more dust than air into her lungs. Beside her, Malcolm was in a similar state. She could not see Raúl, back against the wall. Or anything else either; there was that much dust in the air. But she could hear him.

"Holy shit," Raúl coughed out. Jo was inclined to agree with him.

Gradually the dust cleared and Jo was able to see the extent of the damage.

Her gambit had worked even better than she hoped. The ceiling had fallen in across two-thirds of the store on their side of the van. Rubble filled the space between them and the hole, but it looked to be climbable. Better still, Jo could see the night sky through the hole in the ceiling.

They could get out.

"It worked," Malcolm said. He almost sounded surprised.

"Did you have any doubt?" Jo replied. She stood up and dusted herself off, then started forward toward the debris pile and the hole leading to freedom. "Come on," she said.

Behind her, Malcolm chuckled. "A little," he said. Jo looked back to see him grinning.

Raúl had a tough time of it, with his broken arm. But Malcolm was able to help him over the worst of the debris. Getting up onto the roof was another matter. Jo had to lie down on the roof and take his hand, then pull hard while Malcolm gave him a boost from below.

Raúl was skinny, but he still outweighed Jo by a good twenty kilograms or so, and the angle was awkward. For a moment, she was not sure she would be able to get him up, even with Malcolm's help from below. But finally he managed, and Malcolm quickly pulled himself out as well.

Looking over the top of the building toward the street, Jo saw Agent Moore and her two companions coming out of the building, coughing loudly. One of the agents' legs was twisted and stiff, clearly broken. Agent Moore and the other man had their arms over his shoulders, supporting him as he stumbled toward the street.

They slowly lowered the injured agent to the ground, then Agent Moore turned to look back at the building. She mouthed what could only be a curse as she surveyed the damage. Then she looked up and froze as her eyes met Jo's gaze. Her eyebrows rose and her lips compressed into a thin scowl as she raised her pistol.

Jo dropped into a crouch and cursed. "To the back!" she said, grabbing Raúl by the shoulder—his good one, fortunately—and propelling him toward the back of the store. Malcolm followed as balls of heated plasma began firing over the front edge of the building.

Fortunately, the angle was too acute for Agent Moore or her uninjured colleague to get a good shot at them. Even more fortunately, the shop buildings lining the street were set one against each other for most of the block, so it would take some time for the agents to get around back to find them.

A narrow alley ran between the back of their building and the back of the next street's shop buildings. A dumpster sat against the wall of their building, and Jo was annoyed to see a door in the back of the building across the alley. And every other building she could see. Of all the rotten luck. Muttering under her breath, Jo lowered herself down onto the dumpster, which thankfully was closed at this hour of the night, then reached up to give Raúl a hand in doing the same.

In moments they were on the ground in the alley.

"Ok now what?" Jo asked.

"Now," Malcolm said as he looked quickly back and forth down the alley, "we find a manhole and get down into the storm sewers."

Jo blinked. "You're kidding."

"No way man. Fuck that," Raúl said. He was looking pretty haggard, and Jo could not blame him for not wanting to do any more climbing.

"You don't have to come," Malcolm said, giving Raúl a level, icy look. "It'll probably be better for you if you don't, to be honest."

Raúl snorted. "Yeah right. Do I look stupid to you, cabrón?" He pushed himself forward, thrusting his jaw up at Malcolm. "Even if I trusted you not to sell me out if you get caught, you owe me. For the job and for the van."

Malcolm shrugged and turned away. "Fine. Don't say I didn't warn you."

He set off walking down the alley. Jo hurried to follow. After a moment, she heard Raúl follow as well.

"We'll need flashlights."

Behind her, Raúl spoke up. "I have one. Never leave home without it."

The alley widened between two smaller buildings. Off to the side, not far from the back door on the building on the left, was a manhole cover. Malcolm stopped before it and crouched down. Jo and Raúl joined him.

"The hard part," Malcolm said, "is getting it open. We'll need something to pry it up with."

Jo frowned and looked around. Aside from dumpsters here and there, there was nothing in the alley that looked as though it would be useful for that. "I'm not sure..." The sign on the back of a door one building over announced it as a lumber store. That brought a smile to her face. "Wait here."

Jo hurried over to the door and tried it. Locked. The lack of hinges meant it opened inward. Maybe she could kick it in. Jo stepped back and took a deep breath. Then she kicked as hard as she could, striking the door just below the doorknob with her boot.

The door did not move.

"Impressive," Raúl said as he stepped up next to her. He smirked at her and reached into his pocket. "Step aside," he said. He crouched in front of the door and pulled a small piece of metal out of the inner pocket of his jacket. He inserted the metal piece—a lockpick, Jo assumed—into the keyhole and began working it around.

After a minute or so, Jo heard a soft click and the doorknob turned.

Raúl grinned and pushed the door open, swinging his arm wide in a grand offer for her to enter.

Jo rolled her eyes. "You're quite a character, Raúl. Good with tech and with a lockpick. I would not think those went together."

"You would be surprised, señorita," he replied. He opened his mouth to say something more, but a ruckus down the far end of the alley drew his attention. He shrank back against the alley wall. "Shit, I think they're coming."

Jo blanched. Even if he was wrong, there was no time to dilly-dally. She ducked into the store. It only took a moment to find what she needed. When she emerged from the store and hurried back to Malcolm's side, he gave her an incredulous look.

"I was thinking more like a prybar," he said.

"Beggars can't be choosers."

He shrugged, conceding the point.

The piece of wood she picked out was about a meter long and two centimeters on a side. It just barely squeezed into the little hole on the side of the manhole cover. Jo and Malcolm took hold of the board and pushed down.

A sharp cracking sound issued from the board and for a moment Jo thought her bright idea was going to fail completely. Then the manhole cover moved upward slightly and they were able to slide the board further in, allowing more purchase. Shortly, they raised the cover enough that Malcolm was able to bend over and get his fingers under the cover's edge. From there it was a quick process to slide it aside.

Jo wiped her brow, panting from the exertion, and looked between Malcolm and Raúl. "I'll go first and help Raúl down. I'm not sure I could move the cover into place anyway."

Malcolm nodded.

Jo sat on the edge of the manhole and dangled her feet into the blackness below. The hole opened beneath her like a gaping maw and she had to push aside a surge of fear. Raúl handed her his flashlight, which helped, but still there was something about the descent into the sewer below that seemed creepy.

Swallowing hard, Jo kicked her feet around until she found the ladder rungs built into the side of the shaft, then she slid slowly downward.

24

——————

# UNDER THE WORLD

The ladder went down a bit less than five meters before ending on a concrete landing. Jo stepped away from the ladder and shined the flashlight around.

She stood in a small alcove off the main sewer tunnel. The tunnel itself was maybe four meters across and two and a half high. Narrow walkways ran along each side of it, with the main flow-way for the storm water in the center. Ever so often, Jo saw narrow spans crossing the flow-way, allowing access across the tunnel, for maintenance, no doubt.

No one else was in sight. Not that she really expected there to be, but the NSA Agents had been very savvy to date. Jo did not put it past them to think of looking in the storm sewers for their quarry. Speaking of which...

"All clear," she called up.

Raúl made a few grumbling noises as he lowered himself down onto the ladder. Making the descent one-handed took him quite a bit longer than it had Jo. But once he got low enough that she could help him with his balance, things sped up.

"Hurry up," Malcolm called down from above. "They're coming."

In response, Raúl let go of the ladder and dropped the last meter to the ground. He stumbled as he landed, almost falling over onto his bad shoulder before Jo grabbed him. He flashed her a small grin of thanks then slid out onto the walkway in the main tunnel.

Above, Malcolm dropped the board they used to pry up the

manhole cover down into the tunnel. Then he quickly descended the ladder, pausing only to move the cover back into place.

"Turn out the flashlight," he whispered harshly when he reached the bottom. "They might see the light through the holes in the cover."

Jo complied, and they were plunged into blackness. Faint, almost imperceptible light streamed through the cover holes, but it did little to alleviate the gloom. The soft trickle of water flowing down the central flow-way in the tunnel combined with the sudden pounding of Jo's heart made an uncomfortable harmony as they waited there in the black.

Then other noises intruded on that harmony. Jogging footsteps and voices, muffled and almost inaudible from having to pass through the cover. The noises got louder and Jo slowly found she was able to understand a little of what the voices were saying.

"...can't have just vanished." That sounded like Agent Moore.

"They didn't come out at my end," replied a deep male voice, probably belonging to her unwounded comrade.

"Bollocks," Agent Moore replied, and a metallic clang rang out, as though two pieces of metal had struck each other. She sounded frustrated; Jo took a certain satisfaction in that.

There was a long silence, then Agent Moore said, "Keep looking. They have to be here somewhere."

The voices gradually trailed away, growing impossible to understand again. Then, after several moments, they faded completely.

Jo let the breath she was holding go in a long exhalation and was comforted to hear Malcolm and Raúl do the same. Her eyes had adjusted to the faint light while they waited and she could just make out Malcolm's features where he stood at the base of the ladder. Their eyes met and he nodded to her; she thought she saw a smile on his lips.

When she flicked the flashlight back on, the smile was not present. All business, Malcolm stepped out of the alcove and looked both ways down the tunnel. After a moment's consideration, he turned left.

"This way," he said.

"Do you spend a lot of time in the sewers these days, Malcolm?" Jo asked.

He snorted. "Hardly. But they crisscross the city and allow movement without being seen so some of my acquaintances have taken to using them from time to time. If we can get to the areas they use, we ought to be able to make contact."

"And you're sure that's the right way?"

Malcolm looked back at her and shook his head. "No. Flashlight?" He held out his hand to her.

Jo shrugged and passed the light over to him. If he was going to lead the way he would need it more than she. Malcolm accepted the light with another small nod, then set off down the tunnel in his brisk, quick walk. The flashlight's illumination quickly faded, leaving Raúl and Jo looking at each other in growing darkness.

Raúl shrugged. "Beats being up there," he said, with a gesture toward the ladder.

That much was certain. Jo hurried to follow Malcolm and tried not to think about what might be lurking in the darkness beyond the light's glow.

The next several hours were a nightmare. Not so much because of the oppressive darkness, though that was not pleasant. Or the occasional sounds of scurrying animals. Rats, Jo thought, but who knew. Or the ubiquitous smell of pooling water and mildew, and other more foul scents that Jo managed, through a herculean force of will, to not quite ignore.

No, the worst part was not knowing where the hell she was. Jo could handle the others, but that ignorance ate at her more and more as time went by. Even if she had climbed up a ladder and stuck her head out, Jo felt certain she would still have no idea at all. That ignorance left her helpless in Malcolm's hands, and it was just infuriating. She was not used to being helpless. The fact that, over the last week and a half, she had felt more helpless than in command certainly did not help matters.

So Jo felt more than a little relief when, at the junction between two identical tunnels—really they could have been any of the dozens of tunnels they had traipsed through all night—Malcolm stopped and sighed, his shoulders slumped in defeat.

"Forget it," Malcolm said, his voice thick with fatigue. "We must have turned the wrong way. I'll never find them down here. Let's find a place to lay low, and we can try again in the morning."

"Hell yeah, man," Raúl said as he pushed his way past Malcolm and Jo toward the nearby alcove and ladder. "I've had enough of these stinking tunnels."

Jo was inclined to agree about the tunnels. But where were they going now?

"Do you have a place in mind, Malcolm?"

He nodded. "There are plenty of little motels that don't ask many questions and aren't strict about checking IDs. That's mostly where I've been for the last couple weeks. Since the raid we can't trust any of the old safe houses."

Jo frowned and nodded. That made sense.

A few minutes later, Malcolm pushed the manhole cover back in place and they surveyed their new surroundings. The street was free of traffic and lined by just a few low, unlit buildings that were spaced well apart from each other. It was still night, but a faint glow to the east, beyond the mountains, announced dawn's approach. They must have spent longer in the tunnels than Jo thought.

"Where the hell are we?" Raúl asked.

"My guess is somewhere in the south side," Malcolm replied, "past the Spaceport."

"Great," Jo muttered.

South of the Spaceport, the neighborhoods became progressively less safe. Though Law Enforcement did their best, some of the neighborhoods had become overrun with gang activity in recent years. Most people who did not *have* to go there did not.

There was nothing for it but to follow the plan though, so they set off down the street. Three blocks down, they came upon a seedy-looking motel. Just as advertised, the proprietor did not look very hard at them or ask for their IDs. He simply accepted a few bills from Malcolm without comment and handed over an electronic room key.

The room was tiny and smelled of a mixture of old trash, urine, and smoke. Two tiny beds stood against one wall and a couch, ratty and looking like it was barely able to hold together, sat beneath the room's lone window. In the back of the room, a counter with a sink was mounted to the wall, along with a standard sized mirror. Adjacent to the sink was a door leading into a small bathroom.

Jo winced just looking around the place, but at least the bathroom was marginally clean.

"I've seen worse," Raúl said in a nonchalant tone, though Jo noted an expression of distaste on his face, too.

"I just hope the shower works," Jo replied.

She felt covered in grime and sweat. It reminded her of the horrible few days she spent as the NSA's guest. She shuddered as the memories came back. No need to go there.

A small pile of towels rested in a rack on the wall next to the sink. She picked one out, went into the bathroom, and turned on the shower water. Then she closed the bathroom door and proceeded to wash her cares away.

Or at least her dirt.

She emerged from the shower several minutes later feeling refreshed and at least slightly more human. The concept of putting on the same grimy clothes she had been wearing gave her pause, though.

It flashed through her head that she should have planned things out a bit better. Somewhere in the back of her head she knew going into the encounter at the Parque that she would not go through with it. She should have listened to that part and packed a bag or something. Never mind the unrealistic logistics of it all, she spent several moments chastising herself before forcing herself to stop; she was just delaying putting those clothes back on, and there was no choice in the matter.

When she stepped out of the bathroom into the main room, Raúl was already curled up on one of the beds. He was fast asleep, though he murmured and wiggled from time to time. Once he groaned, probably from the pain in his arm.

Malcolm sat on the couch resting his chin on his fist and clearly fighting sleep. Seeing her, he gestured toward the second bed. "Take the bed, Jo. I'm fine with the couch."

Jo thought about protesting, but the couch truly was a rickety setup. At least the bed looked halfway comfortable. She sat down on the edge, facing Malcolm. Their eyes met and they were silent for a moment. Malcolm looked tired, harried, but determined. Jo did not want to think about how she looked; she had avoided looking in the bathroom mirror for that very reason. It could not be good, though.

The silence weighed on her and she looked away, past Malcolm toward the window. "What's the plan?"

Malcolm shrugged. "That *is* the question, isn't it?" His expression became severe, nearly a scowl. "The organization has been...disjoint-ed...since the raid."

Jo felt a surge of guilt even though she knew the raid was not her fault. All the same, Malcolm had lost friends, either to prison or to the morgue, the night he had brought her to meet them. What did he think about that?

Almost as if he was reading her mind, Malcolm added, "People are not going to be happy that you're involved again, Jo. If this is going to work, I need to know everything that's going on with you."

Jo swallowed. "Malcolm, I didn't - "

He held up a hand and she fell silent. "Frankly, Jo, after last night I'm not sure how much *I* can trust you, and I know you. If you don't give me something to tell my people that will help them feel comfortable with you..." He trailed off.

"What?"

Malcolm did scowl then. He took a deep breath and said, "They may just decide to cut you loose, let you take your chances on your own."

# 25

## NO TELL MOTEL

Malcolm's words hit Jo like a prizefighter's punch. She recoiled, almost feeling a pain in her gut as their impact landed home. He could not mean he would just cast her to the winds! Not after she had...

Jo looked back into Malcolm's eyes and felt a chill. No, *he* would not cut her loose. But his associates would feel no compunction about doing so. She was in almost as delicate a situation as when those aliens came aboard Pericles. One wrong move and it could all fall apart. But this time, there would be no getting out of it, she was sure about that.

"What do you want to know, Malcolm?" Her voice sounded wooden, defeated, to her ears.

"Everything."

In a fit of snark, Jo was half tempted to tell him about the time she had cheated on her math test in third grade. But she knew better than that. All the same, she could not completely prevent a little smirk from twisting her lips.

Malcolm raised an eyebrow. "I'm serious, Jo."

"I know. I just had a random thought is all." She took a deep breath and nodded.

It took a half hour or so to tell Malcolm about everything that had happened. She started with meeting Reynolds at La Chupacabra and ended in the Parque when she fought off DiStefano. Malcolm listened attentively, nodding in appropriate moments and affecting surprise—

genuine, Jo was sure—several times. Finally she came to the end and he leaned back, gingerly she noticed, against the back of the couch.

"I never believed you were on Gagarin," Malcolm said. "But I didn't suspect..." He shook his head and blew out a deep breath. "I'm sorry you had to go through that, Jo."

She blinked, surprise stealing her thoughts for a moment. When she found her voice, she only managed to blurt out, "What?"

Malcolm gave a little half-shrug. "Do you think I could wish that on anyone?"

Jo shook her head, not trusting herself to speak again just yet.

Malcolm smiled slightly. "I suppose I can understand why you agreed to cooperate. Given the same choice, I cannot say I would have done differently." He leaned forward again, resting his elbows on his knees as he looked intently into Jo's eyes. "So why did you change your mind?"

The question hung in the air for a minute before Jo answered.

"That's the wrong question, Malcolm." His eyebrow quirked upward, but Jo continued before he could say something else. "I did not change my mind. I simply allowed myself to accept the decision I made after you dropped me off at home." She looked away from his piercing eyes, toward the blank vidscreen on the wall opposite the beds. "I could intellectually understand why Chandini and the others took the actions they did, but I knew in my heart it was not right. And once our new friends up there learn what happened..." She pointed toward the sky and left the thought unspoken. There would be hell to pay once the aliens found out what had been done to their helpless ones.

Malcolm nodded. "Fair enough." He stood then, his long limbs bearing him quickly from the couch and toward the door. Jo gave a start of surprise, at the fact he had moved as much as from the rapidity of his activity.

"Where are you going?"

"Out." Malcolm looked at her gravely. "I need to make contact with my people, figure out where we can all meet to determine our next move."

"That can wait. You need to rest, too."

He shook his head. "I'm ok. And no, it can't." Malcolm smiled again, and this time his smile was more genuine, warm. "Get some rest, Jo. I'll be back in a few hours."

Then he slipped out the door.

Jo had more than half a mind to get up and follow him; the rest of her screamed out in outraged annoyance at being left in such an impotent position. But fatigue weighed down on her. She was going on two full days with only a few restless hours of sleep. The command decision-making part of her brain, honed through years of training and study, whispered to her that she was in no condition to be making good decisions right now, and she would need to be if she was to help Malcolm in this. Beyond that, she did not know any of the people he would have to contact. And if he was right, her presence, before he had a chance to smooth things over, might just make a tense situation untenable.

All that flashed through her head in a few seconds. It hurt to admit it—not physically, but it hurt her ego—but the best thing to do was to let Malcolm deal with things for the moment.

And to get some sleep while she could.

Despite the objections of her ego, Jo felt a deep, relaxing satisfaction as she reclined on the bed. The mattress was lumpy, stiff, and probably half her age. But just then it seemed the most comfortable thing she had ever felt.

She acknowledged the irony of that sentiment with a small inward smirk, then she drifted off.

---

Jo awoke slowly. At first it did not register to her where she was. She was in a bed, and it was damned uncomfortable.

But a bed where?

She stretched, feeling her back pop slightly as she moved joints that had become stiff from the mattress' lumps. Then she sat up and looked around, and it all came rushing back: the events of the previous night, their predicament with both the authorities and the underground, everything.

It was almost enough to make her lie down again and go back to sleep.

The thought seemed to generate aches of protest from her back and neck, though. So instead, she stood up. Slowly. She really was sore in the middle of her back; she must have slept wrong.

"Those mattresses suck." The words were muffled, as though the speaker could not enunciate properly.

Jo turned her head to see Raúl in the back of the room. He wore nothing but a towel wrapped around his waist, and he was brushing his teeth at the sink. He had more muscle tone than she would have thought, as scrawny as he was. Whatever points that might have won him vanished, though, beneath the weight of an ugly-as-sin tattoo that dominated the left side of his chest and upper abdomen.

Really? A dragon? He could not come up with anything better than that?

Jo shook her head and snorted out a half laugh. The reflection of Raul's eyes in the mirror met hers and he grinned before spitting out a mouthful of toothpaste. Jo pointedly looked away.

"Where did you find a toothbrush?"

Raúl gargled some water before answering. "The front desk has a few odds and ends for sale."

"Really?" Jo was surprised. That was the sort of thing one expected from a more upscale hotel, not a dive like this place.

"I know, right? Who would have thought?"

Raúl finished up at the sink and walked out into the room, where he stripped off his towel and bent over to pull his pants on. Jo turned her back on him; that was something she *definitely* did not need to see. Instead, she picked up the plasma pistol from where she left it on the nightstand and tucked it into her belt at the small of her back.

"So what's Robert's deal?" Raúl asked. "Or Malcolm? Which is it?" He sounded curious, but his words also had a probing quality to them, as though he was hunting for some lever he could use to his advantage here.

Jo rolled her eyes, but did not look back at him. "Malcolm."

"Ah." There was a brief pause, punctuated by the ruffling of fabric. "It's safe to turn around."

Slowly, with no small amount of trepidation, Jo turned back toward Raúl. Thankfully, he was true to his word, and almost dressed as he had been last night; he was lacking his shirt still but at least he had his pants on. His expression was amused as he met her gaze again.

"I would not have figured you to be so shy," he said.

Jo snorted. She did not need to answer that, so she just changed the subject. "How's the arm?"

Raul's amusement faded as he looked down at his arm, which hung limply at his side. It must have been a bitch to shower and get his pants on with the broken limb hampering things, but clearly the shirt was not going to happen without help. "Hurts a bit less. I can move my fingers a little, but..." He gave a little helpless shrug that ended in a wince.

"Here, let me help you with that," Jo said. She stood and picked up his shirt.

Getting Raúl into the shirt was a delicate operation that involved a lot of grunting and muttered curses. Jo winced sympathetically as she helped guide the broken arm into its sleeve, but Raúl managed to be at least slightly stoic about the whole thing. After the shirt was in place, Jo grabbed one of the bath towels and helped him create a makeshift sling. It was not much, but it would do until they were able to find real medical attention for him. Although where that would come from, Jo had no idea.

"How did you get into this line of work, Raúl?"

He sniffed softly and shrugged. "Which line of work is that? I don't normally do high speed chases through the city, if you know what I mean."

Jo just looked at him. After a moment, he lowered his gaze. "Yeah. Well, I never was very good in school, y'know? But I could tinker. And I knew computers. People just sort of started asking me to do little things here and there for them. Before long, it became a steady business."

"I see."

Raúl shook his head, his eyes flashing with...irritation? Jo must not have succeeded in keeping the disapproval out of her tone. "Most of the stuff I do is legit. But sometimes someone like Robert...Malcolm...needs a little somethin' extra. It pays a bit better, so I figure no harm no foul, right?" Raúl sighed, sank down onto his bed, and leaned forward, his eyes focusing on the floor. "After last night, tho..." He shook his head. "No way I can go back to legit work now."

Jo winced. Another person hurt because of her secret. The numbers were beginning to add up. "I'm sorry," she said softly.

Raúl looked up, surprised. "What you got to be sorry for? I knew what I was getting into soon as Malcolm mentioned the tracker." He grinned again. "Not the first time I've had to duck to avoid the long arm of the law. I'll be ok."

"I hope so. But this is - "

The doorknob rattled.

Jo spun toward the door, her heart in her throat. Behind her, Raúl leapt to his feet. She could feel his tension almost as acutely as her own. Jo glanced around quickly, and just as quickly ruled out flight. If it was the authorities at the door, there was no way they could make an escape. She flexed her hand around the grip of the plasma pistol, and waited.

The door opened and Malcolm stepped into the room.

Tension flooded out of Jo in a rush. She let out a breath she had not realized she was holding and took her hand off the weapon. Behind her, she heard Raúl blowing out a breath as well.

Malcolm looked quizzically at the two of them.

"Expecting someone else?"

"Just thought for a second you were the Feds."

Malcolm's eyebrow quirked upward. "They don't know the ID I'm using. We're clean, for the moment." He smiled then and kicked the door shut behind him.

Only then did Jo notice he carried two large bags. She recognized the name on the side of the bags: Lerotte's. A high-end department store.

"Doing a little shopping?"

Malcolm nodded. "You had to leave quickly. I figured you could use some clothes."

Jo's eyes widened and she grabbed the bags away from him. She pulled their contents out and spread them on the bed, her spirits rising higher every second. Two pairs of jeans, three t-shirts, two nicer collared shirts in subdued colors. A light leather jacket. Socks. A pair of sneakers; those would be much better than the dress shoes she wore to the meet in the Parque. And undergarments. All in her size. Finally, down at the bottom of the bag, were deodorant, lipstick and blush, a hair brush, and soap. Real soap, not the crap cheap motels throw in the bathrooms.

She looked back at Malcolm, a surge of emotion welling up. Right then, she could have kissed him. A part of her mind recalled how good he was at it, all those years ago. She suppressed that thought ruthlessly, but not before she felt a little flush run through her.

"Thank you," she said, feeling it was a bit too little to say.

Malcolm returned her smile with one of his own. "I hope I remembered your size correctly." He settled down onto the couch and leaned back, weariness written all over him. "I managed to make contact with my colleagues. They're sending a guy over to pick us up. He'll be here in half an hour," he glanced at Raúl and added, "with a first aid kit. That should get you through until we can get you to a doctor."

Raúl made a little half-shrug, then sat on the edge of his bed.

Jo stood and grabbed fresh underwear, a pair of jeans, and a t-shirt, and was mildly annoyed to realize she was grinning almost like a schoolgirl as she did so. "In that case, I'm going to go change." She paused, then grabbed the soap and deodorant as well. "And take another shower."

# 26

# TRANSIT

Jo felt like a new person when she walked out of the bathroom.

The new jeans were slightly tight, but that was not so unusual with denim. The t-shirt was loose and comfortable. She took a moment to brush out a few tangles in her hair, which as always reminded her why she kept it short, while she studied herself in the mirror over the sink.

Could be a lot worse; the design on the t-shirt, a dog with its tongue lolling out in a grin, was not what she would have picked, but beggars cannot be choosers.

"What did your contact have to say?" she asked, looking at Malcolm's reflection in the mirror.

She immediately wished she had not said anything. He gave a little jerk and blinked; her question must have awoken him.

"Not much." He paused then, suppressing a yawn with the back of his hand, stood up and moved his arms back and forth vigorously, getting his blood flowing. "We lost several good people in the raid, and almost all of our equipment and data. We're still trying to pick up the pieces, but it's hard to stay in contact with everyone."

Raúl peered at Malcolm intently, curiosity on his face, but he remained silent. Smart guy; you could learn a lot by just shutting up and listening. Sometimes more than those around you think you have.

Jo put the brush down and turned to face the two men, frowning.

"Surely there was more to it than what I saw the other night. I thought you said they had people all over the world."

Malcolm gave a half-shrug and spread his hands in a gesture of helplessness. "It's complicated. When we lost Becky and Lars, we - "

A knock at the door cut off his words.

Malcolm's face, bone-weary a moment ago, hardened as he turned to look out the peep hole; no security cameras in this place. After a moment, he relaxed, the sudden tension leaving his shoulders as quickly as it came.

"It's our guy." He reached for the doorknob, then paused and looked back at Jo and Raúl. "Isaac can be a bit oversensitive sometimes. A little touchy. Just be careful what you say to him."

Jo crooked an eyebrow at him.

"You'll see why," Malcolm said.

Then he opened the door. Jo immediately understood what he meant.

---

ISAAC WOULD HAVE BEEN TALL, but he stood with a stoop that left him only slightly taller than Jo. From his wrinkles, deep enough to be almost cracks in his face, he was getting on in years, pushing a hundred-ten, maybe a hundred-twenty. He had hair only on the left side of his head. It was thin, stringy, and gray. The right side of his head was a mass of burn scars, stretching from his neck, halfway down his jaw, then up to his temple. Where his ear should have been was just a hole.

Jo could understand why he would be touchy; it must be horrible going through life so disfigured, and he would scarcely want it pointed out. Why had he not had reconstructive surgery? It was easily obtained, and inexpensive.

But then, inexpensive for some was a king's fortune for others. Perhaps he lacked the money. After all, he wore simple, almost nonde-script clothing.

Or at least, at first glance it was simple. But when Jo looked closer it became clear his cloth was high quality. The kind of quality that is satis-fied to abstain from flashiness in favor of simplicity and functionality. A subtle musky odor surrounded him, faint enough that Jo almost did not notice it, but effective enough that it perked her interest almost before she realized what was happening.

She was forced to re-assess her initial impression. Isaac was a man of some means, but he preferred not to show it.

Intriguing. Who was he, really?

"Hmmph." Isaac spared Malcolm barely a glance, instead giving first Raúl and then Jo a thorough look-over. "That's her, huh? Thought she'd be prettier, the way you go on about her."

Malcolm flinched slightly, then flashed Jo an apologetic half-grin.

Isaac pursed his lips for a moment, then nodded slightly to himself and looked past Jo toward Raúl. Isaac sized him up then held out a small satchel to Malcolm. "Patch him up and meet me downstairs. I'm double-parked," he said. Then he turned and walked away, toward the stairwell leading down to the Motel's parking lot.

"Abrupt, isn't he," Raúl said. From his tone he was not sure whether to be amused or angry.

Jo could relate.

Malcolm wasted no time, but hurried over to the bed and upended the satchel. As first aid kits go, it was bare bones. A few bandages, some gauze, and a small spool of medical tape. But it did have a pair of stainless steel plates to use as a splint, and within a few short minutes they had Raúl's arm done up far better than it had been.

Malcolm stepped back from Raul and took a second to admire their handiwork, then cleared his throat and turned toward the door. "We'd better get moving," he said, over his shoulder. "He might just leave without us."

It took a minute to gather their meager belongings and make their way to the parking lot. Isaac already had his vehicle started. He sat in the driver's seat with the window rolled down. As they approached, he stuck his head out and scowled at them.

"They're not paying me by the hour. Get a move on."

He was certainly a pleasant fellow.

Isaac's car was small, more a coup than a sedan. Whoever got in the back seat was going to be crammed in tightly. But there was no help for it, so Jo pushed forward the passenger seat to climb in.

"I'll take the back, Jo."

She looked at Malcolm incredulously. "With your long legs?" She shook her head. "I'll be fine." Then she climbed in.

Malcolm took a moment to settle up at the Motel office, then they were off.

Very quickly, Jo began to regret not taking Malcolm up on his offer. It was not the tight confines of the rear seats that got to her; Raúl was skinny, so even though they were forced to sit close to each other by the car, they did not have to get that close.

No, the problem was Isaac.

Or rather, the fact that he never even considered activating the automatic navigation system, and he drove like a madman on a race track. He took corners much faster than he should have, pressing her and Raúl into each other. And he tended to brake suddenly. Throughout, he spewed curses at the other drivers that would put the saltiest of starliner pilots to shame.

Before long, Jo began to feel bruised from the constant rocking around and getting shoved into the side of the car, or into Raul's bony shoulder.

And poor Raúl. He must have jarred his injured arm a dozen times or more by the time they finally stopped in front of a nondescript commercial building on the west side of town.

The building was three stories tall and square, with stucco siding and a flat roof. Thin windows that reminded Jo of arrow-slits in a medieval castle marked the building's levels, and a single pair of swinging glass doors set in the center of the first floor offered entrance. A sign over the door read "The Ortega Building". There was a small sign to the right, which presumably listed the various organizations housed there.

Taken as a whole, the building could have been removed and set down in any commercial block of just about any city without causing any comments at all, except about the mechanism required to move it.

Jo could see why the organization, or the underground, or whatever they called themselves, would choose this place to re-organize itself.

"Well, here we are." Isaac took the car out of gear and looked over his shoulder at Jo. "Hope you know what you're doing, girl."

Irritation, born from the ride and amplified by his tone, flared up. "I can manage just fine, Isaac," Jo replied, not trying to keep the acid from her tone. "But thank you for your concern."

He silently met her gaze for a few seconds, and Jo could almost see his wheels turning. Then he surprised her. He shook his head and chuckled. His smile made his disfigured face suddenly bright, and the glimmer of youth shone from his eyes for a moment.

"Watch out for this one, Malcolm," he said, nudging Malcolm with his elbow. "She might give Pedro a migraine."

Malcolm just shook his head and got out of the car. Jo and Raúl followed as quickly as they could, with all the twisting and contorting that maneuver required.

No sooner were they out than Isaac drove away. Jo felt certain he was still laughing to himself.

# 27

# NEGOTIATION

**P**edro could hardly be considered a man, at least to Jo's way of thinking. He was maybe twenty-five, with the kind of baby face that made her doubt he had to shave more than twice a week.

He had the tanned features and dark hair one would expect from the Central or South Americas, high cheekbones in a round face, and dull brown eyes. His jeans, complete with a multitool in a leather pouch, work boots, and simple collared shirt gave him the look of a working man, but when Jo shook hands with him, his palms were smooth like a person who spends little time at manual labor.

But for whatever reason, Malcolm deferred to him. As much as he deferred to anyone, anyway.

"The famous Captain Ishikawa," Pedro said as he released her hand. "I'd say it's nice to meet you, but," he glanced at Malcolm and frowned slightly, "frankly we could all have done without that honor, I think."

Jo scowled, but Malcolm spoke before she could fire back.

"That's not fair, Pedro. The NSA was watching her, yes, but we knew that. They followed *me* back to the House from her place, not her."

Pedro's frown deepened a little, but then he sighed and nodded. "Of course." He looked back at Jo, managing, if not a smile then at least less of a frown. "My apologies for my rudeness. Will you sit?"

He gestured toward the center of the room, where a leather-upholstered couch and a pair of stuffed chairs clustered around a coffee table that was inlaid with a standard-sized display and control pad. Jo nodded and selected one of the stuffed chairs. As she sunk into its comforting embrace, she surveyed the room more closely.

It was located on the second floor of the Ortega Building, then down a long corridor from the lift and around a corner to the right.

As she had followed Malcolm down the corridor, Jo was struck by the generic decoration of the place as well as by its emptiness. Doors to a number of offices lined the corridor, with placards announcing Chiropractors, Lawyers, Accountants, an Artist's studio, and a Catering Service, though Jo presumed they did their actual cooking elsewhere. But no one else entered the corridor at all. It was the middle of the day; surely *someone* else besides them had work to do.

But Jo never saw anyone.

Pedro's office—who knew if it was his, or a shell company's, or what, but Jo thought of it as his anyway—bore the label "McKenzie and Velaquez, Architects" on its placard.

The door had opened as they arrived, and they were greeted by a man and a woman dressed in workout clothing, as though they were going to the gym, except that they wore pistols in shoulder holsters and the woman carried a hand-held weapons scanner. Malcolm they let enter without comment, but they subjected Jo and Raúl to the weapons scanner and a pat down, even after Jo surrendered her plasma pistol.

All that to get here, to meet with this kid.

He knew how to decorate, Jo had to admit. The central area of the offices, where they sat, had hardwood floors that were covered by several rugs that hailed from Persia, unless Jo missed her guess. A few paintings of nature scenes and wildlife hung on the walls, their colors matching those of the rugs and the upholstery of the furniture perfectly.

"First thing's first," Pedro began.

"Yeah," Raúl said, "Where's my money?"

Pedro blinked. "I was going to suggest we have a doctor look at your arm, actually."

"Oh." Raúl flushed slightly, embarrassed.

Pedro tapped the control pad. A moment later, a man walked into the room from further back in the offices. He was tall, just over two meters, and carried himself with a professional air that was enhanced by his sport coat and tie.

"Is the patient here?" he said, then seeing Raúl, and his arm, he smirked slightly. "Of course. I'm Doctor Connors. Will you follow me please?"

Raúl nodded and stood again. He paused to look back at Pedro before following the Doctor out. "Don't forget my money."

"Don't worry, Mr. Ramirez. You'll be fully paid for your trouble."

With another nod, Raúl left the room. A few seconds later, the sound of a door shutting from the back of the offices confirmed his departure, and Pedro turned a baleful eye on Malcolm.

"What the hell, Malcolm?" he said, his tone less civil now that Raúl was out of earshot. "I can understand you bringing her into this. But *him*? We can't trust him to keep his mouth shut!"

"There wasn't much choice at the time. And then afterwards..." Malcolm spread his hands. "What did you want me to do, ditch him, injured, where the NSA would pick him up? They would never believe he wasn't with us from the beginning, and you know what that would mean for him."

Pedro frowned again, then looked down at the coffee table and nodded. "You are right, of course. Well," he perked back up with a quick inhalation and directed his gaze at Jo. "We're in quite a pickle here, Captain, because of your new friends up there." He gestured toward the ceiling vaguely. "And your other friends in Geneva."

"I would not call them my friends."

Pedro smiled faintly. "No, of course you wouldn't. Regardless, since the raid, more than half of the people in our organization have vanished; either they left town or they decided they've have enough, and we'll never hear from them again. Or they're dead or caught. Between that and losing our base and equipment, it's been a difficult couple weeks around here."

Jo frowned, troubled. "I had the impression your organization was larger than just this cell in Quito."

"Oh it is," Pedro replied. "Problem is, I don't know how to get in touch with the others."

"Come again?"

Pedro looked down at the coffee table, abashed. Malcolm spoke in the intervening silence.

"There is not much communication between the branches, for obvious reasons. The branch leaders know who the other branch leaders are, but aside from that..."

What was this, amateur hour?

"You've got to be kidding me," Jo said, exasperation making her tone sharp, biting. "You never put together a contingency plan, in case you lost one of those leaders?"

"Of course we did," Pedro replied, flushing with what Jo hoped was embarrassment, though it could just as easily be anger. "We did not, however, plan to lose both the branch leader and her second. Now, with Becky taken and Lars dead..." He left the rest unsaid.

Jo blinked. She had not realized that Lars was the second; he looked like just a guard.

"So you're telling me we're screwed."

"Not in so many words - "

"There are emergency contingencies," Malcolm interjected, "but they take time to work. We put a message out to the other groups as soon as the raid happened. But it will take another week or so before we hear back from them; they have to revamp their security, move to their alternate safe locations..."

"Ok," Jo said. "So we get some new terminals up, redo the presentation, and line up the press. By the time that's ready to go, the others should be up and ready for it, in case we need support."

The two men looked at her silently. She began to get a sinking feeling in her stomach. Like there had not been enough hits already.

"What?"

Pedro cleared his throat and looked at Malcolm, almost pleadingly, Jo thought.

"The NSA took all of our data storage units in the raid, Jo," Malcolm said softly.

"And you don't have a backup."

"We do. The problem is, its location is a tightly held secret - "

"And only Becky and Lars know where it is," Jo finished. "Shit."

The two men nodded.

Unbelievable. This really was amateur hour.

"Well, gentlemen, I wish you would have been more open about your little organization's planning abilities earlier, before I decided to pick the side that's doomed to failure." Jo leaned back in the chair and pressed her fingers to the sides of her temples. She was beginning to get a headache. "What do you propose we do now?"

There was a long silence. Too long. One of those two had better say something that approximated a plan soon, or Jo was going to lose it.

"I think at this point we need to consider the Pericles issue a lost cause and - "

Jo rose from her seat in a towering fury. "Don't even *think* about going there, Pedro!" She jabbed her index finger at his face, and he recoiled, his eyes widening in surprise and, she hoped, a bit of fear. "I didn't throw away my career, my livelihood, and risk getting killed or thrown in prison over this just so you candy-asses can throw in the towel at the first sign of trouble!"

Malcolm cleared his throat, "Jo - "

She shot him her best "I'm the Captain, I'm pissed, and you better shut up and do what I say" look. His mouth shut with a satisfying click of teeth and he sunk back in his seat a little.

Jo looked back at Pedro. His wide-eyed stare had given way to an expression of chagrin. He refused to meet her eyes.

"Well?"

Pedro swallowed, then shook his head. "It's not a matter of not wanting to do anything, but without - "

"Without Becky you're impotent."

Pedro grimaced. For a second, Jo thought he was going to contest her statement, but then he just nodded.

"Well." Jo crossed her arms over her chest. A plan was beginning to form in her mind. It was ludicrous. Insane, even. But these were desperate times, and maybe they called for a little insanity. "In that case, we'll just have to get Becky back."

The look of stunned incredulity on Pedro's face was priceless.

# 28

# JAILBREAK

The van was old.

Old enough that it could not support a database implant uplink, and they had been developed before Jo departed Gliese on the run back to Earth that had changed everything. Jo supposed it would not have been difficult to upgrade the van's electronics, but for whatever reason its owners never bothered to. Now that Citizens For Liberty—she finally found out what they called themselves, though she still called it the Underground, at least in her own head; CFL seemed a bit trite—used it, Jo had no doubt its electronics would never be upgraded. The lack of connectivity suited their need for stealth and security well.

Jo rolled her shoulders. She and her companions had been sitting in van at their pre-determined location for two hours, awaiting the signal. And the passenger seat, however well padded, was beginning to wear on her. She was developing a kink in her upper back.

"Should be any time now."

Jo glanced aside at her companion in the van's cockpit, a chubby guy dressed, as she was, in a loose black jumpsuit and matching gloves. He had greying black hair, a thick beard, and small, beady eyes. His name was Henri. Over the last week, she had gotten to know him fairly well. Well enough to know that he was cool under pressure, at least theoretical pressure, and that he had little love for the ideals that others in the CFL shared. He was driven by anger. Somehow, some way—he never explained how—the government screwed him, and he was out to screw the government back.

He never explained exactly what he meant by that either.

"You've been saying that for the last hour, Henri," said Raúl, from the passenger area behind them.

Jo was surprised that Raúl was with them. After the doctor fixed up his arm, Pedro gave him money to cover his expenses from the evening, plus extra for his trouble, and lined him up with people who could furnish a new, fake, identity for him. But for whatever reason, he opted to continue providing his services to the CFL. Maybe he wanted to screw the government too.

Or maybe they just paid better than he was used to.

"No sense griping," Jo said. They had known it could be a long wait. Their information was imprecise at best.

Raúl sniffed and went back to monitoring his instruments. When the call came in, he would be the first to see it.

It had taken a while to get Malcolm to agree with her idea, let alone Pedro. The NSA had Becky in their Field Office. The CFL had been able to learn that much from the few contacts they had that still talked with them. But the Field Office was hardly set up for long-term prisoner detention. At some point they would have to move her to a proper prison. When that happened, the CFL would have an opportunity to bust her out.

It was risky. Odds were it would just result in a lot of them getting arrested as well. But if it worked, and they got Becky out, they could get to the backed up data drives and proceed with the plan. The only other alternative was to admit defeat, and Jo was not about to do that.

She was surprised that Malcolm was not onboard immediately. But he eventually agreed, and from there it was fairly short work for the two of them to browbeat Pedro into it.

Not that he came along for the operation himself. He had other things to do.

Jo smirked and shook her head. It was just as well. He was a bit too green for this sort of thing anyway.

Not that Jo was much more experienced in this area either. She was honest enough with herself to admit that much. Leadership, command, organization—those things she could do in her sleep. Blatantly flaunting the law, though... That was still new, and took some getting used to.

A burst of static followed by a series of electronic beeps issued momentarily from the speakers mounted in the van's rear. The noise shut off abruptly, and Jo looked over her shoulder to see Raúl hunched over the workstation there, headphones pressed to his ears while he quickly jotted down notes on the workstation's interface pad. He must have unplugged the headphones for a short while, and who could blame him? Even the most ergonomically designed unit could become uncomfortable over time.

Raúl finished transcribing and looked up. His expression was tight, nervous, and he appeared a bit pale. Meeting Jo's gaze, he nodded quickly.

"Three minutes."

JAQUELINE MOORE PEERED at the transport van through her windshield and scowled. It was bad enough she had to take part in this bit of busy-work, but did it really have to be scheduled on a Sunday? Not that she cared for Sundays more than any other day, really. Her parents attended Mass regularly, but she had long ago left that superstition aside. But this Sunday was supposed to be a day off, and she got few enough of them that she did not relish the thought of losing even one to work.

Especially not to mindless work.

But that was how it went sometimes. Two weeks ago, she had been riding high. She had silenced a potentially huge security leak, was responsible for taking down the largest CFL cell ever discovered, and had secured the cooperation of a well-placed informant who could no doubt lead her to even more arrests in short order. As a result, she had received commendations from the entire chain of command, up to and including Deputy Director Chandini. There was talk of early promotion for herself and Jesús, and maybe a transfer away from this God-forsaken pit of a city to someplace more livable.

And then it all went to hell.

"Fucking DiStefano," she muttered under her breath.

The driver, a rookie agent in a nondescript navy blue suit with a weak tie, whose name she forgot, looked at her curiously. "Ma'am?"

"Nothing. Just keep driving."

The rookie blanched and looked back to the street ahead, his lips compressing into a tight scowl. Jackie almost felt ashamed; she probably did not need to have used so cutting a tone. But she was not in the mood to talk, at least not to the likes of him. The fact that she was stuck with him until Jesús recovered - if he ever did; Ngubwe's plasma bolt had taken off most of his kneecap - just made the situation more annoying.

But she did have to work with the guy. Jackie sighed and looked back at the rookie again.

"Sorry. It's been a tough week."

He flashed an understanding smile at her. "I can only imagine." They rode in silence for almost a full minute, then he piped up again. "Is it true Chandini threatened to send you to Titan for life?"

Jackie blinked. Where had he heard *that* one? Ah, the water-cooler rumor mill. She had always hated that.

"No. Not even close."

Chandini *had*, in fact, threatened her if she failed to correct the situation quickly. But not with anything as pleasant as being stuck on Titan for the rest of her life. She almost shuddered as she recalled the conversation, but forced herself to stillness quickly. It would not do to show weakness in front of the rookie.

"That's good. I'd hate to see that happen to you." The rookie smiled at her again. He was actually not bad looking; she had not noticed that before. "You know, I... OH FUCK!"

He slammed on the brakes and their vehicle fishtailed, almost losing control completely as the wheels struck a leftover puddle from yesterday's rainfall.

But Jackie hardly noticed. Her whole attention was riveted ahead, as she watched her life end.

---

THE TRUCK SLAMMED into the side of the prison transport van, sending the van careening sideways for several meters before it slammed into the metal and concrete guardrail separating the edge of the street from the pedestrian walkway beyond. An assortment of people, from businessmen in expensive suits to vacationers in shorts and t-shirts, leapt away from the impact zone, lest they get crushed.

Jo was relieved to see the guardrail held; they were not there to hurt anyone, after all. Not if they could help it.

She glanced aside at Henri, who nodded curtly. Then they both pulled dark ski-masks down over their faces and he put the van into gear.

In the intersection ahead, traffic had come a standstill. The truck effectively blocked most of the oncoming lanes, and those that were not quickly blocked themselves as cars screeched to a stop. Some of them contained the other teams in their little raid, Jo knew, but still she felt exposed as they sped toward the scene.

Henri slammed on the brakes as they came even with the truck, then put the van in park and hopped out. Jo followed, drawing her plasma pistol as she did.

The prison van driver and the man riding shotgun were visible through the cracked plastiglass of the windshield and side windows. They looked too stunned to do anything right at the moment, but that could change quickly.

To her right, two men in black ski masks like hers hopped out of a stopped car. One trained a rifle on the cab of the prison van—it was his job to make sure the two men in the van did not do anything rash—and the other covered the street to the right.

Jo followed Henri as he hurried toward the back of the prison van, but noticed the truck driver descending from his driver's seat and also shouldering a rifle. Malcolm's eyes glinted with excitement and...glee?...and he shot a wink at her as she passed him before turning his attention to the the street to the left.

Was he any good at shooting a rifle? Jo could not recall; she hoped he had been practicing.

Henri reached the back door and pulled a small roll of what looked like paper out of the pouch on his belt. Unrolling it quickly, he pressed it to the seam where the van's two rear doors met and tapped it in two places, then stepped back. The strip quickly turned red, then a scalding white as light and heat, intense enough that Jo had to step back and look away to avoid being dazzled by the glare and temperature, flowed out of it and into the metal of the doors. Whatever locking mechanism the van had could not stand up to that.

Within seconds, the strip had burned out, leaving only blackened ash marking its place.

Henri glanced at Jo; she could see the question in his eyes. All set?

She nodded and raised her pistol, sighting in on the door and whomever might be inside.

Henri grasped the door's handle and pulled it open.

---

JACKIE THREW the passenger side door open and leapt from the car almost before it came to a halt, drawing her sidearm with practiced speed as she went.

Though there had been speculation about possible trouble with this or another prisoner transfer, she never really expected the CFL to be so bold. Always before they had kept to the shadows, working their little schemes and playing their cloak and dagger games. They would occasionally contribute to something big enough to draw attention to themselves, but they never came out directly.

Which is why it had been so difficult to locate them. If not for the chink in the armor they had revealed during their interaction with Ishikawa...

Jackie scowled. She was involved in this. Jackie knew it instinctively. This sort of direct, aggressive action was exactly the sort of thing Ishikawa would go for. Her bio and psych profile had made that very clear; she was a woman of action, and would not readily sit in the shadows. Jackie had to admit a grudging respect for the erstwhile Captain; a pity she had gone so far off the rails.

But that was neither here nor there. They were not going to get this prisoner. Not on her watch, with that sentence hanging over her head.

All that passed through Jackie's mind in a split second, long enough to hunker down in a crouch behind the car's hood and survey the scene.

Two perpetrators were at the rear of the transport van. They had applied a cutting strip to the doors and would have them open in short order, if their placement was even halfway competent, which Jackie did not doubt for a second. A third peered over the sights of a plasma rifle down the street toward her, but he was mostly focused on the area to her left. It did not appear he had noticed her or the rookie.

Jackie smiled thinly and flexed her fingers around the grip of her weapon. The sentry's oversight was going to doom their whole gambit.

She glanced to her left, where the rookie was just emerging from their vehicle, from the passenger side, the side away from the action, just as the book said. At least the Academy still taught the basics correctly. He was flushed, his eyes narrowed. He was certainly nervous, frightened even, but he did not show it, at least not overtly. Jackie found her initial opinion of him improving. There might be some substance there after all.

A quick series of hand-gestures later, the rookie nodded and slid back toward the rear of the vehicle, crouching to maintain cover. Jackie moved to the front bumper and peaked over again.

The transport van's rear doors were open. The guards inside were cowed, hands raised under the aim of one of the Libertarians, a female. The prisoner, bleary-eyed from her sedatives, was slowly exiting with assistance from the other bandit. Jackie looked back toward the sentry. He was looking backward, toward the prisoner.

It was now or never, and the fool had just given her all the opening she needed.

Jackie made a chopping gesture with her left hand, signaling the rookie to move out. Then she rose and moved around the bumper, bringing her weapon up to a firing position. In her peripheral vision, she saw the rookie do the same.

And then he went down, flung from his feet by a ball of plasma that streaked in front of Jackie from out of nowhere.

Dropping to the ground, she rolled to her right and brought her weapon to bear.

And found herself looking down the barrels of a pair of plasma rifles, the left-most one still releasing a small wisp of post-discharge gasses from its muzzle.

The two men watched her cooly, eyes flat behind their black ski-masks. They stood behind the hood of a car ten meters to her right. How had she not noticed them before?

They had the drop on her. She knew it; they knew it. It only took a second to decide. Chandini's punishment would be bad, yes, but it would not be death. Live to fight another day, and all that.

Jackie, lying there on her belly, raised her hands and tossed her weapon aside.

The men relaxed visibly; the one on the left glanced to the side. Jackie followed his glance and saw the prisoner getting into a van, the one that had followed the truck to the scene. The woman who had covered her exit from the transport and the un-attentive sentry were close behind.

A moment later, the van doors closed, its motor started, and it sped away.

The sound of a motor off to her right drew Jackie's gaze back in that direction. The two riflemen were also gone, their car speeding away after the van.

Jackie got to her feet and retrieved her weapon, and was relieved - and surprised at that - to hear the rookie groan behind her.

"Son of a bitch!" he muttered as he struggled to his feet.

"Glad you remembered your vest."

"Damn right." He stumbled forward to her side and looked around. He whistled softly, then shook his head. "Son of a bitch. We're fucked."

He had no idea how right he was.

# 29

# SETTING THE PIECES

Jackie held herself erect by sheer force of will. Others—most people, truth be told—would wither beneath Chandini's ire, but she would not allow herself to.

She would not.

"...And that is all we know, ma'am." Jackie's supervisor, Viktor Gorshkov, finished the briefing in his usual clipped tones. He managed to keep any hint of emotion out of his words, despite the fact that he was probably at least as embarrassed as Jackie. She had always admired that about him. A consummate professional, Viktor was.

On the wall monitor, Chandini's scowl deepened, which Jackie would not have thought possible a moment ago. "This situation is unacceptable, Agent Gorshkov."

"Yes, ma'am." What else was there to say?

Chandini's gaze left Vicktor and came to rest upon Jackie. She felt a trickle of sweat run down her back and almost let her shoulders slump at the fire in the Deputy Director's eyes. Not so long ago, those eyes had been warm, congratulatory, as Chandini praised Jackie's efforts and went on at length about how bright a future she had.

So much for that.

Chandini's lips pursed for a moment, and Jackie could see the wheels spinning in her head. "Agent Moore."

Jackie stiffened, trying to not look terrified. Here it came.

"You are no longer Agent in charge of this case." It was not unexpected, but hearing the words from the Deputy Director's lips still stung. But that would not be the worst. Chandini continued, "I am taking personal command. I will board a sub-orbital transport ten minutes after the end of this conversation and will be in Quito in two hours."

Jackie could not remember when she had been so surprised. Chandini was coming here? To assume control personally? And to use a sub-orbital ride...

Those were expensive, more costly than standard subsonic aircraft, anyway. NSA travel regulations stipulated subsonic transport except for the highest of emergencies, and even then Viktor, as Section Head, could not just sign off on it; it had to be approved from headquarters.

Of course, Chandini *was* headquarters. But still...

This was a high profile case. Maybe the highest profile case, ever. It should not have surprised Jackie that the Deputy Director would pull out all the stops now that things were going haywire, but it did.

Chandini was saying something else; Jackie missed it in the whirl of surprised thoughts for a moment. "I'm sorry, ma'am?"

Chandini looked askance at her - in truth she had not been looking at her in any other way the entire time, but it just got worse. "Assemble your team, Agent Moore. They must be ready to deploy as soon as I arrive."

"Deploy where?"

The Deputy Director just looked at her silently for a second. Then the monitor went dark, as abrupt an end to a conversation as Jackie could recall in any professional setting.

This was going to be ugly. But at least she was still on the case, still had a job.

In fact, Chandini had not mentioned anything of disciplinary action against her at all. Neither had Viktor.

Slowly, hope and relief welled up within her. They were not going to lop her head off after all. Jackie turned her head away from the monitor to see Viktor grinning at her.

"I told you not to worry," he said, the clipped professional tone he used with Chandini punctuated with more warmth now. It ought to be; they had worked together long enough.

"You did." But she still could not believe it. Why the parole? She new better than to ask. And besides, she knew the answer anyway. She was already read in. She knew the people involved and had some experience with how they operated. And she had a personal stake in making sure this thing turned out the way it was supposed to. She had value, still, and Chandini was never one to waste a resource.

"Get your people ready," Viktor said. "Things are about to get very busy around here."

---

JO HAD NOT STOPPED pacing for hours. At least it felt that way. She did not look at her watch to verify the notion, though. She knew without looking that it would more than confirm her estimate. She had been in what fashioned for a medical waiting room for half a day now, she knew that without any doubt at all.

It was just amusing, or at least felt less pathetic, to tell herself she had only been pacing for a short while and was exaggerating to herself in the midst of her stress.

The analytical part of her mind, the professional part, the part that had seen her through countless stressful scenarios and one or two life-or-death situations over the years, screamed out at her that she was being foolish. Time passes as it will, and she was stupid to deny it. And even more stupid to waste energy in a fruitless exercise. She knew that part of her mind was right, but that mattered not.

She continued to pace.

She did her small, five-step circuit of the waiting area. Not so long ago it had been a small receptionist area where an overly-pompous small business owner could put on aires of importance by having his admin keep potential clients waiting in seats that were just a little too narrow while the climate control kept the room just a little bit too warm. All the better to wear them down before the negotiation got started.

Or at least that's how Jo envisioned the scenario taking place as she paced around. Of course, that notion almost certainly had no relation to the reality of what went on in the office space that the Underground—CFL seemed even more trite, so Jo refused to even think it—leased out.

The office space was in a small commercial building—a different one than Isaac had brought Jo to initially after the escape from the NSA agents—and adjoined a moderately sized park. Jo would have preferred the park not be there. Better a bit more inconvenience on their part getting back and forth from base than to risk children's lives because of their impatience. But then, no one had consulted her on the choice.

Jo stopped before the room's lone window and peered out, her mind whirling through the day's events as she watched the branches in the trees across the street wave in the breeze.

It was hard to believe the recovery had gone so smoothly, almost like clockwork. Very few details varied from the way they had planned it out, and almost before she realized it they were wheeling Becky into the back office, where a medic was waiting. She would undoubtedly be disoriented and, if her experienced came close to matching Jo's, probably hungry and sleep-deprived.

But none of those things required hours of treatment. Well, except sleep. Jo had not seen anyone in quite some time, since a short black-haired man she had never seen before came in to deliver a tray of food. No one told her whether to stay in the waiting area or leave. But Jo could not bring herself to do either.

Dammit, what the hell was going on?

She turned away from the window to resume her pacing, her hands curling into fists as irritation welled up within her. It was well past time she get off her duff and find out something about their status.

And so, naturally, that was when the door from the inner office—the medical room, whatever—opened.

Malcolm and Pedro stepped into the room. Both of them looked exhausted, their clothing rumpled, though Pedro's jeans and short-sleeved green collared shirt faired far worse that Malcolm's black jump-suit from the raid. But worse than that, they were dejected. Malcolm managed a smile of greeting, though it did not pass to his eyes.

"Is she - ?" Jo almost feared to hear it, from the looks on their faces, but she had to know.

Malcolm sighed and flopped into one of the too-narrow chairs that Jo had specifically opted not to use. "Becky is ok. But - "

"But," Pedro interrupted, "she was heavily drugged for the transfer and from appearances was not treated very well before that. She's been in and out of consciousness for the last couple hours, but she finally became coherent just a few minutes ago."

Jo could almost feel the ball beginning to drop. "So what did she - ?"

Malcolm sighed, a sound of defeat if ever Jo heard one. He slumped forward, looking down at the floor. "She told them where the backup drives were stored. She tried to hold out, but..." He shook his head.

That certainly put a damper on things. "Damn," Jo said, which was putting it mildly.

"You could say that," Pedro said. The young man ran his hand through his hair and glanced back at the door to the recovery room, his lips drawing downward into a scowl. Then he, too, sighed. "I'm not sure what to tell you. That's that, I guess."

Jo got a hollow feeling in the pit of her stomach. "What are you saying, Pedro?"

Pedro looked back at her and Jo found herself retreating a half-step before she realized it. His gaze was...almost venomous. "I'm saying we're done here. This whole project was a bad idea from the start, but now..." He shook his head. "That was our last play. There's nothing more we can do. Now we need to focus on rebuilding the organization, recovering from the hits we've taken."

"You can't be serious. You're going to let this happen?" Jo shook her head in denial, but Pedro's expression did not budge in the least. A dreadful realization came over her: he had meant every word. "My God, you are, aren't you. Why the hell did you even get involved in the first place if you're just going to pull out when it gets a little difficult?"

Pedro snorted and made a disdainful gesture toward Malcolm. "Wasn't up to me, Captain. Your silver-tongued friend there won Becky over, and Lars was not far behind. I didn't make the decisions then." He drew himself up and just then he seemed to tower. "I do now. And we have enough *human* problems, injustices that affect actual *people*, not some critters from," he waved his hand upwards toward the ceiling, "up there. We don't need to expend resources that we can't afford to lose on something like this." His eyes narrowed at her, dangerously. "Especially now, after all the damage that's been done."

There it was. She had caught glimpses of it from time to time, but now it was laid bare for all to see. Pedro did not care about the alien babies; they were just animals to him, worth as much as a household cat. Less. He would probably have loved to sign up to work at that damned lab.

The hollow feeling in her stomach became a burning rage at Pedro's callous indifference. His short-sightedness.

She took a step toward him, her fists once more clenched. "You can't be that stupid. They are much more advanced than us. When they learn what we did to their - "

Pedro snorted again. "How are they ever going to learn about it?"

Jo returned the snort. "Secrets this big never stay hidden. You of all people should know that, considering the company you keep."

"And we'll deal with it then, as a people. But in the meantime there are more important issues to tackle." Pedro's stare could freeze a cup of coffee in a second. "You've cost us a lot of trouble, Captain. You and Malcolm." He glanced aside toward Malcolm and, if anything, his gaze hardened. "We've wasted resources, lost equipment, lost people... I've half a mind to turn you both in."

Malcolm rose to his feet. His eyes widened and his expression, resigned, almost defeated before, became suddenly alarmed. "Pedro," he began, his voice shaking. Jo had never heard him speak with such a note of fear in his words before.

Pedro raised a hand toward Malcolm, a gesture Jo presumed was meant to be soothing. "But we all know the NSA won't stop with just you two. Not now, if ever. Turning you in would not help us." He snorted out a bitter-sounding laugh. "Hell, it would probably hurt us more, because you would tell them everything you know about us." He glanced between the two of them. "Wouldn't you?"

"Damn right I would," Jo said through clenched teeth, her rage reduced, but still smoldering within her.

"So," Pedro said, "that leaves us at a bit of an impasse. What to do with the two of you?" He crossed his arms over his chest and raise his left hand to his chin. The index finger tapped idly at his chin as he paused and pondered.

Jo did not trust herself not to flay the boy—he was acting like a boy, whatever his actual age—alive with her tongue. Instead, she managed, in the calm tone she reserved for subordinates who had screwed up royally but who could not be taken to task immediately, to ask, "Have you discussed any of this with Becky?"

Malcolm shook his head quickly, shooting Jo a warning glance.

Pedro either did not notice or did not care. He fixed his gaze fully on Jo and smirked. "What Becky thinks no longer matters. She has been compromised. Until and unless she can be proven not to be turned, or at least to not be a hinderance to our operations, she is no longer in charge. I was next in line, so..." His smirk became a satisfied grin and his eyebrow quirked upward meaningfully.

Son of a bitch. Jo had no response to that.

The silence stretched out for a long several seconds. Then Pedro nodded to himself as though he had settled something in his mind. "I think we are through."

"You already said that," Jo began, but she trailed off when she noticed the stricken expression on Malcolm's face.

Pedro sniffed in disdain. "No, I mean we are through with the two of you. Citizens for Liberty will no longer participate in your little crusade." He snapped his fingers in the air beside his head, and the door behind Jo—the one leading out into the hallway of the building that housed their new hideout—swung open. Two burly men whom Jo recognized from the planning and preparation for the jailbreak walked into the room and took up station on either side of the door, arms crossed over their chests in an intimidating manner.

"These gentlemen will escort you out and give you sufficient funds to set yourselves up somewhere." He affixed first Jo and then Malcolm with a hard stare. "Do not try to contact us again."

He turned on his heel and walked back toward the inner door.

"You're not worried we'll go to the Feds?"

Pedro chuckled softly at Jo's question.

Of course they would not go to the Feds. If they did, they would just be dooming themselves. Sure, they could cause some damage to the CFL, but they themselves would never see the outside of a cell again. If they were even that lucky. The CFL would not turn them in, but they had no reason to fear Jo and Malcolm doing so themselves.

The rage re-ignited from its smolder, burning with an intensity that could melt steel. "You son of a bitch!"

The only reply to Jo's outburst was the solid—and final—click of the door swinging shut behind Pedro.

# 30

# ALONE

Jo stalked into the motel room and hurled her bag across the room. It struck the wall with a resounding thud and for a moment almost seemed to stick there before falling to the floor. She did not want to consider what was on the wall that could possibly have made it do that.

"Calm down, Jo," Malcolm said from behind her. He pulled the door closed with a solid click of the lock. "We can't be going off the handle, here."

"What?" Jo turned on him with her best 'I'm the Captain and you have really pissed me off' look. This time she did not need to fake it. She was gratified to see him recoil a bit. "*What* did you say?"

Malcolm raised his hands in front of himself in a placating gesture. "If we're going to get through this, we need to be calm. Think things through. I can - "

"Stow it! Just stow it, Malcolm!" Jo was half-inclined to march over there and smack him silly. This was all his fault. All of it. If he hadn't gone and...

*And what? Tried to do the right thing?*

Snarling, Jo forced that little voice in her head away before it stole her fury. Anger was all that kept her going right then. She needed it.

Malcolm just looked at her silently, his face smooth. But his eyes told a different story. He was stricken, stricken to the core, and beyond his fear she could see guilt and concern. For her wellbeing, she was sure. Jo's momentary fury at him left and she slumped down onto the edge of the bed.

It was hard as a rock. Typical.

"What are we going to do?" she asked, and inwardly cringed at the despair, the hopelessness that she heard in her own voice. "I gave up my career—my *life*—for this. And now it's over?" Horrified, Jo heard her voice break at the end. She was not going to cry. She had not cried since her father died, and she had promised herself...

She could not help it. Tears welled up, and she could not suppress a sob. That first one unleashed the floodgates. She sagged down, cradling her face in her hands and wept. She wept for herself, for Malcolm. For the helpless babies that were being destroyed. For everything.

At some point, Malcolm sat next to her on the bed and pulled her close. She fell asleep weeping on his shoulder.

----

THE NEXT MORNING DAWNED CLEAR, with only a few high stratus clouds in an otherwise pristine sky.

Any other day, Jo would not have noticed so much. But today, the beauty of the new day kindled something within her. Looking out the motel window toward the sun as it slowly peaked above the mountains to the east, Jo felt the despair and grief from the previous night wash away. Yesterday had been horrible, yes. But today was a new day, and could be better.

She turned away from the window and sipped at her coffee—Malcolm had slipped out before she woke and returned with it, along with bagels—and found herself wishing the same could be said of the motel room.

It still sucked.

She had thought the motel they crashed in with Raúl was bad, but at least that place had been cleaned sometime in the previous year. This place stunk and had dust on every horizontal surface. If she had been in a state to notice last night, there is no way she would have consented to stay there. She felt grimy just looking at the room, but she did not even think about using the shower. There was no telling what had taken place in the bathrooms of a place like this.

But there had been little choice last night; by the time Pedro's men were finished with them it was late and they could either use this place or wander around for a while trying to find someplace else. That prospect was even more unappealing than the conditions of the motel.

All the same, it was a good thing they weren't staying.

"Ok, what's the plan?" Jo had a couple ideas, but none of them were very appealing or likely to succeed. Hopefully Malcolm had come up with something.

He rolled his shoulders in an almost-shrug. "First we need to find a place where we can stay for a while. Settle in. Then," he ran one hand through his hair in the same way he did back as a non-qual on his first starliner when he could not answer a superior's question, "we find some more support."

Oh great. He had no more clue what to do than Jo did, and between the two of them he was the expert in the underworld.

They were so screwed.

Her doubt must have showed on her face, because he smiled in a manner that Jo supposed was meant to be comforting. "It'll be ok, Jo. I know some other people. We can get a team together, figure out a way to make some money - "

"I'm sorry. What? We're not trying to start a business here, Malcolm."

Malcolm sighed and looked down at the floor. "Jo, I think you need to face the fact that we've lost."

"Like hell."

Malcolm scowled, the first genuine emotion he had shown since leaving Pedro last night. "What would you have us do, Jo? We've only a little money, no contacts, no friends. No way to fight, or even find out what the NSA is doing with those eggs." He spread his hands helplessly. "They beat us. I'm sorry, but it's true."

Jo snorted. "I thought you said there were other underground cells all over the world."

"There are, but - "

"Pedro doesn't speak for all of them. We'll just head on down to Australia and make contact down there. They may still want to help."

Malcolm looked at Jo for a long moment. Surprise, then excitement flashed across his face. Then that faded back into resignation.

He shook his head. "It wouldn't work, Jo. I've only ever dealt with the cell here in Quito. I wouldn't know how to get in touch with the Brisbane group. And even if I did," he sighed, "Pedro will send word to the other cells that we can't be trusted. They will not give us the time of day."

"We should try anyway."

Malcolm rolled his eyes. "And how will we get there?"

Jo blinked. "What do you mean? We just hop on a plane and go."

"They take biometrics at every airport, Jo."

"Oh crap." Jo had forgotten about that.

Malcolm nodded. "I've not left Quito, except by car, in eighteen months, for security reasons."

Jo found herself biting her lip in frustration, something she had not done since she was a girl, and forced herself to stop. This was going to be even more difficult than she thought. "Well, we'll figure out a way. We have to keep going, Malcolm."

"I don't see how. I think it would be best to take some time to get our feet back under us first. Get some cash flow, make some new contacts."

"How much time do you think those eggs have? If I were Chandini I'd be making preps to close up shop right now."

Malcolm had no response to that. He simply frowned and looked away. Truth told, there was merit to his notion; it was hard to be effective without a solid footing. But there was no time! All the same, the obstacles seemed insurmountable.

There had to be a way. There was always a way.

"Well," Malcolm said as he rose from his seat, "we won't figure it out right this second. For now, let's find a better place to hole up."

Jo could not argue with that. Just the thought of leaving this place behind lifted her spirits considerably.

 

THEY EMERGED from the motel room into the morning sunlight, and the earlier optimism Jo felt watching the sunrise returned. She slung her bag over her shoulder and inhaled deeply, reveling in the fresh morning breeze for a moment and letting her mind go while Malcolm went to the motel office to settle the bill.

The motel was nondescript, easily exchanged with any of a million similar places, except for its level of upkeep; just a row of rooms with doors opening onto a small parking lot and the office at the far end. At this time in the morning, the parking lot was next to empty and Jo imagined most of the rooms were as well. This place struck her as more of a place where people come for just a short time at night with people they have no intention of seeing again, or with whom they do not wish to be caught. She had heard a term once: No Tell Motel. It summed the place up perfectly.

Jo shook her head, smirking at the judgment she was making. She was not so different than those Johns and cheating spouses at this point, was she? On the run, fearful of being caught.

But at least she was trying to do something good.

Malcolm returned, the resignation and grimness gone from his face now that they were taking action. "We're all set."

They set off walking.

The motel was on the outskirts of one of Quito's northern suburbs, though suburb was probably the wrong word for it. Most suburbs were fairly well-to-do and nice, while this place could charitably be called down on its luck. It was strange to see the closed businesses, the boarded up buildings, the destitute-looking people so close to the wealth and extravagance of one of the world's greatest cities.

"How did this place get so run down?"

Malcolm eyed a man with hungry eyes who watched them as they walked past. For a moment Jo almost thought the fellow was going to do something, right there in the daylight, but instead he looked away, defeated.

"I heard that there was some sort of scandal with the town's mayor and a large business owner. Millions of credits embezzled, or some such."

"That wouldn't drive the entire town to poverty," Jo said. "Not unless it was in isolation. This..." She gestured to yet another house that looked as though it was barely standing. "This is horrible. Why hasn't anyone done something?"

Malcolm raised an eyebrow at her. "They are. Most of the people here are on public support of some sort or other. The local chamber of commerce is trying to encourage businesses to return..."

"...but it takes a lot of encouragement to get someone to be the first to go into a situation like this," Jo finished for him.

Malcolm nodded. "Becky told me about some of the projects the CFL was doing here to try to pull the people out of their learned help-lessness. Progress was...slow."

Jo mulled that over as they walked. She should not have been surprised; she had seen poverty on every world she had visited. Some had it worse than others, but the poor were always there. And, it seemed, would always be there. It was sad, but she had more immediate things to worry over at the moment.

After a couple of kilometers, they came to an intersection with a larger road and turned south. It took a moment, but Jo realized it was Highway 35.

"Is that safe house you mentioned before near here?"

Malcolm looked sidelong at her, confused, for a moment. Then he blinked in surprise. He looked around at the buildings and signs on the road, and grinned. "It is. About five clicks ahead, and then left another couple of kilometers."

"Is it continuously manned or just available for whomever needs it?"

Malcolm's smile grew until it nearly stretched ear to ear.

# 31

# A HOUSE IN THE VALLEY

After another kilometer, the dilapidated buildings Jo had almost become accustomed to walking past grew more sparse until they passed a lone refueling station at the extreme southern end of the pitiful little town. Then it was just her, Malcolm, and the open road.

Jo was tempted to feel guilty that she did not even know the name of the little island of despair they had just departed. But she would very likely never lay eyes on it again, one way or the other.

It actually became pleasant, walking along the empty road under the midmorning sun. It reminded Jo of good times in the past, with her family from the starliner. Hiking the Vine Peaks of Talos. Braving the winds along the eternal terminator of Gliese. Watching the aurora on Centauri.

Those and a hundred other wonders that the planetbound never get to see. Never dream of seeing, because they do not know they exist. Or if they do, they dismiss them as fancy or something beyond a person's reach. It truly was a blessed life Jo had been dealt. Or rather, that she had chosen. Even if all of this turned out poorly, which it seemed it was going to however she tried to keep her spirits up, it had been a good life, and she was thankful for it.

The trick was to make sure things did not turn out poorly.

Small clusters of buildings, businesses and residences, began to appear, one and all in much better repair than those in the shanty they had left behind. Before long, the road resembled more a typical suburban stretch of highway, with businesses and strip malls interspersed with crossroads leading to residential subdivisions. It was like stepping forward in time from some godawful place in history back to modern times.

They reached a busy crossroads. Two refueling stations stood catty-corner on either side of the intersection, and opposite them two competing fast food joints, each catching traffic heading in one of the main directions. The traffic had gotten heavier, but was still far and away from what could be expected down in Quito proper. Still it was substantial compared to what they had seen for the last couple of hours.

"We go left here," Malcolm said.

The street was named Vía de la Valle, and true to its name over the next couple kilometers it wound its way higher into the mountains along the side of a steep grade into a sheltered valley. It was immediately clear that this was a more upscale community: large houses perched higher up the side of the hill, surrounded by carefully sculpted grounds complete, in many cases, with swimming pools. Schools, churches, restaurants, and all manner of other businesses and entertainments were visible down in the valley and along the side of the hill, all beautifully designed and maintained. Jo was immediately struck by the contrast with where they had just been.

"Amazing that things are so much different here, only a few kilometers away," she mused as they stopped for a breather. "I did not expect the safe house to be so impressive."

Malcolm chuckled, wiping the sweat off his brow with the back of his hand; it had grown quite warm as the morning turned to afternoon. "It is not one of those." He gestured toward a particularly large house perched atop a rise not far away. "Our place is down in the valley. We'll take the next road down. It's not far now."

That was good to hear.

Of course, not far is relative, as Jo decided when, an hour and a half later, they finally reached the bottom of the valley. By then she was wet with sweat and feeling quite parched. Why had they not stopped back at those fast food places? At the time it did not seem a big deal, but she was feeling the lack of sustenance now.

Jo normally walked a lot, at least compared to most people she knew, but she was all hiked out. Her feet were throbbing and her legs felt rubbery, and she wanted nothing more than to flop down onto a chair and drink a river. And then eat a cow.

She looked longingly at an outdoor shopping center ahead that sported no less than three different restaurants. "Can we get a bite to eat?"

Malcolm pursed his lips, then shook his head. "The house is stocked. Better that we keep a low profile."

Jo understood the notion, and agreed with it. But damn if she did not feel like taking another step. At least Malcolm looked about as beat as she did, but he voiced no complaint, just kept on hiking. She adjusted her bag on her shoulder and followed.

---

MALCOLM HAD NOT BEEN ENTIRELY truthful about the safe house.

It was no mansion, to be sure, but it was one hell of a nice place. At least from the outside. Two stories tall, with a large front porch and quaint, welcoming architecture, it sat on a secluded lot a hundred meters or so from the nearest neighbor. Somewhere Jo heard the trickling of running water, and she presumed a stream ran somewhere through the grounds. Whoever owned this place had some money to his name. Jo wondered how the Underground had gained use of it.

The door was locked, naturally, but the security system had not been updated to accommodate database implants. Or at least, it still retained just a simple keypad so a person could enter the security code manually. Whether an implant would work or not was anyone's guess, but it did not matter. Malcolm knew the code, and within moments they were inside.

Less than a minute later, Jo flopped onto an incredibly comfortable leather couch in the first floor's spacious living room. Spacious did not even begin to describe it, actually. It was almost as big as Jo's entire condo, and was impeccably decorated with tasteful artwork on the walls, a couple of nice sculptures, furniture that all looked at least as comfortable as the couch, and a large brick fireplace with a televid display above the mantel.

"This," Jo said, "is one hell of a safe house."

"Thank you," said a voice from behind her.

Malcolm froze where he stood, halfway into sitting in one of the stuffed chairs near the fireplace. His eyes widened in shock, in sudden terror. In confusion.

Jo sat bolt upright and looked behind her, toward the hallway leading deeper into the house.

Isaac stood there, dressed casually in jeans and a burgundy collared shirt and holding a glass filled with an amber fluid—scotch?—In each hand. He looked at them with something that could either be irritation or amusement and said, "Welcome to my home. Would you like a drink?"

# 32

# NEW ALLIES

Jo was speechless.

Apparently Malcolm was as well, because his only reaction was to fall into the cushions of his chosen chair as though his legs had given out from underneath him.

Isaac smirked and walked over to them. As he rounded the couch, he said, "I assumed you would make your way here."

He paused and, leaning over, held out a glass to Jo. She took it with a trembling hand and took a long drink.

It was scotch. And good scotch, at that.

Isaac turned away, toward Malcolm. "I hoped you would not. It was a foolish thing to do. Pedro wasted no time in spreading the word. If anyone else were to find you here..." He left the rest unsaid, instead handing the glass to Malcolm, who accepted it silently but did not drink immediately.

Isaac snorted loudly and took a seat in the other stuffed chair. "So. What should we do with you two, hmm?"

The fact that he bothered to ask the question thawed the ice that had formed in Jo's stomach at his approach. If he was not sure whether to put them out, turn them in, or let Pedro know what they had done, maybe there was a chance they could get out of this without having something worse happen to them.

Then it hit her. This was not just an opportunity to avoid further trouble. He said if anyone *else* had found them it would be trouble. Maybe... Maybe he would help them?

It was too much to hope for, but Jo found herself clinging to that hope like a life vest.

"What..." She cleared her throat and took another sip of the scotch, then started again. "What did you mean this is your house?"

Isaac looked at her like she was daft. "I meant what I said, girl. It's my house. It's owned by a company that I own. So therefore..." He shook his head and rolled his eyes. "I see you listen just as well as you make friends."

His tone was scornful, but Jo expected little else, based on their last meeting. She also suspected his gruff exterior was a cover for what lay beneath, based on their last meeting. All the same, that comment stung.

"We'll be on our way then, Isaac," Malcolm said. He rose from his chair.

"Sit down, boy," Isaac snapped and gestured peremptorily for Malcolm to do just that.

Malcolm complied, his expression wary, worried.

Silence loomed for a while, Isaac looking at the two of them in turn and them watching him. Jo was reminded of the exhilarating yet terrifying moment when the aliens first stepped aboard Pericles. What were they? What did they intend? They were armed, as her people were. Was their meeting to end in bloodshed?

Finally Isaac broke the silence. "Pedro..." He broke off and shook his head with a disdainful smirk. "Pedro is even more a fool than the two of you. But at least you're honest about your foolishness. Pedro, though." He paused, looking Jo straight in the eye. "He sees power games more than anything else. He's always wanted to be in charge and now he's found a way to do it. Makes me wonder why he's with CFL at all; he misses the point entirely."

That little spark of hope that seemed too much to cling to now grew into a flickering flame within Jo. "What are you saying, Isaac?"

His eyes narrowed. "I'm saying, girl, that Pedro doesn't speak for all of us." He snorted softly and managed a half-grin. "Or at least, not for me. We all thought this alien business stank to high heaven and we needed to help make it right. I for one—and I'm more than just one—still think that, regardless of what that boy says." Isaac stood up, abruptly. "Make yourselves at home. We'll talk more later."

He walked out of the room, moving quickly in spite of his hunched posture. As he disappeared down the hallway, he said over his shoulder, "Bedroom at the end of the hall is mine. Don't let me catch either of you in there."

Jo, speechless once again, looked back at Malcolm. His jaw hung wide open; he could not have looked more shocked if Jo suddenly sprouted feathers and flew away.

---

IT SHOULD HAVE BEEN A VERY comfortable night. The house was comfortable enough, the bed soft enough, the blankets thick enough. But Jo found she was unable to sleep. She tossed and turned all night, unable to make sense of the sudden turn in her fortunes. To go from having nowhere to turn to suddenly having an ally again, and from such an unexpected source, had her thoughts and emotions in a whirl. Finally, sometime late in the night—or rather, early in the morning—she drifted off into a fitful slumber.

Her dreams were strange, a mixture of being chased and finding a hidden treasure, and other things she could not recall when she finally awoke to the early morning sunlight streaming in through the window. She stretched, luxuriating in the expanse of bed and blankets, and was tempted to just lie there. She was certainly tired enough; her eyes felt gravelly, as though she had not slept at all.

But there were things to do, and suddenly it seemed there was hope for the future. So, regretfully, she got up and went about the morning routine. She lingered perhaps a bit too long in the shower, but it was so good, and considering the circumstances a little indulgence was probably warranted.

She felt like a new woman when she donned freshly-laundered clothes and descended the wide stairwell to the house's first floor and turned into the kitchen. And boy was it a kitchen: spacious, state of the art, immaculately clean, and perfectly organized. A person could make some real art in a kitchen like that. She was the first one down, apparently, so she put on a pot of coffee and looked through the cupboards for something to eat.

A few minutes later, while she was busy scrambling some eggs, Isaac walked into the kitchen. He was fully dressed in slacks and a white collared shirt and tie, and looked as though he had been up for a while. He raised one eyebrow as he saw what she was doing.

"I do appreciate a woman who knows her way around the kitchen," Isaac said.

Jo rolled her eyes, but found herself chuckling. "Do you want some eggs?"

"Don't mind if I do." He pulled out one of the stools that rested next to the counter and took a seat.

Jo scooped some eggs onto a plate, pulled a fork out of the drawer, and slid both across the counter to him. "Why are you helping us, Isaac? Really."

He shrugged. "Doesn't really matter, does it? What matters is you're not as out in the cold as you thought you were."

That was hardly satisfactory, but Jo had to admit he had a point. "So what happens now?"

Isaac shrugged and took a bite of his eggs. He chewed slowly and swallowed, then nodded approvingly. "Not bad, girl. You might have a future."

Then he grinned, showing his teeth, which were shiny white and perfectly straight. Jo had not noticed that about him before, but she was hardly surprised. Aside from his burn scars, Isaac was the image of understated wealth. At least as long as you did not look at his house. He stood and walked around the counter to a cupboard, where he retrieved a glass, then poured himself some water from the sink.

"In a little while," he said after taking a shallow drink, "I have some people coming over. Friends of mine," he looked at her and raised an eyebrow, "and of yours. We'll have a palaver and decide how to proceed, then we'll be off."

"Off where?"

Isaac snorted and sat back down on his stool. He cast a withering glance at her, then went back to eating his eggs and said nothing more.

---

Isaac disappeared after breakfast without saying another word. He simply returned his plate to the sink and grunted at Jo, again giving her a look of disapproval, as though she had said or done something to offend him. Then he left, leaving her to wonder what the hell had just happened.

Not long after, Malcolm rose from the evening's rest and came down to the kitchen, clad in a bathrobe. Jo was just about done cleaning up from her and Isaac's breakfast when he arrived, looking around the kitchen curiously.

"How are you feeling?"

Jo shrugged and, not trusting herself to speak, just kept on scrubbing at the pan she had used to cook the eggs. Malcolm gave her a curious, wary look, but said nothing more. He just grabbed some bread and jam and made himself some toast, then he left to get ready for the day.

It was not that she did not want to talk with Malcolm. It was more that Isaac had her baffled. What was he playing at?

He put on a show of being an uncaring, callous old man—though truth be told he was not really all *that* old—but there was clearly much more going on with him than that. He worked for, or rather with, the Underground, but he was more than willing, eager even, to break with them as soon as he disagreed with what they were doing. And yet he allowed them to use his home, or at least one of his homes, as a safe house. It could not be that hard to trace the house's ownership, and if the NSA or another agency found out how the house was used it would doubtless cause no end of trouble for him. He was a walking contradiction.

It was intriguing. And unsettling. If he was so willing to go against the Underground after clearly having cast his lot with them, how eager would he be to back Jo and Malcolm if they got in real trouble?

Jo gritted her teeth and attacked a particularly stubborn bit of grit on the pan. She hated answering to someone else for her wellbeing. Absolutely hated it. It was much better to be in charge, to make her own decisions and rise or fall based on that, not someone else's whims. Which she supposed is why she loved being Captain so much, and why she was good at it.

It did not take long to finish cleaning up, and she stalked away to freshen up before Isaac's friends arrived.

She might as well not have. Isaac was coy about exactly when his guests were to arrive, or who they were. So there was little to do except wait. Fortunately, the house was marvelously equipped with all the amenities a body could want, so Jo spent the morning and most of the afternoon camped out in the upstairs library with a book tablet that she had always meant to read but never got around to.

At one point, not long after lunch, the strangeness of her situation struck her. Only now that she was a wanted fugitive did she finally have free time to read. Even during the year-long shifts aboard ship, she generally kept busy enough with her duties that reading eluded her. Or she just kept herself entertained with other things. But now, with maybe her life literally on the line, she found the time. It was odd.

Finally, as the sun was beginning to sink below the mountains to the west—at first it surprised her because it was still early, but then she remembered they were deep in the valley—Isaac came to join her in the library.

"They will be here in about an hour," he said.

Jo tapped the tablet display and put it to sleep, then stood and returned it to its places on the small shelf that held Isaac's reading collection. "Will you tell me now who I've been waiting for?"

Isaac smirked. Or was that a half-smile? "I wouldn't want to spoil the surprise."

With that, he left her alone again.

Jo sighed. This cloak and dagger bit was starting to get very tiresome. Very tiresome indeed.

---

Jo took a few minutes to freshen up and change into clean clothes.

Not that the clothes she had on were particularly dirty, but after having been on the run so often lately, Jo found she had become attentive to every little blemish and wanted her shirts, at least, as clean as possible. And she wanted to make a good impression on whomever these mysterious visitors were, and the t-shirt she had on was not going to do the trick. When she descended the stairs in a nice, conservative collared blouse and slacks, she felt more than ready to face whatever came with at least a bit of dignity.

She was not prepared for Malcolm, as she entered the living room.

He had, over the last couple weeks, become as rumpled as Jo felt, even during their short stay with the Underground. Planning Becky's rescue had taken so much time and effort that neither Jo nor he had been able to get much rest.

But this evening he had apparently decided to become human again as well. And he did it with style.

He wore dark blue, pleated slacks and an off-white shirt, open at the collar, and over that a sports jacket that fit well enough that Jo wondered if it had been tailor made for him. Overall, he projected an image of understated style, and it was hard not to stare.

Malcolm turned to face Jo as she entered the room and smiled, inclining his head in greeting, but he did not say anything. His eyes spoke enough, though, as they gave her a quick, approving once-over. In spite of herself, Jo felt a little rush of pleasure at his approval.

Enough of that. They were not first-tour crewmembers on a their first run away from their parents, playing at romance anymore. She was the Captain, and he...

Well, he wasn't in her crew anymore, was he. And she was not the Captain.

That admission pained her, all the more because she had never allowed herself to think it before. She was no longer the Captain. For good or ill, that part of her life was over. Even if she managed to come through this without being crucified by the NSA or any number of other government agencies, it was beyond unlikely that McAllister would take her back on.

It was like a piece of her died. Or rather, like a piece of her had already died, and she just now realized it. The momentary pleasure faded, replaced by a sense of loss more profound than she would have thought. It was just a job, after all.

*Right. Go on telling yourself that.*

Malcolm's smile faded a bit. "Jo? Are you alright?"

Jo forced a smile onto her lips. She nodded. "Yes. Just thinking." She took a deep breath and walked over next to him. "Do you know - ?"

The doorbell rang then, drawing her eyes toward the entranceway.

"I think we're about to find out," Malcolm replied.

# 33

# ISAAC'S STORY

Jo was prepared for a lot of things. She was not prepared to see Isaac walk into the living room followed by Becky and a tall, skinny man in his middle years with black hair that was greying at his temples. Both Becky and the stranger were dressed well: she in grey slacks and a light blue collared shirt, he in a dark grey sports coat and matching slacks, with a somber tie to complete the ensemble. And they both wore serious, if not quite grim, expressions on their faces.

Isaac, for his part, was dressed more casually, in a grey sweater pulled over a white collared shirt, and khakis. He nodded familiarly to Jo and Malcolm as he lead the other two into the room and said, "Good evening. I believe you already know Becky."

She smiled and nodded in greeting to the two of them. Jo thought her smile grew a tad more warm when she greeted Malcolm, but she was not sure.

Isaac continued, "This is Jervis. He is the leader of the CFL compound in Brisbane."

Jo was taken aback. She realized her mouth had fallen open in astonishment and quickly shut it, but noticed that Malcolm took a bit longer to recover. "Nice to meet you," she managed. She glanced quickly from Jervis to Becky to Isaac and back. "You..." She swallowed and tried again. "You're with the Underground in Australia?"

He nodded, looking more than a little amused.

"How...?" Jo turned her gaze on Isaac, baffled.

He smirked in response. "I think we'd better sit down. And get some drinks. This will take a while."

---

"When I was thirty, I became a millionaire."

Isaac said the words as though they had little meaning, and mattered even less. But they hit Jo like a ton of bricks. She had known a number of people who were well-to-do. Hell, Harold did pretty damn well; he probably made a million or more per year as COO of McAllister. But he did not flaunt it, and he certainly never talked about it. On those occasions when his salary or wealth came to be hinted at, he always deflected the subject, as though it was not something to dwell on. Like it was a sacred subject, not to be discussed.

She had never met someone who was so matter-of-fact about his wealth as Isaac.

He smiled knowingly at her, his brow lifting. "I know. I am supposed to be ashamed of the fact that I made more money than most people can ever hope to earn in their lifetimes." He shook his head, snorting. "Bollocks. I made a lot of money then. I've made even more since, and I'm not the least bit ashamed to admit it, or shove it in anyone's face who tells me I should be."

Jo glanced at Malcolm, unsure how to proceed. He sat next to her at Isaac's dining room table, across from Isaac, Becky, and Jervis. Jo saw that he was as taken aback as she. And no wonder. She had just met Isaac a couple weeks earlier. He probably had known Isaac for a year or more. But then, she had suspected from the start that he had money; his clothing gave him away back at the motel. If Malcolm had not taken note...

Jo smirked. Men often failed to notice obvious things like that, though. Was she really surprised that Malcolm had?

Isaac's brow quirked upward, but instead of commenting, he raised his glass, filled with two fingers of scotch on the rocks, and took a sip. He remained silent as he lowered the glass to the table, looking at Jo with a challenging stare.

She took a breath and asked, cautiously, "But you were so casual before. A simple car. Unobtrusive clothes. And..." She gestured with her left hand toward Isaac's burn scars without realizing she was doing it. Abashed, she pulled her hand down and took a sip from her own glass, scotch again, to cover up her slip.

"And I never had my scars repaired," Isaac said, completing her thought. He looked down at the table, where he cradled his glass in his hands, and for a long moment was silent. Then he sighed and said, more softly, "I keep them as a reminder."

Again Jo glanced at Malcolm. His eyes met hers, his expression as questioning as she was sure hers was. But neither he nor she voiced the obvious question. For her part, Jo figured Isaac would explain in his own time, if he wanted to.

And so they all sat in silence for a while. How long, Jo was unsure. They simply sat looking at each other, occasionally taking a sip from their glasses until finally Isaac smirked slightly.

"As I said, I made my fortune very early. I studied Engineering in University and went to work at a promising design firm in Madrid. But after a few years, I had an idea for a new product and it became clear to me that my firm had neither the ability nor the inclination to make anything of it."

Isaac sipped at his scotch again. "So I started my own business. Within two years, my product was gaining market share at a spectacular rate. We were beating the competition in both quality and ease of use, and they became frightened." His eyes twinkled and he grinned at her. "I entertained, and turned down, no less than three different offers to buy my company, and the rights to my invention. The lowest of the offers was for over a billion credits."

Beside her, Malcolm choked on a sip of his scotch. Jo could not blame him. A billion credits was...unimaginable.

The merry twinkle that, for a moment, had lit Isaac's eyes faded, as did his smile. He looked at Jo, his expression becoming as grim as a mortician. "Less than a month after I refused the last offer, a swarm of government regulators descended on my business. They found us guilty of violating regulations I had never heard of before. Hundreds of citations against dozens of rules that, from what I could tell, had either only been enacted within the last several weeks or had not been enforced in decades. The fines bit into my cash flow for that quarter, but I was able to continue. But,"

his tone became flat, bitter, "the next quarter there were even more citations, more fines. I tried to appeal, but was rebuffed. I filed lawsuits requesting redress, but all were denied because there was no violation of the law, only of regulatory rules. With all of my time and spare cash flow going to deal with the never-ending violations, I began to lose market share to a new competing product, one that was disturbingly similar to my invention. I tried to sue for patent infringement, and was denied because my competitors had been issued a patent that super-seded my own."

Isaac's nostril's flared, and Jo could see the rage, still red hot after all those decades, within him. "Finally, I had no choice but to close the business and sell off the assets. But that was not enough to pay off the debts I had accumulated in starting up and in trying to fight the harassment."

"Were you...?"

Isaac shook his head. "When all was said and done, I still had a goodly amount of money left. Enough to live comfortably. But I was ruined, all the same." He drew a deep breath and drank again, draining his glass completely. When he spoke again, his voice was quiet, somber. "Have you ever heard of an early twentieth century writer named Ayn Rand?"

Malcolm shook his head, but the name rang a bell in Jo's head, somewhere.

Isaac smiled slightly at Jo's recognition. "In her book, *Atlas Shrugged*, the businessmen, the successful people, have enough of the burdens foisted upon them by the world and go on strike, bringing society down so it can be rebuilt. I only read that book a few years ago, and I will tell you it is tripe."

His eyebrows lifted, and that sarcastic smirk Jo had seen him wear several times returned. "I agree with some of the principles she discussed, but it could never work. There are too many idealistic, naive young people who come of age and want to do great things. Too many people who would never quit trying no matter what." He looked down at the glass he held cradled in his hands and tumbled the ice around for a second. "And too many men like me."

Isaac went silent and his face twisted into a grimace. He worked his jaw for a long several moments as he fought to hold back some deep emotion that Jo could only guess at.

Beside him, Becky leaned forward and gently took the glass from his hands. She stood and moved over to the liquor cabinet—she moved stiffly, with a pronounced limp, Jo noticed—and refilled Isaac's glass, then returned it to him and sat back down.

"Thank you, my dear," Isaac said, and took another drink, smaller this time, barely more than a sip. Then he drew a deep breath and looked back up at Jo.

"It was obvious what happened. My competitors were large conglomerates with deep fingers into government power, and they used that power to shut me, an impudent upstart, down so I could not threaten their position. I resolved to never let that happen again. So, I started over. But this time I spent most of my time courting favor in Geneva: contributing to campaigns, dining politicians and regulators, supplying favors, that sort of thing. By the time I had a new product to offer, I had a firm cadre of cronies in the government, and this time they were able to shield me. Over the next forty years, I became a behemoth. Growing my influence, and with it my marketshare. Eventually, I became big enough that the major conglomerates that once tried to destroy me welcomed me into the club with open arms."

He shuddered. "Along the way, of course, I had to eliminate my own competition, whether by acquiring them or forcing them out. I knew that I was committing the same sin that had been done to me, and ignored it. To use a term from the Bible, I actively seared my conscience so that eventually I never even felt a hint of guilt as I loosed the power of government to bring them down and enhance my own standing. Until one of them forced me to see what I had done.

"Peter Henderson was his name. He had a promising software company that was on the rise. And, like me, he refused to sell. So I crushed him. Or rather, I had my cronies in Geneva do it. They even managed to find a little known criminal statute that would allow them to prosecute. Not only did he lose everything he had built, but he spent five years in prison. All for daring to challenge me. My friends," Isaac smirked bitterly. "Not friends. I had no friends, only business associates and co-conspirators. They all cheered what I had done to Mr. Henderson, lifted it up as the greatest coup in memory. And it was. But when he got out of prison, he was fixed on revenge. He did not blame the prosecutor, or the bureaucrats who had snuffed out his business. No, he knew where the blame truly fell, and he came to find me.

"And find me he did. I was in Fiji, along with my daughter, Helen, her husband, and their newborn baby. It was Helen's birthday and I decided to take them all on a trip to celebrate. It took everything I could muster to convince them to come; we had not spoken in years, not since her mother and I split, and she was angry with me. But somehow I convinced her husband that I wanted to make amends—I really did—and they came for a week of fun in the sun." Isaac's voice broke and he lifted his hand to his mouth to cover up a small sob. "Oh how I wish they had not."

It took a minute or more for Isaac to compose himself, but when he did it was obvious he still was holding back strong feelings. His lips were tight and Jo thought he trembled a bit. But his eyes were resolute as he raised his head and looked her in the eye.

"I had security guards, of course, but what I did not know was that Henderson had, before University, served with an elite unit of the armed forces. My guards were no match for him. And so he burst into my villa, brandishing a gun, as I was preparing to serve dinner to my family. He cursed me—oh how he cursed me—as a thief and a coward. He spelled out every detail of what had happened to him in prison, how his wife had left him. But worst of all, he told me he would have been content to lose a fair competition with me, if only I had allowed it. All those things rang true, but it was this last that struck a part of my conscience that I did not know still existed, for that was exactly how I felt when they had destroyed my first company, all those years ago."

Isaac sighed, a sigh so filled with regret and remorse that it almost broke Jo's heart to hear it. "I tried to tell Henderson that I understood, that this was not the end for him. That he could start again and over-come, as I had. He just laughed and said he would rather die than be a soulless wretch like me." His voice caught again, but he did not look down this time; he let the tears well up openly. "I noticed the remote detonator in his free hand a second before he pressed the button. He was wearing five kilograms of explosives beneath his shirt."

Jo gasped in shock.

Isaac continued. "I was standing behind the counter. It was made of marble, and shielded me from most of the blast. Helen and her family, though..." He looked away then, revealing his scars more fully for Jo's eyes. "Even without these," he gestured to the scars, "I could never forget. But they are a reminder, nonetheless."

# 34

# THE BIRTH OF A MOVEMENT

"Jesus Christ," Malcolm breathed. "I had no idea..."

"Of course you didn't," Isaac snapped. Back to his regular, considerate self again, it seemed. "It's not a story I tell to just anyone." He scowled at Malcolm, but after a second mollified his expression. "But it is important you two know, so you will understand why I do what I do."

He took another long draw from his glass, and Jo found herself mimicking him. It was good scotch, but even were it not, she would not have cared. Not after hearing Isaac's story.

"What did you do?" Jo asked after swallowing. *And how did you not die yourself,* she did not ask. She never married, and had no children, but she could hardly imagine the pain of his loss.

*I would just curl up and die.*

Isaac shrugged. "I recovered, such as it was. Spent weeks in the hospital and months learning how to walk again. The board appointed an interim CEO while I was recovering, and they kept me apprised of what was going on with my business, but as you can imagine I did not care a whit. I don't think I have to tell you how much pain I was in; I was burned over sixty percent of my body, but even worse, I kept seeing the expressions on their faces when Henderson listed my sins against him. The disgust, the loathing, from Helen and Avi both. That was my last image of them before they died, and it haunted me."

He emptied his glass again, but when Becky reached over to refill it he waved her off. "There are several paths a man can take when his soul is laid bare for him to see, in all its ugly truth. He can repent, change his ways. He can double down on his path, convincing himself that he is not as bad as it appears. He can go mad, or end it all."

Isaac chuckled ruefully. "He can grow enraged and blame the world and everyone around him for his state. Or he can do what I did, and run away. It was the cowardly way, but it was all I could think to do. I left, went to the earth and roamed from one den of iniquity to the next. For years I lost myself, or tried to, in drink and women and drugs; whatever I could think of to dull my mind, to not think about what I had done, what I was, what I had lost.

"But slowly, I came out of the pit of self-pity that I had dug and began to notice the world around me. I saw—really saw, for the first time—how many people were being held back from what they could be, what they could have. Wicked men, men like me, wielded power that kept them from advancing. And why were they able to do it?"

He jabbed a finger up into the air to emphasize his point. "Because we, all of us, allowed it. We invested excessive power in bureaucrats and a government far from us, and entrusted them to oversee things for the good. But we forgot that they are just people, and people look out for their own interests first."

"As well they should," Becky murmured.

"Of course," Isaac replied. "But when a person with power is insulated from the consequences of his decisions, as most in government are, and particularly when he is spending not his own money, but someone else's..."

He shook his head. "Then his perspective gets warped and he begins to think his self interest really *is* the interest of everyone. Then he grows power-hungry and corrupt, and unethical men like me are able to buy him to do their will."

He leaned forward, fixing Jo with a steely stare. "But if we limit his power, put bonds on the economic influence government is allowed to wield, we can maybe stop the cycle of corruption and despotism, bring back honesty in business and competition. If we unfetter normal people so they are able to pursue their dreams without being crushed from above, we can all be better off."

It all clicked into place, like a puzzle going together. "*You* created Citizens For Liberty," Jo said.

Isaac bowed slightly in his chair. "Took you long enough to figure that out, girl."

"But..." Malcolm stopped and shook his head, clearly perplexed. "I don't understand. You don't have a hand in any of the decisions. You're around the periphery. Hell, I've spoken with you five times in a year and a half. Counting today. If you're the founder - "

" Why aren't I in charge?" Isaac finished for him.

Malcolm nodded, and Isaac rolled his eyes.

"The point, boy, is to *dilute* power. Spread it back to the people so Smith's invisible hand can actually work. Doesn't do much good for an organization devoted to liberty to itself have a despot, does it?"

Malcolm did not answer, but from his expression he remained confused. Jo could relate completely. Why not have the man whose vision created the organization lead it?

Isaac looked between the two of them and sighed. "I suppose I shouldn't be surprised. You starfarers are even more inclined toward hierarchy than us, what is it you call us, planetbound?" His eyes twinkled and he chuckled briefly. "Perfectly understandable, of course. A ship needs a Captain. But, and here's the point," he leaned forward again, "*people* do not."

Isaac sat back in his chair, expectantly. Jo really wished she had a good response ready, but she had nothing. Glancing aside, Malcolm was similarly silent. Isaac sighed again.

"Maybe this will help you understand," Isaac said. "For a while, I was indeed the leader. As the CFL spread from Bangkok, where I first had my revelation, to other cities, I was ecstatic, and happy to direct its efforts. You have to understand that I truly thought I was alone when I realized what a poison the philosophy of collectivism is. But as more and more people joined us, or began expressing similar values, it was like mana from heaven for my soul."

He smiled faintly. "At first, CFL was open about its goal, and I proudly proclaimed the cause of liberty to all that would hear it. How foolish I was. The forces of collectivism and despotism—they are the same, of course—have no tolerance for dissent, and especially for philosophies that differ from their own. We were pilloried in the press and I was dismissed as a madman who had cracked under the pressure of losing my family the way I did."

*Maybe he did.* Jo suppressed the thought ruthlessly, but was not successful in preventing it from registering on her face, as Isaac looked askance at her for a moment and then burst out laughing.

"You're wondering if they were right?" He laughed again, and shrugged. "Maybe. Maybe I have gone off the deep end into extremism. To that, I will quote a mid-twentieth century politician—a politician, if you can believe it!—who said 'Extremism in the defense of liberty is no vice'." He lifted an eyebrow at Jo. "Hmm? What say you to that?"

Jo shrugged. "I'd say I'm waiting for you to get to the point. What does this have to do with our situation now?"

Isaac's mouth shut with the clack of teeth striking each other, and his smile vanished. He stared at her for a long moment, then nodded. "You're right, of course." Looking back at Malcolm, he said, "Suffice it to say that before long I became the public face of CFL and then shortly thereafter we were driven underground. I'll spare the gory details; you likely read about them in your history books in school..." He drifted off, then cursed under his breath. "No you probably saw them on the tele-vid, or read about them after you got back from one of your cussed trips to the stars."

Under his breath, but still loud enough that Jo could hear him, he muttered, "I keep forgetting they're both older than me, damn them."

That took Jo aback, and she found herself sinking back into her chair as though pushed there, her surprise was so great. She thought back over her life, and her travels. Like most starfarers, she was born aboard a starliner, and raised there. Her entire existence until her age of ascendency had been a series of year-long shifts, with years of cryosleep in between shifts, and then months of upkeep at the destination worlds where she was able to see and experience something of planetbound life before she set out again. She had gone through one major overhaul that took her from ages 8 to 12, but aside from that most of her childhood years had been spent aboard ship. When she turned 16 and was able to choose her life, she chose to remain.

Not all starfarer children did, and that caused their parents no end of heartache as they struggled with an impossible decision: what was more important to them, the life they loved or the children they loved? Most picked their children, but some managed to find a happy medium, doing short runs from Earth to Centauri or somesuch, where they would only miss a few years here or there. Families whose children left were the main reason McAllister had to recruit new hires at all.

For Jo, there had never been a question. She loved navigating the stars, running the ships, seeing new worlds. But she had never considered the other side of it.

What did the planetbound think of her people, the starfarers, and the lives they led? By Earth standards, Jo had been alive for several centuries, and yet she had not reached her sixtieth waking year; not even middle aged! She had never before considered that some might be resentful of a starfarer's apparent longevity.

She opened her mouth to protest that she had not lived nearly as much as Isaac assumed she had, but he beat her to it, raising a silencing hand before he spoke.

"I know, I know. Time dilation. You don't have to tell me." Isaac snorted and made a gesture that screamed, "Hey, what can you do?" Then he went on. "Point is, about fifty years ago, CFL went underground and I had to scramble to get my investments out of public view before they were all confiscated."

Jo did some quick math in her head, then double-checked it to make sure she was correct. If what Isaac said was true, and she had no reason to believe it was not, that meant he was at least a hundred-twenty, if not a hundred-thirty years old. Not excessively old by any stretch of the imagination; people had been known to live to a hundred-fifty these days. But he definitely had a baby face, strange as that seemed when she thought about it.

"For a few years after that," Isaac continued, pulling Jo's attention back to his story, "people in CFL looked at me like I was a God. My every word was a command, and no one was willing to do a damn thing unless I gave the go ahead. I realized that I had created my own little kingdom and it was in danger of becoming just another petty despotism, just like the government CFL was created to temper. So I stepped down. Disappeared. I left Bangkok and didn't tell anyone where I was going, except for a trusted few. I've moved around, living off my investments, starting a new company or two here and there. And ever so often I check in on a CFL compound to see how things are going."

Isaac scowled. "Unfortunately, some of the leaders were entirely too bright, and figured out who I am." He glared at Becky, who smiled beatifically. Isaac rolled his eyes. "But I suppose that's not entirely bad. It let me step in now, where it matters."

He stood up then, pushing his chair back with the soft sound of the chair legs scraping against hardwood. "I've seen, and caused, a lot of injustice in my life, but I have never before seen anything as despicable as what's going on with those alien eggs."

His eyes grew hard as he leaned forward and smacked the tabletop with his palms. "CFL is *my* baby, and I'll be *damned* if I'll let some snot-nosed punk like Pedro pull it out of this just because he has his panties in a bunch."

He drew a deep breath, then gave Jo a look that was all business, full of command. "So. How can we help you?"

# 35

# SCHEMES

"Well," Jo said, glancing at Malcolm for support, "that is the question, isn't it? Your files are gone, as are the backups. No one's going to take our word for what's going on, so we'll have a hell of a time blowing the lid on this thing now." She paused, looking back at Isaac, then at Becky and Jervis. "Unless you have another copy of the files hanging around somewhere?"

Becky flushed and lowered her eyes, clearly ashamed. "No," she said. "They're all gone."

Jo nodded. "And I expect your mole's been picked up already. If you recorded from his implant, the meta-data - "

Jervis interrupted her. "No, we were quite thorough in removing all identifying data. As of this morning, he is still quite well, and at work with no one the least bit suspicious of him."

"That can't last."

Jervis shrugged. "You may be surprised."

Jo pursed her lips, pondering. Maybe the mole could make another recording, or get some other piece of evidence that they could use to take this thing public. It might work.

"I see those wheels turning, girl. Might be you should rethink that plan."

Jo looked at Isaac askance. "What plan is that?"

He rolled his eyes. "This is not my first rodeo, girl. You're thinking we can just proceed as before, try to get a press conference going. Maybe with some new piece of evidence or somesuch." He snorted. "Not going to happen. Before, they didn't know we had them. But now they know we know, and they'll be ready for it."

"So what would you suggest?"

Isaac spread his hands and gave her a knowing smile that did not touch his eyes, and remained silent.

Wonderful. Real helpful.

"Think, girl. What's the core of the problem?"

Jo frowned. "They're mistreating the eggs."

"No. What's the *core* of the problem?"

Where was he going with this? Sudden movement from the side brought her gaze to Malcolm, who sat bolt upright in his chair as though he had been poleaxed. His eyes were wide; he looked dumbfounded.

"They're not returning the eggs home, like the aliens asked us to."

Isaac's eyebrows rose high on his head and he pointed at Malcolm in approval. "Precisely. Now," he settled back into his chair and pulled it close to the table again, "how can we help you?"

"You know where the lab is, and you have a mole who could help us get inside."

Isaac's eyes were positively twinkling as he nodded in response to Malcolm's words.

Malcolm frowned. "But that doesn't do us any good. We're stuck here in Quito. Unless you wanted to have your people go it alone?"

Jervis spoke up. "We are quite capable, mate. But I think you'll want to be there won't you?"

"Then I don't see - "

"I have a plane," Isaac said.

Malcolm blinked, then grinned. "Ok, that takes care of that. It still doesn't help. Even if we could get them out of the lab..." He trailed off, his eyes growing even wider as he turned to look at Jo.

What he was getting at sunk in, and Jo felt like her stomach had fallen out of her body and struck the floor. He could not be serious.

Could he?

"The biggest problem I see," Isaac said, "is transportation off planet. That is beyond my realm of expertise." He grinned. "Do either of you know a trustworthy pilot?"

And, just like that, the entire caper came together in Jo's mind.

# 36

# RECRUITING

Carlton pulled the throttle to idle and eased back on the stick, lowering his airspeed to just above stall speed while he applied a touch of right rudder. A moment later he felt the barest hint of contact as his wheels touched down on the runway.

Dead on centerline, as always. Or at least, as always in his mind. But what the mind conceives and reality dictates are not always the same. He had flown more than his share of rough landings, landings so hard he felt like his back had nearly been thrown out from the impact.

But not tonight. Tonight, he nailed it, and he could not help smiling in spite of the circumstances.

"Delta Seven Five Zero Four, take taxiway Charlie."

The ground controller's voice was bland, unemotional, almost as though he did not know who he was addressing, or what was going on. Very likely he did not, not exactly. But he had to have noticed that Carlton had been given priority clearance through the traffic pattern, had been allowed to cut in line ahead of half a dozen planes filled with hundreds of travelers with connections to meet. He must surely be wondering who Carlton was to rate such treatment, though you could not tell from his tone or inflection.

Hell, Carlton wondered that himself as he acknowledged the taxi orders and turned his craft off the runway. He had never received orders like he had this day.

Well, almost never.

Carlton frowned and shook his head, forcing himself to not think about those initial weeks after Pericles' last docking. He and Alison had put that behind them, and done a great job of it too. Maybe he was just getting a promotion; Delta's Director of Pilot Training had his office in Boston, conveniently, and the airline's brass could certainly pull the strings needed to get Carlton preferred treatment.

But he had never heard of someone getting that treatment just to learn he had been promoted a step up the ladder. Doubts lingered as he stopped the craft in front of a ground traffic director, who stood with his glowing guide rods crossed in an X over his head in front of the craft, and powered down the engines.

He took a few minutes to secure the craft's systems, then stepped out of the cockpit and activated the controls that opened the craft's hatch and extended the boarding stairs. He stepped out onto the top step and froze cold.

Parked just past the port wing was a large black limo. Alison stood beside it, looking confused. Flanking her were a man and a woman he did not recognize, both dressed in business casual though the woman looked less than comfortable with it. They both wore calm, serious expressions that revealed nothing.

What the hell was going on?

---

"Where are the boys?" Carlton whispered to Alison.

They sat beside each other in the back of the limo - it was luxuriously appointed, Carlton was forced to admit. Their two guides, or guards, or whomever, were up front and the privacy screen was up, so if he did not know any better he could almost pretend he and Alison were out for a fancy night on the town.

Almost.

"They're staying at Greg and Kiko's house," Alison replied. Carlton felt a surge of relief that faded as Alison spoke again. "Carl, what the hell is going on? I got a call to meet you here tonight, that you had something important to tell me?"

Carlton frowned, his worry growing stronger by the moment. "First I heard of it, babe. I thought I was here for a meeting of some kind. I was thinking maybe it was a promotion, but I've never heard of this being done just to promote a guy."

Alison frowned as well and clasped his hand tightly.

Through the windows, the city of Boston flashed across Carlton's vision and he thought back to all the months he had spent here, during his down time between training sessions on Luna. He had grown to love this town. It had such a different feel than Quito, the only other city on Earth he had lived in. He distinctly did *not* think about his last months there, or at least he tried not to. But it was hard to forget, even if he tried his best to act as though it had never happened. Especially after the news of what had happened with the Captain - with Jo - dwelling on those sorts of things was not worth it.

"Where are they taking us?"

Carlton began to shake his head, but stopped. He recognized the building they were stopping in front of from the news a while back. It was the headquarters of Sturdivant Sequencing, a pharmaceutical firm that had made headlines not long before he and Alison moved to Boston. What were they doing here?

The car stopped and, a moment later, one of their guard/guides opened the door, gesturing for them to get out.

"Mr. and Mrs. Hersch," said the man, in a deep Australian accent, "they're waiting for you."

---

Carlton saw who was in the room he and Alison had been led to and promptly turned around to leave.

"Carl, wait. Please listen to me for a minute."

"Hell no, Jo! I don't want anything to do with this," he said over his shoulder. He grasped Alison's hand to lead her away and was surprised to find her resisting. He looked back at her, ready to snap at her to hurry the hell up. But then he saw the expression on her face and he pulled up short. "What's wrong? We need to get out of here right now."

"Carl," Jo said. "You know me. You know I didn't do those thing they're saying."

He knew no such thing, but he sure as hell did not want to stand around and debate it. Whatever she was in to, he wanted no part of it. "I thought I did. Come on, Alison."

Alison pulled her hand from his grasp and Carlton felt his jaw drop from shock. "Just give her a minute," Alison replied, her eyes locked on Jo as though both wishing she were not there and wanting to believe her at the same time. "Please."

Carlton muttered a curse under his breath. They were going up the river if they spent too much time with her. But he couldn't refuse Alison's entreaty. So instead of leaving he took a seat at the table.

They were in a medium-sized conference room, about five meters square with doors on either end, that was dominated by a standard-issue conference table, complete with controls for the wall televid display to the right. There were even glasses and a pitcher of ice water on the table. It was almost like a real conference.

"Ok, Jo," Carlton said, only realizing after he said it that he had left off the honorary Captain for perhaps the first time ever. "What do you want that's worth risking our kids growing up with parents in prison?"

Alison cast a disparaging look at him as she sat down beside him, but he could tell she did not fully disagree. This was one hell of a risk to take, meeting with a fugitive. For her part, Jo at least blanched, whether from embarrassment or anger was hard to tell. Carlton hoped the former.

"It's not just what *I* want," Jo said, and pressed a button on the table's control panel.

A moment later, the door he and Alison had not entered through opened, and Malcolm walked into the room.

Carlton's jaw hit his chest.

---

"THIS IS INSANE."

Malcolm—Carlton still could not wrap his mind around the fact that his late friend was sitting there, alive, at the same table with them— raised an eyebrow. "Why?"

"You want to waltz into a secure NSA facility."

Malcolm and Jo both nodded.

"Steal back the stuff those cat-men gave us."

Again nods.

"And then you want me to help you fly them up to Gagarin."

More nods.

Carlton threw his hands up, for a moment speechless. "Why would I ever even think about doing something like that?"

Jo—when did she stop being the practical one?—leaned forward in her chair. "Carl, there isn't much time. As soon as the NSA is done with its experiments, they're going to kill all the embryos and dispose of them, and they'll just disappear."

"So?"

Jo blinked. "What do you mean, so? Don't you see how wrong what they're doing is?"

Carlton sighed and looked away. He saw it just fine. He was just as appalled as they were, but what they were asking...

It was crazy. And not just crazy, dangerous.

If it was just him, he might be inclined to help. He probably *would* help. But he had Alison and the boys to think about. He couldn't go gallivanting around, flaunting the law. It's not like he could just hop on a starliner in a month or two...

Oh shit.

"Son of a bitch," Carlton breathed, and he looked back at the pair that until tonight he had thought he knew so well. "You're going to steal a freaking starliner to take those things back home, aren't you?"

Poker faces from them both, but Jo flinched just a hair. That was exactly what they were going to do.

Carlton stood up. "You are both certifiable, you know that? You'll be lucky if they only lock you up and throw away the key."

"Carl, stop." It was the first time Alison spoke since Jo and Malcolm had described the situation, and their plan.

He looked at her and his heart sank. She had *that look* on her face. Every woman has it, that look specific to her that she reserves just for her husband, which says she's going to be stubborn.

"Babe, don't tell me you're actually considering this?"

She stopped with *that look*, but her tone was no less serious. "What if it was little Malcolm?"

Carlton blinked; her question took him aback. For that matter, it seemed to take Malcolm by surprise as well, as he gave a little start and his eyes widened. Or maybe it was the fact that he had a namesake.

Whatever. That was not the point.

"This has nothing to do with our son, Alison."

"But what if it did? What if he was stuck somewhere and the people we trusted to bring him back instead abused him, and maybe were going to kill him?"

That hit him like a ton of bricks. Just the thought of something like that happening to their little guy, to either of their little guys... It both terrified and enraged him at the same time. He realized he was making fists and forced his fingers apart.

Alison could see it on his face. "We need to do this, Carl."

"But it's such a risk."

She gave him *that look* again.

He sighed and nodded. When she was right, she was right.

# BRISBANE

The airplane lifted off the tarmac, blazing away into the Boston night, and Jo sank back into her chair with a sigh of mixed relief and trepidation. It was done; Carl was onboard, and the way ahead was clear. Except it was not. Eight million things could still go wrong, and any one of them could spell the end of their little caper, and more than likely the end of *them* as well.

Little caper. She snorted softly to herself. Had there ever been a *bigger* caper than this?

"It went well then, I take it?"

Jo turned her head away from the porthole next to her seat and looked at Isaac, seated in his chair across the jet's small aisle. She nodded. "He's onboard."

"And you're sure he won't betray us?"

This time her snort was loud enough to carry throughout the plane's cabin. "Carl is nothing if not loyal, and discrete. Alison as well."

Isaac frowned, but said nothing more; he sipped at his drink instead.

The plane's attitude eased from the steep nose-high angle of its initial climb into a more moderate cruise climb to its assigned altitude, filling Jo was a greater sense of ease. However much she had travelled, she had never grown particularly comfortable with airplanes. At least not in the way that she was with spacecraft. A starliner could not just suddenly drop out of the sky; it flew on an orbital trajectory through the galaxy, even when its engines were not firing. Nor did it ever really deviate from a straight-and-level attitude. An airplane, though... Cut off those engines and they were all going down. It was not a particularly comfortable thought.

All the same, it was a good thing Isaac had access to this jet. He had been unclear whether he owned it or had just hired it, but regardless, travel through the general aviation sections of the airports had much less security hoops to jump through than the commercial side, so they were able to avoid the damning identification process that had left Malcolm stranded in Quito for so long.

"So now what?" Isaac asked. "Straight on to Brisbane?" Facing him, catty-corner to Jo in his own seat, Jervis perked up, interested.

"I don't see why not," Jo replied. "We have a lot of planning to do, and we'll need access to your personnel and information to do it." She inclined her head to Jervis, who grinned.

"Way ahead of you, mate," he said. "My people are gathering up as we speak; even bringing the mole in."

"Just who is the mole?" asked Malcolm, who sat opposite Jo, directly across the aisle from Jervis.

Jervis just smiled. "Wait and see. I guarantee you'll love it."

Malcolm frowned but did not reply.

---

Jo AWOKE to the airframe shuddering as the landing gear touched the runway. It took her a moment to realize where she was; at first the unfamiliar faux-wood of the cabin's ceiling made her blink in surprise, and she felt a momentary panic. Then memory returned and she relaxed. A bit. Through her little porthole, the world quickly slowed as the pilot applied the brakes, then turned off onto the taxiway.

"Welcome to Bris-Vegas," Jervis quipped.

He looked wide awake, as though he had gotten a good night's sleep, showered, had breakfast, and was ready to get going. It made Jo want to hit him. Twenty-plus hours on this little plane—lavish as it was, it was still small—was not her idea of comfort, no matter how soft the seats and how far they reclined. She had a kink in the middle of her back, between her shoulder blades, and her skin felt sticky; she was in dire need of a shower.

Jo sat up, pushing the button to raise her seat to a sitting position, and rolled her shoulders. "What time is it?"

Jervis grinned at her. "Ten o'clock. Right on schedule." He glanced up forward, toward the cockpit. "I really ought to fly in one of these more often. It's more timely than the commercial birds."

From his seat, Isaac snorted. "You would not like the bill." He looked as ruffled as Jo felt; clearly he had just awoken as well.

Jervis shrugged. "Likely not."

Malcolm and Becky were still asleep, for a wonder. After the plane stopped and the flight crew opened the hatch, they had to shake the pair of them awake. Amazing.

The sun shone down brightly as Jo exited and descended the stairs. Lately she had mostly spent her time in the northern hemisphere when she was not actually on the equator in Quito, so Jo found herself a bit disoriented at first. Her instincts wanted to tell her that the sun, nearing its zenith in the sky to her left as she left the plane, was pointing her toward the south. It took a moment to recall that, as Australia sat, the ecliptic plane lay to the north. It made her pause for a moment to re-arrange her thinking.

A van was waiting for them outside the Fixed Base Operation— Reliant Aviation, it was called—and they piled in. The driver was a lanky man with greying blond hair and a wry smile who greeted them with a cheery "G'day" but said little else. As soon as they were all inside, he put the van in gear and set off.

Jo settled back onto her seat and looked at Jervis. "Why do you call it Bris-Vegas?"

He chuckled and shrugged. "We've called her that for years," he said. "Centuries. Started because of the casino downtown by the river and all the tourists who came through. The casino was destroyed in the Tribune Wars, but the name stuck anyway."

That made sense, to an extent.

The rest of the ride was filled with small talk. Jervis pointed out landmarks as they drove past and shared tidbits of local lore; in general he seemed to like playing the tour guide. Maybe it was because so few opportunities arose to do so. Jo recalled a bit of Australian history; not much, but a bit. Brisbane, during the Tribune Wars, was reduced nearly to rubble. The seat of State government had moved during the wars, and there was no reason to move it back after. Trade had moved on as well, and other cities further up the coast - Townsville and Cairns, if she remembered correctly - drew in the tourists that had once flocked to Brisbane. Over the years, the city had been rebuilt, but it never regained the stature it once had.

Which seemed to make perfect sense for their context, as Jo thought about it. The NSA's lab would need to be near a town or city for logistics support, but ideally not a large one. Large cities meant lots of people, and lots of people meant more people who might find out about the place, or accidentally linger too close, or cause any number of problems. A modest town would be a much more suitable place for a secret facility.

"So how far is the lab from here?"

Jervis looked sidelong at her. "A good two days' drive."

Jo blinked, and set aside the theory she had just been contemplating. "Ah."

Jervis smirked slightly, and chuckled. "It's a big country, mate."

---

THE VAN LEFT them in front of a small commercial building in Brisbane's western suburbs. It was low, only two stories, painted a faded shade of blue, and windowless except for a few small openings at the corners of the second floor. Not exactly inviting.

But then, the neighborhood was not that great, either. Not that it was run down per say, but everything was just noticeably in a state of slight disrepair. The paint was starting to peel, the grass had not been mowed in a couple weeks, the windows were smudgy. Not completely neglected, but just little enough maintenance that a person knew things were not going as well here as they could have been.

Jo looked around and frowned. "Nice place."

Jervis gave her a little smile and shrugged slightly. "It's not much, but it's home." He turned and led the way to the building's front door. "Shall we?"

Becky and Isaac moved to follow without comment. Malcolm remained and shared a glance with Jo.

"You alright?" he asked.

Jo nodded.

"After you." He swept out his arm gallantly, indicating she should lead the way.

Jo could not help but laugh as she followed the others into Jervis' lair. Malcolm did as well.

# 38

# THE MOLE

Jervis was right. Jo fell in love with the mole immediately.

Well, not really in love, but for a moment there she was not sure. He was handsome enough, certainly: young, tall, with striking features, darkly tanned skin, dark hair and eyes, and a dashing smile. But what made her heart soar was his clothing.

He wore the uniform of a security guard, and it exactly matched those of the guards in the video Malcolm and Becky showed her, back in Quito.

"Jo, Malcolm," Jervis said as the mole entered the little room, "meet Winston. He is a member of the security detachment at the lab."

"Very pleased to meet you," Jo said, and smiled broadly. She had assumed the mole was an engineer or scientist, or maybe a technician. For him to be in security there...this made their task so much easier. Hopefully. She could not help but let some of her optimism carry into her tone as she greeted him and shook his hand, and she cringed inwardly.

Beside her, Malcolm smirked, and merely said, "Hello," before shaking hands with the man.

They sat down around a long conference table that dominated the room, Jervis at the head to Jo's left and Isaac at the other end, with her and Malcolm in the middle to Jervis' right. Winston waited for the rest of them to sit then took a seat opposite Jo, moving with the ease of a man who keeps in good shape. Becky was not in this meeting, which Jo found surprising at first. But after thinking it over quickly, it made sense. She would not have known who this man was, and she did not need to know. Malcolm and Jo needed to know; they would be working with him, and Isaac...well, Isaac could apparently know whatever he wanted. His status as the CFL founder afforded him that, Jo supposed, even if he did not make use of it much.

The room was on the second floor, down the hallway and to the left from a control center that was very similar to Becky's in Quito, if not quite as robust and technically up-to-date. That made sense too, since Brisbane was at best tertiary when it came to the monitoring and control of the Earth-Luna space sectors. All the same, for what it was, the control center was impressive: efficiently laid out, apparently well maintained. Jo was beginning to suspect that more than a little of the funding Becky and Malcolm described came from Isaac's shell companies as much as from any legitimate businesses that sought the CFL's help. One control station of Quito's capability was one thing. If all the CFL sectors had command and control setups like Brisbane's, and Jo suspected they did, that would take a hell of a lot of money to establish and maintain, not to mention the bureaucratic know-how to make the required purchases without showing up on some agency's radar.

It was pretty impressive.

"So..." Jo looked from Winston to Jervis and raised her eyebrows. It was their show. Time to see what they had.

Jervis smiled knowingly and gestured for Winston to proceed. The security guard cleared his throat and, inclining his head briefly toward Jervis, said, "Activity has increased severalfold in the fortnight. The scientists are working three shifts; word is there is massive pressure coming down from above to finish the current projects, and then we'll be shutting down altogether. In the meantime, they've nearly doubled the security force." He shook his head. "Something's got them spooked."

That checked with the chart. Chandini had to know there was a possibility they were going to blow the whistle on the whole thing or take more direct action. She, and her superiors, would be stupid not to get rid of the evidence as quickly as possible. Jo was actually surprised - pleasantly surprised - they had not simply pulled chocks already.

"How much time do we have?" asked Malcolm.

Winston shrugged. "I'm not a techie." He frowned thoughtfully for a few seconds, then perked up. "But I heard a couple of the senior engineers talking as they left a few days ago. Sounded like they only thought a month, maybe a little more."

Jo smiled. "Perfect. That's all the time we need."

Winston looked at her askance. "Ma'am, this is a maximum security facility. We all have greater than Top Secret clearance."

"So do I."

He did not look impressed. "You *did*. You've been specially flagged in the system, you know. Everyone in security knows your face on sight." He glanced at Malcolm and added, "Both of you. And even if they didn't, they've got crack troops on security detail. If you think you can just waltz up there without thorough planning, you've got another thing coming."

"Ah, but we have an ace in the hole," Jo replied, giving Winston a sharp, meaningful look.

He snorted. "I'm just a guy who stands watch. I don't have authority over anyone but myself." He leaned forward and tapped his fingertip against the top of the table. "Point is, you're going to have to plan this to the tee. Even with my help. And even then, I wouldn't give greater than a 50-50 chance of getting in, getting your video, and getting out again without being caught."

Video? Jo blinked and looked at Jervis. "You didn't tell him?"

Jervis returned her look with one of annoyance. "I've been with you this whole time. When was I supposed to tell him?"

Winston frowned in confusion. "Tell me what?"

Jo sighed. "We're not going in to get video."

She explained, and his jaw dropped. He remained silent for almost a full minute after she finished. She was about to lean over and shake him when he finally shook his head and spoke again.

"You're insane."

Jo opened her mouth to speak, but he cut her off, standing and wagging a finger at her as he spoke.

"You are bloody bonkers. If you think..." He trailed off and just looked at her incredulously for a moment, then he snorted and threw up his hands. "To hell with this. I'm out of here." He turned toward the door.

And found Jervis blocking his way, his arms crossed over his chest.

"Where do you think you're going, mate?"

"Away from her," Winston replied. "I pass you information, not..." He drew a deep breath and said, more calmly, "Look, I can't be involved in this sort of thing. I'm fucked if I do."

Jervis scowled at him. "You're fucked if you don't."

"But -"

"No. Listen." Now it was Jervis who was wagging a finger - right in Winston's face. "*You* came to *us*, mate. Said what was going on in there was some fucked up shit. Said you wanted to help put a stop to it. Well now's your chance."

"Bollocks. I meant getting the word out, not some loopy scheme to rob the place!"

Malcolm spoke up, his deep voice carrying easily across the room despite the fact that he barely spoke above a whisper. "We tried that. It didn't work. There are no other options."

Winston scowled and shook his head. "No. Fuck this."

He moved to push past Jervis and then...something happened. Jo couldn't see, it happened so quickly. One moment Winston looked as though he was going to push Jervis aside and get through the door. The next, after a confusing twisting of limbs that happened too quickly for her eye to follow, Jervis had him pinned face-first against the wall, his arm pinned behind his back while Jervis grasped his throat in a choke-hold.

Winston's eyes were wide in shock - no less so than Jo's were, she was sure - and he made little choking sounds as he tried to speak.

But Jervis talked over him, quietly into his ear. "You listen, mate, and listen well. You're tied to us. You're going to help with this. If you don't... If you betray us, or do anything that hampers this operation, I will personally see to it that the authorities know *exactly* what you've been doing for us this last year. And about your other little side job." Winston's eyes widened even further, in stark, naked fear. "Are we clear?"

Winston nodded. Or tried to. But it was clear enough.

Jervis released him with a quick shove that sent him staggering back toward the chair he had abandoned. He caught himself from falling by placing both hands on the chair back and stood there, doubled over and breathing in deep gasps of air for a while, his eyes darting between the four of them in fright.

Jo was surprised to find she was standing. A familiar tingling excitement swept through her, the byproduct of adrenalin, she knew, and she had to force her arms not to tremble as she, too, took hold of the table's edge. She leaned forward and looked Winston in the eye. He met her gaze reluctantly, but her patented Captain stare held him once he did.

"I know this plan scares you, Winston," Jo said. "Believe me when I tell you if there were any other way, I would take it. But what Malcolm said is correct. The video you got out of there before is gone; the NSA took it. We have no evidence, and no time to gather any more. If we're going to prevent the wholesale slaughter of those creatures, this is the only way."

He was starting to get his breath back, and more importantly, she could see he was beginning to understand, and accept.

"Help us, Winston. Please."

Winston held her gaze for another long moment, then dropped his own gaze to the tabletop and nodded. Good. There was a chance that Jervis' strong arm tactics would be enough to make him go along well enough. But there was also a large chance that Winston would find some subtle way to betray them that they would never know. Far better to use reason to convince him to give his help; then he would go all in for the mission.

Of course, it would have been better if Jervis had not jumped the gun, and she could have convinced Winston straight off. They were back to amateur hour again, it seemed. Jo turned a baleful eye on Jervis, who did not even have the grace to acknowledge the unspoken rebuke. He just shrugged back at her and made a little "Get on with it" gesture.

Jo had to stop herself from grinding her teeth.

# 39

# COUNTING THE COST

"**A**re you sure about this, Jo?"

Jo turned toward Malcolm in surprise and quirked an eyebrow at him. "It's a bit late to ask that question, don't you think?"

It *was* late. In every sense of the word. They had spent a long afternoon and evening analyzing the layout of the lab - Camp Tycho, Winston called it - and planning their incursion. Jo had not realized how bone weary she was until Jervis at long last declared an end to the day and had an assistant lead her and Malcolm to their quarters: a pair of simple bunk rooms in the rear corner of the building, one on either side of the hall from the other. The mere act of walking toward her bed suddenly allowed all the efforts of the day to fall upon her, and it was all she could do to not sink to the floor and fall asleep right then and there.

But she made it, back to her room. And was about to go in and flop down on her bed - and to hell with brushing her teeth or getting out of her clothes - when Malcolm asked the question.

Malcolm smirked in amusement for a brief moment, but quickly became all seriousness again. "I'm serious. Have you really thought about what we're about to do?"

Her head hurt; too much thinking for one day already. "Yes, Malcolm. I've thought it through. That's all I've been doing for days now. Weeks."

He shook his head. "I don't mean planning. I mean thinking." He took a half-step toward her. "Think about what we're about to do. And I don't mean the fact that we're about to steal those eggs back."

Jo rolled her eyes. "Then what do you mean?"

"You studied the starmap their Captain gave us. Their system is two hundred and sixty-three light years away. If we're successful and get the eggs aboard Agrippa, and then manage to get underway and out of the solar system..." He shook his head. "Even taking time dilation into account, we're talking about a seventy year trip, give or take. One way."

"Yes."

"No one's ever been in cryo-suspension that long. They've never even done *tests* for that long a suspension. Even if all goes well..." He pursed his lips. "On the trip from Gliese to Earth the passengers are in suspension for about eight years, and age six months. On this trip, we'll age almost six years."

Jo snorted. "Six years is nothing."

Malcolm raised an eyebrow.

She sighed, and nodded. She opened her mouth, but Malcolm beat her to it.

"And that's even assuming we awake at all. How much life does Agrippa's reactor have left? Can it even remain hot for seventy years?"

"That's not an issue," Jo said. "I checked. Agrippa is one of the newest fusion drive ships. They burn a lot more efficiently than the plant we had on Pericles. She should be good for as long as we need."

Malcolm nodded, conceding the point. "Fine. But there are still other potential problems. I operated one of those new plants once, a few years ago. They're highly automated, but it's much different from what I'm used to. Even if I can make it work, what if..."

"So look up the technical manuals and study up. They're not classified or anything." She drew a deep breath to try to dampen the annoyance his questions were beginning to invoke. "Look, Malcolm, I know the risks. What would you suggest? We just put the eggs aboard and send it burning off on automatic? Hope the aliens find it and figure out what to do with it?" She shook her head. "That's just silly."

"It'll be on automatic most of the trip anyway."

"Except for the most important part: contact. We need to be there, to explain what's happened. To apologize."

"Even if it means not coming back? We won't have fuel for the return trip. If they're unable, or unwilling, to refuel us, we'll be stuck there.

Forever." He shivered slightly, and Jo was tempted to do the same. "Are you really willing to take that risk?"

That thought had crossed Jo's mind once or twice, and it terrified her. To live out the rest of her days - and there would not be very many of them - so far away from anyone and anything familiar. To die alone, maybe at the hands of the very beings she was trying to do right by. It was not something she wanted to even think about. But Malcolm was right: it was a very real possibility.

So what was she supposed to do, shrink away from that possibility? Maybe if there was another alternative...but there was not. Jo had to believe that these beings, advanced as they were, and as honorable as they appeared during their brief meeting aboard Pericles, would see that she - that they - were trying to do the right thing, and treat them accordingly. And even if they did not, it would be worth it to prevent an even worse impression when they eventually learned the truth of what humanity did to their babies.

As for the rest... she would have to deal with those issues as they came up.

Jo nodded. "It's not an unreasonable risk to take, considering the circumstances."

Malcolm just looked at her for a moment, staring her straight in the eye. Jo felt a rush of warmth and had to work hard to keep from flushing at his direct, frank gaze and his subtle musky smell. He had not looked at her like that since... No, she was *not* going back to that again. She squared her shoulders and forced that bit of excitement down firmly beneath a mantle of professionalism. Or at least she tried to. But tired as she was, it was more difficult to do that than she would have thought.

Finally, Malcolm spoke. "You are remarkable, Jo. Do you know that?"

She realized she was smiling, she hoped not girlishly. "So I've been told." She snorted out a half-laugh. "Remarkably stupid."

Malcolm laughed as well. And then, before she realized it was happening, he was holding her tightly, gently. His mouth pressed against hers, and she surprised herself by returning the kiss fiercely. Time seemed to stop until finally, with a regret that she felt down to her bones, she pushed him back to arms' reach.

Malcolm drew a deep breath; Jo noticed he was shaking. For that matter she was rather breathless herself.

"I've missed doing that," Malcolm said softly.

Jo nodded. Not-so-deep down inside, she had missed it too. But it simply was not feasible, with them on different ships. And then he got transferred onto her ship and it became inappropriate. They had both been adults, put it behind them. But apparently not that far behind.

*It's the stress. You're just clinging to the familiar as a coping mechanism.*

Jo suppressed the thought, but it rang true enough that she could not ignore it completely. Now was not the time for this. Maybe later, after they had put this business behind them and had time to actually think, to feel, without the threat of the gallows hanging over their shoulders.

"Get some rest, Malcolm," she said. "It's going to be a long day tomorrow."

He nodded agreement, but she saw regret...and need...in his eyes, and for a moment she thought he might try to kiss her again. She was not sure how she would react to that.

Instead, he turned and went into his room. The click of the door's latch snapping into place seemed to ring with a note of finality that made Jo's heart sink.

# 40

# THE BEST LAID PLANS

Jo's head hurt. Again. The sort of hurt that comes from thumping her mind against the wall repeatedly for days without the wall giving an inch. It made her empathize with migraine sufferers a bit more, as piercing as the ache was.

She looked across the table at Jervis and Isaac and scowled. This was getting very old. Hell, it was well past old; it was decaying in a grave.

It had been three days, and she had not seen the outside of the CFL building. Of its innards, she had seen little else besides the conference room where she had met Winston before, her quarters, and a small mess hall down the corridor. They had not let her back into the operations center. If she did not know better, she would have suspected they did not trust her, and wanted to keep her from seeing anything more than she absolutely needed to.

*That makes good sense.*

Her scowl deepened. Of course it made sense; she would probably do the same in their place. What she was about to embark upon was risky. If she was captured...again...their best hope would be for her to have only limited information that she could pass along to the NSA when they inevitably broke her. It was not a pleasant thought. Certainly not one she wanted to acknowledge or give credence to, however much she understood it.

"Now comes the hard part," said a voice from Jo's right.

She turned her head and looked past Malcolm, who as always occupied the chair next to her, toward the last member of their small planning cell. A chubby woman of middling height who hailed from the Indian subcontinent from her facial features and skin tone, she wore her black hair down past her shoulders and had a severe face that made her look as though she was never content with anything. Her clothing was nothing to brag about: an off-white collared shirt and jeans that could have been bought at any department store. Her only jewelry was a thin silver necklace, and a matching silver wedding ring. She was Jervis' second and his chief of operations, and she had displayed a remarkable penchant for details so far.

"I'm glad you think getting the incubator out of the lab will be easy, Shani," Malcolm replied in a wry tone.

Shani rolled her eyes and glanced at Jervis, who smirked but remained silent.

"Up to this point in the operation," Shani said, "it is not much different than other operations we have undertaken in the past." Malcolm's mouth opened, but she went on before he could speak. "Tighter security, but the basic premise is the same. However," she looked between Malcolm and Jo with a deep, steady gaze, "we've never transported something off-plant before."

"That's all been arranged already," Jo said, trading looks with Isaac. "Right? Carl will pick us up and get us to Gagarin. From there we just load the incubator onto Agrippa and get underway."

"Just like that."

"Yes."

Isaac cleared his throat. "I have no doubt your man will come through, Captain," he said. "My company has already begun making the arrangements that will see him where he needs to be. I am curious, however, as to just how you intend to make off with a starliner. Surely the passengers will object?"

Jo found herself grinning mischievously. "This is why I told Winston we had plenty of time." She picked up a pitcher of water that rested in the middle of the table and poured herself a glass, then took a sip. "It takes just over two weeks to fuel a starliner for departure. The fueling process is potentially hazardous, so we don't begin loading cargo and passengers until the procedure is complete and the fuel tanks have settled. That means we'll have a window of three or four days between completion of fueling and onload."

Shani pursed her lips. "How long does cargo loading usually take?"

Jo shrugged. "A week. After that, there are two days of underway preps, and then off she goes."

"So if Agrippa is scheduled to depart on the 28th of this month, we need to be off by the 19th, or try for the next ship."

Jo nodded.

Shani frowned. Jo could see her running the numbers in her head. It was the 5th now. Two weeks. Could they pull this off in two weeks? There were a lot of preparations to make, details to see to. They would not get much rest, but it was doable. It had to be.

Jervis looked troubled. "So you're thinking to take the ship during the fuel settling timeframe."

Jo nodded.

"Won't that be dangerous? I expect you have to let the fuel settle for a reason."

Malcolm piped up. "There is some risk of over-pressurization and an explosion if the engines are brought online too soon after fueling." He held up a calming hand as Isaac opened his mouth to speak. "But the risk is small, and there are procedural steps we can take to minimize it. There is an emergency reactor and engine startup procedure just for cases like this." He smirked. "Well, not quite like this, but you get the idea."

Jervis nodded slowly, exchanging a doubtful glance with Isaac. "Ok, but you'll still need two days to get ready for underway."

Jo shook her head. "That's mostly for stowing consumables, moving the crew in, filling out paperwork. With just the two of us, we shouldn't need more than the minimal consumable load the company always maintains aboard the ship. And we're sure not going to file a flight plan."

"Fine. But surely you can't just walk aboard a starliner and fly away. There must be security."

Jo nodded. "There is. Only the ship's Captain can authorize a reactor startup, or disengage the docking mechanism."

"Ok," Jervis said, trading glances with Shani, who completed his thought. "So how do you intend to get past that?"

Jo's smile stretched ear to ear. "I'm Agrippa's Captain."

All eyes around the table widened. All jaws dropped in confusion. It was brilliant.

"Harold Jameson transferred me from Pericles to Agrippa a few weeks ago. When he did that, IT added my account to the list of those with authority to get the ship underway."

The silence that followed was not as satisfying as Jo thought it would be. Jervis, Isaac, and Shani all traded incredulous, doubting glances. Why doubting? Jo looked aside at Malcolm, who was staring at her as though she was daft.

After several seconds, the silence became a bit too much. "What?"

"Jo," Malcolm said, "you're not the Captain anymore."

"I know that. So?"

Isaac cleared his throat carefully. "So..." He stopped and smiled apologetically. "The company has certainly removed you by now. They won't be foolish enough to maintain a fugitive from the law on their security access lists."

Shani looked disgusted. "Really?" she said, her tone dripping scorn. "This was your plan?" She shook her head emphatically. "Forget it. We're fucked if we go for this."

They did not see. But then, Jo should have expected it. None of them had the sort of access she had enjoyed. None of them knew the inner workings of McAllister's security like she did. She had to force herself to stop from grinning even wider.

Jo held up her index finger and wiggled it slightly. Shame, shame. "I would agree with you, Shani, except for one thing."

Shani's eyebrow quirked upward, but she did not speak. She merely gestured for Jo to continue, her doubting frown saying all that needed saying.

Jo explained. "Harry transferred me personally. I was with him when he did it, and I watched him enter his access code."

The doubt left Shani's face, replaced by incredulous surprise, followed by a wide, conspiratorial smile. Beautiful.

# 41

# MAZEL TOV

Jackie pressed her finger against the call box controller and settled back into her chair, to wait. Her heart beat rapidly; the part of her mind that was linked to her implant took note of the rapid beat and shouted an alarm, her heartbeat was so much higher than normal for her resting state, but she ignored it. She simply watched the televid display and waited, her heart literally in her throat.

After what seemed forever, the display flashed to life, revealing a man in his mid-youth, just as Jackie was. Well-built, with a strong, handsome face and a winning smile, he could have been on the cover of a news-zine. And he had been. His hair was bleached blond, nearly white, but that was to be expected from a man who spent most of his time on a surfboard in the tropics. He never had been one for a real job, but somehow he was the one with all the money.

Jackie pushed the angry thoughts that threatened to burst through aside with a grimace that she did not quite hold in.

"Jackie," the man said,

"Steven," she replied by way of greeting. "Is Celeste there?"

Steven's lips turned down into a frown, an unnatural-seeming expression that turned his handsome, joyous face into something cold, bitter. "She's getting ready," he said. He glanced offscreen and paused for a moment before looking back at Jackie with an expression that screamed accusation. "This is a big day for her, you know. She cried for an hour when I told her you wouldn't be here."

Steven's words hit her like a physical blow. The last thing she ever wanted to do was hurt Celeste. She would cut her heart out before doing that. But... But duty called, and some things took precedence, whether Jackie liked it or not.

*And you wonder why you lost your daughter.*

That thought was too much like the accusation in Steven's eyes. "Just put her on."

Steven scowled, and for a moment Jackie thought he would just disconnect the call. Part of her would not have blamed him if he had, and she braced herself for the screen to go black.

Instead, he nodded and said, "Just a sec." Then he tapped something offscreen and his hold pattern flashed up onto the televid. It was an image of Steven, smiling and giving a thumbs-up, riding his surfboard through the tube of a breaking wave. Probably on the North Shore, knowing him.

Several minutes passed before the televid sprang back to life. Celeste sat there, beautiful in her bat-mitzvah dress - her father insisted on keeping his traditions, even though Jackie had turned her back on religion - her dark brown locks, so similar in tone to Jackie's own, pulled back from her face by a pair of berets. She looked sad. No, angry. It was like a lance through Jackie's heart.

"Hi baby," she said.

Celeste snorted loudly. "Don't bother, Mom," she said. "I'm only talking to you because Dad made me."

"Celeste, I really wanted to be there, but..."

"If you wanted to be here," Celeste snapped, "you would be. But you're not. And I'm the only girl whose Mom ditched her on the most important day of her life."

Oh, but there would be far more important days in the future, Jackie wanted to say, and I'll be at all of them. But she knew that would be small comfort. And maybe not even true. She had always told herself she would be there for Celeste, but it was one thing to lie to herself; it was another to lie to her daughter.

"I'm sorry," Jackie said, as plainly and honestly as she could. "I want you to know I'm proud of you."

"Yeah, whatever," Celeste said.

Then the screen went black. Celeste had cut the line.

Jackie hung her head as tears welled up. She sat that way for a long time. Or at least it felt that way, but when she raised her head and pushed herself back from the call box, a glance at the chronometer on the wall - she had her implant chronometer turned off, like normal; it was a terrible distraction - she found that only a couple minutes had passed.

She stood and smoothed her blouse and slacks. Best to not look disheveled. Then she turned and strode through the doorway toward the rest of her office's working spaces. She did not look at the window adjacent to the call box. The view of Earth, continually spinning around like a dish caught in a vortex, had never set her stomach at ease. But today of all days, the image of her home swirling around as she stood on a station tens of thousands of miles away, on a mad quest to apprehend a woman who probably had far too much sense to ever show her face here... That image would have made her break down and weep for what she had given up to be here,

As she drew a deep breath to calm herself, Jackie could not help but wonder whether it was worth it.

42

———

## UNDERWAY

Two vans.

Two vans did not seem enough, to Jo's mind. Not for the task that lay ahead. A half-dozen people, and all their equipment, would completely fill the first. The second was mostly empty, to transport the objective, as Jervis had taken to call it. It seemed like a caper of this magnitude would require more. But then, how much help would more people be? Her crew on Pericles only numbered over a dozen because of the various crewmembers' children, and they had charge of the starliner for an entire year.

*Not the same thing.*

But it was not that dissimilar, in principle. A group of people working as a team to accomplish a goal. If the team became too large, the group dynamic could break down as dissent and social loafing interfered with operations. Jo understood that, but it was easier to accept in the familiar environs of a starliner than here, well past the line of criminal behavior.

Jo shoved the doubt aside. It just came from her own nervousness, a natural reaction to a wholly new set of circumstances. It was not an easy thing to do. She watched as Jervis' men loaded the last of their equipment into the vans. As they slammed the tailgates shut, she found herself swallowing despite the fact that her throat was dry. She felt like a new hire, just getting underway for the first time. Or at least, she felt how she imagined they would feel, how they had described it to her.

Having grown up on the starliners, she never got to experience that apprehension, not in the same way they did.

"Nervous?" Isaac's tone was wry, but beneath that concerned, the way an older captain might feel for a pilot standing her first qualified watch on the bridge without an instructor to keep an eye on her.

Jo smiled slightly at that tone and looked back at him. He stood in the doorway leading from the CFL headquarters' loading garage into the building proper, and was dressed simply, in a white collared shirt and khakis. He seemed particularly partial to that combination. He met her gaze and smiled ever so slightly as she shrugged. "I'd be lying if I said no," Jo replied.

Isaac nodded. "Good. Means you're not nuts." He walked forward to her side, on a small concrete landing above a small flight of stairs that led down into the garage proper, where the two vans were parked. "Though some here would probably disagree with that assessment."

"I might just agree with them."

Isaac snorted. Or maybe he chuckled. Or maybe both. His lips turned upward more broadly as he patted her on the shoulder and gave it a gentle squeeze. "The plan's good," he said. "Simple, straightforward. Nothing fancy to screw up, and you'll have our best people with you. You'll be fine."

Jo returned the smile, but shrugged. "We'll see."

Isaac was right: it was a straightforward plan. As far as Jo could see, the greatest risk ran in the rendezvous with Carl. The closest civilian airfield to Camp Tycho was only a couple hours' drive away, just outside Alice Springs. But that would be too obvious a place to go, so they had selected a field to the north, near Darwin. It was a long drive, though. The map predicted about eighteen hours. A lot could happen in that time; there were plenty of ways for the NSA to find them, and once they did...

Jo suppressed a shudder. That did not bear thinking on. What would be, would be, and she needed to focus on doing whatever she could to make sure the mission turned out well, not poorly.

She turned her eyes back to the floor of the garage, where her team, dressed casually in clothes that would not garner any attention between here and Camp Tycho, was forming up. Jervis stood to the side, along with Shani; they would not be going along, of course. He had higher-level responsibilities to deal with and Shani...well, she was not cut out for field work, that had become clear very quickly. For organization and planning though, she was a whiz.

To Jervis' right was a slight woman with greying hair and amber-brown eyes named Courtney who, so the others in Brisbane said, could crack any safe or cypher known to man. Jörgen, tall, blond and ugly, with a face like a cinder block and a body to match, knew about computers and security systems. Thomas and Grant were brothers. They were both young and muscular, and had they look of military men; it helped that they bore a number of weapons visibly, and likely many others that she could not see. From the word around headquarters, they were very good in a fight.

And then there was Malcolm. And her.

Jo felt decidedly out of place and inadequate, right then. That was a feeling she knew well; it was an old companion, often encountered but rarely journeyed with for long. She had encountered it as that scared young newly-qualified pilot who took watch alone for the first time; when she had conned the ship into port the first time, even under that Captain's watchful eye; when she had taken command and every member of her new crew eyed her with uncertainty as they made their first assessments of her qualifications and quality.

She had proven equal, more than equal, to every one of those situations, but knowing that did not make the anxiety go away. It never did, not until it decided to leave of its own will, not hers. But while it decided when exactly to do that, she had work to do.

Jo cleared her throat and raised her voice. "Are we ready?" Silent nods from her team and a quick smile, somewhat forced she noticed, from Malcolm, who stood apart from the others a small distance, were the only response. Jo inhaled and paused, collecting her thoughts. This was one of those times when the leader is supposed to make an inspirational speech. She had never been good at those.

"We've got a tough job," she said, "one that I never thought I would be involved in. If you'd asked me six months ago, I was going to remain on Earth for another couple years, treading water until my ship got out of the yards and I could go home again." That evoked some strange looks from the assembled people, planetbound all. Few of them could understand how a ship was a crew's, and especially her Captain's, true home no matter where they came from or how long they might stop planetside from time to time. "I never wanted anything else than to travel the stars, see what is out there. I certainly never thought I would give it all up to get into politics planetside."

A smattering of chuckles answered her. Courtney wore an open grin of amusement; the two brothers matching smirks. At least they had some sense of humor. That would be helpful.

Jo paused again, a sudden upwelling of emotion forcing her to get control. She had never said it straight out like that - she would never again be Captain. At least, not on a ship she did not steal. It was one thing to know it; it was something else entirely to admit it aloud, to others. She surprised herself in the depth of loss that the telling drew out from within her. So much for being at peace with it.

Jo sniffed and forced a half-smile onto her face. "But there are some things you can't turn away from. Some things that make it impossible to just go along, safe in your own little world. Or at least there are for me. What's happening in that lab is wrong, more wrong than anything I've ever heard of before. Our first encounter with intelligent aliens, and we treat their children like..." She paused, suddenly finding herself out of words. The silence lingered for a long several seconds, then she drew herself up and made her face hard, taking on her best 'Captain Means Business' expression. "It has to stop, and we have to stop it."

She was surprised by the applause as she walked down the stairs to her waiting team. Not just from them, but from everyone present: the men who had manhandled their heaviest gear into the truck, Jervis, Isaac, the pair of mechanics who had just finished giving the vans a final once-over, a few interested CFL members who had come just to see them off. Everyone clapped for her little speech as though it had been the most inspirational thing ever.

Even Malcolm was clapping. He wore a broad, proud grin as she stepped off the final stair. "Great speech," he said quietly as he fell in alongside her.

Jo snorted, but she could not help but smile. The anxiety was gone, eclipsed by a warm glow of satisfaction.

It was time to get underway.

**43**

---

## CAMP TYCHO

Two days of driving does not sound like much, in the abstract. But what Jervis failed to mention in his description of the distance, or rather what Jo failed to truly appreciate, was that it was almost literally two days—two entire twenty-four hour periods— from Brisbane to Camp Tycho. Past the mountains to the city's west and into the Outback beyond where the settlements were few and far between, and then further still, into the vast desert that dominated the continent's interior.

They stopped only for fuel—those stops were few enough that they carried extra fuel cans within the vans so they could ensure they made it to the next one—and for calls of nature. Fortunately, the vans were large enough that they were able to lie down in the back and sleep in shifts. But the sleep was short and fitful, as more often than not the van would hit an uneven patch of pavement or a pothole and jar the sleepers awake. By the time they reached their first rally point, two hours from the Camp, Jo was exhausted.

The rally point lay within a small box canyon that descended into the earth beside a butte—Jo had no idea if they called them that Down Under or not, but that was the only word that came to mind—that stood out from the flat countryside like a beacon. At first she had objected; it was too prominent a landmark. Surely stopping there would leave them visible to tourists, patrols, you name it. But the canyon was deep and would shield them from prying eyes, and there was no other option that would even come close to offering good concealment for a long way in any direction. They needed to rest after the long drive or they would certainly fail, and this was the best place for it. It was a risk, but a reasonable one.

All the same, Jo made sure to set a watch up near the canyon's entrance before putting everyone in the rack.

THOMAS BROUGHT the van to a halt behind a small rise and turned off the engine. In the passenger seat, Jo peered out the windshield toward the top of the rise, where the glow of electric lights a small distance away eclipsed the stars.

It was a beautiful night: clear and dark, with no moon. They had made sure of that during the planning process. With a few weeks before Agrippa would be ready to sail, Jo's little team had the luxury of selecting the night of a new moon for the caper. Convenient.

Of course, no moon meant little with all the high-powered security lights ringing the place. That was where Winston came in. Assuming he came through and was not discovered. That was just one of the many things that could go wrong tonight, but Jo actually felt good about Winston's role. He had as much to lose as any of them, maybe more, if this thing went south.

Jo glanced down at her wrist chronometer and frowned. Five minutes until the second van was due to arrive.

They had waited until just after sundown and staggered their departure from the box canyon in order to draw less attention. Maybe ten minutes after leaving, they had cut off the road and set off cross country toward this, the second rally point. It would not have been so bad except they had gone without headlights, or lights of any kind. Thomas drove using lowlight goggles, but even still he had twice almost driven into a ditch that would have been impossible to get out of.

Jo lowered her window and craned her neck to look behind, straining to make out the other van.

It should have been a relief to not see a thing. That boded well for their plan, at least for the initial phase. But instead all she felt was dread. If they had hit one of those ditches, the plan was shot. She had planned for a contingency, of course. She, Thomas, and Jörgen could, probably, accomplish the mission on their own, with Winston's help. But it would take longer and the risk would be far greater than with the whole team. And worse, they would have to leave one of the team behind. The incubator was too large, it would take up the entire back of the van. Thomas knew that, and had accepted the risk. But the thought of just leaving him behind where he would certainly be nabbed by the NSA, whether he chose it or not, made Jo's stomach lurch. That was not a choice she wanted to make.

So it came as a great relief when, a moment later, the second van pulled up next to them and shut down.

Everyone piled out of the vans and quickly got about their jobs. Grant and Thomas checked their weapons, then slung their rifles across their chests in tactical mode and split off, jogging off in separate directions to do a quick sweep of the immediate perimeter.

They would subdue any patrols or individuals they found nearby. Not kill. Subdue. Jo had been prepared to fight hard on that matter, back in Brisbane during the planning, but was surprised when Grant beat her to it.

"Better to not hurt or kill anyone, if we can help it," he said. "That gets messy fast."

Watching the two brothers disappear into the night, Jo hoped they remembered that.

Malcolm walked up and held out her pack. It was black, just like the fatigues they all wore, to better blend into the night. She accepted it with a quick nod, took a minute to pull a black knit hat out of the pack, then slipped the straps over her shoulders. Then she pulled the hat on and rolled it down until it covered her face completely, except for her eyes, and touched the pistol on her hip. Better to not hurt anyone, but there was being humane and then there was being stupid.

Of course, Jo was not entirely sure if she *could* shoot another person, if it really came down to it. Hopefully she would not have to find out.

She reached into the van and pulled her night vision goggles from where she had left them on the dashboard. She had not bothered to wear them during the drive; she had tried for a short while but found them heavy and disconcerting to wear. But there would be little choice about using them now. Slipping them onto her head overtop the mask, she adjusted the straps and hit the power switch.

It was like someone turned on the sun. What a moment ago had been lost in shadow was now clear, down to the little pimple on Court-ney's chin before she pulled on her own mask.

Jo took a moment to survey her team. Everyone looked ready. As soon as the brothers finished their sweep, they would make the signal to Winston. And then...

The soft sound of boots on rocks behind her made Jo jump. She spun around, hand landing on the grip of her pistol, and found Thomas —she thought it was Thomas, but it was hard to tell with his mask down—standing there, his rifle held at the ready. Jo could not see his eyes behind the lenses of his goggles, but his tone when he spoke was disapproving.

"You make more noise than a herd of teenage girls," he said, his voice low and serious, businesslike.

Jo blew out in a mixture of relief and exasperation, but nodded. This was a job that required stealth, at least in the initial stages. She needed to keep that in mind.

Thomas returned the nod and joined the group. A moment later, Grant emerged from a hollow of ground a few meters off to the left. Pretty impressive. Jo would not have thought it possible to hide with the goggles making everything so bright, but he managed it somehow.

Training. Lots of training.

He exchanged fist bumps with Thomas, who gestured for them all to huddle up.

"The position is secure," Thomas said in that same low tone of voice. "Looks like they have beefed up security since our last brief from Winston, though. I counted a half dozen guard posts." He paused and looked at Grant, who nodded, confirming the count.

Jo cursed softly. "Is it too much?"

Thomas did not answer for a long moment. Then he shook his head. "No. They're spread out enough that we ought to be ok if we can take two of them down. But we're going to have to move quickly. Once Winston cuts the power, there will be a few minutes of confusion. In that time, you'll have to get the vans in and out of sight, or we're done."

"What about the guards?"

"We'll take care of it."

He said no more, and Jo decided she did not want to know. "Alright," Jo said, "everyone ready?"

Again, nods all around.

"We'll wait for your signal," she said, and Thomas nodded.

The two brothers departed swiftly, again disappearing like ghosts despite the better visibility from Jo's goggles. She shook her head at their prowess, then stuck up her index finger and made a little circle in the air.

Mount up.

She got back into her van and turned on a small wireless receiver that lay in the console between the two front seats. A moment later Malcolm joined her, taking the driver's seat. She was not sure because of his mask, but she could have sworn he was grinning.

"What?"

Malcolm turned to her and made the little finger-circle again. "Really?"

Jo rolled her eyes but did not reply.

Malcolm just chuckled and started the motor.

And then they sat, awaiting the signal that would set the path for the rest of their lives.

# 44

# IN AND OUT

It seemed to take forever, but when Jo checked her wrist chronometer only about ten minutes had passed when the wireless receiver clicked five times.

A second later, the lights over the hill went out. All at once, and completely. A second or two later, the sound of an explosion reached them, causing Jo to jerk upright in surprise. That was not part of the plan.

She was about to signal Grant and Thomas to fall back, but the van next to hers sped off toward the crest of the hill. Courtney and Jörgen apparently had no qualms about proceeding.

Jo and Malcolm shared a quick look.

"I guess we go," he said, and floored it.

As they crested the hill, Jo immediately saw the source of the explosion. At the rear of the camp, an outbuilding was ablaze. It was too far to see, but she was certain people were rushing to fight the fire. And were those high-tension power lines running into that building?

Well, that was one way to turn out the lights.

The ride across the desert to the camp was bumpy, jarring, dangerous, terrifying, exciting, and blessedly short. Their rally point lay only a couple kilometers from Camp Tycho's main gate, and they covered the distance quickly. Not quickly enough to catch up with Courtney and Jörgen, though. Malcolm drove all out, but whichever of those two was behind the wheel drove like a madman. Madwoman. Whatever.

Very quickly, they reached the road again and turned toward the gate. The barrier was wide open. Jo looked as they sped through and saw three guards lying still on the ground. A second guard post lay a half-kilometer to the east, near the bend of the camp's fenceline. It was hard to tell without binoculars, but there was no movement there. Jo presumed those guards were in a similar state. She hoped they were not dead, but at the same time she had to be impressed with Grant and Thomas' handiwork.

And then they were through, and speeding toward the camp's main building a bit less than a quarter kilometer away. Lights were beginning to come back on around the building, but just a few and those were not particularly bright. Emergency lighting, run on batteries and usable mainly to guide people out of the building in an emergency.

Jo found herself surprised. An important outpost like this must surely have a backup generator somewhere.

*Like in that outbuilding?*

The explosion made all the more sense, if that were so.

Malcolm turned left, hard, and it seemed never took his foot off the accelerator because for a second Jo thought the van was going to turn over. But then it steadied up and she gave him a hard look. Or at least she would have, had her goggles not obscured her eyes.

"Sorry," Malcolm said. He did not sound it.

They turned again, toward the side of the main building where, from the schematics Winston showed them, a group of loading docks was located. And sure enough, as they rounded the corner the docks came into view, along with Courtney and Jörgen's van, which was already parked before the first dock. Jörgen stood watch at the base of the stairs leading up to the dock doors, and Jo saw Courtney already at work on the door's control pad, doing her thing. Malcolm eased their van into place beside theirs, and he and Jo hopped out.

"Took you long enough," Jörgen hissed.

"You drive like a maniac," Malcolm replied, his tone a mix of awe and annoyance.

Jörgen snorted. "Wasn't me."

Courtney chuckled softly, from where she was working the lock. "Just because you two are pansies... Aha! Got it!" The door's control panel beeped—apparently the emergency power fed the doors too, which made sense—and she turned back to Jo and the two men. "We're in."

---

THE CORRIDOR STRETCHING AHEAD LOOKED familiar, and no wonder. It was the same corridor Winston had filmed through his implant. Of course, it looked the same as a million other corridors in buildings everywhere, but all the same it felt like a place Jo had known forever.

As though a few weeks now constituted forever.

Ahead, the corridor bent to the the right. If the video recording was any indication, the guard post leading to the lab itself lay not far beyond the bend.

"Wait here," Grant hissed.

He and Thomas had joined back up with the group at the loading docks, per plan, and led them through the dark and mostly deserted corridors, using the route the group had agreed upon and memorized during their planning session. The two looked pristine in their fatigues, as though they had not just been running through the desert and fighting with armed guards. Apparently their reputation was well-earned, but there had been no need for their skills to this point. The only people the group encountered were janitorial personnel and one man in a white lab-coat who had evidently been working the midwatch. They all surrendered without a fight or found themselves tied and gagged before they even knew the group was nearby.

That lack of resistance would likely not last, if the guard post remained manned. And there was no reason to think it would not be.

Jo nodded, and Grant and Thomas moved toward the bend on swift feet that nevertheless made little if any sound. Those were some nice boots they had on.

Thomas reached the bend first and paused. He pulled something out of one of the pouches that were built into his web gear, a little camera from the look of it, and fed it to the very edge of the bend where it could just peek around the corner. He studied the camera's screen for a second, then retracted it and turned back to Grant. He held up four fingers.

Grant nodded and moved up next to his brother.

Jo could not see precisely what they did next, but they took out gadgets of some sort and slid them around the corner. A few seconds later a pair of dull THUMPs echoed down the corridor, followed by the softer sounds of bodies hitting the floor.

Thomas darted around the corner. Grant turned toward the rest of the group and waved for them to come along, then followed his brother.

Jo traded looks with the other three.

Courtney just shrugged. "They know their stuff," she said, then she hurried to catch up with the brothers.

They did indeed. When Jo reached the guard post, she found Grant zip-tying the last of the four guards' arms and legs together behind his back. The other three were trussed up the same, and gags shoved in their mouths despite the fact that they were still unconscious. A strange odor lingered around the guard post, sweet but with the undertone of something burnt or rotten, almost rancid. The leftovers of whatever had knocked the guards out, Jo surmised.

Grant looked up as she passed and Jo thought he grinned. "Stun drones," he said. "Same as we used outside."

That was good to know. At least no one was getting badly hurt. That was the last thing Jo wanted.

"The lab should be just ahead," Malcolm said.

Jo nodded. "Let's keep moving."

As before, the brothers led the way, rifles at the ready. Also as before, there was no resistance until they emerged onto the catwalk that ringed the research area.

Stepping out onto that catwalk felt almost like stepping into a dream. More like a nightmare. As Jo looked down into the darkened room—bright to her through her lowlight goggles, but lit only faintly by emergency lights—she could not suppress a shudder over what had happened there. Such an atrocity, and for what? What purpose did it serve, considering the aliens had given their technology freely? All they asked was the safety of their children, and this was how humanity responded.

No. Not humanity, just bureaucrats in positions of power within the government. Had humanity, or even humanity's representatives in the Assembly, been consulted there was no way this would have happened. But the government had to have its secrets, didn't it.

Right then, Jo found herself agreeing wholeheartedly with Isaac's whacky dogma. Almost.

Jo shook her head, reminding herself to keep her mind on the business at hand. This was no time for philosophizing.

"Contact left," Thomas whispered.

Jo looked that way and saw a number of men and women in lab coats standing in a loose group on the machine shop portion of the lab floor. Of course, Winston had told them the researchers were working three shifts so it was not exactly a surprise to see them. What was a surprise was the immediate impulse Jo had upon seeing them.

These were the perpetrators of the atrocity. They had not made the decision to start the project, but they had participated willingly. They could not claim to be "just following orders". They were criminals of the highest degree.

She almost ordered Grant and Thomas to kill them all. Only the certainty that they would have done so without hesitation stopped her.

That, and because vengeance was not why she was there. Those monsters would receive justice, one way or another. But that was not hers to dispense, and certainly not without a trial.

"Can you disable them like the guards?" Jo asked, and received only a derisive snort in response.

Then Grant and Thomas went to work.

---

Jo STEPPED through the little airlock into the chamber where the NSA stowed the incubator, her heart in her throat. This was it, what she had come here for.

*Are there any eggs left?*

Jo froze midstep, her blood going to icewater at the thought. She had never even considered that. The NSA had been doing its experiments for months, and was on the verge of wrapping up. Why would they keep any of the eggs intact, if that were the case? Much easier to dispose of those that would not be needed for their ghastly research. Oh Lord, please let them not have done that, or this all would be in vain.

Steeling herself for the worst, she pushed through the inner airlock door and stepped into the chamber beyond.

The incubator stood just as it had in Winston's video, from this angle apparently untouched and undamaged. Jo could not restrain herself from darting to its side and pressing the button the alien Captain showed her, the one that opened the incubator's lid.

It cracked open with a slight hiss of escaping gasses and light mist poured out, like dry ice melting. Jo lifted the cover the rest of the way up and peered within, waving with her free hand to clear the mist away. What she saw within broke her heart.

When the alien captain turned the incubator over to her, it had been full of eggs, dozens of them. Now... Now the incubator was less than half full. Tears borne of fury and sadness over what had been done welled up, despite Jo's attempts to stop them. No, she was not going to break down. This was business, and she had to see it done.

It did not help that she could not wipe the tears away, with her goggles on. It took a minute of deep breathing to regain her calm.

"Fucking bastards." That was Grant. He stood to Jo's left, and was looking over her shoulder into the incubator. Jo had not noticed his approach, so caught up was she in her burst of emotion.

Jo nodded in agreement, then closed the lid with a solid click. "Well," she said, feeling proud of how steady her voice sounded at least to her own ears, "we'll make things right, won't we."

"Damn right." He cleared his throat, then said, "The next room's clear. One of them got to the exit, though, and Thomas had to shoot him."

Jo's breath caught in her throat. "He didn't..."

"No. Got him in the thigh. He'll be alright in a few weeks."

Jo nodded. That would have to be good enough. It was too much to hope that *no one* would be hurt in this venture.

She turned away from the incubator and moved a few paces away with Grant following at her side. As she left, Malcolm moved around to the back side of the incubator, where the researchers had installed their power feeds and probes.

On the far side of the room, Courtney stood next to a safe inlaid in the wall, tapping her foot impatiently. Next to her, Jörgen worked on a computer console. This was why Jörgen was on the team; according to Winston, within that safe lay the rod the alien Captain gave Jo, along with the incubator.

The rod contained the starmap to their home system and the recorded message for his fellows, and the safe was wired with extensive security algorithms that had to be bypassed before Courtney could even begin to crack it. It would be beyond useless to make off with the incubator without that rod.

Jo hoped Jörgen was a good as everyone said.

Then again, so far the rest of the team had more than proven their worth, so she had no reason to doubt it.

"I think we have it under control here," Jo said to Grant.

He nodded and turned on his heel, then disappeared through the airlock leading into the medical lab section, where Thomas was waiting. Together they would reconnoiter, as they called it, through the lower level corridors that the team would need to use to get out of the complex.

Jo watched him go and tried not to think of all the things that could go wrong with the team split up like this. But they needed to know what lay ahead. They would not be able to move as quickly with the incubator in tow. Good thing it had that hovering system, or moving it would literally take forever; it was very heavy.

"Um...Jo, we've got a problem." Malcolm stuck his head up from behind the incubator, sounding pained.

"What's up."

"I don't see the hovering units."

Jo blinked, dread surging within her again. "What do you mean?" She hurried over to Malcolm's side and squatted down next to him.

He pointed to two open spaces within the incubator's innards. "The hovering units were here and here, if you recall."

Jo bit back a rebuke. She recalled all right. She had been furious when she learned that Malcolm had opened the unit up and tested the controls while they were still underway on Pericles. He had insisted it would cause no harm. He was just observing what did what, and anyway he had already opened it once, to analyze its power needs and install a power supply. But it was one thing to go into it to make sure it kept power. It was another thing to go tinkering inside it just to see what was what. That was an unacceptable risk to take. After Malcolm's transgression, she had ordered the incubator locked away in cargo stowage, and changed the code to allow only she and her fellow Duty Captains access to it.

"You can't be sure that was the hovering system, not after only that one look."

Malcolm leveled a direct stare at her. Or what passed for a level stare beneath his goggles. "That was not the only look I got. You are not quite so clever with codes as you think you are."

Jo's jaw dropped open in shock. He had not!

But even beneath his mask, it was obvious Malcolm wore that self-satisfied smirk that always annoyed Jo to no end. He had. That insubordinate, obstinate fool of a man! She bit back a snarl and stood, moving over to the incubator's control panel. She tapped the control that the alien Captain used to put the incubator into hover.

Nothing happened.

Aw hell.

She tapped it again. Still nothing.

"Son of a bitch."

Malcolm nodded, also standing. "Told you."

Jo had to restrain herself from hitting him.

# 45

# GETAWAY

"Now what?" Jo wished she did not sound quite so plaintive.

Malcolm looked around the room for a second, then spread his hands helplessly. "I suppose we could try to lift it. We could probably carry it out as a group."

Jo just looked at him for a moment, then turned away in disgust. They were never going to get out of there without handcuffs on if they tried to move the incubator that way. "See if you can find something to lever it with," she said over her shoulder. Then she stalked over to where Jörgen and Courtney were working.

At least things were going better there.

As Jo approached, Jörgen pumped one fist over his head. "And that, my friends, is how we do that," he said and stepped away from the console. Turning toward Courtney, he made a little half-bow and said, "Over to you."

Courtney just shook her head and pulled her safecracking tools out of her pack, which lay on the floor next to her. Then she got to work.

"Well done," Jo said. She meant it; that was quick work. Pretty impressive.

Jörgen merely nodded in reply, but from the way his mask moved Jo was pretty sure he grinned.

"See if you can help Malcolm. We're going to have to carry or haul that thing out of here," she jerked her thumb at the incubator, "and we'll need a lot of mechanical assistance."

Jörgen's smile, if that's what it was, vanished. "Fuck."

"Yup."

He moved quickly over to Malcolm's side, and the two of them began talking. Brainstorming, Jo assumed.

Jo reached into the cargo pocket on her left thigh and pulled out the wireless unit from the van. "Thomas," she said into the microphone.

A burst of static preceded Thomas' voice. "Go."

"See if you can find a cargo loader, or a dolly, or something. We're going to have to move the incubator the old fashioned way."

A few seconds of silence passed. Then Thomas replied, "Roger," and the wireless went dead.

Jo checked her wrist chronometer. They had been inside the lab complex for fifteen minutes. How long before responders put out the fire in the outbuilding? How long before someone thinks to check on the lab?

She shook her head. They were running out of time, and this snafu with the incubator might just doom them all.

---

ONCE AGAIN, it was Grant and Thomas to the rescue. That was getting a bit old, actually.

Courtney made short work of the safe, and turned the rod over to Jo with a professional nod. Jo turned the rod over in her hands and inspected it; no sign of damage. But just to be sure, she pressed each button in turn and watched first the starmap, then the alien Captain giving his speech, then the first few frames of the technical schematics. A bit of her tension went away. The thing still worked. That was good. Key, in fact.

Jo took off her pack and zipped the rod inside, then donned it again.

And then they all gathered around the incubator and tried to come up with a plan. They had gotten precisely nowhere when Thomas strode through the airlock door from the medical section. Or at least Jo presumed it was Thomas since he seemed to be the one to take the lead.

"We found a wheeled cart," he said. It *was* Thomas. "But it will never fit through that airlock."

Jo groaned and looked back at the incubator, sitting there in all its massive glory.

"Well," Jörgen said, not even a hint of enthusiasm in his voice. "We'll just have to lug it through the airlock then."

"I'll get Grant," Thomas said.

A minute later, the four men had the incubator lifted up in the air to waist level.

"It's not so bad," Grant said, though the strain in his voice put the lie to that.

"Shut the fuck up," said his brother. Thomas turned his head to Jo. "Hold the doors open."

And so Jo held the inner door open and Courtney took the outer, and with a lot of grunting, cursing, and sweat, the men got the incubator out into the medical lab and to the cart the brothers found.

Cart was a misnomer. It was more a small platform with wheels on it. The thing was maybe a meter on each side, and did not look particularly sturdy.

"That's not going to work," Courtney said as she eyed it skeptically.

"Not much choice," Grant said, through gritted teeth from the sound of it.

The men lowered the incubator down onto the little cart with sighs of relief. Jo more than halfway expected it to collapse, but to her amazement the little cart held, and before long they were off.

To say it was slow going would be an understatement. It seemed one end of the incubator or another overbalanced and struck the ground for every ten meters of progress they made, to everyone's consternation.

There was never a hope that Thomas and Grant could scout out ahead. It required all four men to keep the incubator even slightly balanced. So the task fell to Courtney, who sounded decidedly unpleased with the notion. But with little choice in the matter, she darted ahead, wireless in hand to warn of threats to the front.

The minutes stretched out, and Jo felt more and more certain that they would be set upon and captured at any moment. Surely there were interior security cameras. And surely those cameras also received power from the emergency supply. Someone in the security shop would vector guards down upon them at any moment, and they would be done.

Except that did not happen.

Somehow, they made it through the lower level corridors to a long, circling ramp that led up to ground level. They stopped at the top of the ramp to give the men a break from pushing, and Courtney came to rejoin them.

"Mostly clear ahead," she said. "But I'm not sure for how long. I heard some guards go past down the main corridor a minute or two ago. Said something about somebody not calling in their hourly sitrep."

"Son of a bitch," Thomas said. "We gotta move. Now!"

Of course, there is moving and there is moving. Move they did, but it was not nearly as fast as Thomas clearly wanted. Hell, as any of them wanted, Jo included. But there was only so much speed the heavy and awkward incubator would allow. By the time they turned onto the main corridor that ran through the complex, Jo was about to jump out of her skin.

Surely the guard Courtney saw would have found the ransacked guard post outside the lab by now. They would have divided their forces, one or two tending to their comrades while the others went on to check the lab. And then...

"Contact rear!" Grant's voice cut through Jo's thoughts. He was at the front of the incubator, working to keep it from hitting the deck. Consequently, he was looking behind the team and saw them first.

Jo spun around. A group of four guards was sprinting down the corridor behind her team, weapons in hand but not yet brought to bear.

"Halt!" ordered the guard in the lead.

As though responding to the guard's order, Thomas let go of his purchase at the rear of the incubator and turned to the rear, bringing his rifle to bear on the approaching guards.

They scattered before Thomas fired his first shot, the lead guards leaping forward onto their bellies, the guards in the rear diving for cover in a crossing passageway. Thomas fired anyway, a steady stream of superheated particles that kept the guards' heads down, at least for the moment.

"Move!"

Malcolm and Jorgen redoubled their efforts. They had to, because Grant left his position on the incubator and took a knee, adding his own fire to his brother's. That was not going to work. Jo hurried back next to Malcolm and helped him push the incubator from behind.

"Courtney," Jo shouted. "We've got trouble. Get the vans started!"

"Right."

She sprinted ahead and turned left at the next intersection. The loading docks lay just a couple dozen meters past that intersection. They could still make it, if they pushed hard.

From astern, the sound of rifle fire interspersed with curses pushed Jo to greater effort. She glanced over her shoulder; the brothers were holding the guards down well, covering each other as they retreated in time with the incubator. But it was only a matter of time before reinforcements arrived, and then the balance of power would shift.

The intersection to the loading docks was so close now. Just a few moments more.

And then guards appeared from further ahead, and Jo's heart sank.

"To the front," Malcolm shouted.

Almost immediately one of the brothers shifted his fire ahead and sprinted forward to the side of the incubator. Again, the approaching guards took cover, but these were more numerous, and a few returned fire. It was far off target, at least for now, but it was more than the nothing the guards to the rear were doing. And it was only a matter of time before they sighted in better.

But the intersection was just ahead.

"Gotta take a hard left here," Jo said.

Jorgen nodded and pulled with all his might. The little cart the incubator rested on squealed in protest; its wheels were on casters and so could rotate freely, but the immense weight resting on them and the incubator's forward momentum worked against Jorgen's attempt. The cart twisted, lining the incubator up with the crossing corridor, but it kept moving forward down the main corridor.

"Damnit."

Jo and Malcolm spoke as one and pushed. Jo pushed until she felt she would launch herself to the moon if only her feet were not solidly on the ground. Slowly, ever so slowly, the incubator's motion changed, veering to the left. Jo almost thought they were going to make it.

And then the incubator slammed side-on into the corridor wall, its rear half extending out into the central corridor in plain view of the guards.

Jo muttered a number of carefully selected curses and ducked behind the bulk of the incubator as the guards to the front renewed their fire. They were more precise this time, and the forward brother joined her in taking cover.

"I'm going to have to take the gloves off." It was Grant. That meant

Thomas stood alone in the main corridor, at least for the moment, covering the rear.

Jo nodded. She hated it, but there was no choice, not if they were going to get out of there with their skins intact. "Do it."

Grant nodded once and then let his rifle drop down into its tactical sling. He pulled two grenades from where they hung off the webbing on his chest and yanked the pins out with his teeth. Then he stood and threw them both toward the guards approaching from the front. He immediately turned and raised his rifle, shooting back down the corridor toward the guards Thomas had pinned down. Jo knew without asking that he was no longer shooting to keep their heads down; he was shooting to take the guards out.

Multiple shouts of chagrin and outright fear preceded the grenades' explosions by a second or so. After that, the rifle fire ended and the only noise coming from that area of the corridor were screams of sudden agony. From the other direction, Grant's shifting fire joined with Thomas' brought forth equal cries of pain as his shots struck home. Jo wanted to cover her ears, but she could not. If this was the price to be paid for humanity's penance, then so be it.

Or at least, that's what she tried to tell herself. It was better than listening to the screams.

THE VAN SPED through Camp Tycho's main gate, passing the still prostrate guards as though they were not even there.

Jo slumped in the passenger seat and did not look over at Thomas. A lot of men had just been badly hurt or outright killed. She had not done it herself, true. But she had given the order, and the guilt of that weighed on her soul.

Was it worth it? Could she really think what she had allowed Thomas and Grant to do was justified?

She glanced over her shoulder, toward the incubator in the back of the van, and tried to reassure herself that it was. A few had been hurt, some wrong had been done, but it was all for a good cause. To right an even greater wrong that had been done.

Sure, those guards had not perpetrated that wrong personally. But they had aided and abetted those who had. They were cogs in the monstrous machine that had done this, like the ancient German guards at Auschwitz.

Somehow, that line of thinking did not make Jo feel much better.

**46**

---

# AIRLIFT

Carlton blew the landing. Blew it completely. For a moment, he thought he may have blown out one of the tires, the landing was so hard. A second later, with the craft slowing and responding to rudder commands as normal, he shelved that idea. But damn, he had not landed that badly since... Hell, not since before his first solo.

He was nervous as hell.

It had taken a lot of doing to get here. He had filed half a dozen separate flight plans, all of them legitimate, taking students from Luna to Earth then to Gagarin and back with landings in ten separate airfields all across the globe. It was all legal, and completely normal. He had embarked on training flights like these countless times over the last year.

The only problem was there was no student in this flight. The student did not exist. Carlton had, with help from one of Isaac's companies, completely fabricated the hopeful young man who was not flying this night, right down to his Social Security Number. He even had a photo ID, somehow. He was an average looking guy; he would go unnoticed pretty much anywhere in the world, which Carlton supposed was the point. He was no expert, but all the documentation Isaac's people created looked pretty legit, and impressive, to him. The folks from the company had assured him that he was correct, and the documents would stand up to the deepest scrutiny.

It made Carlton wonder exactly what those people, and their company, really did for a living. He decided he did not want to know.

"Delta Eight Seven Kilo Lima, taxi to parking on Charlie." The voice in his headset could have been any one of a thousand controllers, anywhere in the world, except for the Aussie accent.

Carlton acknowledged and steered the craft to the taxiway and then to a small hangar on the far side of the field. Delta kept little hangars on most of the larger airfields around the globe, just for circumstances like this. Training flights often landed late, requiring the pilots to spend the night, and leaving the expensive craft out in the open just invited mischief, whether from vandals or thieves or just bad weather. Maintaining a hangar was relatively inexpensive compared to losing a transorbital transport, so it just made sense.

Ground personnel met his craft at the entrance to the hangar, which opened at an electronic command from the craft, and guided him in with their glowing batons. Then they left him in peace to shut down and close up the hangar. They worked for the airport, not Delta, and had no interest in what he did as long as he didn't violate any airport rules. Which was just as well, considering.

Carlton secured the craft's systems and hit the keystroke that would close the hangar door, then climbed the stairs from the craft to the interior of the hangar. As he did, the parallel between this night and the night, weeks ago, when he met Jo and Malcolm in Boston struck him.

The whole thing was just so surreal. Was he really doing this? He had meant what he said then: it was insane. Morally correct, absolutely. Necessary, very likely. But insane nonetheless. He was covered; there should be no way to link him to what Jo and Malcolm were up to, from what he could see. But it was still a huge risk.

At least Alison had plausible deniability. Worst case, she and the boys would be ok. Slightly-less-bad case, McAllister had called periodically over the last year, trying to lure both of them back. If it looked like the heat was going to come down, they could just...slip away on a starliner.

Maybe.

There was no sense griping or worrying over it now. He had made a commitment. Jo and Malcolm were relying on him, and if he backed out now they were screwed. Completely. He could not do that to them.

Squaring his shoulders, Carlton strode across to the door that led from the hangar to the parking lot beyond. Next to the door was a trio of key rings hanging from small hooks. Delta always kept cars for visiting aircrews to use to get to and from the hotel, if necessary. He took a moment to log the car out using a terminal near the door then took one of the key sets, fished one particular key off another set, and exited the hangar.

Before he got in the car, he flipped through the keys, really just small cards containing encryption algorithms that would tell the door's computer to unlock, and fingered the one that he had taken from the second set inside the hangar. Then he shrugged and got in the car.

He drove away with the windows rolled down and the music blasting. In the wake of his car's passage, that one key, the key to the hangar door, fell to the ground and settled at the edge of the road.

---

JÖRGEN FOUND the key after only a few minutes of looking. The truly impressive part is that he never appeared to be searching for it at all. He was simply walking down the road, slowly, but then it was late at night or very early in the morning depending on one's perspective, and then stopped to tie his shoe laces. When he stood up, a single infrared flash from one of the gadgets he wore on his belt signaled his success.

Jo lowered her spyglasses and whistled softly. "He's good." Like she did not know that already, after everything that had happened the last several days.

Beside her, Thomas chuckled, but did not reply.

The vans sat back a kilometer from the airfield's fenceline, inside a small copse of trees that provided extra shadows and cover from prying eyes and passing aircraft. The NSA surely had surveillance craft up, or would soon enough if they did not already, which seemed highly unlikely. Jo's team sat there for an hour before sending Jörgen out to clear the way, watching for even the smallest hint that security had been notified about them. But again, the secrecy of the NSA's operation at the Lab appeared to be working for Jo and her team. In any other situation, every law enforcement agency on the continent would have been called by now, every airfield shut down or at least tightly monitored...

But doing that would bring up questions as to what was going on. Questions that would be too hard to dodge, especially since the news media would inevitably descend on the scene. No, just like the car chase in Quito, their pursuit now would be a job done strictly within the NSA's confines. Which gave Jo a significant advantage. As long as she did not squander it.

Jo raised her spyglasses again and waited the second or two it took them to focus in on the hangar building. Jörgen was fiddling with something next to the door. Why did it take so long to unlock a simple door? What was he...

The lights went out all over the airfield.

Jo's internal monologue shut up.

"That's the signal," Thomas said, and started the van up.

Jo quirked an eyebrow at him, but did not argue. Jörgen had said he would signal when the hangar was ready; she just had not realized it would be so dramatic. That was certainly his signal. But damn...

It was a good thing this airfield was not busier. Many of the busier fields had control towers manned twenty-four seven, and grounds crews on call all night. But they had picked this one specifically because the tower shut down, and with it the rest of the airport, at 01:00 each night. No one would be around to notice the power outage. And by the time everyone returned at 05:00 - just two hours from now, said Jo's inner monologue in annoyance - Jörgen would have reset the lights and the only record of their outage would be on the electric bill at the end of the month.

Thomas drove slowly back through the copse and across a short field until he reached the road. A short distance later, he came to the road leading to the airfield entrance and turned right, headlights off and driving by lowlight goggles, as he had the whole way from Camp Tycho. It was still unnerving, but Jo found herself less fidgety over it than she had been. Good timing on that, since she was about to leave the van behind for good.

They passed a darkened sign naming the field, and a low, squat building next to the control tower that Jo presumed was the airport administration building. A quick turn to the right brought them onto a long road that circled the runway and led past a number of hangars and buildings containing air and space-craft maintenance, rental, and flight training facilities. Or at least that's what Jo presumed they were; that was the typical fare for businesses at airfields. Somewhere there was probably a small cafe or restaurant, where pilots flying in from other airfields in the region could get their "Hundred Dollar Hamburgers".

She found herself smiling as she recalled Carl bitching about that old monicker. It made no sense, he always said, since no one had used dollars, or dinars, rubles, or whatever for centuries. But just as seafaring terminology and tradition lived on in starliners and other spacecraft, so did other old time sayings elsewhere. It was hardly surprising. He never wanted to hear that, though.

Thomas stopped the van in front of the Delta hangar and secured the engine. Wasting no time, Jo hopped out and pulled open the side door, allowing Courtney and Malcolm to spill out. Both stretched for a moment, restoring circulation to limbs that had been squeezed between bags of equipment and half-empty jugs of fuel for several hours, while Grant pulled the second van in beside them.

No one spoke; they all knew what to do. Grant, Thomas, Malcolm, and Courtney headed to the rear of Grant's van and began unloading the incubator while Jo headed into the hangar.

She found the interior still dark and stopped just within the door, suddenly hesitant to proceed for fear of running into something.

"Jörgen?" Jo called, quietly as she dared.

The noise of someone moving in the blackness to her right preceded his voice by a second. "Looks like your man did his job," Jörgen said.

That was good. Not that Jo expected Carl to lay down on the job, but in a caper like this... She shook her head. That did not bear thinking on. All was well, that was what was important.

"Step to your right."

Jo moved to obey instinctively. Or maybe it was the tone of quiet command in Jörgen's voice. Or the fact that he had lowlight goggles on and she did not. Regardless, a second or two after she moved, the light from outside, faint though it was, was blocked out by the forms of her teammates lugging the incubator through the door. Like her, they paused a short distance inside the hangar. Unlike her, they were panting. That damn thing was right heavy.

The door shut with a solid-sounding click and then, a second later, the interior lights turned on.

Jo winced, blinking at the sudden brightness while her eyes adjusted.

"Fuck, man," Grant snapped, his voice strained from the effort of carrying the incubator as much as from sudden annoyance. "At least warn us!"

Jörgen sniffed, but remained silent.

"Come on, let's get this damn thing loaded," Thomas replied.

Carl's craft had a cargo hatch in its underbelly. It was lowered, forming a short ramp into the craft's rear, where its small cargo hold lay. It was, in fact, a very small cargo hold. The incubator almost did not fit inside. And wouldn't that be a suitable bit of irony, if they went to all the trouble of stealing the damn thing only to be unable to make a getaway because they picked the wrong kind of vehicle? It took several long minutes of grunting, cursing, and adjusting, but eventually they managed to get the thing in and secured.

Jo glanced at her wrist chronometer. 04:15. That took a lot longer than she thought. They were cutting it close.

"Thank you all," she said to her team, and gave them a weary smile.

Somber nods, and a grin from Malcolm, were the only responses. This bunch had never been particularly talkative; that was Jo's only complaint about them.

"Do you two need anything?"

Jörgen glanced at Courtney and quirked an eyebrow at her. She shrugged in response and turned her gaze to Jo. "Just don't screw the pooch up there," she replied. "Don't want all my effort wasted."

Jo could not help but smile a bit wider at that. "I'll try not to." She shook hands with first Courtney then Jörgen and added, "Be careful out there."

They nodded and, without another word, turned and walked to the door. Jörgen pressed the door's control pad, and the lights turned off. A moment later, the door opened and they were silhouetted for a second in the comparatively brighter light outside. Then they were gone, and the door clicked shut once more. The lights turned back on.

Jo breathed in deeply and turned to the remainder of her team. "Right. Let's get onboard and get ready."

# 47

# GAGARIN STATION

Carlton parked the company car in its spot outside the hangar and turned off the engine. But instead of getting out, he sat there, staring at the building. He was not sure how long he sat there—he normally kept the chronometer function of his database implant turned off because he was still not used to the text perpetually hovering there in his vision—and he did not care.

He had done his best to treat this morning like any other. He got up at the usual time, went for his morning jog, had a hearty breakfast, and drove leisurely back to the airfield. Just as he would—and as he always had—during any training flight. But try though he might, the butterflies were now threatening to burst out of his stomach like the alien creature in that ancient screen play a buddy of his found, way back when.

This was no ordinary day. No amount of pretending would make it that way, either.

Up until now, it had been all fun and games. Sure, he had pulled a fast one on the company. But all that had really done was net him a few extra hours in the cockpit. Hell, that shell company—it could have been real for all Carlton knew—had even paid for the fake trial student's lessons, so it's not like he had cost Delta any money.

Now, though. Now the shit got real. If he got on that craft and piloted it up to Gagarin with Jo and her friends onboard, that was it. Yeah, he had a cover story built into the plan. Jo had made sure of that. But even he could see it was flimsy. The NSA would see right through it.

*But would they be able to prove it?*

Carlton snorted at his own thought. The NSA did not need proof. Not for something like this. There would be no arrest. No trial. That would blow the whistle on the whole thing. Most likely, he would just vanish. And maybe Alison and the boys as well.

Right then, Carlton almost started the car back up with the intention of going to the admin building and blowing the whistle on the whole thing himself. Let Jo and Malcolm fry, and to hell with those alien eggs; they were not his problem. But the image of Alison's face, the disapproval and contempt in her eyes when she learned what he had done—and she would—gave him pause. He had given his word to Jo. To Alison. And damn it all, they were both right. This needed to be done.

Carlton just hated being the one to do it.

Some time later, he inhaled deeply and flung the car door open, then stepped out. It was time to get it done.

---

THE PREFLIGHT CHECK of the craft's exterior was routine. The engine outlets, vertical stabilizers, ailerons and flaps on the wings, orbital maneuvering jets, and docking apparatus were all in good shape, as expected. That much was good. Jo and her pals had at least not made a mess.

Carlton smirked slightly and keyed open the crew access hatch, then waited while it opened and the boarding ladder folded out, smooth as silk. Then he climbed up and began his check of the interior.

As normal, he gave a quick sweep of the small passenger compartment—empty, as to be expected on this flight—and then proceeded to the cockpit. Settling down into the left seat, he inserted his Delta identicard and tapped the main console, and the cockpit displays flashed to life. A quick scan showed all was as he had left it the previous night. Fuel state was sufficient to get back to Luna with more than the required fuel reserve, let alone to Gagarin, in accordance with his flight plan.

Satisfied, Carlton tapped the console and called up the engine start procedure. He was halfway through it when he felt a hard piece of metal press against his right temple.

"Do exactly as I say," Jo said, her voice calm and cold. Almost as cold as the metal of the plasma pistol she held to his head, but then Carlton had never particularly liked guns.

---

THE ATMOSPHERE outside the cockpit windows changed quickly from a normal sky blue, to navy blue, and then to black as the craft propelled itself upward into orbit. Carlton focused on that, and on his instruments, and tried to ignore the fact that Jo had not taken the pistol off of him since she first joined him in the cockpit. Oh, she had taken it away from his temple—she had to so he could don his headset and talk to flight control—and settled down into the copilot's seat. But she had kept the gun leveled on him the whole time.

She had to, of course. Every aspect of the flight was recorded, from power-up to power-down, by recorders within the craft's systems and by audio and visual recorders in the cockpit and passenger compartments. It would not do to make it look like Carlton was anything but her hostage, doing her bidding against his will, or he would be screwed in the post-incident investigation. And there would surely be one. Concealing the fact that she had gotten up to Gagarin with her prize in his craft would be nigh on impossible. At least this way allowed a slim chance that he would not share in the blame.

Yeah right. And pigs could launch themselves into orbit.

"You're not going to get away with this, you know that," Carlton said, trying his best to look and sound nervous but not out of control. "Security will nab you as soon as we dock."

"Let me worry about that," Jo growled, and waggled the gun at him. She was overdoing it a bit.

Carlton rolled his eyes. "Put down the gun, Jo. We both know you're not going to shoot me."

She glared at him. "We do? I can fly this crate too, you know."

He snorted. "When's the last time you logged an hour in the pilot's seat? Fifteen years ago?" He glanced sidelong at her. "Longer?"

Jo's lips compressed into a scowl and she did not respond. She also did not lower the gun.

The console beeped and Carlton glanced down. The display told him what he already knew from the lack of g-forces. Orbital insertion was complete; the main engines were secured and the orbital maneuvering thrusters were powering up. Right on schedule. The familiar feeling of free-fall began to register in the pit of his stomach as the craft coasted along on its low earth orbit trajectory. It was strangely calming, that little bit of queasiness. Carlton had lived with it, off and on, for most of his life. It was like an old friend, in a way.

This was no time to be enjoying zero-g's though; there was work to do, and a hostage role to play. Carlton tapped in the command to execute the burn that would place them on an intercept trajectory with Gagarin Station and paused, his hand poised over the Execute touch-button. He turned his gaze on Jo again.

"This is nuts, Jo. Think about what you're doing. I haven't deviated from my flight plan. There's no need for anyone to know what's happened here. Put the gun away and we can forget the whole thing. I'll figure a way to get you back from Luna quietly. Honest. Mum's the word."

"I'm not alone." Carlton dropped his jaw open, affecting surprise, but Jo spoke again before he could retort. "And even if I was, we both know what you said is not true. You're supposed to have an under-instruction. Where is he?"

Carlton winced and looked away. "That's not really a deviation," he began, but stopped when Jo snorted loudly. Rolling his eyes, Carlton said, "*She* got space-sick yesterday and bailed." In spite of his situation, he shook his head and snorted out a half-chuckle. "You believe that? Kid never even bothered to go up once before signing up for orbital flight training. Now she's out a bunch of credits and I've wasted a lot of time." He sighed. "But that's why they call them Trial training flights. Separates the serious from the wannabes." He looked back at Jo and his momentary mirth fled. "Don't try to deflect the subject. What do you hope to accomplish with this?"

Jo just continued to stare at him. She made a little gesture with her gun toward the Execute touch-button.

Carlton sighed and hit it. The console beeped in response and the orbital maneuvering thrusters fired for a long several seconds before cutting out. On the navigation display screen, the craft's orbital track updated to reflect its new heading toward Gagarin. Estimated Time of Arrival, fifty minutes.

It was going to be a long flight.

EVERY TIME he made an approach to Gagarin, or any of the other geosynchronous space docks, Carlton found himself unable to not stare in awe at the sheer size and complexity of the thing.

A starliner was one thing. Pericles was about two and a half kilometers long, and she was an older model, smaller than the new Gorshkov class that started rolling off the lines while he and Alison were on Gliese last. But, big as the starliners were, the station dwarfed them. Large enough to dock a dozen starliners at once, with room left over for smaller private transports aplenty and a special section for military vessels, the station was probably forty or fifty kilometers long. The thing could easily be mistaken for a small moon, if one was not looking too carefully.

A small and oddly-shaped moon, though.

The main living and administrative spaces were a series of six stacked rings, several kilometers in diameter and all connected to a central hub by a like number of support struts that also served as passageways. Each pair of rings rotated slowly in opposite directions to generate g's within the ring and null out the station's net angular momentum, just like the rings on a starliner. From the rings, the hub stretched out in both directions, one side pointing right at Earth, the other out into space. The Earth-side of the hub contained the station's reactor complex and planetary communications gear. The other side contained the docking facilities, and was considerably larger.

The mooring apparatus was arranged radially, with four starliner-sized ships able to dock on each level. The arrangement was ingenious: great clamps with four passages that locked into the ships from the bow and stern, linking up with each of the four airlocks in the starliners' rings. The clamps themselves were mounted on drives that turned them, and the rings they were attached to, in order to generate g's within the ships and the transition area on the station. This made loading and unloading cargo and personnel significantly easier.

Looking up as they approached, Carlton could make out a number of starliners moored there. The sight made him heartsick for a moment. He loved his life, and his job planetside, but there was something about just blasting away to see what lay out there, among the stars...

*What the hell are you thinking?*

Carlton glanced over to the copilot's seat, where Jo sat. She was no longer watching his every move, but she still held the pistol pointed squarely at him. She was good at this; he almost forgot for a moment that it was all just an act.

At least for her part. The closer they actually came to Gagarin, though, the more it felt like he really was the prisoner, the hostage. He had been roped into this by her. By Alison. And they did have a point. But dammit, it was so much to risk. After this, he may as well dream of flying using his own two arms as ever think seriously about getting back aboard a starliner. Or doing anything at all that did not involve the inside of a prison cell, if he was lucky.

*You gave your word.*

And that was why he had even blasted off with Jo aboard. But now, just moments away from the intercept point where Station control would take over and guide the craft into its designated docking bay, that suddenly did not seem like a good enough reason.

*Alison is thinking with her heart. I need to think with my head. For both of us.*

He hated thinking what he was thinking. But it was the only thing that made sense.

Carlton glanced at Jo again. She was looking upwards and to the right. He followed her gaze and saw a lone starliner docked on level three of the mooring rings. Agrippa, he was sure.

She was distracted. It was now or never.

The craft's transponder controls were to his left, from Jo's perspective behind the control stick. Slowly, so as to not draw her attention with an obvious movement, he moved his hand from the stick to the controls. Carlton swallowed, hesitated. Either way, there was no going back after this. Drawing in a quick breath, he changed the code entered into the transponder from 2570, which was what traffic control had assigned him, to 7500.

His craft had officially been hijacked.

## 48

# WELCOME WAGON

The craft rotated ninety degrees and Jo had to brace herself for a moment against the sudden acceleration. This was always the worst part, the final docking. Station Control's guidance systems were always more jerky than when a pilot was running things himself, or even when the onboard autopilot handled ship's guidance. Someone must have left out consideration for the crew and passengers when he designed that algorithm; no doubt that designer had never been on a small transport craft, or cared about much except getting the code completed ahead of schedule so he could get the bonus stipulated in his contract.

Definitely a government operation.

Beside her in the cockpit, Carl winced as the thrusters fired to arrest the craft's rotation. "Hate this part," he muttered.

Jo worked hard to keep an amused grin from her face. "Shut up," she said. She still had to be in character, for his safety.

Carl shot her a withering glance. He was good at this game.

Too bad they would never be able to sit down over a drink to reminisce over this one. It would have made a good story to tell.

The craft lurched as the docking apparatus locked on from above. Then the only sensation was that of a small forward acceleration as the mechanism overhead began to pull them into the waiting hangar bay.

Unlike larger ships, which could not be accommodated in a bay, orbital transport craft like Carl's were always docked within one of hundreds of bays in the station's administrative support rings. It made onload and offload easier, with g's in place and an atmosphere to breathe. It also made for less of a jarring transition for the planetbound who travelled to and from the surface of the planet below. For the purpose of this trip, their hangar bay assignment was ideal: number 657, on the "upper"-most ring, closest to the starliner mooring facilities. The less real estate she and her team had to cross with the incubator, even bundled up so as to look like just another piece of cargo, the less chance they would be waylaid.

The craft came to an abrupt halt and a humming sound reverberated through the hull as the hangar bay doors slid shut behind them. Then came a louder hiss as atmosphere—not Earth normal, but breathable for a good long time without bad side effects—flooded into the bay. Then the craft slowly lowered to the bay floor, and the grapple released them and retracted into the docking mechanism proper, where it remained housed in the ceiling directly over the craft.

"Well," Carl said, eyeing her with thinly-veiled contempt. "We're here."

Jo frowned and shook her head, but kept the pistol pointed at him. "I'm sorry it had to be this way, Carl," she said.

In truth, there was no other way to have it, not without jeopardizing his safety. But she hated to have their last interaction play out this way, feigned or no. Because it would be their last interaction, ever. Whether she was successful or not, whether she got the eggs onto Agrippa and away, whether the aliens killed her or not, whether she returned victorious to Earth, he would not be alive to see it. Jo found herself biting back pre-emptive tears for the loss of such a dear friend.

Carl's only reply was a cynical smirk.

Jo waggled the pistol at him. "You first."

He complied, getting up from his seat and leading the way back into the small passage between the cockpit and the passenger compartment, where the crew access hatch allowed ingress and egress. Past his shoulder, Thomas, Grant, and Malcolm were on their feet at the front of the passenger compartment, waiting to get moving.

Carlton feigned shock at Malcolm's presence. "Malcolm," he gasped. "How? Why?" He looked between Jo and the once-dead man and managed to look convincingly dumbfounded. She never knew he was such a good actor.

"It's a long story, Carl," Jo said, "and we don't have time for it. Open the hatch. And then I must apologize, but we're going to have to tie you up and leave you here."

Carl reached out and activated the hatch controls at Jo's command, but froze at the mention of tying him up. He had been frowning for most of the last hour. Now he was *frowning*. Carl shook his head, but before he could say anything, Grant sprang at him from behind. In seconds, the brawny Aussie had Carl pinned on the ground. Less than a minute later, Carl was back on his feet, his hands bound behind him with zip-ties. He worked his jaw slowly, his frown now an all out scowl.

"I'm sorry, Jo," he said, softly.

That took her by surprise. What did he have to be sorry for?

A moment later, she found out.

---

THROUGH THE OPEN ACCESS HATCH, the thud of booted feet running carried, followed by a terse shout in a deep baritone.

"The craft is surrounded. Release the crew and come out with your hands up!"

The shouted command was like a smack across the face. Jo had to stop herself from cringing away from the force it exerted on her psyche. How? She gave Carl a forceful look, the one she knew from experience would break even the hardest of space dogs from their silence.

"What did you do?"

Carl met her gaze for a moment, but that was all, before turning his eyes to the floor of the craft. "I tuned the transponder to the hijacking code."

"Son of a bitch!" Thomas growled through gritted teeth; he looked ready to kill Carl right then and there. His brother looked the same. Malcolm was not far off.

Jo could sympathize, but she was in command. She had to remain cool, in control if they were going to get out of this with their skins intact, let alone if they were going to accomplish the mission.

"Why, Carl? You were going to be free to go your own way. There was no reason - "

His snort cut her off. He looked back up at her fiercely, his eyes narrow and burning with a deep anger. "Like hell. If I didn't turn you in they'd find out. They'd know, sooner or later." Jo opened her mouth to protest; they had given him all the cover he would ever need. But he beat her to it. "You're leaving, Jo. I have to *live* here, and I'm not going to do it as a fugitive." He looked away again, but Jo could tell it was more out of defiance than from shame. "I won't do that to Alison, or my boys."

It stung. More than that, it filled her with a fury that she had seldom felt before, and even then not in years. But...

But he was right.

It was dreadfully unfair of her to ask this much of him. She could run roughshod over the law, because she was leaving. Malcolm too. Thomas, Grant, Jörgen and Courtney, the others in CFL...they had all volunteered, decided of their own free will to join the cause, without having to be asked. Carl and Alison though were content to live their lives in Boston and neither bother nor be bothered. Until she had imposed on them. The fact that she had no alternative did not matter; she had upset their lives, and she could not blame Carl for doing what he thought was best for his family.

She nodded slowly. "I understand."

The other members of her team looked at her incredulously. All except Malcolm. His expression had softened as Carl spoke, and he nodded at Jo's words. He understood as well.

"We're going to have to gag you, Carl," she said.

He nodded.

Jo looked at Grant. "Do it. Don't make it too tight."

The fighting man scowled and grabbed Carl by the scruff of the neck, then dragged him into the passenger compartment. The soft sound of scuffling issued for a few seconds, followed by Carl crying out, "Ow" momentarily before his voice was muted by the gag. After another brief period, Grant rejoined them next to the hatch.

He gave Jo a quizzical look in response to her glare. "What? He'll be fine."

Jo rolled her eyes.

Thomas had taken up position just inside the hatch. He peeked out for a second, then hurriedly pulled his head back under cover. "Half a dozen men," he reported. "Looks like station security regulars. Riot Gear and rifles."

Malcolm frowned. The worry in his eyes mirrored Jo's own. "Can you handle them?"

Thomas just grinned.

---

Jo would not have believed it had she not seen it with her own eyes.

Grant and Thomas, working as one and moving with a speed and precision that she could not begin to comprehend, took down the assembled security forces with apparent ease. One moment, the law men were ringing the craft. The next, and almost before the two flash-bang grenades the brothers threw out had finished going off, they were down, unconscious, with their hands zip-tied behind their backs and their weapons gathered into a tidy pile at the base of the craft's boarding ladder.

It was all Jo could do to avoid gaping like a schoolgirl. As it was, she was certain her jaw was going to be bruised from striking her upper chest so hard before she could get herself back under control.

"How the hell did you do that?" Malcolm sounded breathless, and as stunned as Jo was.

Grant smirked. "Jervis didn't send us along for our good looks." He did not have a scratch on him, and he was not particularly attractive, at least not to Jo's taste. But right then she could have kissed him, and his uglier brother too.

Instead she just rolled her eyes. Or she would have, if she was not still looking from unconscious body to unconscious body in amazement.

Thomas broke her out of it. "They'll be sending backup. We need to be out of here in three minutes or we're screwed."

"Right." Jo shook herself and slung her pack over her shoulder. Then, holstering the plasma pistol she had held on Carl, she darted down the boarding ladder into the hangar bay.

It was not a spectacularly large space. About twenty meters long and thirty wide, long enough to accommodate a basic orbital transport like the one Carl picked them up in, it nevertheless was as well-outfitted as the larger bulk transport hangars. Along both side walls hung fuel hoses, hoses for O2 and water replenishment, and those for sanitary pumpout. At the front of the bay was parked a mechanized loader alongside firefighting gear.

And, of course, there was a windowed-off control space, about five meters up the front wall. It was fully manned, of course, and Jo could see a number of pale faces watching them with wide eyes. Three pale faces, actually. One of them, the supervisor, no doubt, was obviously shouting something, but the other two just stood there as though struck dumb. And considering what Grant and Thomas had just done, Jo could not blame them. Finally, the supervisor shoved one of the other two and punched down, probably activating a communications circuit. He began yelling again. Jo couldn't hear him, but he was no doubt calling for help.

"Everything's under control here, situation normal," Grant said, his tone highly amused as he watched the supervisor's antics from Jo's side.

She glanced sidelong at him, perplexed. He caught her gaze and rolled his eyes. "No one remembers the classics anymore," he muttered. Then, more loudly, he pointed at the loader. "Get that thing started up!"

Jo moved to obey and was halfway to the loader before she realized that he had given an order and she had taken it. That was not right. She was in command, not...

She looked back and saw that the three men were gone, vanished into the cargo hold in the back of Carl's craft. Of course, it made sense. They were all stronger than her. It would be difficult enough getting the incubator out of the craft with all of their muscles. If Malcolm or Thomas were driving the loader instead of her, it might be impossible.

It still stung a bit.

Whatever. There was work to do.

If you've seen one loader, you've seen them all. That was what Jo had always thought, and she was not disappointed with the unit in their hangar. Its controls were simplicity itself. And it did not require a data-base implant to start it, thank God. In less than a minute, she had it running. Thirty seconds later, she met the men at the bottom of the cargo ramp.

Between the three of them, they could just barely lift the incubator, but it was a good thing they did not have far to go to meet her, or they would have either dropped it or been forced to lay one end down and drag it to her. Jo had no idea how delicate the incubator's innards were —not very, she would wager, based on how well it had kept running through all the abuse the lab rats had put it through—but she knew enough about complex mechanisms to know they were designed to function at a certain attitude, and if you tipped them over or left them at a bad angle for long enough, that could cause trouble.

It was a moot point now. After another few seconds of moaning and groaning, along with a goodly number of curses from all three men, they had the thing secured onto the loader's twin arms.

There was no time for the wicked to rest on their laurels though. No sooner had they gotten the incubator squared away than Thomas and Grant hurried over to the main hatch leading into the station's innards. Malcolm paused only to pick up a pair of plasma rifles from the small pile at the bottom of the boarding ramp. He handed one to Jo and shouldered the other, then ran to follow the two brothers.

Jo put the loader in gear and floored it. The damn things were not all that fast, but she easily caught up to the men as they ran down the adjoining passage toward this level's central corridor. From there it should not be too far to the access tunnel to the Station's central hub, where further transport lifts would take them to Mooring Level Three, where Agrippa was docked.

It was all coming together. They just needed their luck to hold out for a little bit longer.

# 49

# GHOST TOWN

The main corridor was deserted.

That was odd. Jo checked her wrist chronometer. 1100. It was far too early for traffic to have died down this much. Where was everyone?

A chill ran down her spine as she looked left and right down the passageway. It was wide, wider than any corridor on Pericles. But then, the station handled a much larger volume of personnel and cargo than a starliner could ever dream of. The ring they had docked in was large enough that the corridor's curvature was hard to see unless you focused more than a few meters away; then, the slow upslope in each direction became obvious. Past a few hundred meters in either direction, the floor met the ceiling, apparently, the portions of the ring beyond hidden from view by its curvature. It was often disconcerting to the planetbound who were used to the ground, or the sea, curving downward in the distance, but to Jo it was natural as the stars in the night sky, even as far removed from it as she had been these last two years.

The corridor was illuminated at intervals by recessed lights in the ceiling and by lit signs labeling the passageways that crossed every few tens of meters. Artwork from the various regions of Earth and of the other colonized worlds hung at regular intervals, and potted plants as well as the occasional sitting area gave the place a warmer feel than the uninitiated might expect from a space station. But, just as people had long ago learned that it paid dividends to design starliner living quarters as comfortably and naturally as possible to increase morale and productivity, the same held true for stationary bases. People simply responded positively to beauty, to natural things. And so they were included.

Jo preferred to focus on the fact that it made life aboard more peaceful than on the practical reasons for doing it.

Not that it mattered at this moment. The fact remained that the corridor should have been bustling with activity, or at least have *some* people scurrying to and fro.

"This is bad," Grant said, echoing Jo's thoughts. "They must have locked down this section when we docked."

That little chill in Jo's spine became a icy shard of fear. "What do we do?"

Grant exchanged a look with his brother, who shrugged. Grant grunted and returned the shrug, then looked back at Jo with serious eyes. "We go on. Be ready; this could get ugly fast."

With that, he stepped fully out into the corridor and turned right, moving at a brisk jog toward the lift, which should lie two hundred meters ahead on the left. Thomas remained still for a moment, then gestured for Jo and Malcolm to get moving; he would bring up the rear.

Jo swallowed and drove the loader out into the corridor, following Grant's lead. Malcolm hurried to follow, walking briskly to keep up.

At each crossing passageway, Jo expected troops to jump out and ambush them. But that never happened. She continued along in her loader, driving at a pace that just matched Grant's jog, and within moments they reached the lift leading to the station's central hub.

It took a few moments for the lift to arrive in response to their call, giving Thomas plenty of time to catch up. He looked tense, no less so than his brother. Neither of them looked tense enough, though, to match the anxiety coursing through Jo's veins.

"This doesn't make any sense," she said. "If they've locked the section down, why aren't they coming to get us? Why is the lift working?"

Grant shook his head; he had no answer to give. Even Malcolm looked perplexed.

"Nothing for it but to keep going," Thomas offered.

That was the problem, though. The lift was the only way to get to the central hub. Oh sure, there were emergency access tubes, but they were merely ladderwells, and the hub lay a few kilometers above them.

It would be a difficult climb for an unencumbered person, even though the g's would gradually reduce as they neared the hub and the centripetal acceleration from the ring's motion faded. But they were far from unencumbered; it would be next to impossible to haul the incubator up a ladder. Maybe if its floating units, or whatever the researchers had decided to call the devices within it that had allowed the aliens to just push it through the air while it levitated off the deck, were still functioning. But with those units removed...

That left just the lift. More and more, the lift began to feel more like an invitation to arrest, or execution, than a passage to the station's hub.

The lift doors opened; Jo expected to be looking down the barrel of a plasma rifle or a slugthrower. Instead there was only the empty rectangular chamber of the lift itself. She exchanged glances with the men, then drove the loader into the lift. Again unto the breech, and all that. The men followed, and the doors slid shut behind them.

A moment later, they sped upward toward the station's hub.

---

THE FEELING of gradually reducing g's was always disconcerting. This was one aspect of space travel where the planetbound faired the same as starfarers. No matter how long most people spent in space, whether in zero-g or simulated, they never developed a way to adjust to gravitational differences on the fly, without at least a few moments of disorientation. Try though she might, school her mind though she had, Jo had always been one of those "most people". She found herself swallowing to put down a growing queasiness as she felt herself grow lighter and lighter; it felt like her breakfast was going to come up along with the rest of her.

She had never actually gotten space-sick, though she knew a fair number of colleagues who had. But it sometimes took a large effort of will not to. It did not help that she was already on-edge, nerves frayed. For a moment the general nervousness she had been feeling erupted into terror - not of being caught or killed but of humiliation. If she lost it here, she would never live it down. Oh, Malcolm would never mention it. And Thomas, at least, looked more than a bit queasy himself so he would understand. But Jo was not sure she would ever be able to look at herself in the mirror again without flinching.

But it was going to happen anyway. She was going to sick-up.

And then she left her seat as the lift came to an abrupt, screeching halt that almost lifted the loader from the deck, it was so abrupt.

Jo landed awkwardly, but not as hard as she would have thought because of the low g's; she estimated without realizing she was doing it that she was at about one-half her normal weight. All the same, the unexpected stop threw her for a loop, and for a few seconds all she could do was look around in confusion, her nausea forgotten.

"Fuck!" Thomas summed the situation up nicely.

# 50

## STUCK IN A BOX

Silence reigned for a minute.

If no one said anything, maybe that would make what had just happened not be real. Or maybe everyone else was as stunned as Jo felt. More than likely the latter.

And why not? One moment they were hurtling toward the station hub, their goal in sight and getting closer by the minute. The next they were stopped, thrown up from the floor by the force of their stopping. It was enough to put anyone off her game.

Finally Malcolm spoke up. "Maybe it's a mechanical problem." He neither looked nor sounded like he really believed that, but he really hoped it was true.

Grant snorted loudly. Thomas was a half-second behind. The looks they gave Malcolm were dubious, almost scornful, as though they could not believe he would say something so stupid.

"I think we all know that's not what happened," Jo said. She slid off the loader and walked to the lift controls, near the doors. The control panel was dark, lifeless. It was not going to work. All the same, she hit the button for the hub level. Nothing happened.

Jo stepped away from the panel and frowned.

"Now what?" muttered Thomas.

"At least the lights are still on," Grant replied.

As though his speaking had somehow jinxed it, the lights picked that precise moment to flicker and for a moment Jo thought they were going to extinguish completely. Then the small display screen at the top of the control panel flickered to life, revealing a woman's face. She wore a satisfied smile and her eyes shone with victorious glee. Jo recognized her immediately.

Chandini.

"You've led us a merry chase, Captain Ishikawa," Chandini said. Jo blinked, surprised at the audio, before she remembered the speakers mounted in the lift's walls, to accommodate those who desired music through the several-minutes-long trip from the ring to the central hub.

Jo did not bother to answer; there was no way Chandini could hear her, regardless.

The Deputy Director surprised her, though. "No need to pout," she said, her smile growing just a tad bit more broad. "We've been waiting for you for some time."

"What the fuck does that mean?" Grant said, from Jo's left.

The Director's smile did not flinch, but her eyes darted toward Grant. "It means, Mr. Gilford, that there were only a few courses of action left to the good Captain, and only one place to turn if she followed the most illogical option."

They must have rigged a microphone in the lift somewhere. But where... And then Jo about smacked herself. The emergency call button. There had to be a microphone in there, else the passengers could not call for help if something went wrong. Stupid. But then, Jo had felt stupid a lot lately, so why should this day be any different?

Chandini's eyes turned back to Jo. "You did not actually think you could get away with something like this, did you?" She definitely sounded amused.

Jo found herself crossing her arms over her chest, defensively. "I sort of did, yes."

The Deputy Director smirked. "I'll be seeing you shortly," she said. Then the screen went dark.

---

"Fuck me," Grant said. "How the hell did she know who we are?" He looked at Thomas, who shrugged, spreading his hands helplessly.

"Maybe your organization in Brisbane is not as secure as you think," Malcolm offered.

The brothers both cast baleful looks at him, but said nothing. From the expressions on their faces, it was clear they were not dismissing Malcolm's conjecture out of hand.

"Never mind all that," Jo snapped. "They'll be coming. If they don't just bring the lift back down on remote." By now, they were well above the ring's upper levels. It would be far more efficient to just bring the lift back down, and given they had the ability to stop it, Jo could not see why they would not do that very thing, and quickly. "Any ideas how to get out of this?" Lord knew she was coming up blank.

Grant and Thomas looked at each other and frowned a similar frown. Right then, except for the fact that Grant had a goatee and Thomas was clean shaven, they could have been looking in the mirror, so similar they looked. Neither spoke; it was like they were working out the details by telepathy or something.

But there was no time for that sort of thing.

Apparently Malcolm felt the same. He raised his plasma rifle and fired a shot into the control panel. It blew out in a shower of sparks and slag.

"Well that'll help," Thomas said in a wry tone.

"More than you might think," Malcolm said. "The internal relays in the controls interface with interlocks in the station's transit control system. If those relays are not functioning, they won't be able to order the lift back down." He paused, frowned, then shrugged. "Or at least, it will take a bit longer for them to be able to do it."

Jo blinked, surprised. She did not know that. Where had Malcolm learned it?

He noticed her expression and quirked an eyebrow at her. "Engineer, remember?" He grinned in a self-deprecating manner. "We don't get the sexy shore jobs you pilot-types get. I did a stint or two on these stations, back before I joined you on Pericles."

"Right," Grant interrupted. "Not to spoil the stroll down memory lane or anything, but..." He left off the rest, but his meaning was clear. *What the hell does that have to do with us getting out of here?*

A very good question, and from the smug look on his face, Jo suspected Malcolm knew the answer. He grinned and gestured toward the ceiling, where the hub access doors were situated. "Shall we get out of here then?"

By the time the lift would have reached the station's hub, all of the ring's centripetal g's would have gone away completely. That meant the doors to the lift could be placed anywhere, since everyone and everything within would essentially be just floating around. Given that, it made perfect sense to place the hub access doors in the ceiling and keep the ring access doors on the side walls. Personnel and objects could simply float into the lift from the hub, and as the rotational g's built up, slide down one of the walls to the floor. By the time they reached the ring, they could walk or be pushed out, just like on any lift planetside.

Which was all well and fine, except that now neither set of doors opened to much of anything that was of use. The side doors just faced the side wall of the lift shaft, and the hub doors pointed up. A long ways up. But that was where they needed to go, so...

"You want us to climb up the rest of the way," Grant said.

Malcolm nodded. "There are access ladders along the shaft, between the chutes for the lift cars."

"What about that thing?" Thomas said, nodding at the incubator, resting on the loader's twin arms. "Can't exactly haul that up a ladder. It weighs a ton."

"No, it *weighed* a ton. Down there." Malcolm pointed downward, toward the floor and the ring below. "Here, it's about half that, and it'll be less the closer we get to the hub."

The brothers looked dubious, but Malcolm was right. It could work.

"We've got rope," Jo said, coming to Malcolm's aid. "Two of us can climb to the next landing and pull while the other two lift up from below. It will be difficult at first, but..."

Thomas snorted. Loudly. "It'll be well past difficult."

Malcolm spread his hands in a helpless gesture. "Do you have a better idea?"

Thomas was right. Difficult did not even begin to describe it.

Even at about half its normal weight, the incubator still had to weigh a good thirty or forty kilograms, easily. Grant and Thomas, lifting together, could get it up fairly well, but they could only reach halfway to the hub access doors, and later less than halfway between landings of the ladder. That left Malcolm and Jo to haul the delicate machine the rest of the way. They took care to use two strands of rope for redundancy, and to tie it off securely enough that the thing was not going to leave the rope's grip for anything short of someone coming up and actually cutting the rope with a knife.

All the same, for the first several landings, the only thing Jo could think of was what would happen if they lost it somehow. The incubator would fall, and fall far. Depending on how they lost it, it could actually fall into a neighboring lift chute, so it would fall all the way to the ring, to its certain destruction. Even the shorter fall to their stranded lift would likely damage it badly, and after several landings the height became such that it was probably academic which fate would be worse for the incubator. Jo did not even want to think about that; about what it would mean to, well, to *everything*.

Fortunately, the higher they got, the lower the g's. After a dozen or so landings that required what was probably excessive amounts of effort to bring the incubator up, the device's weight had lowered to the point that just one man could lift it up from below, and then haul it up from above.

Regardless, all things considered it was tiring work, both physically and mentally. But finally, after what seemed an age but was in reality probably less than an hour and a half, they made it to the top of the shaft. There they paused at the hub access doors to catch their breath, and to consider.

"They're going to be waiting on the other side of these doors, you know that," Thomas said.

Jo nodded. In all likelihood he was entirely correct.

He frowned. "I don't have much practice fighting in zero-g." Thomas glanced at his brother, who shook his head. He had no training in it either.

"If it's any consolation, you probably have more idea how to go about it than I do," Jo replied, earning a look in return that said it was not any kind of consolation at all, and thank you very much. She shrugged. "I don't think station security usually trains for zero-g trouble either, so we'll be on equal - "

Malcolm snorted. "Really think it'll be station security coming after us?"

Jo paused. He had a point. The NSA had not involved locals before;

they would want to keep things hush-hush, so they would use their own goons. Probably the same goons, actually, so there was a good chance it was Moore waiting for them. Did *they* train for zero-g combat? There was no way to know, and Jo would accomplish nothing sitting around bellyaching over it.

It was time to go.

Jo took a deep breath. "Alright, let's move. Remember, we're heading to the transport tube in the center of the hub. The transports have cargo mounts to carry the incubator, and will get us to the starliner levels in just a couple minutes."

"Assuming they're not shut down too," Grant said. Wasn't he just a ray of sunshine.

"We'll deal with that when we come to it," Jo said, trying to sound confident despite the fact that her stomach was doing backflips in her belly from nerves. "Everyone ready?"

Nods all around.

"Ok, let's do it."

She nodded at Malcolm, and he pushed himself over to the center of the access doors. He tripped their actuating assembly, and a moment later the doors slid open.

# 51

# HUB

Past the hub access doors was a wide expanse of open air. In a different environment, it would have been impossible to navigate. But in zero-g, it was child's play to push off from the doorway leading into the lift and propel themselves outward. Or rather, inward.

As many times as she had been here over the years, the central corridor of the station—of all five stations, really—always took Jo's breath away. It stretched apparently endlessly in both directions with only the transport tubes in its center to break up the hub's expanse. In eight locations around the hub's circumference, constantly moving as the ring they led to rotated, were pairs of matched doors, identical to the ones Jo and her party came through, but no one else was immediately visible. The area was well-lit by lighting bolted to the walls in every direction, but still it seemed a place of mystery, as odd as it was compared with normal existence on board ship or planetside.

Jo looked back as they floated toward the transport tubes in time to see the doors they had passed through close, sealing them in. There was no turning back, even if they had been so inclined.

It only took a few moments to reach the central transport tubes, and Jo was relieved to find a transport sled waiting ready to receive them at this level's station. The sleds were designed to move cargo as well as people, and it only took a few minutes to latch the incubator in place, and then the four of them strapped in to the couches in the forward area of the sled. A few seconds later, after Jo selected their destination level on the control console, they were off, heading "upwards" toward starliner level three, where fate awaited them.

The acceleration was impressive. Jo felt herself pressed forcefully against her couch, a familiar sensation that very nearly matched the force she felt on initial liftoff from any number of launch complexes, except that this acceleration lasted a fraction of the time. She barely had time to register the force and brace herself against it before it was gone, and the sled had moved from the station into the transport tube, hurtling toward its stop several kilometers away.

In just a short couple of minutes, the sled's brakes fired and it veered off of the main tube, causing Jo to once again brace herself against acceleration forces, although this time she felt as though she was going to fly forward out of her seat and past the sled's bow. And then, just as soon as it came, the acceleration was over and the sled coasted to a stop at another station, identical to the one they departed except for the large sign that read, "Starliner Level 3A" off to their right.

They sat there for a moment, in silence.

"I can't believe they let us get this far," Jo said finally. She had been more than half-convinced that they would meet nothing but the ends of rifles as they emerged from the hub access doors. The fact that they had made it this far without molestation was amazing. Troubling. What was going on?

"Maybe they did not expect us to get out of the lift," Malcolm replied. Though his tone and expression were doubtful in the extreme.

"More likely they're lying in wait ahead," Thomas said as he and Grant unclipped from their restraint harnesses and kicked themselves up out of the sled. They both unslung their rifles and panned about, looking down their sights carefully for threats.

Jo frowned.

They had a good point. Chandini certainly would have had a backup plan at the ready. It went beyond naiveté to expect anything else. Given that near certainty, though, Jo felt a surge of guilt. She and Malcolm would be blasting away onboard Agrippa. The brothers would be left on their own, to fend for themselves.

To be imprisoned or worse.

She shook her head. She could not be a party to that. Unhooking her harness, she kicked herself upward to join them. "You two stay with the sled," she said as she became level with them and placed her hand on one of the sled station's support girders to halt her ascent. "Malcolm and I will take it from here."

The brothers gave each other long looks, then Grant spoke. "Yeah, that's not going to happen."

Jo glanced between the two of them. They both looked resolved, serious as hell. "There's a lot more trouble here than we planned on," she said. "I need to keep going, but you don't have to."

Grant just laughed, a bitter but strong sound as he looked at her as though she was daft.

Thomas sniffed. "You don't get it, Jo." That was the first time he had ever called her anything other than Captain or Ma'am.

Jo quirked an eyebrow at him.

"Jervis did not assign us to this; we volunteered." Grant nodded agreement, but let his brother speak for them both. "We've always wanted to do something important, and this..." Thomas spread his hands and trailed off.

Silence loomed for several seconds, and then Grant, glancing with momentary chagrin toward his brother, took up the conversation.

"First Contact," he said, his voice awed. "This is something we—all of us, all of humanity—have been dreaming about for centuries. And now it's happened and our dumbass government is going to fuck it up." He shook his head. "We can't let that happen, not even if it means we..." He swallowed and shrugged, looking down at the sled and its cargo. "Well, you know."

Thomas swallowed and nodded. "We'll see you to the ship. No matter what."

Right then, Jo could have kissed them both. As it was, she felt tears welling up, unbidden.

This was not what she wanted.

They were young, just getting started, with so much to look forward to. It was too much, what they expected her to accept from them. How did that old phrase go? The last full measure of devotion. That was what they were offering; likely what all of them would give, herself included, and likely without achieving their goal.

She could accept that for herself—she had come to peace with it somehow, sometime—but not for them. She had no right to do so; it was her burden, not theirs.

She shook her head, but Malcolm spoke from behind her, stopping her protest. "We all knew what we were getting into, Jo. You're not alone in this; never have been."

Grant nodded, smirking. "Look at it this way. Someday, they'll name high schools after us." He looked aside at his brother, then his smirk became a peaceful smile that he turned to include her and Malcolm as well. "All of us."

She almost broke down then. Almost. But years of training, and especially her years as Captain, came to her aid. She steeled herself to calm and wiped the budding tears away before she realized what she was doing.

They were right, of course.

And even if they weren't, it was too late to turn back now. There was no way any of them, even the brothers, would get off the station without a fight, or at all. Might as well get about their job then.

Jo inhaled deeply, then nodded. "Ok. Let's head out."

# 52

# ROUND AND ROUND

The Starliner levels were arranged differently from the ring levels. Each level was actually divided into two, about three and half kilometers apart. Level A attached to the bow of the starliner; B to the stern. Within each sub-level there were no rotating doorways, no rotation at all.

Zero-g ruled until one actually reached the loading rings, which turned along with the starliner's two living and cargo rings to generate artificial gravity in the loading sections of the station and aboard the starliner itself. Consequently, navigating from the sled station to the loading ring access tubes was a bit more complicated than from the station to the station rings.

Once Jo's party left the sled station, they had to maneuver around the outside of the transport tube complex until they reached their desired berth—Berth Three—and then they could push themselves "upward", using guide cables to maintain their course, until they reached the access doors on the hub's outer wall.

"This is terribly inefficient," Grant muttered as they touched down, for lack of a better word, adjacent to the doors. "Floating cargo around like this?"

Jo smirked and gestured toward the hub's inner wall adjacent to the doors. Embedded into the wall was a large conveyer-belt looking device, with davits where standard-sized shipping containers could be strapped.

"No one ships large cargo loose, like we have it. It all goes into containers, and has a different access to the ship."

She gestured upward along the axis of the hub, where a few tens of meters away were larger doors that led into separate tubes, specifically designed to ship cargo into the loading rings, and then downward toward a separate set of connections that led from the hub wall toward a different sled station than they had used. From its size, it was built only for cargo containers.

"The sled we took was for passengers, and for their personal baggage."

Grant blinked. Then his eyes widened as he tracked toward where she was pointing. At first, she thought he was impressed by the size and elegance of the design. Then he scowled, surprising her. "You mean to tell me we could have just hidden ourselves away inside a cargo container and saved all this sneaking and stalking and maybe getting shot at?"

Jo recoiled slightly, his irritation getting the better of her for a second. Oh, it was understandable, considering what he and his brother faced. But it was so wrong.

"There is no way to open those containers from inside, Grant," Jo said as gently as she was able. He opened his mouth to protest, but she held up a hand, silencing him. "And they are all lined up a month or more before loading, and are all inspected. Even if we could have put ourselves into one and shipped it, we would either have suffocated within it or been killed by the scanning devices."

Those were particularly high-energy, and were the reason why one did not ship pets or other livestock aboard starliners, at least not as cargo. Each ship carried a small number of cryo-suspension units that could accommodate animals, but the waiting list to get into one of those was long.

And for good reason. The last thing one would want to do was to bring an alien creature onto a different world. Some number of pets or other domesticated animals were likely to escape, and they would have no natural predators on the new world. Even just a few members intro-duced from an alien species could have cataclysmic consequences for the world's ecosystem.

Grant nodded slowly, the bitterness that had flooded into his gaze leaving as quickly as it came. He gestured toward Thomas, who pressed the control pad for the loading ring access doors. A moment later, with a slight gust of air as the pressure between the loading rings and the hub equalized, the doors opened.

Jo's group proceeded onward.

***

THE ACCESS TUBE stretched a kilometer or more away from the hub proper, running straight and true, and wide enough for a dozen or more people to float in file down its entire length. But now, as before, there was no one else visible anywhere. This was not so unusual; procedure dictated that the ship be cleared of personnel and only minimal personnel allowed within the loading rings during fueling and settling. And most of the loading ring personnel would be stationed within the cargo holds: security guards, inventory clerks, and the like. There would be no need for commuter assistance personnel until time to load the passengers next week. So Jo fully expected to encounter only electronically secured access doors the whole way into the ship.

All the same, for whatever reason, the lack of people made Jo nervous. Looking aside at her compatriots, she was not the only one. Time for a pep talk. She turned around to face the others, her momentum continuing to push her backwards toward the end of the tube. But Thomas spoke before she was able.

"They're waiting for us up ahead." It was a statement of fact, not a question. There was no doubt in his eyes.

Next to him, Grant had a similar look. Dread, but below that steely determination.

Jo nodded. "Only a fool would not have people stationed at the access hatches, and these people are not fools. Agrippa is the only starliner leaving in the next two months. Where else would we go?"

No one responded for a minute or so. Finally, Grant said, "Why not have them stationed on the ship itself?"

That was one thing that had worried Jo to no end. If that were the case, there was a good chance they would never know it until far too late. Worse, they would never know whether they had cleared the ship or not. Even if they made it out of the solar system, they would potentially be placing themselves into cryo-suspension with hostiles onboard, ready to do them in while they were helpless.

Of course, that would doom the hiding troops to live out the rest of their days on a starliner that was hurtling off toward a far distant star. Jo found it hard to believe NSA people had the expertise to operate a starliner at all, let alone navigate it back to Sol. No, that would likely be a suicide assignment.

Hard to motivate a person to take a job like that.

Especially when one of those sexy warships moored a couple dozen kilometers above Agrippa could just as easily get underway and blow Agrippa out of the sky.

That was not likely, though. It would mean spreading word far and wide about what was going on here.

Or maybe not. It would be easy to just make up a cover story that seemed plausible and give the order. To call what ran down Jo's spine right then a chill was to call a glacier a little pile of snow.

That was an angle she had not ever really considered before. She had presumed the NSA would keep this in-house, to avoid bad press and maybe to avoid losing face with other Agencies.

But what if they deemed stopping her so important that they threw all that to the wind?

There was no way to know. And, frankly, she could not worry about everything; that would leave her incapable of taking action at all.

An old friend had once said, "Sometimes you have to just grab sack and go for it."

Walter had always been a colorful guy, but off as his turn of phrase was, he had a good point. Fortune favors the bold, and all that. Sometimes there was nothing for it but to just go and give it your all, and see where things end up. Endlessly fretting accomplishes nothing.

Jo shook her head and replied to Grant, "Safety precautions, remember? No personnel are allowed aboard ship for another day. They would be putting their people in greater danger, and what benefit would they gain?"

Grant pursed his lips, considering. Then after a moment, he nodded. "Makes sense. Once we're on the ship, they've lost a bit of the initiative, too. Best to keep us off the ship. And they'll do that by meeting us at the airlock."

Jo nodded.

"Ok then. We'll hold them off long enough for you two to get aboard. I hope you have some way to stop them from following after that, though." The implication was clear: he and his brother would not be around to offer resistance for long after shots started flying.

Jo swallowed, but kept her Captain In Charge face on full display. "As soon as we're through, I'll close all airlocks and break seal with the forward and aft loading rings. That should buy us enough time to initiate an emergency reactor startup and get underway." She frowned, a thought occurring to her.. "You could come with us, you know. Four will not use much more resources than two. There's no need - "

Thomas cut her off. "Don't think we haven't considered that one." He and Grant exchanged a long look that ended in mutual shrugs. "If we see a way to make it aboard without jeopardizing the mission, we'll take it," Thomas said finally. "But don't wait for us."

There was not much left to say after that.

---

THE REMAINDER of the journey to the loading rings' hub passed uneventfully. Just as with the station itself, the loading ring access tubes were arrayed radially, with the lift access hatches revolving slowing around the hub's circumference. Also as in the station hub, there were separate lifts and accesses for cargo and for personnel.

Jo's group took care to avoid the former in choosing a lift, and before long they were ensconced in a lift, smaller than the they had used earlier but still spacious enough to easily accommodate the incubator's bulk.

Along the side wall of the lift was a pallet, latched in place on the "floor" where they could strap the incubator down. Loaders, smaller cousins of the unit from the docking bay, would be stationed adjacent to the lift doors at the bottom of the passageway; there would be no need to lug the weight of the incubator all the way to the ship.

And good thing, too.

As always when entering a lift from the zero-g side, the wall seemed to come up and crash into them—gently—and they found themselves pressed up against it until they pushed themselves down to the lift's "floor". The g's were not much, not yet, but they were enough to at least give them a sense of up and down. From the looks on Grant and Thomas' face, that was quite a relief.

Agrippa's rings were only a kilometer across and the loading rings had been sized to fit her, so the trip to the lower level and the main access airlocks was quite a bit quicker than the trip up the station's ring had been, as was the increase in g's. In just a couple minutes Jo found herself flexing her muscles and working her joints as they hit full Earth-normal acceleration. It felt good, but also a little awkward, even after such a comparatively short time in zero-g.

And then an electronic chime announced the lift's imminent arrival at Deck One.

Grant and Thomas unlimbered their rifles and raised them to a ready position. Malcolm did the same as Jo got the pallet unlatched from the deck. It was time to meet their fate, whatever it was.

# 53

# THROUGH THE FRONT DOOR

The lift doors opened.

Beyond lay the antechamber leading to the two personnel access airlocks in Agrippa's forward ring. Wide, spanning a good third of the loading ring's circumference, and deep, a good hundred meters or more from the lift entrance to the far wall, it was for the most part open, save for a few structural columns at regular intervals, and brightly lit by recessed lights in the ceiling. Jo had seen the personnel staging area countless times, but it always struck her, in the hours before passenger loading, as a lonely place. Sad.

Today, it struck her as ominous.

On the bright side, the wide-open area made it nearly impossible for anyone to sneak up on her group, at least from within the area that was not rendered invisible by the ring's curvature. But it also meant they would be clearly visible to any watching eyes. And there were many of those, lurking around. The company had myriad security cameras installed, covering every square centimeter of the area, or as close to it as they could. Same with the access tunnels she had just departed, and the lift. Jo had no illusions that they had somehow managed to sneak in here unobserved. Maybe if they had not been discovered earlier. But now...

For a heartbeat, she considered ordering Malcolm to hit the up button, retreating to Carl's orbital transport, and fleeing back to the planet. Just as quickly, she dismissed that thought. It was foolhardy in the extreme. There was no chance at all that they could make it back to the craft without being intercepted.

If there was any hope, it lay in moving forward, toward Agrippa. Yes, she was at a disadvantage here, but if she could get through the airlock and aboard the ship, that all changed. With the access codes Jervis' IT people had programmed in for her—codes that were, to any but the most intimately observant eye, authorized by Harold Jameson himself— she could render the ship impregnable. Or close enough to it. Close enough to get the thrusters and reactor online, and get them the hell away from here.

Hopefully.

"We going or not?"

Grant's words jerked Jo out of her reverie. She realized with a start that she had taken a step forward and was now blocking everyone else's path. Flashing him an apologetic smile, she darted out of the lift and turned left to where the loaders should be parked.

She expected... Well, she was not sure what she expected. But silence and a complete lack of action was not it.

As she cleared the lift doors, Grant and Thomas surged forward. They spread out wide to the left and right, sweeping the area over the sights of their rifles. After a few seconds, they glanced at each other. Despite being separated by a good fifty meters, they seemed to communicate complete sentences with the slightest expression; a second later, Grant waved her and Malcolm onward.

She hopped up into the loader—thank God it hadn't been moved— then carefully drove it into the lift car and slipped its arms under the pallet holding their precious cargo. Backing up out of the lift, she looked over her shoulder.

Malcolm looked decidedly awkward with his rifle up against his shoulder as he watched her back the loader up, but he wore the grim expression of a man who means to do business with a weapon. Right then, Jo could not tell how much was feigned and how much real.

Jo cleared the lift door, and turned the loader hard to the left and depressed the loader's accelerator, pressing the machine to greater speed toward the hatch at the far end of the room. It led to the extendable tunnel that linked up with the airlock in Section Four of Agrippa's forward ring, Ring A. That was the section that housed the crew living spaces during cruise flight, and the alternate control station. From there, she would have the same controls as existed on the bridge, which was located on Agrippa's hub. She could start up the reactor, engage the maneuvering thrusters, burn the main engines...whatever she needed. And it was only a few hundred meters away.

They advanced steadily, Grant and Thomas on the flanks, Malcolm at her side, the loader humming along nicely. As they drew within twenty meters of the airlock hatch, Jo imagined that they would meet no further opposition. That Chandini had been so flummoxed by their trick on the lift that she had not been able to re-deploy her forces in time to intercept Jo and her team. They were going to get aboard Agrippa, Grant and Thomas as well as Malcolm and her, and make a clean getaway, and then it was off to the stars, and no more worrying, no more grief and concern. She would return the aliens' babies home and be regarded a hero by alien and human alike.

If only.

---

THEY WERE CLOSE, less than twenty meters away from the airlock hatch, when Jo heard it.

Booted feet. Running. And getting louder.

She glanced aside and, past the curvature of the floor, saw a flicker of movement off to the right. Looking left, the same, except the flickering became figures running toward her party. Figures that were dressed in black assault gear, body armor and everything, and carrying rifles. About a dozen troops total; more than enough to take her little group down.

Except Jo had just seen Grant and Thomas defeat a half-dozen men, men who were presumably well trained, without effort. Maybe...

The two brothers shot glances at each other, and Jo saw the hopeless resolve on their faces. They were outmatched and the brothers knew it. They did not hesitate though, bless them.

Grant shot Jo a hard look and shouted, "Go!" And then he ran forward to meet the troops approaching from the right. Thomas took left.

Jo wanted to tell them there was still time; they could get to the airlock before the troops reached them. But she knew the truth.

Without something to hold them back, the troops would gun them all down well before she could get the door open.

So she floored the accelerator, and the loader lurched forward. It surged past Malcolm, who had broken into a run as soon as the troops came into view.

"Get on!" Jo shouted, and he obliged, leaping onto the side of the machine as it passed him.

If they had far to go, he probably would have fallen, as precarious as his perch was, but as it was they crossed the remaining distance to the airlock in just a few seconds. Even still, he looked relieved when he dropped back to the floor. Jo swung the loader around to put at least some of its bulk between them and the approaching troops and took it out of gear.

Just then, rifle fire erupted from Thomas' direction and the loud THUMP of a flash-bang echoed from Grant's. Jo looked and saw the two men crouched behind separate columns. Thomas' troops scattered in the face of his fire, darting to find their own cover while shooting back, wildly from all appearances. Two of the men approaching Grant were down, stunned by the grenade. The remaining four split up, moving two by two toward his flanks.

It was not going to take long at all to overwhelm the brothers.

"Hurry, Jo!"

Malcolm grabbed her shoulder and pulled. She slid from the driver's seat and had to catch herself to keep from sprawling out onto the floor. Irritation flashed through her, sublimating the fear that had reared up when she heard the troops coming. She almost gave him a tongue lashing, but the deadly serious expression on his face, the tightness around his eyes that bespoke his own fear, drew her up short. He was right, of course. This was no time to screw around.

She nodded to him instead and turned to the airlock control pad. He shouldered his rifle and sighted in on Thomas' troops. Maybe he could help hold them off.

Malcolm's rifle barked, but Jo paid it no heed. Fishing her old holo-card from the cargo pocket on her thigh, she pressed it against the control pad. The pad flashed a message in red: security code validation required. Now was the moment of truth. Harold's access codes should have given the IT guys all the clearance they needed to make her access codes work. It had been so logical; everyone agreed it would work, and their test runs had been flawless.

But it was one thing to hack into the system from afar so Jo could verify the codes worked on a remote workstation. This was something else entirely. If those codes did not work...

She wiped sweat from her brow and tapped in the ten digit alphanumeric code: P3R!CL3S:). Not super-inventive, that. But it was easy to remember and appropriate.

The system seemed to process the code for hours, though in truth she knew it took less than a second.

The control pad flashed green and the doors began to open. It was like being thrown a lifeline while drowning. They were in. It was going to work.

Jo glanced over her shoulder. "Malcolm, come on -" Her words stuck in her throat as she turned her head back to the now open airlock, and the tunnel beyond that led to Agrippa's outer airlock door.

Agent Moore stood just inside the doors, dressed in black combat fatigues with her hair pulled back from her face. She wore a grim expression and had her plasma pistol in hand, held at the ready and pointing right at Jo's head.

"Hello, Captain Ishikawa," she said, in a tone that would freeze molten steel.

# 54

# STANDOFF

Malcolm spun around, bringing his rifle to bear on Agent Moore, but held up short as she made a little tsking sound and flexed her fingers on the grip of her weapon. Her index finger slipped into the trigger guard; she was ready to shoot.

"Chandini would rather I take you two alive," she said, "but if you prefer otherwise..."

Another flash-bang detonated off to the right. Jo hoped that meant Grant was gaining ground against his group of troops, but right then that was the least of her concerns.

"You know," Moore said, "I thought Chandini had lost it when she deployed us up here. There was no way you would be stupid enough to show your face." She pursed her lips and gave a little shake of her head. "Guess I was wrong."

"Put down the gun, Jaqueline," Jo said in her vintage Cool Under Pressure Captain voice.

Moore snorted. "Not going to happen. You're caught; might as well admit it to yourselves now." Her lips twisted into a sneer. "So close, and yet so far."

Jo glanced toward Malcolm. He had lowered the barrel of his rifle so it aimed at the floor near Agent Moore's feet. Probably did not want to give her a reason to shoot; not a bad plan, considering there was no way she would miss at this range. All the same, it would have been nice if he were a bit more ready, just in case. She drew a deep breath and looked Agent Moore directly in the eye.

"Neither Malcolm nor I want to hurt you." The sneer returned again; she, at least could not hurt Agent Moore, and they both knew it. Jo tried another tack. "Do you even know why you're here?"

Agent Moore's eyebrow quirked upward. "I'm apprehending fugitives who - " Another burst of rifle fire from Thomas' direction, too many bursts to have just come from him, interrupted her. The multitude of shots made her lips turn upward into a small smile; her people were winning, and she knew it. She continued, " - who are attempting make a getaway after having stolen government property. Not to mention having disclosed classified material, evaded arrest, and assaulted a number of Federal officers." Again with the tsking sound. "You two are going away for a very long time." Her eyes flicked toward Malcolm. "Put down the rifle, Ngubwe, before you make me nervous."

Malcolm made no move to comply, bless him, but his rifle barrel did lower a few centimeters. His scowl would have turned Medusa to stone, but it did not phase Agent Moore in the least.

Jo shook her head. "So you really don't know." Typical, and not unexpected. Agent Moore was a worker bee. She did not need to know what was going on, not in detail. She just needed to know enough to help her catch her query. And to not ask questions beyond that.

"We encountered aliens, when we were out on Pericles."

Surprise, followed by confusion and irritation, flashed across Agent Moore's face. And was that perhaps a bit of wonder, quickly suppressed?

More gunfire, this time in Grant's direction. It was much closer now.

"They were stranded, dying. They gave us their eggs—their babies— and asked us to return them home. We turned them over to the NSA when we returned, along with the tech they gave us in payment. And do you know what Chandini did?"

"Shut up," Agent Moore said through clenched teeth. She flexed her fingers on the grip of her gun again. "Turn around and get down on your knees."

Jo did not move; she kept staring straight at Agent Moore's eyes. She had flinched a little bit at the word babies. "Chandini sent them to that lab in Australia, the one we raided the other day. They took those eggs and cut them open. Experimented on the alien babies inside and discarded them like so much rubbish." Again, the slightest of flinches. Jo took a small step forward. "Do you have any children, Jaqueline?"

Agent Moore retreated in time with Jo's advance. "Get down on your knees. Now!"

She had flinched again, even more noticeably, and her tone was suddenly less certain than it had been. So, she was a mother; rather surprising, actually. Not that she had attracted a mate, but that she had chosen to have a child. She seemed far too focused, too ruthlessly intense about her work, to have that side to her. But then, people had many layers about them, apparently even government stooges.

Jo pressed on, advancing once again. "We're not stealing from the government, Jaqueline. We're rescuing the surviving babies. Bringing them home." Time to play the trump card. "What would you want most if your child was trapped and in danger? Wouldn't you want someone to help, if she could? Wouldn't you do anything to rescue him?"

Agent Moore's hand trembled. "Her," she said softly.

Jo advanced again; she was almost within arm's reach. "If someone hurt your little girl, if he killed her and tried to claim it was in the name of science, what would you do to that person when you found out?"

Agent Moore's frown deepened. Almost too softly to hear, she murmured, "I'd kill him."

"So you see," Jo said, "we're not just trying to save these babies. We're trying to save the rest of us as well."

For a second, Jo thought she had gotten through, that Agent Moore would understand and let them past.

And then that second passed.

Agent Moore shook her head. "No," she said. And then, more strongly, she added, "No. You've broken the law. Even if you think you're doing the right thing, there are ways to go about it that don't involve doing what you've done." She drew in a breath and squared her jaw, returning Jo's stare with a determined look of her own. "Get down on your knees now, or I'll put you down." She glanced aside, toward Malcolm. "Both of you -"

Jo did not let her finish the order. No sooner had Agent Moore's eyes left her than Jo bounded forward and to her right, removing her head from the path of the pistol's barrel and aiming a roundhouse kick at Agent Moore's navel.

Agent Moore's eyes flashed in surprise and she darted away. She was quick, very quick. But not quick enough. She had only just begun to move when Jo's boot struck her. She bent over double and stumbled backward from the force of the kick, couching as the breath left her lungs.

She still clutched her pistol, though.

"Malcolm, get the loader," Jo ordered as she stepped forward and grabbed at the gun in Agent Moore's hands.

From the corner of her eye, Jo could see Malcolm hesitate for a second, clearly torn between helping her and getting their cargo to the ship. That second quickly passed and he shouldered his rifle and hauled himself up into the loader's control chair.

More rifle fire, followed by a loud cry of pain, Jo could not tell from where exactly, covered the sound of the loader's motor shifting into drive. Not that Jo had the time to pay attention to it.

Stunned as Agent Moore was, she was obviously well-trained and in control of herself. The moment Jo's hand touched the pistol, she squirmed and twisted, almost succeeding in evading Jo's grab. Only getting her second hand down around Agent Moore's wrist prevented it; as it was, the pistol came perilously close to pointing at Jo's chest before she managed to force it away.

And not a moment too soon. The pistol barked, and superheated plasma lanced out, the heat of its passage charring Jo's fatigues and causing her to grit her teeth in pain as her skin burned along her lower left ribs, and impacted with the ceiling.

Jo twisted her hips, using the force of her momentum to pull Agent Moore off her feet and send her sprawling to the floor off to Jo's side. The impact jarred the pistol loose; for a moment Jo had a hold of it, but only for a moment. Then she lost her grip and the weapon dropped away and skittered across the floor toward Agrippa's airlock.

Agent Moore noticed and tried to push herself up onto her knees, to go after it. Jo's boot in the small of her back stopped that quickly enough.

Jo pressed down, forcing the other woman to the floor, and pulled her own pistol from its holster on her hip. "Don't move, Jaqueline."

Beneath her, Agent Moore closed her eyes. "Just do it."

Jo took a second to glance behind her and saw the loader still at the mouth of the tunnel, motionless. Where - ?

And then she saw Malcolm, standing beside the loader with his arm wrapped around Grant. The fighting man was bleeding from a cut on his temple and his left sleeve was torn away, revealing a painful-looking burn that ran down most of his upper arm. He moved stiffly on his right leg, as though he was having troubling bending it.

Where was Thomas?

Malcolm met her eyes and must have seen the question there. He shook his head, his face grim.

Sorrow, and cold anger, welled up with Jo; she could see the same thing, magnified a thousandfold, in Grant's eyes beneath the physical pain. Jo's heart went out to him. She had never had a blood brother, but she had a large extended family among her fellow starfarers. She knew how it was to lose a loved one. Her eyes flickered toward Malcolm again, and she recalled the agony when he had died, those months ago. Except that he had not really died. Thomas would not come back from the dead, like Malcolm had.

But there was no time to dwell on that now. "Move it," Jo said in as commanding a tone as she could muster—and that was quite commanding, all things considered.

She turned back to Agent Moore and pressed her pistol to the back of the woman's head. Then she reached down with her left hand and felt along her waist until...there. Handcuffs. Never leave home without them. A couple seconds later, Jo had Agent Moore's hands cuffed behind her back, and she shoved her against the wall so she would be out of the way.

Then Jo hurried back to the loader, and her two comrades. From the corner of her eye, she saw disbelief on Agent Moore's face.

# 55

# PURSUIT

Rifle fire greeted Jo as she met up with Malcolm and Grant. She flattened herself again the tunnel wall and peeked out, and saw several men in black advancing quickly, those in front on one knee and laying down covering fire for those behind. She did not take time to count, but there must have been a half-dozen or more.

The fact that Grant and Thomas had taken down half the force was pretty impressive, all things considered. But not impressive enough.

"We need to get this door shut," Jo said.

The men nodded agreement. Jo took a minute to look them over. Malcolm was sound, and had his rifle. Grant was without his weapon, and badly wounded. But his eyes burned with fury and determination. Jo's own rifle lay where she had left it, up on the driver's seat; far too exposed to get it right this moment.

Jo pressed her pistol into Grant's hand then looked him and Malcolm in the eye. "Cover me. I'll get the loader in here and then we'll seal the door."

Malcolm looked as though he was going to protest, but then he nodded. Sometimes he was a very smart man. He helped Grant lean up against one edge of the door, then he took station on the other. Jo drew a deep breath and nodded.

The two men began to fire. Instantly, the advancing troops stopped. Those in the clear ducked behind the closest cover they could find. The others returned fire, but it was more sporadic than a moment before; they had to be careful not to hit their fellows as they darted out of the line of fire.

It was by no means a clear dash to the loader driver's seat, but it was only a couple of meters, and there would not be a better time to go. So Jo went.

She almost got shot immediately; a plasma ball just missed hitting her in the face, but the act of flinging herself onto the driver's boarding ladder got her head out of the way in time. Still, the heat of the passing shot singed her. Again.

Twice in less than a minute.

That was too much good luck for any one person. Jo scrunched down as tightly as she could, shoved the motor into gear, and floored it.

Fortunately, Malcolm had managed to get the loader aligned with the door before he got back down to help Grant, so flooring it was all the thing required to surge through the door into the tunnel beyond.

"Malcolm!" Jo shouted as she rocketed past him.

Nothing else needed saying. She stopped the loader and turned around on the seat in time to see the door shut as Malcolm activated the control pad on the inside of the tunnel.

Or rather, in time to see the door almost shut. The two halves of the door slid out from their housings on either side of the doorway, but very quickly began to shudder and jerk until they finally stopped with a half-meter of open space between them.

"Son of a bitch," Jo breathed. The door's operating mechanism must have been damaged by all the plasma bolts. Lucky they moved at all, if that were the case. More loudly, she said, "Malcolm, help Grant up here. That's not going to slow them down much."

Malcolm was way ahead of her. As soon as the doors began to move, he darted across the opening—and almost got shot for his effort—to Grant's side. Again looping his arm around Grant's shoulder, Malcolm half-pulled half-carried him toward Jo and the loader. He paused only for a brief moment to look back as Jo spoke. Then he breathed a curse and redoubled his effort.

In a moment they had Grant perched on the driver's seat next to Jo. She had to squeeze over, and even then he only got a very narrow bit of the seat, but it was the best they could do on short notice, and he had plenty of handholds.

"Hold on," Jo said, earning a nod from Grant and a look that screamed, "I'm not stupid." She quirked an eyebrow at him, then hit the accelerator again.

---

THREE HUNDRED METERS does not seem like much, but when you are running from a bunch of goons with guns who are intent on shooting or arresting you, it seems like forever. Or at least it did to Jo. At its best, the loader was not slow; a tad faster than the average running man. But right then it felt like she was riding a tortoise, with a half-dozen hares coming up fast from behind.

She looked back over her shoulder several times during the drive down the airlock tunnel. At first, the only things moving were Malcolm as he labored to keep up—he gave up on that early on and just hopped up onto the boarding ladder below Grant—and Agent Moore. She managed to push herself up onto her feet and got over to the inner door's control pad, but all her blind tapping at it was to no avail. The door operating mechanism must have been completely shot, because it did not move at all.

That was good.

Not good enough, though. Shortly, troops began squeezing through the gap, and soon a quartet of them joined Agent Moore in the tunnel. They paused a moment to free her hands from the cuffs, and to grab her pistol from where it had fallen—and why had Jo not thought to grab it? Then they were off at a sprint.

"Well that didn't take long," Malcolm noted, his voice tight with strain. "Where are the others? I could have sworn there were two or three more still up."

Grant adjusted himself on his precarious perch, and hissed in pain as he jarred his injured leg. "Probably going to the other personnel airlock," he said, gritting his teeth.

"Crap."

Jo ran the numbers in her head. Airlock 2 lay a quarter of the way around the ring; a walk of a little less than a kilometer. But the troops would not have to walk. The loading rings had transport trams, similar to the intra-ring transport system aboard the starliner itself. The tram would get them to the airlock entrance in a minute, maybe a little more.

Then it was a short sprint to the inner door, then three hundred meters to the junction with Agrippa.

"It's going to be close," Jo said, "but once we're onboard I'll be able to seal the ship's hatches. We should be secure, then."

"Unless they override it." Grant was always so cheerful.

Jo shook her head. "Can't do it. Safety interlocks prevent access without permission from within the ship itself."

"Ok. But they could - "

A plasma ball shot past, interrupting Grant's words and making him duck down reflexively.

"Son of a bitch," Malcolm cursed. "Are they stupid? You don't shoot rifles inside an airlock tube. It could cause a breach!"

Jo glanced back again, and saw one of the pursuing troops had lagged behind the others. He bent over to pick something up; his rifle. Looked like his fellows had upgraded him.

Jo's group was almost to the outer door, and the junction with Agrippa; just thirty meters to go.

"I'm going to need to hop off to get the door open," Jo said to Grant. "Can you drive this thing with your leg?"

He took a second or so to answer, considering. Then he nodded.

"Good." Jo shot him a half-smile. "Looks like you're coming with us after all."

He just grunted, scowled.

Fifteen meters. Ten. Five.

Jo stopped the loader and hopped off. She did not bother with the ladder; it would be too much trouble to dislodge the men, and it was not that far a drop, nothing she had not done before. So naturally, she rolled her ankle painfully as she landed.

"Dammit," she muttered.

She may have broken something - or had she just sprained it? No time to worry about that now. She forced herself to push past the pain and limped over to the control pad.

Moment of truth. Again. She swiped her holocard and entered the code again.

The screen flashed red, then a fake-sounding female voice said, "Access Denied."

Oh hell.

"What's the problem?" Malcolm asked.

Jo tried again. Maybe she had mis-typed.

"Access Denied."

"Son of a bitch," Jo said for what felt the hundredth time that day. "Their techs must have seen the code I used back there and changed it, or removed its access."

"Isn't there a backup?" Grant asked.

Jo scowled. "Just Agrippa's internal access codes. I'm not sure if they'll work out here or not."

The two men looked at her flatly. Right. Only one way to find out.

Jo replaced her personal holocard and pulled the other one, the one that IT had made specifically for Agrippa's network, from her pocket. She took a deep breath, then swiped it and entered the code.

There was a long pause. Too long. It was not going to work.

Then there was an electronic beep and the screen flashed green. The same female voice said, "Welcome Aboard. Enjoy your flight."

The door began to open. They were in.

# 56

# AGRIPPA

The relief Jo felt as she closed Agrippa's inner airlock door was palpable, like she had been carrying a couple tons and suddenly threw them off.

It only lasted a second. There were still a thousand things that could go wrong, not the least of which involved the other troops boarding Agrippa through the second personnel access airlock. If they did not just come in through the cargo airlocks. Or the airlocks in Ring B. Or if they were not already onboard the ship. Or if...

*Stop it. No time for this.*

Jo turned back to the men. Malcolm was helping Grant down from the loader, which he had parked on the far side of the airlock access parlor. It took up a good chunk of the available room; Jo was fairly certain they were not going to be able to maneuver it through the ship's corridors either. Starliners had a lot less interior volume than the Station.

"We don't have much time," Jo said, in her best no-nonsense Captain voice. "Get the reactor started up, Malcolm. Grant and I will secure the ship and get us underway."

Malcolm nodded, his expression focused. She could tell he was already stepping through the startup procedure, re-checking in his mind which steps he could reduce or eliminate altogether, how to best trim down the amount of time needed to get them up and running. "I'll be in touch," he said.

And then he was off, sprinting down the corridor toward the lift to the ship's hub and then to the reactor, two kilometers aft of the rings.

Jo did not stop to watch him go, but instead turned to the control workstation adjacent to the airlock doors. She brought it to life with a tap, then entered her access code. It had been too soon after using the code in the tunnel for it to have been compromised, or so she hoped, but all the same she experienced a moment of dread after she tapped ENTER, while the ship's network processed it.

No need. The Command Access screen popped up, and she smiled with satisfaction. From this screen, she could access all basic ship's functions. Some of the more specialized things, like starting up the maneuvering thrusters and the main engines, had to be done from the Bridge, located in the ship's hub, or in Control, here in Ring A. But this screen provided all she needed for her immediate purposes. First thing, she severed the ship's network connection with the station.

There. Now no one from outside could interfere. Or at least, it would take them some time to do so. Until she actually detached the Station Support Umbilical, there would still be a physical network connection, but it would take an IT type a fair amount of time to force a software link. Or at least that's what Shani's people had said. Here's hoping they were correct.

"How long will the startup take?" Grant asked.

"I'm not entirely sure," Jo replied absently as she tabbed through to the airlock status screen.

"What?" He sounded shocked, chagrined. "What do you mean you don't know? Don't you do," he made a sweeping gesture with his hand, "this for a living?"

Jo chuckled and gave him a wry smile. "A normal startup takes four hours." Grant's jaw dropped open, a look of dread coming over his face. Jo continued before he could interject. "But we don't have four hours, so Malcolm is going to use the emergency procedures, and skip a number of steps from them. He thinks he can have the reactor up in a half hour, maybe forty-five minutes."

Grant swallowed. "If he doesn't blow us all up."

Jo shrugged. "There is that, yes. Don't worry. Malcolm is very good at what he does."

On the display, the remaining seven ship's airlocks showed red - all were open. Jo frowned and tapped over to security, then called up the video feeds from the airlocks and their access parlors. All showed clear, except...

Jo's heart skipped a beat. The troops were clearly visible in Ring A's second airlock camera. They were sprinting down the tunnel, less than thirty meters out. In a rush, Jo tapped back to the airlock status screen and hit the command to close Airlock 2 and lock out its local controls. On the security feed, the doors began sliding closed. The troops redoubled their efforts, pushing themselves as fast as they could go.

"Come on," Jo murmured. The door was almost closed.

With a final leap, the lead trooper hurled himself through the swiftly contracting space, landing inside the airlock a heartbeat before the outer door closed. On the security feed, he lay still for a moment, then he pushed himself to his feet and rolled his shoulder, where he had landed. Then he turned toward the control pad on the wall and tapped it.

Jo smirked. Good luck with that, buddy.

The trooper tapped the control pad again, and again, clearly growing agitated when it did not respond. Then he turned around and stopped cold.

Beside her—Jo had not noticed his approach—Grant snorted. "Didn't think about the inner door, did he?"

Jo shook her head. "Apparently not." She tapped the command to close the remaining airlocks, feeling quite smug for a second.

"We're not going to just leave him in there, are we?"

The smugness faded. Grant had a point. If they left him in there, he would suffocate before too long; there were no standard ventilation ducts into the airlock, for obvious reasons, just equalization blowers. But did they dare let him aboard? He was just one man, but he could still make a lot of trouble. And fat chance he would just leave if they opened the outer airlock door for him.

Crap.

"We'll figure it out later. For now, we're secure. We need to get the incubator and loader stowed, then get up to Control so I can get us underway."

---

AGRIPPA'S CONTROL room was more spacious than on Pericles, but the basic layout was the same: support workstations at the front of the room, facing the main display screens, and the command station at the rear on a slightly raised platform. Sitting in the command chair felt like coming home, even if she *was* stealing it. That thought did not feel at all comfortable, but she pushed it from her mind. Can't make an omelet, and all that.

The maneuvering thrusters warmup procedure took five minutes. During that time, she shifted the ship's electrical loads from station power to the ship's electrical distribution system—at this point just the battery, but it had plenty of juice to keep them for a while—and opened the Shore Power Breakers. Then she secured the other connections— water, sanitation, atmospheric—and initiated the umbilical separation procedure.

Very shortly, the only thing connecting them with Gagarin Station would be the airlock tunnels. She would wait for the maneuvering thrusters before detaching them.

"Looks like they're bringing in cutting torches," Grant reported. He sat at the piloting support workstation and had brought up the security feed. The external cameras from both Airlocks 1 and 2 showed the troops bringing in a lot of heavy gear. He was right; those looked like cutters. Grant pursed his lips. "They don't have suits. Doesn't seem too smart of them. We could just pop the connection, and they'd be..." He trailed off and looked back at Jo with a faintly sick look on his face.

She could understand. It was one thing to shoot a guy. It was another to subject him to the vacuum of space. Jo once saw what happens to a person in space; she never wanted to again. The worst part is that the person would be aware, feeling his blood vessels explode all over his exposed skin, his lungs burst, his blood boil. It was a bad way to go.

"We're not barbarians," Jo said. Reaching over to her command control pad, she pulled up the communication feed to Airlock 1's external control pad. A soft beep indicated the system's readiness, and Jo looked toward a small camera mounted at eye level off to her right. "Call your men back, Jaqueline," she said.

On the security feed, Agent Moore—she had been clearly visible on the security camera, if only because she was the only one not wearing a helmet—gave a surprised jerk and whipped her head around to look at the airlock control pad. Then she walked briskly over and touched the control pad.

The sound was poor, but Jo could hear the sneer in her voice as Agent Moore responded. "Not a chance."

Jo shrugged. "It's your choice. In one minute, I'm going to open the outer door to Airlock 2, so your man can leave. Thirty seconds later, I'm breaking the soft seal between Agrippa and the Station. I highly suggest you have your outer doors closed before that happens."

Agent Moore laughed. "You'll do no such thing. Your reactor won't be ready for at least another hour," she replied, "and we control the airlock couplings."

That's what she thought. "Coupling requires linkup from both ends, Jaqueliine. Once I release mine..." She left the rest unsaid.

Agent Moore did not reply, but on the security feed Jo thought she could see uncertainty appear on her face.

Grant cleared his throat. "Not to tell you your job or anything, Captain," he said, "but she's right, isn't she? The Reactor's not up yet. Can we get underway without it?"

Jo smiled, trying to appear confident, for Grant's benefit, despite the butterflies doing flips in her stomach. What she was about to do... Well, it was not anything she would ever have considered, ever, before today. It was just not done. "The maneuvering thrusters will be online in a minute, and we have plenty of juice in the battery. We can get underway on the thrusters and get clear of the station while Malcolm finishes the startup."

Grant just stared at her for a long several seconds. "That sounds...dangerous."

Jo shrugged. "It is." That was an understatement. "But so is everything on this mission."

"Have you done this before?"

She paused. "No." Grant's face fell a bit, and Jo put on a confident smile. "We can't fully light off the main engines until we're well clear of the Earth-Luna system anyway. It'll be fine. I'm a great pilot."

Grant nodded slowly, licking his lips. He looked positively unnerved. Funny how a guy could face down a squad of armed men without flinching, but a little thing like getting underway without full propulsion sets him all on edge.

Jo snorted inwardly. It set *her* on edge. On the razor freaking edge.

What she was about to do was one hundred percent against about fifteen different procedures and regulations, precisely because it was so dangerous.

Oh well. It was not like she had not violated an ass-ton of regulations already in the last few days.

Jo hit the comms control again. "Thirty Seconds, Jaqueline. What's it going to be?"

Agent Moore did not answer. Or at least, she did not answer Jo. Her head was cocked to one side, and from time to time her lips moved; she was talking with someone; her superior most likely.

"Fifteen seconds." Jo began to feel irritated. It would be one thing if Agent Moore forced Jo to decouple, and thus kill her, as the ultimate "Fuck You" to Jo and her mission. It would be something else if Agent Moore and her troops died because she was talking too damn much!

Finally, Agent Moore nodded and touched the control pad. "You win, Captain. As soon as our man is free, we're pulling back."

Jo blew out a breath she had not realized she was holding. A second later, her command workstation beeped. Jo shifted to the airlock status control and entered the command to open Airlock 2's outer door. A moment later, the trapper trooper was back with his fellows, and Jo shut the outer door again.

The Station outer doors slid shut, and then a few seconds later Jo released the soft seal couplings.

There was a subtle change in the ship's motion, or apparent lack thereof. They were free. Almost.

# 57

# PILOTING

Maneuvering a starliner away from a Station is a slow, complicated process. Normally, the Station and ship decouple from each other simultaneously, after tugs have attached to the ship's tow points. The Station Pilot, an expert on that particular Station's quirks who augments the crew for underway and docking, issues orders to the tugs, and they carefully extract the ship from the Station's mating tunnels, which never fully retract. The ship's thrusters, much larger and more powerful than the tugs, were never used. The slow process ensured no damage would occur to either ship or Station.

Jo did not have time for any of that.

For one thing, it was not like that Station was going to just oblige and retract the mating tunnels. Oh, the Station personnel probably would - they would not want the Station damaged - but Jo doubted Chandini would allow them. To do so would be to admit defeat, or worse, to allow Jo to get away, and Jo did not see Chandini going there. Beyond that, every moment they lingered was a moment Chandini and her goons could try something else, like, for instance, an EVA into Agrippa's shuttle bay, which lay open to space. It would be damn hard to stop that, and all the mischief they could cause once inside there.

So it fell to Jo to get the ship underway. Herself. Without help.

She had never done that.

"I need to get to the bridge," Jo said. She could operate the thrusters from Control, sure. But the bridge afforded much better visibility and, frankly, she felt more comfortable trying this from there. "Are you ok to stay here?" She looked at Grant.

He looked like hell warmed over. The bleeding had stopped from his head wound, but his face was covered in clotted blood. His eyes were red and it was obvious he was in a great deal of pain: physical, and otherwise. Jo was not sure how he had not shut down completely, considering.

He nodded. "Good to go."

Jo suspected he was lying, but there really was nothing much to be done about it right then. "Ok. Keep an eye on the security feeds. Let me know if you see anything untoward." She pointed out the internal communication pad to the left of his workstation. "Use this channel to reach me."

He nodded again. "Good luck."

"Thanks."

She was going to need it.

---

Like on Pericles, Agrippa's bridge lay in a bulbous protrusion near the forward end of the ship's hub. It took a couple minutes to get there, and Jo sweated every second. But she was reasonably sure the time she spent in transit was not enough to allow Chandini to do anything too bad to throw a wrench in her plans. Hopefully.

The bridge was simply arranged: just a pilot's station forward, with ship's control and diagnostic workstations to the front and left and communications to the right, and the command station, directly behind and above the pilot. Each station was designed like a high-end lounge chair that was hard mounted to the deck, allowing no swiveling, only a forward and aft adjustment. All around the two stations was plastiglass, allowing a 360 degree azimuthal view, as well as a mostly unimpaired view upward.

Being located on the hub, zero-g ruled at the present, but that would not always be the case. During the year of acceleration away from the origin star and of deceleration as the ship approached the destination, the thrust from the main engines would create acceleration forces down the length of the ship. Since the bridge had to be used then as well, the deck around and between the two stations was tiered to act as stairs, and ladders were mounted to allow access from the bridge entrance corridor to the stations.

Jo did not like the bridge during acceleration and deceleration. Working there during that time meant sitting with your back on the floor, essentially. It could be awkward. Zero-g made it a lot easier to maneuver around.

But that was neither here nor there. Jo strapped herself into the pilot's station and keyed the internal comms channel to Reactor Control. "How we looking, Malcolm?"

Malcolm's voice came back clear and strong, but strained. "This plant is nice," he said. "A lot easier to operate than what we had on Pericles."

"Great. What's your ETA?"

There was a short pause. "Going to be another ten or fifteen minutes."

Dammit. Well, she knew getting the plant up very much quicker than normal had been a long shot. As it was, Malcolm was setting a speed record. "Ok. Report when you've completed."

"Yes, ma'am." Jo was certain she heard more than a bit of irony in that. She rolled her eyes.

Next, she keyed up the IMC, which would allow her to talk ship-wide. "All hands prep for acceleration forces. Initiating maneuvering thruster firing."

She paused, in case Malcolm or Grant had any objections. Ten seconds passed with no word. Good enough. She called up the maneuvering thruster controls and took a moment to assess the situation.

The main problem was the mating tunnels, on the Station's Loading Rings. They rotated in time with the ship's rings, being driven by their own turning motors that were synched up with the ship's upon docking. With the ship decoupled, though, The difference in mass between the ship's rings and the Stations' meant that the two sets of structures would begin to change their rates of rotation, relative to each other. Normally this would not be an issue since standard procedure entailed the Station securing rotation and retracting the rings. That did not happen this time, beyond the initial retraction that went along with decoupling. People on the station could not have stopped that if they wanted to; it was automatic, and pulled the mating tunnel back two meters away from the ship to avoid any inadvertent impact before ring retraction.

Jo looked out at the slowly moving tunnels all around her, like the bars of a great cage, and swallowed hard. There was enough mass in one of those tunnels to seriously damage Agrippa. Maybe not cripple her, but it would make driving her very difficult. Not to mention the fact that anyone within those tunnels would be seriously injured or killed by such a collision.

She was going to have to time this perfectly.

Jo reached out for the control stick but had to stop to wipe the sweat from her palm. She was more nervous than... She could not recall when she had been this nervous. Even breaking into Camp Tycho seemed routine compared with this, maybe because she really did not know all the risks involved then, the countless things that could go wrong. But here, in her own element... Jo found she was suddenly terrified.

She should not have been surprised when the communication station beeped just then, indicating the ship was being hailed. That did not stop her from all but jumping out of her seat; she might have, had she not strapped herself in. Jo glanced to the right and saw Chandini's face on the comms display. From the room behind her, she was most definitely onboard Gagarin; in the Station's Control Center unless Jo missed her guess. Unlike the last time, in the lift, Chandini did not look the least bit pleased, or amused. If anything, her expression could be said to indicate a towering fury.

At least she did not look so damn smug anymore.

Jo considered ignoring the hail. But decades of underway etiquette, and no small amount of curiosity, rebelled against that. So she reached over and tapped the console, accepting the hail.

"Deputy Director," Jo said, nodding in greeting. She kept her tone neutral, professional. Might as well keep things cordial, if possible.

"I applaud your determination, but this madness has gone quite far enough, Captain," Chandini said. "Recouple that ship immediately and surrender yourselves."

"Why on Earth would I do that?"

"Jo." Harold's voice intruded into to the conversation. The camera zoomed out a little, and Jo saw him sitting next to Chandini. He looked stressed, worried. He looked to be in handcuffs. "Do as she says, Jo. Please."

Jo sat still, stunned into silence.

"You are surprised to see Mr. Jameson." Chandini said it as a statement of fact. "You should not be. He is in custody because of you."

Bullshit. "Harry had nothing to do with this. He didn't know - "

Chandini chuckled softly. "Someone has to be held responsible. If you make your grand getaway," she said that with oceans of sarcasm, "which you will not, I assure you, the responsibility falls to him." Her lips turned upward in a vicious little smile. "The burden of command. But then, you know all about that, don't you Captain?"

Jo swallowed. So that was how it was going to be. Emotional blackmail. "And how are you going to explain that one?"

"The story writes itself. A corrupt corporate executive plots with his underlings to steal a multi-billion credit ship with the intent of selling it to the black marketeers on Muir Solace. A pity he got caught before he could meet his compatriots in orbit." Her brow furrowed. "And a still greater pity that his accomplices were killed when they refused orders to surrender and heave to." She shook her head. "The CO of the warship in pursuit received a nice decoration and promotion, though. And McAllister's insurance more than covered the loss."

Chandini's words caused a hollow feeling in the pit of Jo's stomach. Of course they would send a warship. She had considered that possibility, and discounted it as being too public, impossible to cover up. Apparently she should not have. Agrippa had no weapons, save for small arms for the crew in case of an encounter with pirates or some internal disturbance. There was no way they could fight off a warship, if one was vectored at them.

The only hope would be to outfly it. Jo did not place much hope there, but it was all she had.

"Thank you for the warning," she said, then looked at Harold. "I'm sorry, Harry." And she meant it. The pain she felt, knowing he was going to take the fall for this, was like a knife in the heart. But she could not turn back. Whatever slim hope she had here, aboard Agrippa, there was no hope at all in surrender.

She looked away from the Comms display and tapped the control stick to port. The starboard side thrusters fired, ever so briefly, pressing

Jo against the side of her seat for a moment, and Agrippa began to move laterally.

"Jesus Christ," someone said in the Control Station behind Chandini. "She's actually fucking doing it!"

"Retract the Loading Rings," ordered an authoritative voice, causing Chandini to spin around.

"No!" she ordered. "Do not touch those controls." Her voice was command itself, and would brook no objections.

But, bless him, the Station Commander—it could only be him, and it *was* a he on Gagarin, a pleasantly efficient fellow whose name Jo could not remember just then—raised an objection anyway. "But ma'am, if she hits those rings, it could destroy the ship and the loading rings both. We'd be risking a hull breach, depressurization..."

"Then the ship gets destroyed," Chandini snapped. She jabbed a finger at him, or at least Jo assumed it was a finger, it was hard to see from the angle. "If you touch those controls you will never see the outside of a prison cell, I promise you."

Silence, the kind of silence that only comes from sudden fear, followed her words. Chandini watched them all for a long several seconds, then turned back to Jo. Her lips were pressed together in a thin, angry line. "Have it your way, Captain."

Just before the comms display went dark, Jo thought for a moment that she saw the faintest shadow of a smile on Harold's face.

---

Jo HAD no time to dwell on the future, whether hers or Harold's. The ship was moving, and the rings were getting closer.

She had been very careful to apply only lateral thrust, and was gratified to see the ship slipping easily away in a straight line from its moored position. That was the first place the maneuver could go wrong, but a quick look around showed that the mating tube couplings had cleared the ship's rings cleanly, at least for the moment. While the port side of the ship was clear, the hub and the starboard side still were in danger.

The hub was the key problem. As long as she did not impart any forward or aft thrust, the starboard side of the rings should clear just fine. The hub, though... Go too slowly, and the mating tunnels would strike the hub straight on. The tunnels were not particularly resilient, and Agrippa's hub had been built to withstand up to 1.5g's of acceleration. But that was mostly in the bulkhead structure. The skin of the ship was relatively thin, to conserve on mass. There was a good chance that a direct impact could breach the hull in several locations, and if that happened...

No sense dwelling on it.

The ship slipped further to port, the hub drawing ever closer to the rotating tunnels. Fortunately, there were only four of them. But...were they speeding up?

Her eyes did not deceive her. The loading rings' rotation had begun to speed up markedly, and showed no signs of stopping. Jo hoped they had cleared all personnel out of them before doing that. Already the g's would be well above Earth-normal. Too much more, and they could injure people.

It would also make Jo's task that much harder. It was one thing to time a constantly moving object. An accelerating object, though...

This was going to be bad.

One hundred meters.

Sweat trickled down Jo's brow and she wiped it away with annoyance. It was just flying.

Fifty meters. One of the tunnels was approaching.

Twenty meters. The tunnel swooped down through her field of vision, passing the hub to port. The next one was coming up quickly. It was now or never.

Jo applied port thrust, a long drawn out burn that pressed her against the side of her seat again for several seconds. Agrippa began moving more quickly, shooting for the gap.

Jo looked up and saw the next tunnel sweeping down toward her at what appeared to be great speed. She cringed; if it struck, it would crush the bridge, and her with it, like an aluminum can. Better than dying in a vacuum.

The tunnel passed directly overhead, perilously near now. Jo braced herself. It would hit in a second.

And then it was past, sweeping down the starboard side of Agrippa's hub with maybe centimeters to spare. If this had been an old science fiction movie, she would have expected a WOOSHING sound, and just then, ludicrous as such a sound effect was in space, it seemed like it would be more fitting than the silent brush with death that had just occurred.

Jo breathed a sigh of relief and applied port thrust again, and, just like that, the starboard side rings were clear as well.

It was time to get the hell out of here.

# 58

# EVASION

Jo keyed the 1MC. "The ship has cleared the Station. All hands report status."

Almost immediately, Grant's voice came over the circuit. "I about knocked myself silly on that last maneuver, but I'm ok."

"Any sign of mischief?"

"No, looks like we're clear."

"Ok. Sit tight. Malcolm will be along in a couple minutes."

"No worries."

Jo turned Agrippa away from Gagarin Station and applied forward thrust, putting the ship on a vector away from the inner solar system in the general direction of Leo, where the aliens' homeworld lay. Then she called up the navigation system and began entering their course data.

A moment later, Malcolm called up. "Reactor's hot, Jo. You should have main propulsion in three minutes."

Tension left her in a rush. That was the final obstacle. With the mains online, the only thing standing between her and success was two hundred sixty-three light years, and a long, long nap. Unless they really sent a warship. Jo keyed the aft radar system and trained the aft upper camera toward Gagarin's upper moorings, where the Navy kept their ships.

No signs of movement up there. Maybe it was just a bluff.

Yeah right. They were not that lucky.

"Ok," Jo said into the comms circuit. "Go back to Control and help

Grant up to the acceleration quarters. Report as soon as you're there and I'll secure ring rotation. We may have to burn the mains early."

The second's pause before Malcolm replied spoke volumes. "This close to the planet?"

He was right to question. The main engines put out one hell of a lot of thrust, and left quite a wake of highly energetic particles behind them. Burning too close to a planetary body could wreak havoc with the planet's ionosphere. On a highly populated planet like Earth, that could translate to all sorts of problems: power losses on orbiting ships and platforms, and maybe on the ground as well, outright destruction of smaller electronics systems, fires, that sort of thing. On the plus side, it would also make for one hell of an aurora for those on the ground.

"I'd rather not, but Chandini just called and threatened to send a warship if we don't heave to, so..." She left the rest unsaid.

"Roger. We'll be up in a few minutes."

* * *

"Starliner Agrippa, this is the United Earth Ship Bunker Hill. You are ordered to heave to and prepare to be boarded, over."

The hail came in loud and clear over the primary intrasystem hailing frequency. Jo had expected to hear it, and dreaded it. But part of her had held out hope that maybe, just maybe it would not happen.

But when, an hour earlier, she gained radar contact on a vessel closing from astern, she knew that hope was false. The ship's velocity exceeded hers, and would continue to for quite some time unless she burned the mains, as small as the acceleration from the maneuvering thrusters was.

She trained the aft lower camera toward the approaching vessel, and cringed.

It was a warship, all right. To the uninitiated, it would be difficult to tell the difference between it and Agrippa, but to Jo's experienced eye it was obvious. The boxy bow, containing the ship's missile battery. The plasma turrets on swivel mounts in three clusters along the length of the hub. The boxy section just aft of the ship's rings—the ship's hangar bay, where it kept its compliment of fighter craft. All pointed to that ship being a one hell of a destructive platform.

On the bright side, interstellar travel being as long and arduous as it was, the typical warship was not equipped for journeys outside the solar system; its fuel and consumables capacity was limited, though it could accelerate a hell of a lot faster than Jo could onboard Agrippa, that was for sure. Its limited range was a small comfort. If it caught her before she could get to an appreciable velocity—and it would—she was screwed.

"Well, crap," Jo muttered.

She keyed the comms circuit down to the crew's acceleration quarters, where Malcolm and Grant were waiting in the mess. "We've got company," she said.

"Warship?" It was Grant. He sounded more energetic than before, more focused. Malcolm had been able to use the hours since their departure from Gagarin to better treat his wounds and get some food—and coffee—into all of them. Jo felt a lot better, as well.

Or at least she *had*.

"Yep. The Bunker Hill."

"Fuck." Silence followed for a few seconds. "We'll be up in a minute."

True to his word, Grant hobbled up the ladder from the bridge access corridor a few minutes later. Malcolm helped him along, but he did surprisingly well, considering his injuries. Well, maybe not that surprising. They were only accelerating at 0.3 g's.

"So, you gonna do some of that pilot shit, or what?" Grant gave her a snarky little grin that did not carry to his eyes. He might look better, and be acting better, but he was still hurt. Badly. And not just physically.

"Hope so," Jo replied, trying a confident smile in return. "The timing is going to be tricky, though." She looked at Malcolm. "Are we all stowed belowdecks?"

He nodded. "The incubator's mounted in one of the cargo bins, just like we did before, and the loader's strapped down. I rigged up a power feed to the incubator, so it should be fine for as long as it needs to be." Which would be quite a long time, hopefully.

Jo nodded, satisfied. That had been Malcolm's other project since their getaway from the Station. It would not do to have the incubator flung around willy nilly as they accelerated and decelerated during their transit to the aliens' star system. The cargo bins were mounted on pivots that shifted with the acceleration forces on the ship, so the cargo was always facing "downward". It made for a better passage that way, and a *much* better offload and unpacking.

"Ok then. Let's surrender."

Their plan was risky. Damn risky. But it was the only one any of them could come up with. Jo secured the maneuvering thrusters and then turned to the comms panel and responded, "Bunker Hill, this is Agrippa. Roger. I have secured my thrusters, over."

The warship's only reply was a terse acknowledgment.

---

BUNKER HILL TOOK station five kilometers off Agrippa's port quarter.

She looked tiny, especially at that distance. And compared with Agrippa, she was. Warships did not need the cargo and consumables capacity of starliners, so while Agrippa measured two and a half kilometers long, Bunker Hill probably measured a half kilometer, total. Consequently, her rings were smaller and rotated quite a bit faster than Agrippa's. But just because she was smaller did not mean she was not tough.

Jo frowned. Five kilometers was a bit further out than she hoped they would get, but it should not matter. Anything inside ten would work. Theoretically.

"Agrippa, this is Bunker Hill, over."

Jo keyed the comms circuit. "Agrippa."

"Standby to receive our boarding party, Agrippa. We intend to come along your port side to your hangar bay and mate up there, over."

Like hell. But she was not going to tell *them* that. "Roger, Bunker Hill. We look forward to seeing you."

"I'm surprised they don't have any fighters out," Malcolm mused, from where he floated to her left.

Jo found herself in agreement, but Grant smirked and shook his head. "No need for fighters to take a pig like us. Standard procedure is to hold them in reserve for dealing with smaller, more maneuverable targets. Besides, no ship captain worth his salt is going to turn over capturing a prize like us to a couple of flyboys. He would never live it down."

Jo looked at him askance; Malcolm did the same.

"What? I had friends in the Navy, once upon a time."

Jo rolled her eyes. Whatever the reason, she was glad for the lack of fighter cover. Had Bunker Hill put fighters out, their plan stood exactly zero chance of working. As it was, Jo figured they had a fifty-fifty shot.

She looked back at the camera display, which was zoomed in tight on Bunker Hill. The ship had one of her plasma turrets trained in their direction, but aside from that, it could have been just sitting there, for all Jo could tell.

"How long to launch the shuttle, do you think?"

Malcolm shrugged. "Five minutes, probably."

"Ok. Go strap yourselves in. We'll be doing some wild maneuvers here."

Malcolm and Grant grinned nervous but excited smiles. The three of them shook hands, and then the two men left the bridge.

Jo pulled the straps tight around her shoulders and adjusted herself in the pilot's seat. It seemed to take forever, but just a minute later, Malcolm called up on the intercom.

"All set."

"Roger. Standby for g's."

She looked back at the camera display. A moment later, a small craft launched from the belly of Bunker Hill: their shuttle, no doubt. It pivoted and fired thrusters, making a beeline for Agrippa. Jo watched the turret closely, hoping and praying that it would...

There. The turret was training away as the shuttle came into its line of fire. Blue on blue makes for a bad day, and all that.

It was time.

Jo grabbed the control stick and initiated maximum thruster burn, pivoting Agrippa's stern until it pointed directly at Bunker Hill. Then she hit the main engine controls.

Full Thrust.

A deep rumbling sound filled the ship and sudden acceleration, well past Earth-normal, pressed Jo back into her seat.

She looked at the camera, still trained on Bunker Hill, and smiled thinly as the ship was obscured by Agrippa's brilliant white wake.

It was not a plasma gun, but it was almost as good. Agrippa's main engines worked by accelerating a large number of charged particles to high relativistic velocities and then channeling them through narrow nozzles in the main engine nacelles. Even if Bunker Hill had a warning, she would not have been able to avoid the wake, as fast as it was traveling, not at that range.

Best case, and Jo fervently hoped they got the best case, the stream of particles would knock them for a loop, taking out their primary systems and causing havoc with their electronics. Worst case...

Well, Jo did not really want to think about it, but worst case, the ship might get torn apart. But that was only likely if she was close. Real close.

Jo grabbed the stick and pulled back, and the maneuvering thrusters pitched Agrippa up ninety degrees, back toward their desired heading and accelerating all the way. As they gained distance and bearing from the encounter site, Jo slewed the aft upper camera back toward Bunker Hill.

She was just emerging from the glowing wake, turning end over end, out of control. The missile battery forward was twisted, like some great fist had punch it from the side, knocking it askew. One of the rings was venting; Jo could see a stream of gasses leaking out. Quite a large stream, actually. Jo cringed. She hoped the ship's interior bulkheads had held, otherwise they were in trouble.

Regardless, that crew had enough to deal with that they were not going to bother Jo and crew anytime soon.

There was no sign of the shuttle.

Guilt crashed onto Jo's shoulders. She had very likely just killed a bunch of people. Dozens, maybe more. The fact that it was necessary, that she had no choice in the matter, did not help. It was one thing to know that people under her command, Grant and Thomas, had killed some people during their mission. They had taken pains to avoid it if they could, using flash-bangs and the like, but she had no doubt some of the troops on Gagarin had been killed.

It was something else when she did it herself.

She was unprepared for it. Completely unprepared.

She was crying. She hated it, but she was. There was no time for this. But she kept right on crying, nonetheless, and did not stop for a long time.

# 59

# ASLEEP BENEATH THE STARS

Jo tapped the cryo-suspension tank's control panel and its semi-transparent lid slid up into place with a soft click. Grant was already asleep, looking peacefully at rest. It was more peaceful than he had appeared in days. Jo glanced to the cryo tank next to Grant's, where Malcolm lay asleep, his tank's lid already frosted over.

She smiled slightly and whispered, "See you in seventy years or so." Then she turned away.

She stood alone in the cryo chamber for a moment, looking at the long line of tanks that normally would house Agrippa's entire crew for the periods of her journey when they were not asleep. Dozens of tanks, crammed closely together to save on space. And only two in use. Three, momentarily.

The pain of her guilt for what she had done to Bunker Hill's crew still hung on Jo like a heavy cloak, but she had herself back under control. It took a while, and she had remained on the bridge alone until the worst of it passed. In that time, she adjusted the engine settings to achieve the normal 1 Earth-Normal g acceleration and verified their course to the aliens' home system was laid in correctly, then she went below to rejoin Malcolm and Grant.

They ate a small victory feast. Although victory was probably not the right word for it, considering how much they had paid to get where they were, and the fact that even now there was a good chance their mission would still end in failure. But there was cause for celebration nonetheless, so they managed.

The following hours contained a myriad of tasks to prepare the ship for their long slumber, from programing the vegetation feeding cycles in hydroponics to securing power and supplies to the cryo-suspension tanks they were not going to use—and there were a lot of them, over five thousand total. The preparations were tiring, but no one complained. They would soon get more than enough sleep to compensate for it.

Jo stepped over to the display screen on the wall near the cryo chamber's door and, one last time, called up the navigation system. The course looked good. Programmed wakeup contingencies were all proper, as was the final arrival wakeup point. Consumable stores were more than sufficient for the trip, and there was no sign of any further pursuit on the sensors. They were, it seemed, in the clear. There was nothing else for her to do but go to sleep.

And yet she was strangely reluctant. Something felt undone, somehow. But rack her mind though she did, Jo could not think of what.

*It's just nerves. Leftover stress from the last few weeks.*

And that was very likely true. She had never been all that good at winding down, and she had been strung out on stress for as long as she could remember lately, it seemed. It was time to put all that aside. Time for rest before the real challenge: meeting the aliens. Explaining, somehow, what had happened.

*Yeah, that's the perfect way to stop being stressed out, thinking about that.*

Jo shook her head and snorted at herself. Enough delaying.

She slid off her fatigues and undershirt, all the way to her bra and panties. Then she slipped into her cryo tank and pulled the thermal blanket up over her body.

This was the part she hated, but she always insisted on being the last one in; it seemed fitting, as Captain. So she had long ago taught herself how to insert her own IV and hook up her own EKG and EEG probes. Finally, she strapped the breathing mask over her face and tapped the control pad—there was one built into the interior of every tank as well as an exterior one, just for this reason. Gas began flowing into her breathing mask and she felt a cool fluid enter her veins from the IV.

Immediately she began to feel drowsy. As always—and she had never been able to stop herself from doing this—she fought the feeling, trying to remain conscious and alert. But the drugs won out, as they always did.

The last thing she saw before drifting off was the tank's lid sliding shut.

# WAKEUP CALL

Electronic beeping slowly intruded on Jo's consciousness. Faint at first, but gradually growing louder, it penetrated her slumber first in her subconscious, evoking odd dreams of being followed by an eternally beeping robot. Slowly, as she began to wake, the fact that she was dreaming registered. People don't dream in cryo-suspension.

Her eyes fluttered open.

The lighting in the cryo chamber was dim to allow her eyes to adjust. Months, or in her case years, of slumber necessitated a gradual return to normal activity. But there was light enough to see, so she found the control pad easily enough. She tapped the controls and, with an audible click and a soft hiss as the tank's atmosphere equalized with the rest of the ship, the tank's lid slowly opened.

Pulling the electrodes from her chest and head, Jo sat up and stretched. She felt weak, weaker than she had ever felt when coming out of cryo-suspension. But then, to her knowledge, no one had ever been under for as long as she had. The massage units in the chamber, though adequate to prevent muscle atrophy during shorter journeys, clearly were not able to prevent it completely during her long slumber.

She managed to stand without too much difficulty and looked around. Malcolm and Grant were still asleep, per the planned wakeup sequence. The Captain is always the last to sleep and first to rise, at least on Jo's ship.

Jo hobbled over to the wall console. She almost fell twice; only reaching the wall and leaning a hand against it stopped her from collapsing completely there at the end. She was in bad shape.

She tapped the display to life and was unable to suppress a feeling of anxiety. The fact that she was standing on the wall that was in line with the longitudinal axis of the ship, and not standing on the ring's outer wall or floating, meant that the engines were firing, decelerating the ship. But were they decelerating at the right star system?

The navigation status display flashed onto the screen, and Jo breathed a sigh of relief. Ship's position plotted exactly on the projected course. They were about three days from the outskirts of the aliens' star system, with twelve hours left on the deceleration burn.

Plenty of time.

She forced herself erect and slowly, carefully, maneuvered over to Malcolm and Grant's tanks and checked their status: five minutes remained on their wakeup cycle.

As their tanks slowly thawed and the two men began the usual pre-waking movements, Jo ran through everything that needed to be done to prepare for the meeting in her mind. There was a lot to do, but the tasks were mostly everyday, easily accomplished. That did not make any of it less important, though.

Soft hisses from each tank announced their opening. Jo put on a smile of greeting as the men groggily rubbed at their eyes and sat up, working their jaws slowly to work the dryness from their mouths. Malcolm was the quicker to throw his feet out of his tank and stand up, but then he had done this countless times.

"Morning, Jo," he said, flashing a grin at her. Then he pushed himself up onto his feet and his knees promptly buckled beneath him.

Jo rushed over and put an arm around his shoulder to help him to his feet. "Easy. Take it slow," she said, as though she was not in about the same shape he was.

Slowly, she got Malcolm up on his feet. He leaned back against the side of his tank and smirked in embarrassment. Jo turned to check on Grant.

And found him siting upright, his feet dangling over the edge of his tank. He was leaning forward slightly, his palms resting on the side of the bed next to his knees. He looked a little green.

"It's normal to feel a little bit queasy," Jo said, trying to sound soothing. "Especially your first time."

He nodded and flashed a slight grin at her. "I'll be ok," he said.

Then he doubled over and threw up onto the floor.

---

THE FIRST THING Jo did after she, Grant, and Malcolm dressed was go up to the bridge and initiate a full forward sensor scan.

Then she went below to eat breakfast.

You do not know hunger if you have never come out of cryo-suspension. And this was the longest cryo-sleep in history; her stomach felt like a black hole had taken up residence.

She hurried to the mess, still a bit wobbly on her feet, and found Malcolm and Grant hard at work snarfing down as much food as they could. None of it fresh, of course, but even powdered and freeze dried tastes like a king's feast after a long cryo-sleep.

"Do you think the plants survived?" Jo asked in between bites of something that tasted of strawberries but was certainly not.

Malcolm shrugged. "With no one to tend them for so long?" He paused, considering. "They probably overgrew their containers a long time ago. Could be at least some of them are ok still. We'll see." He took a bite of his food, chewed with relish and swallowed with a grin. "Grant and I will check on them, and on the other supplies, after this. I presume you'll be on the bridge."

Jo nodded. Wild horses could not keep her away from the bridge for long, not now.

Malcolm chuckled.

Jo took another bite and looked at Grant. He sat silently, eating slowly and with little sign of relish.

Physically, he looked great. His time in cryo-suspension had healed his wounds from the assault on Gagarin; Jo could hardly see the scar on his temple and forehead and he had only a slight limp to show from his leg wound. Aside from a smattering of grey above his ears that had not been there before—ah the joy of aging while sleeping away the flight— he looked the same man Jo had met, all those trillions of kilometers and decades before. But he was subdued, more than the serious, businesslike manner he had about him before. If she did not know better, Jo would say he was depressed.

"You ok?" Jo asked.

Grant looked up from his plate and shrugged slightly. "Just thinking." He paused, frowning slightly as though unsure whether, or how, to proceed. Then he shrugged again. "I wonder what Thomas would think about all this, if he was here."

The question took Jo by surprise, though it really should not have. They may have slept away years, but the passage of those years did not heal the mind the way that their passage in a waking state would. Jo knew that for a fact; just thinking back to the events that led up to Thomas' death brought to mind Bunker Hill, and her crew members who had died at Jo's hand. It was like a knife in the gut still, because she had not really had the time to heal.

Neither had Grant.

Jo forced the surge of guilt and regret down ruthlessly and glanced at Malcolm. He sat quietly, chewing on his food with a pensive expression. He did not look like he had anything to add.

"I don't know, Grant. I," Jo paused to find the right words. "I think he would be proud."

"Yeah, probably." Grant swallowed and looked at the food on his plate for a moment, then sighed and stood, pushing the plate away. He looked at Malcolm and quirked an eyebrow at him. "You ready to do this?"

Malcolm looked surprised. He glanced at Jo quickly, and she gave a little nod. Better to keep Grant busy, if he really was depressed.

Malcolm swallowed down a gulp of water and stood. "Let's go."

The two men took their plates to the sanitizer, then strode out of the mess. As they passed, Malcolm gave Jo a little smile and a wave.

Jo watched them go, concern for Grant weighing on her mind almost as much as her guilt. Almost.

---

JO MADE her way back to the bridge and settled into the command seat. She frowned at the active sensors display, suppressing a surge of annoyance at the lack of results. But then, they were a number of light-hours away still; the returns from her radar sweep would not make it back to the ship for some time.

That did not preclude a passive search, though. Jo keyed in a standard spectral analysis sweep from the two aft observation cameras—she would have preferred to use the forward cameras, which would not have the ship's wake to contend with, but the stern faced the star system, so the forward cameras would not be of much use—and settled back to wait on the results.

A few minutes later, the intercom beeped and Malcolm's voice came through. "Hydroponics is a total loss," he said.

Well. That put a damper on things. "There's nothing retrievable at all?"

"Not enough to make it worthwhile. We'll have to pull the emergency stock from cryo and replant everything."

Jo frowned. That would be a long, involved bit of work, and neither she nor Malcolm was a botanist. Grant certainly would not know his way around a hydroponics plant; very few of the planetbound had a clue about that sort of thing. But then, Grant was not really planetbound anymore, was he?

Curious thought, that.

"Alright. Go ahead and get started. We've got," she glanced at the ship's status display, "nine hours left on the burn. See what you can get done in that time."

"Aye aye," Malcolm replied. The intercom went dead.

Jo spared a minute to consider their situation. The hydroponics gardens supplied most of the food for the crew. Most of the plants were high protein content, and used to make sim-meat—it was a lot more tasty than the planetbound Jo described it to assumed—and the other staples that saw them through.

But the ships carried freeze-dried stores and protein paste tubes for emergencies. The stock should last a good long time.

More importantly, the gardens were the ship's primary atmospheric processing system, scrubbing the $CO_2$ from the crew's exhalations and replenishing the oxygen supply. There were backup chemical systems, and water stores that could be broken down to bleed oxygen back into the air, but their capacities were limited. If Malcolm was not able to restore at least some of the garden, they could have a real problem for the long-term. It helped that her crew was so very small, but it still warranted attention.

Later.

For now, the immediate concern was their mission. Long-term survival was important, but there was a greater than zero chance they would not survive the meeting with the aliens. Making sure that meeting went well, or even went at all, ranked a bit higher on the priority list.

# 61

# ANNOUNCING ONE'S PRESENCE

The aliens' star dominated the bridge's forward observation window. The window was designed to automatically polarize itself to minimize glare from outside, but that ended up blacking out a significant portion of the window. Just as well that starships weren't normally flown from visual cues.

It had been a busy day.

Jo, Malcolm, and Grant spent most of the day working in hydroponics, with just a brief interruption when the main engines cut off, right on schedule. Jo took a few minutes to maneuver the ship to point the system. Then she initiated ring rotation and went back to work with Malcolm and Grant.

They made good progress, uprooting a good third of the dead plants. They would not be able to re-plant for some time; thawing from cryofreeze was a long, delicate process that, if not done correctly, would kill their precious seeds. It was not something Jo had any intention of rushing. Besides, the sheer immensity of Agrippa's interior volume meant they had plenty of time before air quality became a concern, and the emergency rations would last the three of them for months. They could afford to be deliberate.

The three of them were in the crew's mess, enjoying a meal of protein paste, when a warbling alert from the ship's status display on the wall grabbed Jo's attention.

Jo swallowed and exchanged looks with Malcolm and Grant, a sudden mixture of excitement and apprehension flooding her.

"Sensor data's ready," Malcolm said with a quirked eyebrow.

Jo nodded; she had set the alert specifically for that eventuality.

They wasted no time, running out of the mess to the lift for the bridge.

Looking at the polarized window, Jo smirked. They could have done this from Control. But there was just something about being up on the bridge. The enhanced visibility of it just seemed a more appropriate place for a journey of discovery. And besides, the bridge was located on the ship's hub, not in one of the rings. With the main engines secured, they could enjoy zero-g for a time, something they could not partake in on the rings. Might as well have a bit of fun while they could.

"Let's see what we have," she said, and tapped the sensor analysis display to life.

Her earlier passive scan revealed that it was a binary star system. She should not have been surprised by that; far more systems were binary than single-star. But the system's primary star—G-type, with about ten percent greater mass than Sol—out-shined its brown dwarf partner so completely that Jo missed the dwarf with her naked eye.

That was all well and good, but Jo wanted planetary data, and the passive sweep had been inconclusive for planets, except for one probable gas giant at the outer edge of the system's Goldilocks Zone. If there had been more time, she could have gotten more data passively, but the analysis required to eek out planetary effects on the star was a long process.

Which was why they had been awaiting the active radar scan so eagerly.

The computer took a few seconds to compile the data. The system chart, when it popped up, turned Jo's blood to icewater.

"Oh crap," she breathed.

Four planets. The gas giant they had already found and three worlds that were likely rocky but also were far too close to the stars to support life, or at least life like humans or the aliens she had encountered on Pericles. And that was it.

"What do you mean, oh crap?" Grant said.

"Where is it?" Malcolm asked, right on his heels.

Jo shook her head.

"Where is what?" Real fear was in Grant's voice. He was completely out of his element, and if Jo and Malcolm had reason to be worried, how much worse would it be for him?

Jo drew in a deep breath. "The aliens' homeworld. It should be here, but..." She trailed off, mystified.

Grant's eyes widened and he went pale. "It's not here?" He was almost shouting now, and Jo could not blame him. "How could it not be here?"

Jo shook her head. "I know we read the star map correctly." She glanced at Malcolm. "Didn't we?"

He spread his hands helplessly.

"Oh God," Grant said. He pushed himself away from the command station and floated over to the rear of the bridge. He ran his hand through his hair and looked around frantically at the expanse of space all around them. "Oh shit." He was about to lose it.

"Grant," Jo said, moving over to him. "It's ok. Relax."

In a flash of movement, Grant grabbed her by the collar of her underway coveralls. Before she knew what was happening, her shoulders slammed painfully into the plastiglass of the port side observation window. Grant stared at her through eyes that were narrowed into angry, almost murderous, slits.

"We risked everything for this. My brother *died* for this. And now, these fucking alien critters AREN'T HERE???" The last came out in a roar of fury, and of pain so deep Jo felt for a moment she might drown in it of her own accord.

She opened her mouth to reply, but what was there to say? Apparently, she had been wrong, oh so wrong, in her analysis of everything. Maybe the aliens had not meant for them to bring the eggs here. Maybe...

No, that made no sense. She had looked the alien leader in the eye as he—she?—made his request. As he gave them payment. The message could not have meant anything else. Could not! She must have misread the star map. There was no other explanation that made sense.

Jo began to apologize, but Malcolm interrupted.

"You two might want to take a look at this." He sounded calm and cool, as though nothing untoward was going on in the slightest.

Grant gave a little jerk and looked away from Jo, his eyes still seething. "What?" he demanded. His expression said clearly that once he was done with Jo, Malcolm would be the next target of his ire.

Malcolm stood—floated really—with his arms at his side, his face a mask of calm. He gestured toward the sensor display.

Slowly, agonizingly slowly, Grant let up the pressure on Jo's shoulders. He pushed himself away and bobbed over to Malcolm's side.

Jo took a moment to compose herself; her limbs were shaking and she felt a fright she had not experienced in some time. Even her brawl with Agent Moore had not called up this much fight or flight response. But then, she had gone into it reasonably sure she had a chance against Moore. With Grant... Jo did not deceive herself. She had some residual skills from her studies as a youth, but Grant was a trained expert. If he really meant to do her ill, she would not be able to stop him.

She shuddered, then drew a deep breath and forced herself to calm. Well, mostly calm. Then she maneuvered toward the two men.

"I don't get it," Grant said. "What am I looking at?" The fury, the terror, was gone from his voice, replaced by puzzlement and curiosity.

Malcolm smiled ever so slightly and turned his gaze on Jo. "A moon," he said. "One of the gas giant's moons."

It hit Jo like a ton of bricks. Of course! It was well known that a large enough moon revolving around a gas giant could conceivably harbor life, though such places were so far exceedingly rare.

Jo halted herself next to Malcolm—on the far side of Malcolm from Grant—and peered at the display. Sure enough, the gas giant's fourth major moon appeared to be about Earth-mass, though its radius was significantly smaller; it was likely heavy metal rich. That would explain the aliens' compact size and great strength; the moon's gravitational field would be substantially greater than Earth's, at that radius.

Assuming that moon was what they were looking for.

"Track in a camera," Jo said. She sounded a bit breathless, even to her own ears.

Malcolm nodded and brought up the observation camera control screen, then trained the camera toward the moon. It took a long minute or two for the camera to align itself and then track on the small body. Then, finally, the image from the camera came up, and Jo's jaw dropped. Her growing tension flew away, replaced by amazed wonder.

The moon was just emerging from the gas giant's night side. It was covered by a mass of swirling white clouds overtop a mottled blue and green surface.

But Jo had seen that sort of planet many times. What caught her breath, and made her shiver a little, was a glittering ring, clearly a construction of some sort, that seemed to surround the moon. It was thick: from a more acute angle of approach than the one she was taking, Jo surmised it would probably obscure much of the moon itself.

"But what is that?" she asked. "Can you zoom in further?"

Malcolm frowned and tapped the magnification control. A moment later the image zoomed in until the moon took up the entire display. The ring became clear. Jo could see several pylons of some sort that rose from the moon's surface and joined with the ring. They could only be support structures for space elevators, which meant the entire ring had been constructed in geosynchronous orbit. Amazing!

The zoomed-in view revealed a multitude of vessels docking with and departing the ring. It was impossible for her to evaluate what each vessel's purpose was just by looking at them, but Jo found herself calling certain smaller ones tugs, others ferries, and still others cargo carriers. Then a new kind of vessel, larger than the others, got underway, and Jo's breath caught.

She had seen that sort of vessel before. Crescent-shaped, off-white in color, with a small blister on its dorsal section that must have been its bridge, the vessel was the same make as the one they encountered on Pericles, all those years ago.

She traded looks with Malcolm and he nodded. He recognized it as well.

Jo swallowed, a shiver of both excitement and anxiety going down her spine. There was no doubt about it: this was the place.

"Son of a bitch," Grant said.

"That about sums it up," Jo replied, shooting him a quick grin. "I guess we know where we're heading."

Jo adjusted the ship's heading to intercept that one special world. Then she left the bridge.

---

GRANT SURPRISED HER.

He found her an hour later as she was walking down the main

passageway in the crew's section of Ring A, about halfway between Control and the Captain's cabin—her cabin. He approached slowly, almost tentatively, his normal confidence giving way to uncertainty. Jo found herself quirking an eyebrow, odd as his approach was.

Grant coughed and looked at the deck. "Jo, I," he ran his hand through his hair, then hurried on. "I wanted to apologize for how I acted on the Bridge." He paused and looked back up at her. "No excuse." His voice regained some of its normal assurance as he finished, but his eyes carried an unspoken plea.

The apology took her aback. She did not expect one, and really, one was not needed. They had all been through a lot, sacrificed a lot for this mission, but Grant more than she and Malcolm. It was completely understandable that he would feel anger if it turned out that his sacrifice, so large as it had been, was for nothing.

"Thank you," Jo said. "I can't begin to know how you are feeling - "

"I said, there's no excuse."

Jo paused, considering. "That's true. But there is an explanation, and a valid one."

Grant's eyes narrowed as he considered her words, then he nodded quickly.

"I trust nothing like this will happen again." Jo used her Captain-Means-Business voice. Sometimes it helped to assume an authoritative stance, and Grant seemed to be the sort who wanted and needed a hierarchy to belong to.

He nodded again, more deeply. "No, it won't."

Jo held his gaze for a long moment then nodded. "Very well. See that it doesn't."

Grant turned away then, and walked back toward Section B, where Hydroponics was located. He almost wore a smile as he left.

---

AFTER A SHORT NAP, Jo went back on to the bridge and strapped into the pilot's station. The straps were not necessary, but they saved having to constantly adjust herself in the zero-g environment. After a while sitting there staring at the camera display of their destination, she frowned. There was something odd, but she could not put her finger on what. The little voice in the back of her head quipped that the entire situation was odd, but she paid it no heed. Something was missing from the picture. Something that should be there.

She frowned and called up the spectrographic analysis display. The moon's atmospheric conditions were what she expected from her last encounter with the aliens: primarily Nitrogen and Oxygen, with $CO_2$ and Helium levels that were significantly higher than Earth's. That was not it.

Maybe it was just the anticipation of the upcoming meeting, and of her relative inaction now, after so much running around before. Preparations for the meeting were made as well as they could be, and she found she was more hindrance than help down in Hydroponics. Ripping a bunch of dead, dying, or decayed plant matter out of the bins and preparing them for new seedlings was not something she was particularly good at. And besides, someone had to monitor their approach to the moon.

But still...

It nagged at her for almost an hour before she hit upon it. It was so obvious she was surprised she had not noticed it before: the silence. The entire time they drew nearer to the system, and to the moon, Agrippa's communications equipment had not picked up a single signal, in any frequency range, except normal background static. That was unheard-of, in Jo's experience. The channels should have been full of navigational beacons, traffic control, entertainment networks...the list went on. But here there was nothing.

The aliens sure did not seem to be talking with each other.

Jo frowned and looked back at the moon, now fully visible on the gas giant's day side. The mass of vessels docking and getting underway, transiting the area, or just sitting in a stationary orbit, was no less than it had been the first time she saw it. But if that was so, why no radio chatter? Surely an operation as complex as that ring would require an extensive communications network to avoid conflicts and ensure things ran smoothly.

Jo checked the receivers again, then ran the self-diagnostic utility. Everything was in good working order; there was simply nothing to receive. It was very puzzling. Perhaps they did not use radio. But if not radio, what?

That was a rabbit hole with no end, and pointless. Even if the aliens did not use radio channels to communicate, they must surely be able to receive them. It was her broadcast from Pericles to the crippled ship that initiated their first meeting, after all.

Jo glanced at the navigation display: about 10 light-hours from the planet. They should arrive in about a day. Politeness dictated announcing their arrival beforehand, and Jo figured this was as good a time as any. She called up the communications controls again. Now, what did the first contact procedure for starliners say about the communications system? Although it had been years since she accessed the contact protocols aboard Pericles, Jo remembered the keystrokes as though it had happened yesterday. She tapped them in, hoping the algorithms had not been changed.

Her hope was rewarded as the screen shifted to a yellow-bordered command access display. The controls were exactly as Jo remembered from the encounter aboard Pericles. She pointed the directional antennas at the planet then, a couple taps later, the ship's antenna status indications lit up across all bands.

If the aliens had not detected Agrippa already, they would in a few hours. Now there was little to do but wait.

***

THE BEEPING of the proximity alarm roused Jo from a fitful sleep. She was still on the bridge, at the pilot's station. She must have dozed off without realizing it. She began cursing herself for allowing that to happen before experience made her stop. Sleep was a weapon, and a necessity. It would be far worse to push herself past endurance than to grab a little shuteye when opportunity presented itself.

Jo shook her head and, wiping sleep from her eyes, tapped the control pad to wake up the sensor display. Even though she knew intellectually what was out there, she gasped and felt a surge of adrenalin when she saw it on the display. Two crescent-shaped off-white ships just like the one she saw earlier were paralleling her course, one on either side of Agrippa, at a distance of ten kilometers.

It looked as though her message had been received.

# 62

# REUNION

"My God," Grant breathed, his voice hushed, awed.

He was looking out the port side observation window on the bridge at the alien ship in formation with them, his mouth agape.

And who could blame him? Not one but two alien starships—or perhaps warships—running in clear view in a tight formation with your own ship was not exactly an everyday sight. It was one thing to know intellectually what was coming. It was another thing entirely for it to actually happen, for you to definitively see that not only was there other intelligent life in the galaxy, but it was more advanced than man.

Jo could relate. Even though it was not her first meeting with these creatures, she still felt a giddy excitement mixed with primal terror, just looking at them. Of course, even had this been her thousandth meeting with them, she expected her reaction would be the same, considering her mission this time.

"How do we play this?" Malcolm asked.

Jo looked over to where he hovered on the starboard side of the bridge, his arms crossed over his chest in an almost defensive manner and his brow furrowed in thought, or worry. Again, who could blame him, if it was the latter?

Jo shrugged. "Same way as on Pericles. We secure ring rotation and the exterior illumination lights, shine the mooring lights on the airlock we want them to come aboard through, and wait. Unless you have a better idea?"

Malcolm remained silent for a short while, considering.

Grant spoke before Malcolm did. "If it was me, I would not just come over to an unknown vessel just because they shined a spotlight on their airlock."

"Why not? It worked before, and - "

"Before, they were stuck in a lifepod after their ship blew up, right?"

Jo nodded.

"So they had no choice. These guys," Grant jerked a thumb at the ship to port, "do. And they're probably wondering who or what we are, and what we want. If we go making sudden moves like running darkened ship, they might take that as showing hostile intent."

Jo's blood went cold. That would be well past bad. It would not do at all for them to have gone to all the trouble of bringing the eggs back here just to be shot down by the people they meant to deliver the eggs to. She tried to think of a way around Grant's logic, but after a moment she realized he was right. How would she react if one of those alien ships just showed up in the Sol system and started acting strangely? How would United Earth Military react?

"Good point," Jo said. "Do you have a suggestion?"

Grant nodded. "They obviously received our signal. Why don't you play that message you supposedly have in that black flashlight-thing for them over the radio? That ought to show them we are on the level. Then we can work out how to bring them aboard, so we can give them their kids back."

It boggled Jo's mind how she could miss something so obvious.

Shaking her head in chagrin, she said, "I'll be right back," then headed below.

The trip down the lift to Ring A seemed to take forever, though it was only a few minutes. From there it was a quick jog to the cargo space where they had stowed the incubator and loader. The black rod the alien Captain gave her onboard Pericles was right where she left it before hitting the cryo-tank: safely enclosed in a small bin, a few spots down from the incubator, that was meant to hold delicate items that needed to be stored separately.

Feeling an almost reverent rush, she lifted the rod out of the bin and stared at it for a moment. So many monumental things had happened because of the information in this thing, and the precious cargo within the incubator. It seemed odd that such a small device could do so much.

Malcolm's voice over the IMC broke her reverie. "Get up here, Jo. I think they're getting antsy."

Crap. Jo hurried from the cargo space, sprinting toward the lift, and the bridge.

***

Jo GAVE MALCOLM A HARD LOOK. "We need to talk about your definition of antsy."

Malcolm shrugged as if to say, "Hey, don't look at me," but did not reply.

Rolling her eyes, Jo turned away from him and looked out at the alien ships.

Two kilometers. They had maneuvered two kilometers closer and then stopped, holding position on both quarters, as before. They were just drifting along in time with Agrippa, not doing anything. And he called that acting antsy.

*Easy for you to say now.*

And that was true. Had she been up on the bridge when they maneuvered, Jo may have had the same reaction Malcolm did. Maybe. But, and she often forgot this, he was an Engineer, not a pilot. He had little to no experience in the way ships interact and how they maneuver, especially when in close proximity to each other. And it was not like they were dealing with other humans here. He could be forgiven for being a little jumpy.

For his part, Grant looked slightly amused, though there was a tightness about his eyes that belied his little grin. He was more tense than he put on. Hard to blame him there, either. Jo felt it too.

"Ok," she said, and moved past the men toward the pilot's station, and the communications panel to its right. "Let's see how this works."

A few taps on the display called up the first contact protocol display again. She paused and glanced back at Malcolm. He shrugged again, and said, "It's worth a shot."

Jo activated the local microphone and looked down at the rod, at the three little buttons inlaid into one side. The first called up the starmap and the third the technical schematics, their payment. The second was what she needed now, but for some reason she hesitated to play the message. It almost felt like a sacred act, doing that. Like playing the message would consummate everything she had worked for these last weeks. Last decades. Better to not listen to that little voice.

Jo shook her head at her silliness and tapped the transmit button, then she pressed the second button on the rod. The image of the alien Captain's face appeared in the air, a holographic projection, and began speaking in the aliens' language of barks, growls, and hisses. The Captain continued for some time, explaining, Jo hoped, what had happened to their ship and that they had entrusted the eggs to Jo and her crew.

*Of course, he could be saying something else entirely. He could be telling his brethren to kill them and use the starmap to invade Earth, now that humans had been foolish enough to reveal themselves.*

Jo forced such thoughts away. She would not give in to paranoia. And anyway, it was far too late to do anything to avert that invasion, if such was really the aliens' intention. Which it wasn't.

Lord, let it be so.

ONE AIRLOCK LOOKS MUCH the same as any other, but this one held particular importance to Jo. It was here, or at least at the equivalent airlock on Pericles—and they were identical—where she greeted the alien Captain and his crew as they stepped aboard her ship.

*And you almost got your throat ripped out.*

Jo ground her teeth and tried not to remember that part of the first meeting. She drew a deep breath and looked at Malcolm. He floated weightlessly at the airlock control panel, at the ready.

Just as Grant proposed, after playing the message over the radio circuits, he and Malcolm had moved the incubator into position at this airlock. Then Jo secured ring rotation and all external illumination except for the running lights and anti-collision strobes, and turned the mooring spotlights onto the airlock outer door. Then she transferred ring rotation and external sensor control to the airlock workstation and hurried to join Malcolm and Grant here.

The aliens had been stoic in their response to the message, in that they did nothing. At least nothing that Jo could see before she left the bridge. By the time she joined the men at the airlock, that nothing had changed to...nothing.

Jo was beginning to wonder whether they really had received her transmissions, either of them, when the workstation beeped an alert. She tapped the screen and the display shifted to the aft upper camera, which was trained on the alien vessel to starboard. The display showed a small, round object drop from the ventral section of the alien ship and proceed a few hundred meters down then stop completely before advancing at a brisk pace toward Agrippa.

"Looks like they got the message," Grant said from beside her, a certain satisfaction in his tone.

Jo nodded. "They'll be here in a minute. Take station."

And so they arrayed themselves, Jo in the center of the room next to the incubator, Malcolm at the airlock controls, and Grant over to the right. Despite his satisfaction that his suggestion had payed off, Grant looked nervous and downright uncomfortable.

*Probably feels naked without a gun.*

Jo smirked inwardly. Well, maybe not entirely inwardly. Grant had pressed hard to have at least one of them armed, preferably himself, for this meeting.

"It makes sense," he said. "I have the most training. If we need to defend ourselves - "

Jo had cut him off with a shake of her head and a raised hand. "If we need to defend ourselves, we're dead anyway. Even if we fight the ones in the shuttle off, the ships will just open fire. I am not going to risk this meeting going wrong. Not this time."

Grant hated it, but he was forced to concede to her logic, and acquiesced.

Now, looking at him, so obviously ill at ease, Jo knew she was right not to let him grab a gun. He just might shoot before thinking. Not that he had ever even come close to doing that before, but that was just another added risk onto a mission that was risky enough already.

"Everyone ready?" Jo asked, trying to keep her voice calm and in command. She was actually surprised at how well she accomplished that.

Nods all around.

Jo turned her attention to the workstation display. Malcolm had called up the airlock's external camera, and it revealed the alien shuttle on approach. It was remarkably similar to the lifepod Jo remembered from the first ship, with a number of circular protuberances on various locations and strange hieroglyphs that Jo presumed were the aliens' language. The biggest difference she saw was while the lifepod had been roughly spherical, the shuttle was flat on one side. Jo surmised that side housed landing gear of some sort. Maybe it was capable of atmospheric re-enty? Agrippa's shuttle could not do that; no need, or at least so the designers had said. But Jo could see all sorts of useful reasons for that capability.

The shuttle stopped even with the airlock then rotated until the flat side faced the ring's outer edge. A moment later, one of the protuberances bulged slightly, then parted allowing a circular tunnel to cross the intervening distance between the shuttle and the airlock outer door. Just before it reached the airlock, the end of the tunnel warped and convulsed, then settled into a shape that Jo knew exactly matched the airlock's seating surface.

A soft thunk penetrated the hull as the tunnel made contact, followed by a very soft sucking sound that lasted for less than a heartbeat.

The airlock control panel beeped, and a light flashed green.

Malcolm read the display and turned back to Jo, nodding. "Soft seal."

"Very well. Restore ring rotation."

"Aye." Malcolm tapped a control on the workstation and a moment later the faintest hint of a rushing noise reached Jo's ears. "Thrusters firing," Malcolm reported, referring to sets of thrusters mounted tangential to the rings that were used to get the rings started initially.

Slowly, ever so slowly, the bulkhead to Jo's left began moving toward her. It always took a few moments to overcome inertia before...

"Turning motor engaged," Malcolm said.

The wall began to speed up, and a moment later Jo found herself pressed up against it. She slid down to the deck and stepped away from the bulkhead, moving slowly to avoid bouncing off the deck in the extremely low, but steadily building, simulated g-forces. The men were moving similarly. In another circumstance it would be almost comic.

On the camera display, the aliens' tunnel flexed and shifted slightly, but the airlock seal held and soon enough the shuttle was revolving in time with the ring as it slowly built up to its Earth-normal turning rate.

Malcolm did not wait for an order. He tapped the airlock controls, and a red light over the inner door began flashing as the outer door slid open.

Nothing happened for several minutes. Then, just as on Pericles, a doorway opened at the far end of the tunnel. For a second or two, the only thing visible from within the shuttle was a soft white-orange light. But then a pair of figures eclipsed the light and walked onto the tunnel. The doorway shut behind them.

The aliens were just as Jo recalled: short, stooped, wearing grey jumpsuits and breathing masks over their elongated snouts. Their yellow-green, scaly skin seemed to glisten in the tunnel's lighting as they approached. And, as before, they were armed. Or at least, Jo assumed the staff-like handles that stuck up over their shoulders were the grips to weapons of some sort. She shifted on her feet uncomfortably, recalling the feel of the alien Captain's powerful fingers clenching her throat and how those wicked-looking claws had extended from the fingertips of the Captain's free hand.

They hardly needed any other weapons at all, if the aliens meant to do them harm.

Malcolm shifted the display to the airlock's inner security camera as the aliens stepped over the threshold. Their movements became slightly awkward as they crossed from their tunnel into the airlock. Jo recalled that happening on Pericles as well, probably a result of them leaving their artificial gravity field and entering Agrippa's. They recovered quickly, though, and shortly reached the inner airlock door. There they waited for a moment. Then the one on Jo's right - it was slightly larger than its fellow and Jo presumed it was the leader - pulled the staff-looking thing out of its shoulder-harness and rapped the end of it against the airlock inner door.

"Knock knock," Grant quipped.

Malcolm snorted out a little laugh, then tapped a command into the airlock control panel. A moment later a soft hissing sound announced the equalization of air pressure within the airlock and tunnel. He took a moment to read the display then looked back at Jo and nodded. "Equalized. Atmospheres nominal."

"Very well." Jo got back into position and smoothed out her clothes.

Not that coveralls really needed smoothing, but it just seemed the thing to do. Then she looked her little crew over. They had done well. Damn well. Now came the payoff.

She nodded at Malcolm. "Well," she said. "Here we go."

Malcolm tapped the control panel, and the inner door slid open.

# 63

# FROM OUT OF THE BLUE

Ilena Dmitrikov yawned and leaned back in her chair, rubbing at her eyes to ward off sleep.

It had been a long shift, and there were still four hours left to go. Her brain felt fuzzy and it was all she could do to keep her eyes open. It was her own damn fault, of course. She knew better than to stay out late the evening before she had the duty. But it was Jasmine's last day aboard the station, and Ilena would never have forgiven herself if she missed the going away party.

And the after party.

Another yawn burst forth and she kicked her chair back from her station. She needed to stand up. Move around, get the blood flowing.

Her back, stiff from sitting for so long, protested as she straightened. Grimacing, she raised her arms up over her head, the loose white fabric of her uniform blouse falling down around her shoulders as she did so, and stretched the way her Yoga instructors taught her. She went all the way up onto her tip toes, her soft pseudo-leather shoes flexing easily as though part of her skin, and she felt a slight pop from somewhere in the middle of her back. All at once, the discomfort went away and she was left with only a blissful feeling of relaxation.

Exhaling slowly, she lowered her arms and sank back down onto the flats of her feet. Much better.

A sudden sensation, very like someone poking at her with a blunt piece of soft plastic, brought her attention back to her station.

Unless one was logged in, the station did not look like much: just an empty space at the end of a small, oblong room with grey-blue walls and faux-wood paneled floor and ceiling. But to her eyes, the space was alive with data. The readouts from every craft in this sector of the outer solar system, the status of every communications relay, every outpost were instantly available to her if she but reached for them.

She sat back down and slid forward, and found herself surrounded by space in all its immensity. Even just her little portion was awe-inspiring. As always, it took her a moment to re-acclimate, to force down the mixture of vertigo and exhilarated joy she felt as she floated in the void, observing all that occurred. Of course, it was just a simulation, but what did it matter? It still was enough to take one's breath away.

The moment passed, as it always did, and the tugging at her consciousness drew her attention to the far edge of her assigned sector, to the southeast-by-east edge of the Oort Cloud. Two objects that were not present before she went through her wake-up routine caught her eye immediately, as much because they were outlined in glimmering silver, a construct of the sim that was designed to draw attention to new contacts, as because they were so much different than anything else flying.

The first was a long cylinder-shaped craft with several great spheres surrounding its after half and what looked like two rings—rings!—about a third of the way from its bow. The second was larger, off-white, and crescent-shaped.

Ilena frowned. Where had they come from?

A thought reversed the sim image of the two vessels—they could only be vessels—until they suddenly vanished.

She blinked, and the sim began playing forward again.

There was a momentary flash of light and then...something happened. It was like space itself bent and twisted. Ilena would not have noticed except a star opposite the area where it occurred suddenly became distorted and then vanished. In its place was only a reddish-yellow circle that hung there for a second or two, doing nothing. Then, the cylinder-ship shout out of the circle, followed by the crescent, a few seconds later.

The strange circle, or hole, or whatever it was closed abruptly behind them, and space returned to normal.

The sim froze as Ilena realized what she had just seen. A wormhole.

Hyperspace portal. Whatever the different theorists called it, it was supposed to be nigh-on impossible to create. And yet, what else could it have been?

Her earlier fatigue long-since forgotten, Ilena gave quick thought to a report for Headquarters, in Geneva, and reset the sim to current time.

The two objects drifted together, the crescent having taken station off the cylinder's port side. The orbital computations took less time than it took to query for them. They were on an intercept heading for Earth.

The message popped into Ilena's vision and she checked it over quickly, then with a thought sent it flying. They were several light hours away. Conceivably there would be plenty of time for follow-up before the two craft could pose a serious threat, but given what she had just seen there was nothing to be gained from delaying her report for further analysis.

Which did not mean she was not going to investigate further.

The sim zoomed in on the pair of ships and Ilena's breath caught in her throat. At the higher magnification, she recognized both instantly. The cylinder ship was an old Achilles-class starliner. What the hell was one of those doing flying around? The last of them were decommissioned over two hundred years ago, when the Higgs-Carpenter drive rendered their plasma-impulse engines and centripetal rings obsolete.

But the other....

For her entire NSA career, Ilena had seen images of that other ship. Grainy images, by modern standards, shot through old-style telescopic cameras centuries ago. Images of an alien craft that housed beings with the ability to invade a person's mind, turn otherwise good and loyal men and women against their own race. A craft that she and her comrades must constantly guard against.

A craft that now appeared in her sim display.

Ilena swallowed hard against the surge of fear that swept over her. She had to stay under control. Record as much as possible. Any piece of data, no matter how seemingly insignificant, could make the difference between survival and destruction at these beings' hands.

But she had never thought to really see such a craft.

For a full minute, she just watched the two craft drift in formation, every second bringing them closer to Earth. She could not think of what to do. The boogey-man from her earliest training was here.

And she did not know what to do.

Finally, she pulled her attention back and looked to the nearest defense outpost: the Charon battery. The two craft were almost within range. Maybe the battery could intervene.

That small action got the rest of her mental gears turning. She thought out a follow-up message for Earth, including her intentions to intercept with Charon, and sent it, chopping Charon in the transmission. Then she settled back to wait for a response. Local time appeared over the two craft and the battery on Charon when she thought of it, along with the craft's time to Closest Point of Approach at Charon.

Ilena frowned. They would reach CPA in about three hours. There was no way she would receive a reply from Earth in that time.

It was up to her.

Ilena reached out with her thoughts to the Charon battery, and a heartbeat later she was part of the systems on the icy moon. The systems came online at her mind's touch, the weapons began powering up from their long slumber. Death incarnated into plasma, fusion pulse torpedoes, and less exotic missiles and mass cannons came to train on the patch of space where the approaching crafts would pass.

And then she waited.

Gradually, imperceptibly except for her sim-heightened awareness, the craft drew closer. She thought up the countdown timer. CPA in one hour.

Ilena licked her lips in anticipation.

Then something else tugged on her consciousness. Something new, and unexpected. Unexpected because she had not sensed this particular tug in years, since her training back on Titan.

She frowned and cast a thought toward the new stimulus. The communications window flashed open, familiar and set up just as it always was. Her frown deepened. What was it?

And then she saw it. At the bottom of the display, an old group of frequencies and modulation patterns that went out of use more than a century ago. She had always wondered why the NSA bothered to include them in its monitoring algorithms anymore, why they had trained her on them. Looking at the ancient starliner, apparently back from the scrapyard, she suddenly realized exactly why.

The people in charge were expecting an encounter like this.

That spike of fear flooded through her again. Ilena tried to push it away, to no avail. She pulled away from Charon—it was set to go and would take care of itself, only needing her input for the final engagement sequence—and shot out through the void toward the pair of ships. This time she zoomed in as far as she could, until the starliner appeared nearly life-size in front of her.

There, on the port bow. Markings. Hard to read in the dim light from the distant sun, despite the ship's hull illumination lights. But she managed to see the vessel's name: Agrippa.

Ilena recoiled, physically and mentally, and almost pushed herself out of the interface station again.

Agrippa.

It could not be!

But then, the other vessel from her training was there, large as life. Why not the traitorous Agrippa as well?

*What else were you expecting? What else could you expect?*

The thoughts were true, but knowing what ship that was and seeing it for true were two different things. If this was Agrippa.... Was it possible her Captain drove her still, like some ghost ship out of ancient legend?

It was nonsense, of course. Ghosts did not exist, and people did not live nearly long enough for her Captain to still be aboard. But if not...who was flying the famous, cursed ship?

Without realizing what she was doing, Ilena returned to the communications controls and keyed the old channels to life.

The sim in front of her flickered, then coalesced into a quadrilateral of static for a brief half-second before resolving into the image of a more than handsome woman of east-asian descent. Her hair was long, black but heavily streaked with silver, and pulled back from her face into a ponytail. She wore black fatigues of some kind and sat in a chair facing her transmitting station, no doubt. Flanking her were two men: one tall and slender, African, with even more grey than she had, the other shorter and more stocky, of central European descent from the looks of him and only a bit of grey on his temples.

Ilena's heart skipped a beat. She knew those faces. The traitors. On instinct, she moved her thoughts to the Charon battery, but the craft were too far out of range to do any good.

The asian woman smiled ever so slightly before speaking.

"Earth Control, this is Josephine Ishikawa aboard the starliner Agrippa, over." Or at least that's what Ilena thought she said. Some of

Ishikawa's words were indecipherable, a dialect that Ilena had never heard before. The sim did its best to fill in the gaps, but it still was difficult to be certain she had heard correctly.

Ilena licked her lips, trying to restore some moisture to her mouth. What to do? Before she realized what she was doing, she heard herself say, "This is Sol Approach, Haley sector."

Ishikawa's eyebrow quirked upward at the identifier that would be, to her, unfamiliar. "Haley sector, this is Ishikawa, aboard Agrippa. Malcolm Ngubwe is here with me." The tall African nodded gravely. "As well as Grant Gilford." The European flashed a quick smile that almost looked forced. "We've come home, and we've brought some new friends with us. Request safe passage through the solar system, and permission to approach and dock at Earth. We have a lot to discuss, and our friends are eager to meet with Earth's leadership. They pledge non-aggression for the duration of our stay."

Ilena found herself unable to put a coherent thought together for some time, let alone respond. They were really here, the demons and traitors everyone had been warned about. She should just blast them out of the sky. Her superiors would advise her to do just that.

And yet, looking at the Ishikawa woman's eyes, serious but unguarded, and those of her companions, Ilena suddenly found it hard to assign the raving lunatic label to them even though it had been passed down for so many years.

*Why not?*

She did not know how to answer her own thoughts. But something told her that this woman and her crew was not an immediate threat. And besides, there were many more batteries ready and able to unleash death in all its forms the closer to the inner solar system they approached, and they were only two ships. If they were indeed a threat, it would become plain soon enough, and the batteries and ready warships could take care of it.

Ilena made her decision. With a thought, she secured the battery at Charon, putting it back into sleep mode. Then she replied, "Permission granted to transit, Agrippa. For docking, contact orbital approach control on 327.483, modulation Alpha-six-two."

Ishikawa's eyebrows raised and she mouthed the channel identifiers to herself, then glanced at Ngubwe. He frowned but, after a moment, nodded. Apparently the ship's communications array could handle that channel.

Ishikawa returned the nod then faced forward. "Roger, Haley sector. Thank you. Agrippa out."

The transmission winked out. Ilena thought up an update to headquarters and sent it. Somewhere in the back of her mind, she knew her lack of action here might incur the wrath of her superiors, but somehow that seemed alright. She stared for a long time at the old starliner, drifting with its unknowable companion, and some of that fear she had felt before receded, replaced once more by exhilaration.

"Welcome home," she said, to no one, and to everyone.

# MESSAGE FROM THE AUTHOR

Thank you for reading my book. I hope you enjoyed reading it as much as I enjoyed writing it.

Every review helps an author out, so whether you loved this book, hated it, or something in between, please take a minute to tell other readers what you thought. All of the online retailers make it very easy to do, and I would really appreciate it.

Feel free to come say hi at my website or on Gab. I always enjoy hearing from readers, especially since you all are, collectively, my boss.

I also have a weekly podcast, Story Time With Michael Kingswood, where I read stories and talk through some of the latest goings on in my world. I'd love to see you there.

Thanks again. My best to you and yours.

Warm Regards,
Michael Kingswood

# MAILING LIST

If you enjoyed this book and would like word on new releases and special deals from Michael Kingswood, sign up for his newsletter on his website. Guaranteed to be spam-free, you can opt out at any time. And you can rest assured he will not share your information with anyone, for any reason.

https://michaelkingswood.com/newsletter-signup/

# MEMBERSHIP

Michael would like to invite you to become a supporting member of his website. Similar in concept to Patreon, a few dollars a month will give you access to exclusive content, and help him to focus more of his time to writing fun and exciting stories for your enjoyment.

Sign up at his website:

https://www.michaelkingswood.com/membership/join/

# ABOUT THE AUTHOR

Michael Kingswood is 20-year veteran of the US Navy submarine force and a lifelong fan of science fiction and fantasy literature. His work has appeared in numerous collections and anthologies, to include the Fiction River Anthology series from WMG publishing. He holds a bachelors degree in Mechanical Engineering as well as a Master of Engineering Management and a Master of Business Administration. He has four children and currently resides in San Diego.

Find Michael Kingswood online at:

www.michaelkingswood.com
www.gab.com/michaelkingswood

# MORE BOOKS BY MICHAEL KINGSWOOD

### Glimmer Vale Chronicles

Glimmer Vale

Out-Dweller

Tollard's Peak

Robbed Blind

The Falconer's Stairs

Glimmer Vale Omnibus Edition #1

### Stories From Glimmer Vale

Legacy

Hidden Magic

Captive Hearts

Wedding Gifts

Lost Credit

### The Pericles Conspiracy

Passing In The Night

The Pericles Conspiracy

### Dawn Of Enlightenment

Masters Of The Sun

## Novellas

What Lurks Between

The Necromancer's Lair

The Champion

Veritas Morte

## Story Collections

Tales Of Adventure #1

Tales Of Adventure #2

Short Story 10-Pack

A Jar Of Mixed Treats

Short Mystery 10-Pack

Stories From Glimmer Vale, Volume 1

## Short Fiction

Michael has also published a number of shorter works, links to which can be found on his website.